TERRY CARR HAS PICKED
THE WINNER . . .

Nebula Award: Best Novella of 1978
The Persistence of Vision, by John Varley

. . . AND SOME NOMINEES,
TOO

Hugo Award: Best Novella of 1978*

The Persistence of Vision, by John Varley

The Watched, by Christopher Priest

Fireship, by Joan D. Vinge

Seven American Nights, by Gene Wolfe

*The winner of this award was announced in August, 1979, after this book went to press.

The Best Science Fiction Novellas

of the Year #1

Edited by
Terry Carr

A Del Rey Book

BALLANTINE BOOKS ● **NEW YORK**

ACKNOWLEDGMENTS

"The Persistence of Vision" by John Varley. Copyright ©
1978 by Mercury Press, Inc. From *Fantasy and Science Fiction*,
March 1978, by permission of the author and his agents, Kirby
McCauley, Ltd.

"Old Folks at Home" by Michael Bishop. Copyright © 1978
by Terry Carr. From *Universe 8*, by permission of the author
and his agent, Virginia Kidd.

"Shipwright" by Donald Kingsbury. Copyright © 1978 by the
Condé Nast Publications, Inc. From *Analog*, April 1978, by
permission of the author.

"Seven American Nights" by Gene Wolfe. Copyright © 1978
by Damon Knight. From *Orbit 20*, by permission of the author
and his agent, Virginia Kidd.

"Fireship" by Joan D. Vinge. Copyright © 1978 by Joan D.
Vinge. From *Analog*, December 1978, by permission of the
author and her agents, Marie Rodell–Frances Collin Literary
Agency.

"The Watched" by Christopher Priest. Copyright © 1978 by
Mercury Press, Inc., copyright © 1979 by Christopher Priest.
From *Fantasy and Science Fiction*, April 1978, by permission
of the author and his agents, Marie Rodell–Frances Collin
Literary Agency.

A Del Rey Book
Published by Ballantine Books
Copyright © 1979 by Terry Carr

Library of Congress Catalog Card Number: 79-87672

ISBN 0-345-28084-9

Manufactured in the United States of America

First Edition: September 1979

Contents

Introduction
  Terry Carr   vii

The Persistence of Vision
  John Varley   1

Old Folks at Home
  Michael Bishop   54

Shipwright
  Donald Kingsbury   110

Seven American Nights
  Gene Wolfe   153

Fireship
  Joan D. Vinge   211

The Watched
  Christopher Priest   274

Introduction

Many science-fiction writers feel that the novella is the most satisfying form for stories in this genre. They point out that the short story, though offering good opportunities for presenting a single idea in dramatic focus, necessarily limits the wordage for character development and exploration of future settings and societies—whereas the writer of a novella can afford to flesh out these aspects, which results in sf stories that are memorable both emotionally and intellectually.

Full-length novels of science fiction also offer this extra dimension, but because of tradition or public taste, the sf novel frequently concentrates on telling an adventure story in a colorful setting. Many excellent sf novellas have subsequently been expanded by their authors to novel length, resulting in books that are actually less satisfying than the novellas from which they came.

Personally, I have a great fondness for the short-story form, which is why most of my own writing has been in this length—and, indeed, is the reason I've edited so many anthologies. But I've written and often anthologized novellas, so I'm impressed by the greater freedoms allowed by this longer length.

A surprising number of the finest works of science fiction, from H. G. Wells's original version of "The Time Machine" to the stories gathered together in this book, have been novellas. Oddly, however, anthologies of sf novellas have been comparatively rare—and there's never before been a book devoted to the best sf novellas of the year.

This book is an attempt to rectify that situation. It's a companion volume to *The Best Science Fiction of the Year*, which in the past has had to limit the number of its longer stories to one or two per book even though there were *always* several more novellas that would properly have been included in any best-of-the-year list. If *The Best Science Fiction Novellas of the Year #1* appeals to enough readers (i.e., if enough people buy it), we will continue the series.

I hope it does, and I believe it will. The stories in this volume will demonstrate why: they make their own case. Here are six future worlds and many extraordinary people who live in them; their stories are detailed but never padded with irrelevancies.

Enjoy them—and tell your friends.

—TERRY CARR

The Persistence of Vision

John Varley

We begin with a story of the near future that's set in a communal society of deaf and blind people who were born after the German measles epidemic of 1964. Now adults, these people have established a society that reflects their limitations and some surprising new abilities.

John Varley is the author of many excellent short stories and the novels *The Ophiuchi Hotline* and *Titan*. He's currently at work on a sequel to *Titan*, provisionally titled *Wizard*.

It was the year of the fourth nondepression. I had recently joined the ranks of the unemployed. The President had told me that I had nothing to fear but fear itself. I took him at his word, for once, and set out to backpack to California.

I was not the only one. The world's economy had been writhing like a snake on a hot griddle for the last twenty years, since the early seventies. We were in a boom-and-bust cycle that seemed to have no end. It had wiped out the sense of security the nation had so painfully won in the golden years after the thirties. People were accustomed to the fact that they could be rich one year and on the breadlines the next. I was on the breadlines in '81, and again in '88. This time, I decided to use my freedom from the time clock to see the world. I had ideas of stowing away to Japan. I was forty-seven years old and might not get another chance to be irresponsible.

This was in late summer of the year. Sticking out my thumb along the interstate, I could easily forget that there were food riots back in Chicago. I slept at night on top of my bedroll and saw stars and listened to crickets.

I must have walked most of the way from Chicago to Des Moines. My feet toughened up after a few days of awful blisters. The rides were scarce—partly competition from other hitchhikers and partly the times we were living in. The locals were none too anxious to give rides to city people, who they had heard were mostly a bunch of hunger-crazed potential mass murderers. I got roughed up once and told never to return to Sheffield, Illinois.

But I gradually learned the knack of living on the road. I had started with a small supply of canned goods from the welfare, and by the time they ran out, I had found that it was possible to work for a meal at many of the farmhouses along the way.

Some of it was hard work; some of it was only a token from people with a deeply ingrained sense that nothing should come for free. A few meals were gratis, at the family table with grandchildren sitting around while grandpa or grandma told oft-repeated tales of what it had been like in the Big One back in '29, when people had not been afraid to help a fellow out when he was down on his luck. I found that the older the person, the more likely I was to get a sympathetic ear. One of the many tricks you learn. And most older people will give you anything if you'll only sit and listen to them. I got very good at it.

The rides began to pick up west of Des Moines, then got bad again as I neared the refugee camps bordering the China Strip. This was only five years after the disaster, remember, when the Omaha nuclear reactor melted down and a hot mass of uranium and plutonium began eating its way into the earth, headed for China, spreading a band of radioactivity six hundred kilometers downwind. Most of Kansas City, Missouri, was still living in plywood and sheet-metal shantytowns while the city was rendered habitable again.

These people were a tragic group. The initial solidarity people show after a great disaster had long since faded into the lethargy and disillusionment of the displaced person. Many of them would be in and out of hospitals for the rest of their lives. To make it worse, the local people hated them, feared them, would not associate with them. They were modern pariahs: unclean. Their children were shunned. Each camp had only a number to identify it, but the local populace called them all Geigertowns.

I made a long detour to Little Rock to avoid crossing the Strip, though it was safe now as long as you didn't linger. I was issued a pariah's badge by the National Guard—a dosimeter—and wandered from one Geigertown to the next. The people were pitifully friendly once I made the first move, and I always slept indoors. The food was free at the community messes.

Once at Little Rock, the aversion to picking up strangers—who might be tainted with "radiation disease"—dropped off, and I quickly moved across Arkansas, Oklahoma, and Texas. I worked a little here and there, but many of the rides were long. What I saw of Texas was through a car window.

I was a little tired of that by the time I reached New Mexico. I decided to do some more walking. By then I was less interested in California than in the trip itself.

I left the roads and went cross-country where there were no fences to stop me. I found that it wasn't easy, even in New Mexico, to get far from signs of civilization.

Taos was the center, back in the sixties, of cultural experiments in alternative living. Many communes and cooperatives were set up in the surrounding hills during that time. Most of them fell apart in a few months or years, but a few survived. In later years, any group with a new theory of living and a yen to try it out seemed to gravitate to that part of New Mexico. As a result, the land was dotted with ramshackle windmills, solar heating panels, geodesic domes, group marriages, nudists, philosophers, theoreticians, messiahs, hermits, and more than a few just plain nuts.

Taos was great. I could drop into most of these communes and stay for a day or a week, eating organic rice and beans and drinking goat's milk. When I got tired of one, a few hours' walk in any direction would bring me to another. There, I might be offered a night of prayer and chanting or a ritualistic orgy. Some of the groups had spotless barns with automatic milkers for the herds of cows. Others didn't even have latrines; they just squatted. In some, the members dressed like nuns or Quakers in early Pennsylvania. Elsewhere, they went nude and shaved all their body hair and painted themselves purple. There were all-male and all-female groups. I was urged to stay at most of the former; at the latter, the responses ranged from a bed for the night and good conversation to being met at a barbed-wire fence with a shotgun.

I tried not to make judgments. These people were doing something important, all of them. They were testing ways whereby people didn't have to live in Chicago. That was a wonder to me. I had thought Chicago was inevitable, like diarrhea.

This is not to say they were all successful. Some made Chicago look like Shangri-La. There was one group who seemed to feel that getting back to nature consisted of sleeping in pigshit and eating food a buzzard wouldn't touch. Many were obviously doomed. They would leave behind a group of empty hovels and the memory of cholera.

So the place wasn't paradise, not by a long ways. But there were successes. One or two had been there since '63 or '64 and were raising their third generation. I was disappointed to see that most of these were the ones that departed least from established norms of behavior, though some of the differences could be startling. I suppose the most radical experiments are the least likely to bear fruit.

I stayed through the winter. No one was surprised to see me a second time. It seems that many people came to Taos and shopped around. I seldom stayed more than three weeks at any one place, and always pulled my weight. I made many friends and picked up skills that would serve me if I stayed off the roads. I toyed with the idea of staying at one of them forever. When I couldn't make up my mind, I was advised that there was no hurry. I could go to California and return. They seemed sure I would.

So when spring came, I headed west over the hills. I stayed off the roads and slept in the open. Many nights I would stay at another commune, until they finally began to get farther apart, then tapered off entirely. The country was not as pretty as what I had been through.

Then, three days' leisurely walking from the last commune, I came to a wall.

In 1964, in the United States, there was an epidemic of German measles, or rubella. Rubella is one of the mildest of infectious diseases. The only time when it's a problem is when a woman contracts it in the first four months of her pregnancy. It is passed to the fetus, which usually develops complications. These complications include deafness, blindness, and damage to the brain.

In 1964, in the old days before abortion became readily available, there was nothing to be done about it. Many pregnant women caught rubella and went to term. Five thousand deaf-blind children were born in one year. The normal yearly incidence of deaf-blind children in the United States is one hundred and forty.

In 1970 these five thousand potential Hellen Kellers were all six years old. It was quickly seen that there was a shortage of Anne Sullivans. Previously, deaf-blind children could be sent to a small number of special institutions.

It was a problem. Not just anyone can cope with a blind-deaf child. You can't tell them to shut up when they moan; you can't reason with them, tell them that the moaning is driving you crazy. Some parents were driven to nervous breakdowns when they tried to keep their children at home.

Many of the five thousand were badly retarded and virtually impossible to reach, even if anyone had been trying. These ended up, for the most part, warehoused in the hundreds of anonymous nursing homes and institutes for "special" children. They were put into beds, cleaned up once a day by a few overworked nurses, and generally allowed the full blessings of liberty: they were allowed to rot freely in their own dark, quiet, private universes. Who can say if it was bad for them? None of them were heard to complain.

Many children with undamaged brains were shuffled in among the retarded through an inability to tell anyone that they were in there behind the sightless eyes. They failed the batteries of tactile tests, unaware that their fates hung in the balance when they were asked to fit round pegs into round holes to the ticking of a clock that they could not see or hear. They spent the rest of their lives in bed as a result, and none of them complained, either. To protest, one must be aware of the possibility of something better. It helps to have a language, too.

Several hundred of the children were found to have, IQ-wise, what might be thought of as normal intelligence. There were news stories about them as they approached puberty and it was revealed that there were not enough good people to properly handle them. Money was spent, teachers were trained. The education expenditures would go on for a specified period of time, until the children were grown; then things would be back to normal and everyone could congratulate themselves on having dealt successfully with a tough problem.

And, indeed, it did work fairly well. There are ways to reach and teach such children. They involve patience, love, and dedication, and the teachers brought all that to their jobs. All the graduates of the special schools left knowing how to speak with their hands. Some could talk. A few could write. Most of them left the institutions to live with parents or relatives or, if neither was possible, received counseling and help in fitting themselves into society. The options were limited, but people can live rewarding lives under the most severe handicaps. Not every one, but most of the graduates were as happy with their lot as could reasonably be expected. Some achieved the almost saintly peace of their role-model, Helen Keller. Others became bitter and withdrawn. A few had to be put in asylums, where they became indistinguishable from the others of their group who had spent the last twenty years there. But for the most part, they did well.

But among the group, as in any group, were some misfits. They tended to be among the brightest, the top 10 percent of the IQ scores. This was not a reliable rule. Some had unremarkable test scores and were still infected with the hunger to do something, to change things, to rock the boat. With a group of five thousand, there were certain to be a few geniuses, a few artists, a few dreamers, hell-raisers, individualists, movers and shapers: a few glorious maniacs.

There was one among them who might have been President but for the fact that she was blind, deaf, and a woman. She was smart, but not one of the geniuses. She was a dreamer, a creative force, an innovator. It was she who dreamed of freedom. But she was not a builder of fairy castles. Having dreamed it, she had to make it come true.

The wall was made of carefully fitted stone and was about five feet high. It was completely out of context with anything I had seen in New Mexico, though it was built of native rock. You just don't build that kind of wall out there. You use barbed wire if something needs fencing in, but many people still made use of the free range and brands. Somehow it seemed transplanted from New England.

It was substantial enough that I felt it would be unwise to crawl over it. I had crossed many wire fences in my travels and not got in trouble for it yet, though I had some talks with some ranchers. Mostly they told me to keep moving but didn't seem upset about it. This was different. I set out to walk around it. From the lay of the land, I couldn't tell how far it might reach, but I had time.

At the top of the next rise I saw that I didn't have far to go. The wall made a right-angle turn just ahead. I looked over it and could see some buildings. They were mostly domes, the ubiquitous structure thrown up by communes because of the combination of ease of construction and durability. There were sheep in there, and a few cows. They grazed on grass so green I wanted to go over and roll in it. The wall enclosed a rectangle of green. Outside, where I stood, it was all scrub and sage. These people had access to Rio Grande irrigation water.

I rounded the corner and followed the wall west again.

I saw a man on horseback about the same time he spotted me. He was south of me, outside the wall, and he turned and rode in my direction.

He was a dark man with thick features, dressed in denim and boots with a gray battered Stetson. Navaho, maybe. I don't know much about Indians, but I'd heard they were out here.

"Hello," I said when he'd stopped. He was looking me over. "Am I on your land?"

"Tribal land," he said. "Yeah, you're on it."

"I didn't see any signs—"

He shrugged.

"It's okay, bud. You don't look like you're out to rustle cattle." He grinned at me. His teeth were large and stained with tobacco. "You be camping out tonight?"

"Yes. How much farther does the . . . uh, tribal land go? Maybe I'll be out of it before tonight?"

He shook his head gravely. "Nah. You won't be off it tomorrow. 'S all right. You make a fire, you be careful, huh?" He grinned again and started to ride off.

"Hey, what is this place?" I gestured to the wall, and he pulled his horse up and turned around again. It raised a lot of dust.

"Why you asking?" He looked a little suspicious.

"I dunno. Just curious. It doesn't look like the other places I've been to. This wall—"

He scowled. "Damn wall." Then he shrugged. I thought that was all he was going to say. Then he went on.

"These people, we look out for 'em, you hear? Maybe we don't go for what they're doin'. But they got it rough, you know?" He looked at me, expecting something. I never did get the knack of talking to these la-

conic westerners. I always felt that I was making my
sentences too long. They used a shorthand of grunts and
shrugs and omitted parts of speech, and I always felt
like a dude when I talked to them.

"Do they welcome guests?" I asked. "I thought I
might see if I could spend the night."

He shrugged again, and it was a whole different gesture.

"Maybe. They all deaf and blind, you know?" And
that was all the conversation he could take for the day.
He made a clucking sound and galloped away.

I continued down the wall until I came to a dirt road
that wound up the arroyo and entered the wall. There
was a wooden gate, but it stood open. I wondered why
they took all the trouble with the wall only to leave the
gate like that. Then I noticed a circle of narrow-gauge
train tracks that came out of the gate, looped around
outside it, and rejoined itself. There was a small siding
that ran along the outer wall for a few yards.

I stood there a few moments. I don't know what all
entered into my decision. I think I was a little tired of
sleeping out, and I was hungry for a home-cooked meal.
The sun was getting closer to the horizon. The land to
the west looked like more of the same. If the highway
had been visible, I might have headed that way and
hitched a ride. But I turned the other way and went
through the gate.

I walked down the middle of the tracks. There was a
wooden fence on each side of the road, built of horizontal planks, like a corral. Sheep grazed on one side of
me. There was a Shetland sheep dog with them, and she
raised her ears and followed me with her eyes as I
passed.

It was about half a mile to the cluster of buildings
ahead. There were four or five domes made of something translucent, like greenhouses, and several conven-
tional square buildings. There were two windmills turning lazily in the breeze. There were several banks of
solar water heaters. These are flat constructions of glass
and wood, held off the ground so they can tilt to follow
the sun. They were almost vertical now, intercepting the

oblique rays of sunset. There were a few trees, what might have been an orchard.

About halfway there, I passed under a wooden footbridge. It arched over the road, giving access from the east pasture to the west pasture. I wondered what was wrong with a simple gate?

Then I saw something coming down the road in my direction. It was traveling on the tracks and it was very quiet. I stopped and waited.

It was a sort of converted mining engine, the sort that pulls loads of coal up from the bottom of shafts. It was battery-powered, and it had gotten quite close before I heard it. A small man was driving it. He was pulling a car behind him and singing as loud as he could with absolutely no sense of pitch.

He got closer and closer, moving about five miles per hour, one hand held out as if he was signaling a left turn. Suddenly I realized what was happening, as he was bearing down on me. He wasn't going to stop. He was counting fenceposts with his hand. I scrambled up the fence just in time. There wasn't more than six inches of clearance between the train and the fence on either side. His palm touched my leg as I squeezed close to the fence, and he stopped abruptly.

He leaped from the car and grabbed me and I thought I was in trouble. But he looked concerned, not angry, and felt me all over, trying to discover if I was hurt. I was embarrassed. Not from the examination; because I had been foolish. The Indian had said they were all deaf and blind, but I guess I hadn't quite believed him.

He was flooded with relief when I managed to convey to him that I was all right. With eloquent gestures he made me understand that I was not to stay on the road. He indicated that I should climb over the fence and continue through the fields. He repeated himself several times to be sure I understood, then held on to me as I climbed over to assure himself that I was out of the way. He reached over the fence and held my shoulders, smiling at me. He pointed to the road and shook his head, then pointed to the buildings and nodded. He touched my head and smiled when I nodded. He climbed back onto the engine and started up, all the time nodding and pointing where he wanted me to go. Then he was off again.

I debated what to do. Most of me said to turn around, go back to the wall by way of the pasture and head back into the hills. These people probably wouldn't want me around. I doubted that I'd be able to talk to them, and they might even resent me. On the other hand, I was fascinated, as who wouldn't be? I wanted to see how they managed it. I still didn't believe that they were *all* deaf and blind. It didn't seem possible.

The sheltie was sniffing at my pants. I looked down at her and she backed away, then daintily approached me as I held out my open hand. She sniffed, then licked me. I patted her on the head, and she hustled back to her sheep.

I turned toward the buildings.

The first order of business was money.

None of the students knew much about it from experience, but the library was full of Braille books. They started reading.

One of the first things that became apparent was that when money was mentioned, lawyers were not far away. They wrote letters. From the replies, they selected a lawyer and retained him.

They were in a school in Pennsylvania at the time. The original pupils of the special schools, five hundred in number, had been narrowed down to about seventy as people left to live with relatives or found other solutions to their special problems. Of those seventy, some had places to go but didn't want to go there; others had few alternatives. Their parents were either dead or not interested in living with them. So the seventy had been concentrated from the schools around the country into this one, while it was worked out what to do with them. The authorities had plans, but the students beat them to it.

Each of them had been entitled to a guaranteed annual income since 1977. They had been under the care of the government, and so they had not received it.

They sent their lawyer to court. He came back with a ruling that they could not collect. They appealed and won. The money was paid retroactively, with interest, and came to a healthy sum. They thanked their lawyer and retained a real-estate agent. Meanwhile they read.

They read about communes in New Mexico and instructed their agent to look for something out there. He made a deal for a tract to be leased in perpetuity from the Navaho Nation. They read about the land, found that it would need a lot of water to be productive in the way they wanted it to be.

They divided into groups to research what they would need to be self-sufficient.

Water could be obtained by tapping into the canals that carried it from the reservoirs on the Rio Grande into the reclaimed land in the south. Federal money was available for the project through a labyrinthine scheme involving HEW, the Agriculture Department, and the Bureau of Indian Affairs. They ended up paying little for their pipeline.

The land was arid. It would need fertilizer to be of use in raising sheep without resorting to open-range techniques. The cost of fertilizer could be subsidized through the Rural Resettlement Program. After that, planting clover would enrich the soil with all the nitrates they could want.

There were techniques available to farm ecologically, without worrying about fertilizers or pesticides. Everything was recycled. Essentially, you put sunlight and water into one end of the process and harvested wool, fish, vegetables, apples, honey, and eggs at the other end. You used nothing but the land and replaced even that as you recycled your waste products back into the soil. They were not interested in agribusiness with huge combine harvesters and crop dusters. They didn't even want to turn a profit. They merely wanted sufficiency.

The details multiplied astronomically. Their leader, the one who had the original idea and the drive to put it into action in the face of overwhelming obstacles, was a dynamo named Janet Reilly. Knowing nothing about the techniques generals and executives employ to achieve large objectives, she invented them for herself and adapted them to the peculiar needs and limitations of her group. She assigned task forces to look into solutions of each aspect of their project: law, science, social planning, design, buying, logistics, construction. At any one time, she was the only person who knew everything about what was happening. She kept it all in her head, without notes of any kind.

It was in the area of social planning that she showed herself to be a visionary and not just a superb organizer. Her idea was not to make a place where they could lead a life that was a sightless, soundless imitation of their unafflicted peers. She wanted a whole new start, a way of living that was by and for the blind-deaf, a way of living that accepted no convention just because that was the way it had always been done. She examined every human cultural institution from marriage to indecent exposure to see how it related to her needs and the needs of her friends. She was aware of the peril of this approach, but was undeterred. Her Social Task Force read about every variant group that had ever tried to make it on its own anywhere, and they brought her reports about how and why these groups had failed or succeeded. She filtered this information through her own experiences to see how it would work for her unusual group with its own set of needs and goals.

The details were endless. They hired an architect to put their ideas into Braille blueprints. Gradually the plans evolved. They spent more money. The construction began, supervised on the site by their architect, who by now was so fascinated by the scheme that she donated her services. It was an important break, for they needed someone there that they could trust. There is only so much that can be accomplished at such a distance.

When things were ready for them to move, they ran into bureaucratic trouble. They had anticipated it, but it was a setback. Social agencies charged with overseeing their welfare doubted the wisdom of the project. When it became apparent that no amount of reasoning was going to stop it, wheels were set in motion that resulted in a restraining order, issued for their own protection, preventing them from leaving the school. They were twenty-one by then, all of them, but were judged mentally incompetent to manage their own affairs. A hearing was scheduled.

Luckily, they still had access to their lawyer. He also had become infected with the crazy vision and put on a terrific battle for them. He succeeded in getting a ruling concerning the rights of institutionalized persons, later upheld by the Supreme Court, that eventually had severe repercussions in state and county hospitals. Realizing the trouble they were already in regarding the thousands of patients in inadequate facilities across the country as a result of the first ruling, the agencies gave in.

By then, it was the spring of 1986, one year after their target date. Some of their fertilizer had washed away already for lack of erosion-preventing clover. It was getting late to start crops, and they were running short of money. Nevertheless, they moved to New Mexico and began the backbreaking job of getting everything started. There were fifty-five of them, with nine children aged three months to six years.

I don't know what I expected. I remember that everything was a surprise, either because it was so normal or because it was so different. None of my idiot surmises about what such a place might be like proved to be true. And of course I didn't know the history of the place; I learned that later, picked it up in bits and pieces.

I was surprised to see lights in some of the buildings. The first thing I assumed was that they would have no need of them. That's an example of something so normal that it surprised me.

As to the differences, the first thing that caught my attention was the fence around the rail line. I had a personal interest in it, having almost been injured by it. I struggled to understand, as I must if I was to stay here even for a night.

The wood fences that enclosed the rails on their way to the gate continued up to a barn, where the rails looped back on themselves in the same way they had outside the wall. The entire line was enclosed by the fence. The only access was a loading platform by the barn and the gate to the outside. It made sense. The only way a deaf-blind person could operate a conveyance like that would be with assurances that there was no one on the track. These people would *never* go on the tracks; there was no way they could be warned of an approaching train.

There were people moving around me in the twilight as I made my way into the group of buildings. They took no notice of me, as I had expected. They moved fast; some of them were actually running. I stood still, eyes searching all around me so no one would come crashing into me. I had to figure out how they kept from crashing into each other before I got bolder.

I bent to the ground and examined it. The light was getting bad, but I saw immediately that there were concrete sidewalks crisscrossing the area. Each of the walks was etched with a different sort of pattern in grooves that had been made before the stuff set—lines, waves, depressions, patches of rough and smooth. I quickly saw that the people who were in a hurry moved only on those walkways, and they were all barefoot. It was no trick to see that it was some sort of traffic pattern read with the feet. I stood up. I didn't need to know how it worked. It was sufficient to know what it was and stay off the paths.

The people were unremarkable. Some of them were not dressed, but I was used to that by now. They came in all shapes and sizes, but all seemed to be about the same age, except for the children. Except for the fact that they did not stop and talk or even wave as they approached each other, I would never have guessed they were blind. I watched them come to intersections in the pathways—I didn't know how they knew they were there but could think of several ways—and slow down as they crossed. It was a marvelous system.

I began to think of approaching someone. I had been there for almost half an hour, an intruder. I guess I had a false sense of these people's vulnerability; I felt like a burglar.

I walked along beside a woman for a minute. She was very purposeful in her eyes-ahead stride, or seemed to be. She sensed something, maybe my footsteps. She slowed a little, and I touched her on the shoulder, not knowing what else to do. She stopped dead instantly and turned toward me. Her eyes were open, but vacant. Her hands were all over me, lightly touching my face, my chest, my hands, fingering my clothing. There was no doubt in my mind that she knew me for a stranger, probably from the first tap on the shoulder. But she smiled warmly at me, and hugged me. Her hands were very delicate and warm. That's funny, because they were calloused from hard work, but it was still true; they felt sensitive.

She made me to understand—by pointing to the building, making eating motions with an imaginary spoon, and touching a number on her watch—that supper was served in an hour and that I was invited. I nodded and smiled beneath her hands; she kissed me on the cheek and hurried off.

Well. It hadn't been so bad. I had worried about my ability to communicate. Later I found out she learned a great deal more about me than I had told.

I put off going into the mess hall or whatever it was. I strolled around in the gathering darkness looking at their layout. I saw the little sheltie bringing the sheep back to the fold for the night. She herded them expertly through the open gate without any instructions, and one of the residents closed it and locked them in. The man bent and scratched the dog on the head and got his hand licked. Her chores done for the night, the dog hurried over to me and sniffed my pant leg. She followed me around the rest of the evening.

Everyone seemed so busy that I was surprised to see one woman sitting on a rail fence, doing nothing. I went over to her.

Closer, I saw that she was younger than I had thought. She was thirteen, I learned later. She wasn't wearing any clothes. I touched her on the shoulder, and she jumped down from the fence and went through the same routine as the other woman had, touching me all over with no reserve. She took my hand and I felt her fingers moving rapidly in my palm. I couldn't understand it, but knew what it was. I shrugged and tried out

other gestures to indicate that I didn't speak hand-talk.
She nodded, still feeling my face with her hands.

She asked me if I was staying to dinner. I assured her
that I was. She asked me if I was from a university.
And if you think that's easy to ask with only body
movements, try it. But she was so graceful and supple in
her movements, so deft at getting her meaning across. It
was beautiful to watch her. It was speech and ballet at
the same time.

I told her I wasn't from a university and launched
into an attempt to tell her a little about what I was
doing and how I got there. She listened to me with her
hands, scratching her head graphically when I failed to
make my meanings clear. All the time, the smile on her
face got broader and broader, and she would laugh silently at my antics. All this while standing very close to
me, touching me. At last she put her hands on her hips.

"I guess you need the practice," she said. "But if it's
all the same to you, could we talk mouth-talk for now?
You're cracking me up."

I jumped as if stung by a bee. The touching, while
something I could ignore for a deaf-blind girl, suddenly
seemed out of place. I stepped back a little, but her
hands remained on me. She looked puzzled, then read
the problem with her hands.

"I'm sorry," she said. "You thought I was deaf and
blind. If I'd known I would have told you right off."

"I thought everyone here was."

"Just the parents. I'm one of the children. We all
hear and see quite well. Don't be so nervous. If you
can't stand touching, you're not going to like it here.
Relax, I won't hurt you." And she kept her hands moving over me, mostly my face. I didn't understand it at
the time, but it didn't seem sexual. Turned out I was
wrong, but it wasn't blatant.

"You'll need me to show you the ropes," she said and
started for the domes. She held my hand and walked
close to me. Her other hand kept moving to my face
every time I talked.

"Number One: stay off the concrete paths. That's
where—"

"I already figured that out."

"You did? How long have you been here?" Her hands searched my face with renewed interest. It was quite dark.

"Less than an hour. I was almost run over by your train."

She laughed, then apologized and said she knew it wasn't funny to me.

I told her it *was* funny to me now, though it hadn't been at the time. She said there was a warning sign on the gate, but I had been unlucky enough to come when the gate was open—they did it by remote control before the train started up—and I hadn't seen it.

"What's your name?" I asked her as we neared the soft yellow lights coming from the dining room.

Her hand worked reflexively in mine, then stopped. "Oh, I don't know. I *have* one; several, in fact. But they're in body-talk. I'm . . . Pink. It translates as Pink, I guess."

There was a story behind it. She had been the first child born to the school students. They knew that babies were described as being pink, and so they called her that. She felt pink to them. As we entered the hall, I could see that it was visually inaccurate. One of her parents had been black. She was dark, with blue eyes and curly hair lighter than her skin. She had a broad nose, but small lips.

She didn't ask my name, and so I didn't offer it. No one asked my name, in speech, the entire time I was there. They called me many things in body-talk, and when the children called me, it was "Hey, you!" They weren't big on spoken words.

The dining hall was in a rectangular building made of brick. It connected to one of the large domes. It was dimly lighted. I later learned that the lights were for me alone. The children didn't need them for anything but reading. I held on to Pink's hand, glad to have a guide. I kept my eyes and ears open.

"We're informal," Pink said. Her voice was embarrassingly loud in the large room. No one else was talking at all; there were just the sounds of movement and breathing. Several of the children looked up. "I won't introduce you around now. Just feel like part of the family. People will feel you later, and you can talk to them. You can take your clothes off here at the door."

I had no trouble with that. Everyone else was nude, and I could easily adjust to household customs by that time. You take your shoes off in Japan, you take your clothes off in Taos. What's the difference?

Well, quite a bit, actually. There was all the touching that went on. Everybody touched everybody else, as routinely as glancing. Everyone touched my face first, then went on with what seemed like total innocence to touch me everywhere else. As usual, it was not quite what it seemed. It was *not* innocent, and it was not the usual treatment they gave others in their group. They touched each other's genitals a lot *more* than they touched mine. They were holding back with me so I wouldn't be frightened. They were very polite with strangers.

There was a long, low table, with everyone sitting on the floor around it. Pink led me to it.

"See the bare strips on the floor? Stay out of them. Don't leave anything in them. That's where people walk. Don't *ever* move anything. Furniture, I mean. That has to be decided at full meetings, so we'll all know where everything is. Small things, too. If you pick up something, put it back exactly where you found it."

"I understand."

People were bringing bowls and platters of food from the kitchen, which adjoined. They set them on the table, and the diners began feeling them. They ate with their fingers, without plates, and they did it slowly and lovingly. They smelled things for a long time before they took a bite. Eating was very sensual to these people.

They were *terrific* cooks. I have never, before or since, eaten as well as I did at Keller. (That's my name for it, in speech, though their body-talk name was something very like that. When I called it Keller, everyone knew what I was talking about.) They started off with good, fresh produce, something that's hard enough to find in the cities, and went at the cooking with artistry and imagination. It wasn't like any national style I've eaten. They improvised and seldom cooked the same thing the same way twice.

I sat between Pink and the fellow who almost ran me down earlier. I stuffed myself disgracefully. It was too far removed from beef jerky and the organic dry card-board I had been eating for me to be able to resist. I lingered over it, but still finished long before anyone else. I watched them as I sat back carefully and wondered if I'd be sick. (I wasn't, thank God.) They fed themselves and each other, sometimes getting up and going clear around the table to offer a choice morsel to a friend on the other side. I was fed in this way by all too many of them, and nearly popped until I learned a pidgin phrase in hand-talk, saying I was full to the brim. I learned from Pink that a friendlier way to refuse was to offer something myself.

Eventually I had nothing to do but feed Pink and look at the others. I began to be more observant. I had thought they were eating in solitude but soon saw that lively conversation was flowing around the table. Hands were busy, moving almost too fast to see. They were spelling into each other's palms, shoulders, legs, arms, bellies, any part of the body. I watched in amazement as a ripple of laughter spread like falling dominoes from one end of the table to the other as some witticism was passed along the line. It was *fast*. Looking carefully, I could see the thoughts moving, reaching one person, passed on while a reply went in the other direction and was in turn passed on, other replies originating all along the line and bouncing back and forth. They were a wave-form, like water.

It was messy. Let's face it; eating with your fingers and talking with your hands is going to get you smeared with food. But no one minded. *I* certainly didn't. I was too busy feeling left out. Pink talked to me, but I knew I was finding out what it's like to be deaf. These people were friendly and seemed to like me but could do nothing about it. We couldn't communicate.

Afterwards, we all trooped outside, except the clean-up crew, and took a shower beneath a set of faucets that gave out very cold water. I told Pink I'd like to help with the dishes, but she said I'd just be in the way. I couldn't do anything around Keller until I learned their very specific ways of doing things. She seemed to be assuming already that I'd be around that long.

Back into the building to dry off, which they did with their usual puppy-dog friendliness, making a game and a gift of toweling each other, and then we went into the dome.

It was warm inside, warm and dark. Light entered from the passage to the dining room, but it wasn't enough to blot out the stars through the lattice of triangular panes overhead. It was almost like being out in the open.

Pink quickly pointed out the positional etiquette within the dome. It wasn't hard to follow, but I still tended to keep my arms and legs pulled in close so I wouldn't trip someone by sprawling into a walk space.

My misconceptions got me again. There was no sound but the soft whisper of flesh against flesh, and so I thought I was in the middle of an orgy. I had been at them before, in other communes, and they looked pretty much like this. I quickly saw that I was wrong and only later found out I had been right. In a sense.

What threw my evaluations out of whack was the simple fact that group conversation among these people *had* to look like an orgy. The much subtler observation that I made later was that with a hundred naked bodies sliding, rubbing, kissing, caressing all at the same time, what was the point in making a distinction? There was no distinction.

I have to say that I use the noun "orgy" only to get across a general idea of many people in close contact. I don't like the word, it is too ripe with connotations. But I had these connotations myself at the time, and so I was relieved to see that it was not an orgy. The ones I had been to had been tedious and impersonal, and I had hoped for better from these people.

Many wormed their way through the crush to get to me and meet me. It was never more than one at a time; they were constantly aware of what was going on and were waiting their turn to talk to me. Naturally, I didn't know it then. Pink sat with me to interpret the hard thoughts. I eventually used her words less and less, getting into the spirit of tactile seeing and understanding.

No one felt they really knew me until they had touched every part of my body, and there were hands on me all the time. I timidly did the same.

What with all the touching, I quickly got an erection which embarrassed me quite a bit. I was berating myself for being unable to keep sexual responses out of it, for not being able to operate on the same intellectual plane I thought they were on, when I realized with some shock that the couple next to me were making love. They had been doing it for the last ten minutes, actually, and it had seemed such a natural part of what was happening that I had known it and not known it at the same time.

No sooner had I realized it than I suddenly wondered if I was right. *Were they?* It was very slow and the light was bad. But her legs were up, and he was on top of her—that much I was sure of. It was foolish of me, but I really had to know. I had to find out *what the hell I was in*. How could I give the proper social responses if I didn't know the situation?

I was very sensitive to polite behavior after my months at various communes. I had become adept at saying prayers before supper in one place, chanting Hare Krishna at another, and going happily nudist at still another. It's called "when in Rome," and if you can't adapt to it you shouldn't go visiting. I would kneel to Mecca, burp after my meals, toast anything that was proposed, eat organic rice and compliment the cook; but to do it right, you have to know the customs. I had thought I knew them but had changed my mind three times in as many minutes.

They *were* making love, in the sense that he was penetrating her. They were also deeply involved with each other. Their hands fluttered like butterflies all over each other, filled with meanings I couldn't see or feel. But they were being touched by and were touching many other people around them. They were talking to all these people, even if the message was as simple as a pat on the forehead or arm.

Pink noticed where my attention was. She was sort of wound around me, without really doing anything I would have thought of as provocative. I just couldn't *decide*. It seemed so innocent, and yet it wasn't.

"That's(—) and (—)," she said, the parentheses indicating a series of hand motions against my palm. I never learned a sound word as a name for any of them but Pink, and I can't reproduce the body-talk names they had. Pink reached over and touched the woman with her foot and did some complicated business with her toes. The woman smiled and grabbed Pink's foot, her fingers moving.

"(—) would like to talk with you later," Pink told me. "Right after she's through talking to (—). You met her earlier, remember? She says she likes your hands."

Now this is going to sound crazy, I know. It sounded pretty crazy to me when I thought of it. It dawned on me with a sort of revelation that her word for talk and mine were miles apart. Talk, to her, meant a complex interchange involving all parts of the body. She could read words or emotions in every twitch of my muscles, like a lie detector. Sound, to her, was only a minor part of communication. It was something she used to speak to outsiders. Pink talked with her whole being.

I didn't have the half of it, even then, but it was enough to turn my head entirely around in relation to these people. They talked with their bodies. It wasn't all hands, as I'd thought. Any part of the body in contact with all other was communication, sometimes a very simple and basic sort—think of McLuhan's light bulb as the basic medium of information—perhaps saying no more than "I am here." But talk was talk, and if conversation evolved to the point where you needed to talk to another with your genitals, it was still a part of the conversation. What I wanted to know was *what were they saying?* I knew, even at that dim moment of realization, that it was much more than I could grasp. Sure, you're saying. You know about talking to your lover with your body as you make love. That's not such a new idea. Of course it isn't, but think how wonderful that talk is even when you're not primarily tactile-oriented. Can you carry the thought from there, or are you doomed to be an earthworm thinking about sunsets?

While this was happening to me, there was a woman

getting acquainted with my body. Her hands were on me, in my lap, when I felt myself ejaculating. It was a big surprise to me, but to no one else. I had been telling everyone around me for many minutes that it was going to happen through signs they could feel with their hands. Instantly, hands were all over my body. I could almost understand them as they spelled tender thoughts to me. I got the gist, anyway, if not the words. I was terribly embarrassed for only a moment; then it passed away in the face of the easy acceptance. It was very intense. For a long time I couldn't get my breath.

The woman who had been the cause of it touched my lips with her fingers. She moved them slowly, but meaningfully I was sure. Then she melted back into the group.

"What did she say?" I asked Pink.

She smiled at me. "You know, of course. If you'd only cut loose from your verbalizing. But, generally, she meant 'How nice for you.' It also translates as 'How nice for me.' And 'me,' in this sense, means all of us. The organism."

I knew I had to stay and learn to speak.

The commune had its ups and downs. They had expected them, in general, but had not known what shape they might take.

Winter killed many of their fruit trees. They replaced them with hybrid strains. They lost more fertilizer and soil in windstorms because the clover had not had time to anchor it down. Their schedule had been thrown off by the court actions, and they didn't really get things settled in a groove until the following year.

Their fish all died. They used the bodies for fertilizer and looked into what might have gone wrong. They were using a three-stage ecology of the type pioneered by the New Alchemists in the seventies. It consisted of three domed ponds: one containing fish, another with crushed shells and bacteria in one section and algae in another, and a third full of daphnids. The water containing fish waste from the first pond was pumped through the shells and bacteria, which detoxified it and converted the ammonia it contained into fertilizer for the algae. The algae water was pumped into the third pond to feed the daphnids. Then daphnids and algae were pumped to the fish pond as food and the enriched water was used to fertilize greenhouse plants in all of the domes.

They tested the water and the soil and found that chemicals were being leached from impurities in the shells and concentrated down the food chain. After a thorough clean-up and a restart, all went well. But they had lost their first cash crop.

They never went hungry. Nor were they cold; there was plenty of sunlight year-round, both to power the pumps and the food cycle and to heat their living quarters. They had built their buildings half-buried with an eye to the heating and cooling powers of convective currents. But they had to spend some of their capital. The first year they showed a loss.

One of their buildings caught fire during the first winter. Two men and a small girl were killed when a sprinkler system malfunctioned. This was a shock to them. They had thought things would operate as advertised. None of them knew much about the building trades, about estimates as opposed to realities. They found that several of their installations were not up to specs and instituted a program of periodic checks on everything. They learned to strip down and repair anything on the farm. If something contained electronics too complex for them to cope with, they tore it out and installed something simpler.

Socially, their progress had been much more encouraging. Janet had wisely decided that there would be only two hard and fast objectives in the realm of their relationships. The first was that she refused to be their president, chairwoman, chief, or supreme commander. She had seen from the start that a driving personality was needed to get the planning done and the land bought and to foster a sense of purpose from their formless desire for an alternative. But once at the promised land, she abdicated. They would operate from that point as a democratic communism. If that failed, they would adopt a new approach. Anything but a dictatorship with her at the head. She wanted no part of that.

The second principle was to accept nothing. There had never been a blind-deaf community operating on its own. They had no expectations to satisfy; they did not need to live as the sighted did. They were alone. There was no one to tell them not to do something simply because it was not done.

They had no clearer idea of what their society would be than anyone else. They had been forced into a mold that was not relevant to their needs, but beyond that they didn't know. They would search out the behavior that made sense, the moral things for blind-deaf people to do. They understood the basic principles of morals: that nothing is moral always, and anything is moral under the right circumstances. It all had to do with social context. They were starting from a blank slate, with no models to follow.

By the end of the second year they had their context. They continually modified it, but the basic pattern was set. They knew themselves and what they were as they had never been able to do at the school. They defined themselves in their own terms.

I spent my first day at Keller in school. It was the obvious and necessary step. I had to learn hand-talk.

Pink was kind and very patient. I learned the basic alphabet and practiced hard at it. By the afternoon she was refusing to talk to me, forcing me to speak with my hands. She would speak only when pressed hard, and eventually not at all. I scarcely spoke a single oral word after the third day.

This is not to say that I was suddenly fluent. Not at all. At the end of the first day I knew the alphabet and could laboriously make myself understood. I was not so good at reading words spelled into my own palm. For a long time I had to look at the hand to see what was spelled. But like any language, eventually you think in it. I speak fluent French, and I recall the amazement when I finally reached the point where I wasn't translating my thoughts before I spoke. I reached it at Keller in about two weeks.

I remember one of the last things I asked Pink in speech. It was something that was worrying me.

"Pink, am I welcome here?"

"You've been here three days. Do you feel rejected?"

"No, it's not that. I guess I just need to hear your policy about outsiders. How *long* am I welcome?"

She wrinkled her brow. It was evidently a new question.

"Well, practically speaking, until a majority of us decide we want you to go. But that's never happened. No one's stayed here much longer than a few days. We've never had to evolve a policy about what to do, for instance, if someone who sees and hears wants to join us. No one has, so far, but I guess it could happen. My guess is that they wouldn't accept it. They're very independent and jealous of their freedom, though you might not have seen it. I don't think you could ever be one of them. But as long as you're willing to think of yourself as a guest, you could probably stay for twenty years."

"You said 'they.' Don't you include yourself in the group?"

For the first time she looked a little uneasy. I wish I had been better at reading body language at the time. I think my hands could have told me volumes about what she was thinking.

"Sure," she said. "The children are part of the group. We like it. I sure wouldn't want to be anywhere else, from what I know of the outside."

"I don't blame you." There were things left unsaid here, but I didn't know enough to ask the right question. "But it's never a problem, being able to see when none of your parents can? They don't . . . resent you in any way?"

This time she laughed. "Oh, no. Never that. They're much too independent for that. You've seen it. They don't *need* us for anything they can't do themselves. We're part of the family. We do exactly the same things they do. And it really doesn't matter. Sight, I mean. Hearing, either. Just look around you. Do I have any special advantages because I see where I'm going?"

I had to admit that she didn't. But there was still the hint of something she wasn't saying to me.

"I know what's bothering you. About staying here."

She had to draw me back to my original question; I had been wandering.

"What's that?"

"You don't feel a part of the daily life. You're not doing your share of the chores. You're very conscientious and you want to do your part. I can tell."

She read me right, as usual, and I admitted it.

"And you won't be able to until you can talk to everybody. So let's get back to your lessons. Your fingers are still very sloppy."

There was a lot of work to be done. The first thing I had to learn was to slow down. They were slow and methodical workers, made few mistakes, and didn't care if a job took all day as long as it was done well. If I was working by myself I didn't have to worry about it: sweeping, picking apples, weeding in the gardens. But when I was on a job that required teamwork, I had to learn a whole new pace. Eyesight enables a person to do many aspects of a job at once with a few quick glances. A blind person will take each aspect of the job in turn if the job is spread out. Everything has to be verified by touch. At a bench job, though, they could be much faster than I. They could make me feel like I was working with my toes instead of fingers.

I never suggested that I could make anything quicker by virtue of my sight or hearing. They quite rightly would have told me to mind my own business. Accepting sighted help was the first step to dependence, and, after all, they would still be here with the same jobs to do after I was gone.

And that got me to thinking about the children again. I began to be positive that there was an undercurrent of resentment, maybe unconscious, between parent and child. It was obvious that there was a great deal of love between them, but how could the children fail to resent the rejection of their talent? So my reasoning went, anyway.

I quickly fit myself into the routine. I was treated no better and no worse than anyone else, which gratified me. Though I would never become part of the group, even if I should desire it, there was absolutely no indication that I was anything but a full member. That's just how they treated guests: as they would one of their own number.

Life was fulfilling out there in a way it has never been in the cities. It wasn't unique to Keller, this pastoral peace, but they had it in generous helpings. The earth beneath your bare feet is something you can never feel in a city park.

Daily life was busy and satisfying. There were chickens and hogs to feed, bees and sheep to care for, fish to harvest and cows to milk. Everybody worked: men, women, and children. It all seemed to fit together without any apparent effort. Everybody seemed to know what to do when it needed doing. You could think of it as a well-oiled machine, but I never liked that metaphor, especially for people. I thought of it as an organism. Any social group is, but this one *worked*. Most of the other communes I'd visited had glaring flaws. Things would not get done because everyone was too stoned or couldn't be bothered or didn't see the necessity of doing it in the first place. That sort of ignorance leads to typhus and soil erosion and people freezing to death and invasions of social workers who take your children away. I'd seen it happen.

Not here. They had a good picture of the world-as-it-is, not the rosy misconceptions so many other utopians labor under. They did the jobs that needed doing.

I could never detail all the nuts and bolts (there's that machine metaphor again) of how the place worked. The fish-cycle ponds alone were complicated enough to overawe me. I killed a spider in one of the greenhouses, then found out it had been put there to eat a specific set of plant predators. Same for the frogs. There were insects in the water to kill other insects, and it got to where I was afraid to swat a mayfly without prior okay.

As the days went by, I was told some of the history of the place. There were mistakes that had been made, though surprisingly few. One had been in the area of defense. They had made no provision for it at first, not knowing much about the brutality and random violence that reaches even to the out-of-the-way corners.

Guns were the logical and preferred choice out here but were beyond their capabilities.

One night a carload of men who had had too much to drink showed up. They had heard of the place in town. They stayed for two days, cutting the phone lines and raping many of the women.

The people discussed all the options after the invasion was over, and they settled on the organic one. They bought five German shepherds. Not the psychotic wretches that are marketed under the description of "attack dogs," but specially trained ones from a firm recommended by the Albuquerque police. They were trained both as seeing-eye and police dogs. They were perfectly harmless until an outsider showed overt aggression; then they were trained not to disarm, but to go for the throat.

It worked, like most of their solutions. The second invasion resulted in two dead and three badly injured, all on the other side. As a back-up in case of a concerted attack, they hired an ex-marine to teach them the fundamentals of close-in dirty fighting. These were not dewy-eyed flower children.

There were three superb meals a day. And there was leisure time, too. It was not all work. There was time for someone to stop working for a few minutes, to share some special treasure. I remember being taken by the hand by one woman—who I must call Tall-one-with-the-green-eyes—to a spot where mushrooms were growing in the cool crawl-space beneath the barn. We wriggled under until our faces were buried in the patch, picked a few, and smelled them. She showed me how to smell. I would have thought a few weeks before that we had ruined their beauty, but, after all, it was only visual. I was already beginning to discount that sense, which is so removed from the essence of an object. She showed me that they were still beautiful to touch and smell after we had apparently destroyed them. Then she was off to the kitchen with the pick of the bunch in her apron. They tasted all the better that night.

And a man—I will call him Baldy—who brought me a plank he and one of the women had been planing in the woodshop. I touched its smoothness and smelled it and agreed with him how good it was.

And after the evening meal, the Together.

During my third week there, I had an indication of my status with the group. It was the first real test of whether I meant anything to them. Anything special, I mean. I wanted to see them as my friends, and I suppose I was a little upset to think that just anyone who wandered in here would be treated the same as I was. It was childish and unfair to them, and I wasn't even aware of the discontent until later.

I had been hauling water in a bucket into the field where a seedling tree was being planted. There was a hose for that purpose, but it was in use on the other side of the village. This tree was not in reach of the automatic sprinklers and it was drying out. I had been carrying water to it while another solution was found.

It was hot, around noon. I got the water from a standing spigot near the forge. I set the bucket down on the ground behind me and leaned my head into the flow of water. I was wearing a shirt made of cotton, unbuttoned in the front. The water felt good running through my hair and soaking into the shirt. I let it go on for almost a minute.

There was a crash behind me, and I bumped my head when I raised it up too quickly under the faucet. I turned and saw a woman sprawled on her face in the dust. She was turning over slowly, holding her knee. I realized with a sinking feeling that she had tripped over the bucket I had carelessly left on the concrete express lane. Think of it: ambling along on ground that you trust to be free of all obstruction, suddenly you're sitting on the ground. Their system would only work with trust, and it had to be total, and everybody had to be responsible all the time. I had been accepted into that trust, and I had blown it. I felt sick.

She had a nasty scrape on her left knee that was oozing blood. She felt it with her hands, sitting there on the ground, and she began to howl. It was weird, painful. Tears came from her eyes; then she pounded her fists on the ground, going "Hunnnh, hunnnh, *hunnn!*" with each blow. She was angry, and she had every right to be.

She found the pail as I hesitantly reached out for her. She grabbed my hand and followed it up to my face. She felt my face, crying all the time, then wiped her nose and got up. She started off for one of the buildings. She limped slightly.

I sat down and felt miserable. I didn't know what to do.

One of the men came out to get me. It was Big Man. I called him that because he was the tallest of anyone at Keller. He wasn't any sort of policeman, I found out later; he was just the first one the injured woman had met. He took my hand and felt my face. I saw tears start when he felt the emotions there. He asked me to come inside with him.

An impromptu panel had been convened. Call it a jury. It was made up of anyone who was handy, including a few children. There were ten or twelve of them. Everyone looked very sad. The woman I had hurt was there, being consoled by three or four people. I'll call her Scar, for the prominent mark on her upper arm.

Everybody kept telling me—in hand-talk, you understand—how sorry they were for me. They petted and stroked me, trying to draw some of the misery away.

Pink came racing in. She had been sent for to act as a translator if needed. Since this was a formal proceeding, it was necessary that they be sure I understood everything that happened. She went to Scar and cried with her for a bit, then came to me and embraced me fiercely, telling me with her hands how sorry she was that this had happened. I was already figuratively packing my bags. Nothing seemed to be left but the formality of expelling me.

Then we all sat together on the floor. We were close, touching on all sides. The hearing began.

Most of it was in hand-talk, with Pink throwing in a few words here and there. I seldom knew who said what, but that was appropriate. It was the group speaking as one. No statement reached me without already having become a consensus.

"You are accused of having violated the rules," said

the group, "and of having been the cause of an injury to (the one I called Scar). Do you dispute this? Is there any fact that we should know?"

"No," I told them. "I was responsible. It was my carelessness."

"We understand. We sympathize with you in your remorse, which is evident to all of us. But carelessness is a violation. Do you understand this? This is the offense for which you are —." It was a set of signals in shorthand.

"What was that?" I asked Pink.

"Uh . . . 'brought before us?' 'Standing trial?' " She shrugged, not happy with either interpretation.

"Yes. I understand."

"The facts not being in question, it is agreed that you are guilty." (" 'Responsible,' " Pink whispered in my ear.) "Withdraw from us a moment while we come to a decision."

I got up and stood by the wall, not wanting to look at them as a debate went back and forth through the joined hands. There was a burning lump in my throat that I could not swallow. Then I was asked to rejoin the circle.

"The penalty for your offense is set by custom. If it were not so, we would wish we could rule otherwise. You now have the choice of accepting the punishment designated and having the offense wiped away, or of refusing our jurisdiction and withdrawing your body from our land. What is your choice?"

I had Pink repeat this to me, because it was so important that I know what was being offered. When I was sure I had read it right, I accepted their punishment without hesitation. I was very grateful to have been given an alternative.

"Very well. You have elected to be treated as we would treat one of our own who had done the same act. Come to us."

The group lost its discrete circle as everyone drew in closer. I was not told what was going to happen. I was drawn in and nudged gently from all directions.

Scar was sitting with her legs crossed more or less in the center of the group. She was crying again, and so was I, I think. It's hard to remember. I ended up face-down across her lap. She spanked me.

I never once thought of it as improbable or strange. It flowed naturally out of the situation. Everyone was holding on to me and caressing me, spelling assurances into my palms and legs and neck and cheeks. We were all crying. It was a difficult thing that had to be faced by the whole group. Others drifted from everyone there, but only the offended person, Scar, did the actual spanking. That was one of the ways I had wronged her, beyond the fact of giving her a scraped knee. I had laid on her the obligation of disciplining me, and that was why she had sobbed so loudly, not the pain of her injury but the pain of knowing she would have to hurt me.

Pink later told me that Scar had been the staunchest advocate of giving me the option to stay. Some had wanted to expel me right out, but she paid me the compliment of thinking I was a good-enough person to be worth putting herself and me through the ordeal. If you can't understand that, you haven't grasped the feeling of community I felt for these people.

It went on for a long time. It was very painful, but not cruel. Nor was it primarily humiliating. There was some of that, of course. But it was essentially a practical lesson taught in the most direct terms. Each of them had undergone it during the first months, but none recently. You *learned* from it, believe me.

I did a lot of thinking about it afterwards. I tried to think of what else they might have done. Spanking grown people is really unheard of, you know, though that didn't occur to me until long after it happened. It seemed so natural when it was going on that the thought couldn't even enter my mind that this was a weird situation to be in.

They did something like this with the children, but not as long or as hard. There was a consensual lightening of responsibility for the younger ones. The adults were willing to put up with an occasional bruise or scraped knee while the children learned.

But when you reached what they thought of as adulthood—which was whenever a majority of the adults thought you were or when you assumed the privilege yourself—that's when the spanking really got serious.

They had a harsher punishment, reserved for repeated or malicious offenses. They had not had to invoke it often. It consisted of being sent to coventry. No one would touch you for a specified period of time. By the time I heard of it, it sounded like a very tough penalty. I didn't need it explained to me.

I don't know how to explain it, but the spanking was administered in such a loving way that I didn't feel violated. *This hurts me as much as it hurts you. I'm doing this for your own good. I love you, that's why I'm hurting you.* They made me understand those old clichés by their actions.

When it was over, we all cried together. But it soon turned to happiness. I embraced Scar and we told each other how sorry we were that it had happened. We talked to each other—made love if you like—and I kissed her knee and helped her dress it.

We spent the rest of the day together, easing the pain.

As I became more fluent in hand-talk, "the scales fell from my eyes." Daily, I would discover a new layer of meaning that had eluded me before, like peeling the skin of an onion to find a new skin beneath it. Each time I thought I was at the core, only to find that there was another layer I could not yet see.

I had thought that learning hand-talk was the key to communication with them. Not so. Hand-talk was baby talk. For a long time I was a baby who could not even say goo-goo clearly. Imagine my surprise when, having learned to say it, I found that there were syntax, conjugations, parts of speech, nouns, verbs, tense, agreement, and the subjunctive mood. I was wading in a tidepool at the edge of the Pacific Ocean.

By hand-talk, I mean the International Manual Alphabet. Anyone can learn it in a few hours or days. But when you talk to someone in speech, do you spell each word? Do you read each letter as you read this? No, you grasp words as entities, hear groups of sounds and see groups of letters as a gestalt full of meaning.

Everyone at Keller had an absorbing interest in language. They each knew several languages—spoken languages—and could read and spell them fluently.

While still children they had understood the fact that hand-talk was a way for blind-deaf people to talk to *outsiders*. Among themselves it was much too cumbersome. It was like Morse code: useful when you're limited to on-off modes of information transmission, but not the preferred mode. Their ways of speaking to each other were much closer to our type of written or verbal communication, and—dare I say it?—better.

I discovered this slowly, first by seeing that, though I could spell rapidly with my hands, it took *much* longer for me to say something than it took anyone else. It could not be explained by differences in dexterity. So I asked to be taught their shorthand speech. I plunged in, this time taught by everyone, not just Pink.

It was hard. They could say any word in any language with no more than two moving-hand positions. I knew this was a project for years, not days. You learn the alphabet and you have all the tools you need to spell any word there is. That's the great advantage in having your written and spoken speech based on the same set of symbols. Shorthand was not like that at all. It partook of none of the linearity or commonality of hand-talk; it was not code for English or any other language; it did not share construction or vocabulary with any other language. It was wholly constructed by the Kellerites according to their needs. Each word was something I had to learn and memorize separate from the hand-talk spelling.

For months I sat in the Togethers after dinner saying things like "Me love Scar much much well" while waves of conversation ebbed and flowed and circled around me, touching me only at the edges. But I kept at it, and the children were endlessly patient with me. I improved gradually. Understand that the rest of the conversations I will relate took place in either hand-talk or shorthand, limited to various degrees by my fluency. I did not speak nor was I spoken to orally from the day of my punishment.

I was having a lesson in body-talk from Pink. Yes, we were making love. It had taken me a few weeks to see that she was a sexual being, that her caresses, which I had persisted in seeing as innocent—as I had defined it at the time—both were and weren't innocent. She understood it as perfectly natural that the result of her talking to my penis with her hands might be another sort of conversation. Though still in the middle flush of puberty, she was regarded by all as an adult, and I accepted her as such. It was my cultural conditioning that had blinded me to what she was saying.

So we talked a lot. With her, I understood the words and music of the body better than with anyone else. She sang a very uninhibited song with her hips and hands, free of guilt, open and fresh with discovery in every note she touched.

"You haven't told me much about yourself," she said. "What did you do on the outside?" I don't want to give the impression that this speech was in sentences, as I have presented it. We were body-talking, sweating and smelling each other. The message came through from hands, feet, mouth.

I got as far as the sign for pronoun, first-person singular—and was stopped.

How could I tell her of my life in Chicago? Should I speak of my early ambition to be a writer and how that didn't work out? And why hadn't it? I could tell her about my drive. I could tell her about my profession, which was meaningless shuffling of papers when you got down to it, useless to anything but the Gross National Product. I could talk of the economic ups and downs that had brought me here when nothing else could dislodge me from my easy sliding through life. Or the loneliness of being forty-seven years old and never having found someone worth loving, never having been loved in return. Of being a permanently displaced person in a stainless-steel society. One-night stands, drinking binges, nine-to-five, Chicago Transit Authority, dark movie houses, football games on television, sleeping pills, the John Hancock Tower where the windows won't open so you can't breathe the smog or jump out. That was me, wasn't it?

"I see," she said.

"I travel around," I said and suddenly realized that it was the truth.

"I see," she repeated. It was a different sign for the same thing. Context was everything. She had heard and understood both parts of me, knew one to be what I had been, the other to be what I hoped I was.

She lay on top of me, one hand lightly on my face to catch the quick interplay of emotions as I thought about my life for the first time in years. And she laughed and nipped my ear playfully when my face told her that for the first time I could remember, I was happy about it. Not just telling myself I was happy, but for true. You cannot lie on body-talk any more than your sweat glands can lie on a polygraph.

I noticed that the room was unusually empty. Asking around in my fumbling way, I got a rough picture that only the children were here.

"Where is everybody?" I asked.

"They are all out ***," she said. It was like that: three sharp slaps on the chest with the fingers spread. Along with the finger configuration for "verb form, gerund," it meant that they were all out *** ing. Needless to say, it didn't tell me much.

What did tell me something was her body-talk as she said it. I read her better than I ever had. She was upset and sad. Her body said something like "Why can't I join them? Why can't I (smell-taste-touch-hear-see) sense with them?" That is exactly what she said. Again, I didn't trust my understanding enough to go with that interpretation. I was still trying to force my conceptions around the things I experienced here. I was determined that she and the other children be resentful of their parents in some way, because I was sure they had to be. They *must* feel superior in some way, they *must* feel held back.

I found them, after a short search of the area, out in the north pasture. All the parents, none of the children. They were standing in a group with no apparent pattern. It wasn't a circle, but it was almost round. If there was any organization, it was in the fact that everybody was about the same distance from everybody else.

The German shepherds and the sheltie were out there, sitting on the cool grass facing the group of people. Their ears were perked up, but they were not moving.

I started to go up to the people. I stopped when I became aware of the concentration. They were touching, but their hands were not moving. The silence of seeing all those permanently moving people standing that still was deafening to me.

I watched them for at least an hour. I sat with the dogs and scratched them behind the ears. They did that chop-licking thing that dogs do when they appreciate it, but their full attention was on the group.

It gradually dawned on me that the group was moving. It was very slow, just a step here and another there over many minutes. It was expanding in such a way that the distance between any of the individuals was the same. Like the expanding universe, where all galaxies move away from all others. Their arms were extended now; they were touching only with fingertips in a crystal lattice arrangement.

Finally they were not touching at all. I saw their fingers straining to cover distances that were too far to bridge. And still they expanded equilaterally. One of the shepherds began to whimper a little. I felt the hair on the back of my neck standing up. Chilly out here, I thought.

I closed my eyes, suddenly sleepy.

I opened them, shocked. Then I forced them shut. Crickets were chirping in the grass around me.

There was something in the darkness behind my eyeballs. I felt that if I could turn my eyes around I would see it easily, but it eluded me in a way that made peripheral vision seem like reading headlines. If there was ever anything impossible to pin down, much less describe, that was it. It tickled at me for a while as the dogs whimpered louder, but I could make nothing of it. The best analogy I could think of was the sensation a blind person might feel from the sun on a cloudy day.

I opened my eyes again.

Pink was standing there beside me. Her eyes were screwed shut, and she was covering her ears with her hands. Her mouth was open and working silently. Behind her were several of the older children. They were all doing the same thing.

Some quality of the night changed. The people in the group were about a foot away from each other now, and suddenly the pattern broke. They all swayed for a moment, then laughed in that eerie, unself-conscious noise deaf people use for laughter. They fell in the grass and held their bellies, rolled over and over and roared.

Pink was laughing, too. To my surprise, so was I. I laughed until my face and sides were hurting, like I remembered doing sometimes when I'd smoked grass.

And that was *** ing.

I can see that I've only given a surface view of Keller. And there are some things I should deal with, lest I foster an erroneous view.

Clothing, for instance. Most of them wore something most of the time. Pink was the only one who seemed temperamentally opposed to them. She never wore anything.

No one ever wore anything I'd call a pair of pants. Clothes were loose; robes, shirts, dresses, scarves, and such. Lots of men wore things that would be called women's clothes. They were simply more comfortable.

Much of it was ragged. It tended to be made of silk or velvet or something else that felt good. The stereotyped Kellerite would be wearing a Japanese silk robe, hand-embroidered with dragons, with many gaping holes and loose threads and tea and tomato stains all over it while she sloshed through the pigpen with a bucket of slop. Wash it at the end of the day and don't worry about the colors running.

I also don't seem to have mentioned homosexuality. You can mark it down to my early conditioning that my two deepest relationships at Keller were with women: Pink and Scar. I haven't said anything about it simply because I don't know how to present it. I talked to men and women equally, on the same terms. I had surprisingly little trouble being affectionate with the men.

I could not think of the Kellerites as bisexual, though clinically they were. It was much deeper than that. They could not even recognize a concept as poisonous as a homosexuality taboo. It was one of the first things they learned. If you distinguish homosexuality from hetero-sexuality, you are cutting yourself off from communica-tion—*full* communication—with half the human race. They were pansexual; they could not separate sex from the rest of their lives. They didn't even have a word in shorthand that could translate directly into English as sex. They had words for male and female in infinite variation and words for degrees and varieties of physi-cal experience that would be impossible to express in English, but all those words included other parts of the world of experience also; none of them walled off what we call *sex* into its own discrete cubbyhole.

There's another question I haven't answered. It needs answering, because I wondered about it myself when I first arrived. It concerns the necessity for the commune in the first place. Did it really have to be like this? Would they have been better off adjusting themselves to our ways of living?

All was not a peaceful idyll. I already spoke of the invasion and rape. It could happen again, especially if the roving gangs that operate around the cities start to really rove. A touring group of motorcyclists could wipe them out in a night.

There were also continuing legal hassles. About once a year the social workers descended on Keller and tried to take their children away. They had been attacked ev-ery way it was possible to be attacked, from child abuse to contributing to the delinquency . . . It hadn't worked so far, but it might someday.

And, after all, there are sophisticated devices on the market that allow a blind and deaf person to see and hear a little.

I met a blind-deaf woman living in Berkeley once. I'll vote for Keller.

As to those machines . . .

In the library at Keller there is a seeing machine. It uses a television camera and a computer to vibrate a close-set series of metal pins. Using it, you can feel a moving picture of whatever the camera is pointed at. It's small and light, made to be carried with the pin-pricker touching your back. It costs about thirty-five thousand dollars.

I found it in the corner of the library. I ran my finger over it and left a gleaming streak behind as the thick dust came away.

Other people came and went, and stayed on.

They didn't get as many visitors as the other places I had been. They were out of the way.

One man showed up at noon, looked around, and left without a word.

Two girls, sixteen-year-old runaways from California, showed up one night. They undressed for dinner and were shocked when they found out I could see. Pink scared the hell out of them. Those poor kids had a lot of living to do before they approached Pink's level of sophistication. But then Pink might have been uneasy in California. They left the next day, unsure if they had been to an orgy or not. All that touching and no getting down to business: very strange.

There was a nice couple from Santa Fe who acted as a sort of liaison between Keller and their lawyer. They had a nine-year-old boy who chattered endlessly in hand-talk to the other kids. They came up about every other week and stayed a few days, soaking up sunshine and participating in the Together every night. They spoke halting shorthand and did me the courtesy of not speaking to me in speech.

Some of the Indians came around at odd intervals. Their behavior was almost aggressively chauvinistic. They stayed dressed at all times in their levis and boots. But it was evident that they had a respect for the people, though they thought them strange. They had business dealings with the commune. It was the Navahos who trucked away the produce that was taken to the gate every day, sold it, and took a percentage. They would sit and powwow in sign language spelled into hands. Pink said they were scrupulously honest in their dealings.

And about once a week all the parents went out in the field and ***ed.

I got better and better at shorthand and body-talk. I had been breezing along for about five months, and winter was in the offing. I had not examined my desires as yet, not really thought about what it was I wanted to do with the rest of my life. I guess the habit of letting myself drift was too ingrained. I was here and constitutionally unable either to decide to go or face up to the problem if I wanted to stay for a long, long time.

Then I got a push.

For a long time I thought it had something to do with the economic situation outside. They were aware of the outside world at Keller. They knew that isolation and ignoring problems that could easily be dismissed as not relevant to them was a dangerous course. So they subscribed to the Braille *New York Times* and most of them read it. They had a television set that got plugged in about once a month. The kids would watch it and translate for their parents.

So I was aware that the nondepression was moving slowly into a more normal inflationary spiral. Jobs were opening up, money was flowing again. When I found myself on the outside again shortly afterwards, I thought that was the reason.

The real reason was more complex. It had to do with peeling off the onion layer of shorthand and discovering another layer beneath it.

I had learned hand-talk in a few easy lessons. Then I became aware of shorthand and body-talk and of how much harder they would be to learn. Through five months of constant immersion, which is the only way to learn a language, I had attained the equivalent level of a five- or six-year-old in shorthand. I knew I could master it, given time. Body-talk was another matter. You couldn't measure progress as easily in body-talk. It was a variable and highly interpersonal language that evolved according to the person, the time, the mood. But I was learning.

Then I became aware of Touch. That's the best I can describe it in a single, unforced English noun. What *they* called this fourth-stage language varied from day to day, as I will try to explain.

I first became aware of it when I tried to meet Janet Reilly. I now knew all the formative history of Keller, and she figured very prominently in all the stories. I knew everyone at Keller, and I could find her nowhere. I knew everyone by names like Scar and She-with-the-missing-front-tooth and Man-with-wiry-hair. These were shorthand names that I had given them myself, and they all accepted them without question. They had abolished their outside names within the commune. They meant nothing to them; they told nothing and described nothing.

At first I assumed that it was my imperfect command of shorthand that made me unable to clearly ask the right question about Janet Reilly. Then I saw that they were not telling me on purpose. I saw why, and I approved, and thought no more about it. The name Janet Reilly described what she had been *on the outside*, and one of her conditions for pushing the whole thing through in the first place had been that she be no one special on the inside. She had melted into the group and disappeared. She didn't want to be found. All right.

But in the course of pursuing the question I became aware that each of the members of the commune had no specific name at all. That is, Pink, for instance, had no fewer than one hundred and fifteen names, one from each of the commune members. Each was a contextual name that told the story of Pink's relationship to a particular person. My simple physical-description names were accepted as the names a child would apply to people. The children had not yet learned to go beneath the outer layers and use names that told of themselves, their lives, and their relationships to others.

What is even more confusing, the names evolved from day to day. It was my first glimpse of Touch, and it frightened me. It was a question of permutations. Just the first simple expansion of the problem meant there were no fewer than thirteen thousand names in use, and they wouldn't stay still so I could memorize them. If Pink spoke to me of Baldy, for instance, she would use her Touch name for him, modified by the fact that she was speaking to me, and not Short-chubby-man.

Then the depth of what I had been missing opened beneath me, and I was suddenly breathless with fear of heights.

Touch was what they spoke to each other. It was an incredible blend of all three other modes I had learned, and the essence of it was that it never stayed the same. I could listen to them speak to me in shorthand, which was the real basis for Touch, and be just aware of the currents of Touch flowing just beneath the surface.

It was a language of inventing languages. Everyone spoke their own dialect because everyone spoke with a different instrument: a different body and set of life experiences. It was modified by everything. *It would not stand still.*

They would sit at the Together and invent an entire body of Touch responses in a night; idiomatic, personal, totally naked in its honesty. And they used it only as a building block for the next night's language.

I didn't know if I wanted to be that naked. I had looked into myself a little recently and had not been satisfied with what I found. The realization that every one of them knew more about it than I because my honest body had told what my frightened mind had not wanted to reveal was shattering. I was naked under a spotlight in Carnegie Hall, and all the no-pants nightmares I ever had came out to haunt me. The fact that they all loved me with all my warts was suddenly not enough. I wanted to curl up in a dark closet with my ingrown ego and let it fester.

I might have come through this fear. Pink was certainly trying to help me. She told me that it would only hurt for a while, that I would quickly adjust to living my life with my darkest emotions written in fire across my forehead. She said Touch was not as hard as it looked at first, either. Once I learned shorthand and body-talk, Touch would flow naturally from it like sap rising in a tree. It would be unavoidable, something that would happen to me without much effort at all.

I almost believed her. But she betrayed herself. No, no, no. Not that, but the things in her concerning

*** ing convinced me that if I went through this I would only bang my head hard against the next step up the ladder.

***

I had a little better definition now. Not one that I can easily translate into English, and even that attempt will only convey my hazy concept of what it was.

"It is the mode of touching," Pink said, her body going like crazy in an attempt to reach me with her own imperfect concept of what it was, handicapped by my illiteracy. Her body denied the truth of her shorthand definition, and at the same time admitted to me that she did not know what it was herself.

"It is the gift whereby one can expand oneself from the eternal quiet and dark into something else." And again her body denied it. She beat on the floor in exasperation.

"It is an attribute of being in the quiet and dark all the time, touching others. All I know for sure is that vision and hearing preclude it or obscure it. I can make it as quiet and dark as I possibly can and be aware of the edges of it, but the visual orientation of the mind persists. That door is closed to me, and to all the children."

Her verb "to touch" in the first part of that was a Touch amalgam, one that reached back into her memories of me and what I had told her of my experiences. It implied and called up the smell and feel of broken mushrooms in soft earth under the barn with (Tall-one-with-green-eyes, she who taught me to feel the essence of an object). It also contained references to our body-talking while I was penetrating into dark and wet of her, and her running account to me of what it was like to receive me into herself. This was all one word.

I brooded on that for a long time. What was the point of suffering through the nakedness of Touch, only to reach the level of frustrated blindness enjoyed by Pink?

What was it that kept pushing me away from the one place in my life where I had been happiest?

One thing was the realization, quite late in coming, that can be summed up as "What the hell, am I *doing* here?" The question that should have answered that question was "What the hell would I do if I *left?*"

I was the only visitor, the only one in *seven years* to stay at Keller for longer than a few days. I brooded on that. I was not strong enough or confident enough in my opinion of myself to see it as anything but a flaw in *me*, not in those others. I was obviously too easily satisfied, too complacent to see the flaws that those others had seen.

It didn't have to be flaws in the people of Keller or in their system. No, I loved and respected them too much to think that. What they had going here was certainly as near as anyone has ever come in this imperfect world to a sane, rational way for people to exist without warfare and with a minimum of politics. In the end, those two old dinosaurs are the only ways humans have yet discovered to be social animals. Yes, I do see war as a way of living with another, by imposing your will on another in terms so unmistakable that the opponent has to either knuckle under to you, die, or beat your brains out. And if that's a solution to anything, I'd rather live without solutions. Politics is not much better. The only thing going for it is that it occasionally succeeds in substituting talk for fists.

Keller *was* an organism. It was a new way of relating, and it seemed to work. I'm not pushing it as a solution for the world's problems. It's possible that it could only work for a group with a common self-interest as binding and rare as deafness and blindness. I can't think of another group whose needs are so interdependent.

The cells of the organism cooperated beautifully. The organism was strong, flourishing, and possessed of all the attributes I've ever heard of for defining life except the ability to reproduce. That might have been its fatal flaw, if any. I certainly saw the seeds of something developing in the children.

The strength of the organism was communication. There's no way around it. Without the elaborate and impossible-to-falsify mechanisms for communication built into Keller, it would have eaten itself in pettiness, jealousy, possessiveness, and any dozen other "innate" human defects.

The nightly Together was the basis of the organism. Here, from after dinner to time to fall asleep, everyone talked in a language that was incapable of falsehood. If there was a problem brewing, it presented itself and was solved almost automatically. Jealousy? Resentment? Some little festering wrong that you're nursing? You couldn't conceal it at the Together, and soon everyone was clustered around you and loving the sickness away. It was like white corpuscles clustering around a sick cell, not to destroy it, but to heal it. There seemed to be no problem that couldn't be solved if it was attacked early enough, and, with Touch, your neighbors knew about it before you did and were already laboring to correct the wrong, heal the wound, to make you feel better so you could laugh about it. There was a lot of laughter at the Togethers.

I thought for a while that I was feeling possessive about Pink. I know I had done so a little at first. Pink was my special friend, the one who had helped me out from the first, who for several days was the only one I could talk to. It was her hands that taught me hand-talk, all by herself. I know I felt stirrings of territoriality the first time she lay in my lap while another man made love to her. But if there was any signal the Kellerites were adept at reading, it was that one. It went off like an alarm bell in Pink, the man, and the women and men around me. They soothed me, coddled me, told me in every language that it was all right, not to feel ashamed. Then the man in question began loving *me*. Not Pink, but the man. An observational anthropologist would have had subject matter for a whole thesis. Have you seen the films of baboons' social behavior? Dogs do it, too; many male mammals do it. When males get into dominance battles, the weaker can defuse the aggression by submitting by turning tail and surrendering. I have never felt so defused as when that man surrendered the object of our clash of wills—Pink—and turned his attention to me. What could I do? What I did was laugh, and he laughed, and soon we were all laughing, and that was the end of territoriality.

That's the essence of how they solved most "human nature" problems at Keller. Sort of like an oriental martial art; you yield, roll with the blow so that your attacker takes a pratfall with the force of the aggression. You do that until the attacker sees that the initial push wasn't worth the effort, that it was a pretty silly thing to do when no one was resisting you. Pretty soon he's not Tarzan of the Apes, but Charlie Chaplin. And he's laughing.

So it wasn't Pink and her lovely body and my realization that she could never be all mine to lock away in my cave and defend with a gnawed-off thighbone. If I'd persisted in that frame of mind, she would have found me about as attractive as an Amazonian leech, and that was a great incentive to confound the behaviorists and overcome it.

So I was back to those people who had visited and left, and what did they see that I didn't see?

Well, there was something pretty glaring. I was not part of the organism, no matter how nice the organism was to me. I had no hopes of ever becoming a part, either. Pink had said it in the first week. She felt it herself, to a lesser degree. She could not ***. That fact was not going to drive her away from Keller; she had told me that many times in shorthand and confirmed it in body-talk. If I left, it would be without her.

Trying to stand outside and look at it, I felt pretty miserable. What was I trying to *do*, anyway? Was my goal in life *really* to become a part of a blind-deaf commune? I was feeling so low by that time that I actually thought of that as denigrating, in the face of all the evidence to the contrary. I should be out in the real world where the real people lived, not these freakish cripples.

I backed off from that thought very quickly. I was not *totally* out of my mind, just on the lunatic edges. These people were the best friends I'd ever had, maybe the only ones. That I was confused enough to think that even for a second worried me more than anything else. It's possible that it's what pushed me finally into a decision. I saw a future of growing disillusion and unfulfilled hopes. Unless I was willing to put out my eyes and ears, I would always be on the outside. *I* would be the blind and deaf one. I would be the freak. I didn't want to be a freak.

They knew I had decided to leave before I did. My last few days turned into a long goodbye with a loving farewell implicit in every word touched to me. I was not really sad, and neither were they. It was nice, like everything they did. They said goodbye with just the right mix of wistfulness and life-must-go-on, and hope-to-touch-you-again.

Awareness of Touch scratched on the edges of my mind. It was not bad, just as Pink had said. In a year or two I could have mastered it.

But I was set now. I was back in my life-groove that I had followed for so long. Why is it that once having decided what I must do, I'm afraid to re-examine my decision? Maybe because the original decision cost me so much that I didn't want to go through it again.

I left quietly in the night for the highway and California. They were out in the fields, standing in that circle again. Their fingertips were farther apart than ever before. The dogs and children hung around the edges like beggars at a banquet. It was hard to tell which looked more hungry and puzzled.

The experiences at Keller did not fail to leave their mark on me. I was unable to live as I had before. For a while I thought I could not live at all, but I did. I was too used to living to take the decisive step of ending my life. I would wait. Life had brought one pleasant thing to me; maybe it would bring another.

I became a writer. I found I now had a better gift for communicating than I had before. Or maybe I had it now for the first time. At any rate, my writing came together and I sold. I wrote what I wanted to write and was not afraid of going hungry. I took things as they came.

I weathered the nondepression of '97, when unemployment reached 20 percent and the government once more ignored it as a temporary downturn. It eventually upturned, leaving the jobless rate slightly higher than it had been the time before and the time before that. Another million useless persons had been created with nothing better to do than shamble through the streets looking for beatings in progress, car smashups, heart attacks, murders, shootouts, arson, bombings, and riots: the endlessly inventive street theater. It never got dull.

I didn't become rich, but I was usually comfortable. That is a social disease, the symptom of which is the ability to ignore it while your society develops weeping pustules and has its brains eaten out by radioactive maggots. I had a nice apartment in Marin County, out of sight of the machine-gun turrets. I had a car, at a time when they were beginning to be luxuries.

I had concluded that my life was not destined to be all I would like it to be. We all make some sort of compromise, I reasoned; and if you set your expectations too high, you are doomed to disappointment. It did occur to me that I was settling for something far to the downwind side of "high," but I didn't know what to do about it. I made it with a mixture of cynicism and optimism that seemed about the right mix for me. I kept my motor running, anyway.

I even made it to Japan, as I had intended in the first place.

I didn't find someone to share my life. There was only Pink for that, Pink and all her family, and we were separated by a gulf I didn't dare cross. I didn't even dare think about her too much. It would have been very dangerous to my equilibrium. I lived with it and told myself that it was the way I was. Lonely.

The years rolled on like a Caterpillar tractor at Dachau, up to the penultimate day of the millennium.

San Francisco was having a big bash to celebrate the year 2000. Who gives a shit that the city is slowly falling apart, that civilization is disintegrating into hysteria? Let's have a party!

I stood on the Golden Gate Dam on the last day of 1999. The sun was setting in the Pacific, on Japan, which had turned out to be more of the same but squared and cubed with neo-samurai. Behind me, the first bombshells of a fireworks celebration of holocaust tricked up to look like festivity competed with the flare of burning buildings as the social and economic basketcases celebrated the occasion in their own way. The city quivered under the weight of misery, anxious to slide off along the fracture lines of some subcortical San Andreas Fault. Orbiting atomic bombs twinkled in my mind, up there somewhere, ready to plant mushrooms when we'd exhausted all the other possibilities.

I thought of Pink.

I found myself speeding through the Nevada desert, sweating, gripping the steering wheel. I was crying aloud but without sound, as I had learned to do at Keller.

Can you go back?

I slammed the citicar over the potholes in the dirt road. The car was falling apart. It was not built for this kind of travel. The sky was getting light in the east. It was the dawn of a new millennium. I stepped harder on the gas pedal and the car bucked savagely. I didn't care. I was not driving back down this road, not ever. One way or another, I was here to stay.

I reached the wall and sobbed my relief. The last hundred miles had been a nightmare of wondering if it had been a dream. I touched the cold reality of the wall and it calmed me. Light snow had drifted over everything, gray in the early dawn.

I saw them in the distance. All of them, out in the field where I had left them. No, I was wrong. It was only the children. Why had it seemed like so many at first?

Pink was there. I knew her immediately, though I had never seen her in winter clothes. She was taller, filled out. She would be nineteen years old. There was a small child playing in the snow at her feet, and she cradled an infant in her arms. I went to her and talked to her hand.

She turned to me, her face radiant with welcome, her eyes staring in a way I had never seen. Her hands flitted over me and her eyes did not move.

"I touch you, I welcome you," her hands said. "I wish you could have been here just a few minutes ago. Why did you go away, darling? Why did you stay away so long?" Her eyes were stones in her head. She was blind. She was deaf.

All the children were. No, Pink's child sitting at my feet looked up at me with a smile.

"Where is everybody?" I asked when I got my breath. "Scar? Baldy? Green-eyes? And what's happened? What's happened to you?" I was tottering on the edge of a heart attack or nervous collapse or something. My reality felt in danger of dissolving.

"They've gone," she said. The word eluded me, but the context put it with the *Marie Celeste* and Roanoke, Virginia. It was complex, the way she used the word *gone*. It was like something she had said before: unattainable, a source of frustration like the one that had sent me running from Keller. But now her word told of something that was not hers as yet, but was within her grasp. There was no sadness in it.

"Gone?"

"Yes. I don't know where. They're happy. They ***ed. It was glorious. We could only touch a part of it."

I felt my heart hammering to the sound of the last train pulling away from the station. My feet were pounding along the ties as it faded into the fog. Where are the brigadoons of yesterday? I've never yet heard of a fairy tale where you can go back to the land of enchantment. You wake up, you find that your chance is gone. You threw it away. *Fool!* You only get one chance, that's the moral, isn't it?

Pink's hands laughed along my face.

"Hold this part-of-me-who-speaks-mouth-to-nipple," she said and handed me her infant daughter. "I will give you a gift."

She reached up and lightly touched my ears with her cold fingers. The sound of the wind was shut out, and when her hands came away it never came back. She touched my eyes, shut out all the light, and I saw no more.

We live in the lovely quiet and dark.

Old Folks at Home

Michael Bishop

Here's another specialized society of the not-very-distant future, consisting of people in their "senior" years who band together in government-sponsored group marriages. Their world and their social structures are fascinating, but it's the people themselves, each a fully realized human being, who will capture your attention and your love.

Michael Bishop's novels include *A Funeral for the Eyes of Fire* and *A Little Knowledge*.

---

1   *"sold down the river"*

At a stilly six o'clock in the morning Lannie sat looking at the face of her visicom console in their sleeper-cove, Concourse B-11, Door 47, Level 3. Nausea was doing its stuff somewhere down in her plumbing: bubbles and fizzes and musical flip-flops. And Sanders—Sanders, her blue-jowled lummox—he lay sprawled snoring on their bed; if Levels 1 and 2 fell in on them, he'd still sleep, and he didn't have to get up for another hour. But Lannie intended to fight it; she wasn't going to the bath booth yet, no matter how tickly sick she began to feel.

That would wake Zoe, and she wasn't ready for Zoe yet, maybe not for the rest of the day.

Putting her arms across her stomach, Lannie leaned over the glowing console and tapped into the *Journal/Constitution* newstapes. Day 13 of Winter, 2040, New Calendar designation. Front page, editorials, sports: peoplenews, advertisements, funnies.

Then, in among the police calls and obituaries, a boxed notice:

WANTED: Persons over sixty to take part in the second phase of a five-year-old gerontological study funded by the URNU HUMAN DEVELOPMENT COMMISSION. Health and sex of applicants of no consequence; our selections will be based on a consideration of both need and the individual interest of each case. Remuneration for the families of those applicants who are selected. Contact DR. LELAND TANNER, or his representative, UrNu Human Development Tower.

Lannie, still clutching her robe to her middle, held this "page" on the console. After two or three read-throughs she sat back and gazed at the room's darkened ceiling. "Eureka," she whispered at the acoustical punctures up there. "Eureka."

Sanders, turning his mouth to the pillow, replied with a beluga-like whistling.

She wasn't deceived, Zoe wasn't. She read the newstapes, too, maybe even more closely than they did, and if Melanie and Sanders thought they could wool-eye her with this casual trip to the UrNu Human Development Tower, they needed to rethink their clunky thinking. I wasn't born yesterday, Zoe thought. Which was so ludicrous a musing that right there in the quadrangle, on the gravel path among the boxed begonias and day lilics, Sanders craning his head around like a thief and Melanie drawing circles in the gravel with the toe of her slipper, Zoe chuckled: *Clucka-clucka-cluck.*

"Mother, hush!"

"'Scuse me, Lannie, 'scuse me for living." Which was also reasonably funny. So she *clucka-clucked* again.

Sanders said, "What does he want to meet us out

here for? How come he can't conduct this in a business-like fashion?" Sanders was a freshman investment broker. He had had to take the afternoon off.

"Not everyone runs their business like you do," Melanie answered. She was a wardrobe model for Consolidated Rich's.

It was 2:10 in the afternoon, and the city's technicians had dialed up a summery 23° C. in spite of its being the month Winter. The grass in the quadrangle, as Zoe had already discovered by stepping off the path, was Astroturf; and for sky the young Nobles and Melanie's mother had the bright, distant geometry of Atlanta's geodesic dome. On every side, the white towers of that sector of the Human Development complex called the Geriatrics Hostel. Many of the rooms had balconies fronting on the garden, and at various levels, on every side but one(the intensive-care ward), curious faces atop attenuated or bloated bodies stared down on them, two or three residents precariously standing but many more seated in wheel chairs or aluminum rockers. Except for these faces, the Nobles and the old woman had the carefully landscaped inner court to themselves.

"Home, sweet home," Zoe said, surveying her counterparts on the balconies. Then: "Sold down the river, sold down the river."

"Mother, for God's sake, stop it!"

"Call it what you want to, Lannie, I know what it is."

"Leland Tanner," a young man said, surprising them. It was as if he had been lying in wait for them behind a bend in the path, the concealing frond of a tub-rooted palm.

Leland Tanner smiled. More than two meters tall, he had a horsy face and wore a pair of blue-tinted glasses whose stems disappeared into shaggy gray hair. A pleasant-looking fellow. "You're Zoe Breedlove," he said to her. "And you're the Nobles. . . . I thought our discussion might be more comfortable out here in the courtyard." He led them to a ginkgo-shaded arbor on one of the pathways and motioned the family to a stone bench opposite the one he himself took up. Here they were secure against the inquisitive eyes of the balcony-sitters.

"Zoe," the young man said, stretching out his long legs, "we're thinking of accepting you into our community."

"Dr. Tanner, we're very—" Melanie began.

"Which means I'm being sold down the river."

"Damn it, Mother!"

The young man's eyes, which she could see like clear drops of sapphire behind the colored lenses, turned toward her. "I don't know what your daughter and your son-in-law's motives are, Zoe, but it may be that—on down the Chattahoochee, so to speak—you'll find life a little better than it was on the old plantation. You may be freer here."

"She's as free as she wants to be with us," Sanders said, mounting his high horse. "And I don't think this plantation metaphor's a bit necessary." His foot always got caught in that wide, loose stirrup: his mouth.

Only the young doctor's eyes moved. "That may be true, Mr. Noble," he said. "In the Urban Nucleus everyone's freedoms are proscribed equally."

"The reason they're doing it," Zoe said, putting her hands on her papery knees (she was wearing a disposable gown with clip-on circlets of lace at sleeves and collar), "is 'cause Lannie's gone and got pregnant and they want me out of the cubicle. They're not gonna get off Level 3 anytime soon, and four rooms we've got. So they did this to get me out."

"Mother, we didn't *do it* to get you out."

"I don't know why we did it," Sanders said, staring at the gravel.

Zoe appealed to the intent, gracefully lounging young doctor. "It could sleep in my room, too, that's the shame of it: it could sleep in my room." Then, chuckling again, "And they may be sorry they didn't think of that before hauling me up here. Like two sneaky Simon Legreedies, Lannie and Sandy."

"Dr. Tanner," Melanie said, "we're doing this for her as much as for ourselves and the baby. The innuendoes about our motives are only—"

"Money," Zoe said, rubbing her fingers against her thumb like a usurer. "I read that box in the newstapes, you know. You're auditioning old people, aren't you?"

"Sort of like that," Leland Tanner said, standing. "Anyway, Zoe, I've made up my mind about you." Under a canopy of ginkgo leaves he stared down at the group huddled before him, his eyes powerful surrogates for the myopic ones on the balconies.

"Don't take me," Zoe said, "it'll serve them right."

"From now on," the young man said, "we're going to be more interested in serving *you* right. And in permitting you to serve."

Sanders, her son-in-law, lifted his head and squinted through the rents in the foliage. "It's supposed to be Winter," he said. "I wish they'd make it rain." But an even, monochromatic afternoon light poured down, and it was 23° C.

2   to marry with the phoenix

She was alone with young Leland in a room opening onto the garden, and he had pulled the curtain back so that she could see out while they talked. A wingback chair for her, with muted floral-print upholstery. Her feet went down into a pepper-and-salt shag carpet. Tea things on a mahogany coffee table, all of the pieces a dainty robin's-egg blue except for the silver serving tray.

Melanie and Sanders had been gone thirty minutes, but she didn't miss them. It didn't even disturb her that it might be a long while—a good long while—before she saw them again. The ginkgo trees in the garden turned their curious oriental leaves for her examination, and the young man was looking at her like a lover, although a cautious one.

"This is a pretty room," she said.

"Well, actually," he said, "it's a kind of decompression chamber, or air-lock, no matter what the comfortable trappings suggest. Usually I'm not so candid in my explanation of its function; most prospective residents of the Geriatrics Hostel must be introduced into their new environment slowly, without even a hint that a change *is* occurring. But you, Zoe, not only realize from the outset what's going on, you've also got the wit to assimilate the change as if it were no more significant than putting on a new pair of socks."

"That's not so easy any more, either."

He tilted his head. "Your response illustrates what I'm saying. I judge you to be a resilient woman; that, along with my interview with your family, induces me to select you as a candidate for the second stage of our study. I can use a term like *air-lock* to describe this sitting room without flustering you. Because, Zoe, if you decide to stay with us, and to press your candidacy, you'll be very much like an astronaut going from the cramped interior of a capsule—via this room, your air-lock—into the alien but very liberated realm of outer space."

"First a sold-down-the-river darkie. Now a space-man." Zoe shook her head and looked at the damp ring her teacup had made on the knee of her gown. "Well, I'm old, Mr. Leland, but I'm still around. More than you can say for slaves and astronauts, thank goodness in the one case, too bad in the other."

Young Mr. Leland's violet eyes (he had taken those hideous glasses off), twinkled like St. Nick's, but he didn't laugh, not with his voice. Instead he said, "How old are you, Zoe?"

"Sixty-seven. Didn't *they* tell you?"

"They told me. I wanted to see if you would."

"Well, that's correct. I was born in 1973, before the domes ever was, and I came into Atlanta from Winder, Georgia, during the First Evacuation Lottery. Barely twenty-two, virgin and unmarried, though in those days you'd best not admit to the first condition any more than you had now. Met my husband, Rabon Breedlove, when the dome wasn't even a third finished. But a *third* of my life—my entire youth, really—I spent in the Open, not even realizing it was dangerous, the city politicians even said traitorous, to be out there." A few bitter, black leaves adhered to the robin's-egg-blue china as she turned her empty cup.

"And how old is Melanie, then?"

"Twenty-eight or -nine. Let's see." She computed. "Born in 2011, a late child and an only one. Rabon and me had tried before, though. Four times I miscarried, and once I was delivered of a stillborn who went into the waste converters before we had a chance to put a name on it. Boy or girl, they didn't tell us. Then Melanie, a winter baby, when we thought we'd never have one. All the other times was forgotten, a pink and living tadpole we had then, Rabon and me."

"Your husband died when she was eight?"

"Embolism."

Young Mr. Leland stood up and went to the window drapes. She saw how the shag lapped over his work slippers, even though his feet were big: good and big. "The Geriatrics Hostel has two parts, Zoe, one a nursing home and hospital, the other an autonomous community run by the residents themselves. You don't need the first, but you can choose to be a candidate for the second."

"I got a choice, huh?"

"We coerce no one to stay here—but in the case of those committed to the hostel's nursing sector it's often impossible for the residents to indicate choice. Their families make the decisions for them, and we then do the best we can to restore their capacity for reasoned, self-willed choice."

"What does it mean, I'm a 'candidate'?"

"If you so decide, you'll go into one of our self-contained communities. Whether you remain with that group, however, is finally up to you and the members of the group themselves."

"S'pose the old fuddy-duddies don't like me?"

"I view that as unlikely. If so, we find you another family or permit you to form one of your own. No losers here, Zoe."

Very quietly she said, "Hot damn." Young Mr. Leland's eyebrows went up. "An expression of my daddy's."

And came down again into an expression amusingly earnest. "Your husband's been dead twenty years. How would you like to get married again?"

"You proposin'?"

Well, he *could* laugh. With his voice as well as his eyes. She was hearing him. "No, no," he said, "not for myself. For the first septigamic unit we want to introduce you to. Or for the six remaining members of it, that is. You'll have six mates instead of one, Zoe. Three husbands and three wives, if those terms mean anything at all in such a marriage covenant. The family name of the unit is Phoenix. And if you join them, your legal name will be Zoe Breedlove-Phoenix, at least within the confines of the Geriatrics Hostel itself. Elsewhere, too, if things work out as we wish."

"Sounds like a bridge group that's one short for two tables."

"You'll be doing more than playing bridge with these people, Zoe. No false modesty, no societally dictated inhibitions. And the odd number is a purposive stipulation, not merely a capricious way of messing up card games. It prevents pairing, which can sometimes occur on an extremely arbitrary basis. The old NASA programmers recognized this when they assigned *three* men to the Apollo missions. The same principle guides us here."

"Well, that's fine, Mr. Leland. But even with those astronauts, you'll remember, only two of 'em went down honeymooning."

His horsy face went blank, then all his cheek- and jawbones and teeth worked together to split the horsiness with a naughty-boy grin. He scratched his unkempt hair: shag on top, shag around his shoes. "Maybe I ought to renege on the Phoenix offer and propose for myself, Mrs. Breedlove. All I can say to answer you is that honeymooning needn't be what tradition only decrees. For the most part, the septigamic covenant has worked pretty well these last five years at the hostel. And your own wit and resilience make me believe that you can bring off your candidacy and marry with the Phoenix. Do you wish to become a candidate, Zoe?"

Zoe put her cup on the silver serving tray. "You know, Mr. Leland, you shoulda been a comedy straight man." By which she didn't mean to imply that he was even half so humorless as Sanders Noble. No, sir. That Sanders could stay sour in a room full of laughing gas.

"Missed my calling. But do you want to?"

"Oh, I do," Zoe said, taking what he'd served up. "I do."

3 *helen, and the others*

Dr. Leland Tanner made a call on an intercom unit in the sitting room. Then, leaning over Zoe so that she could smell the sharp cologne on him, he kissed her on the forehead. "I'm going out now, Zoe. If you decide to stay, you'll see me only infrequently; your new family will occupy your time and your attention. There's no interdict, however, on associating with the culturally immature. If you like, you can see me or anyone else younger than yourself. Just let me know."

"Then I s'pose I shall, Mr. Leland."

" 'Bye," and he strode through the whipping shag, saluted at the sliding glass doors, and went out into the quadrangle. In only a moment he was lost to Zoe on one of the foliage-sheltered paths, and the calm, curious ginkgo trees held her amazed interest until an inner door opened and a thin woman with close-cropped gray hair came in to her.

"Zoe Breedlove?" A manila envelope clasped in front of her, the newcomer looked *toward* the wingback but not exactly *at* it. A handsome, frail woman with silvery opaque eyes and an off-center smile.

"That's me," Zoe said. The other's eyes focused on her then, and the smile firmed up. The woman navigated through waves of carpet to a chair opposite Zoe's, and they faced each other across the tea service.

"I'm Helen," the woman said. "Helen Phoenix. Parthena and Toodles wanted another man, I think, but I'm happy Leland found somebody who won't have to compete with our memories of Yuichan. That would have been unfair to you."

"Yui-chan?" The word sounded foreign, particularly to a dome-dwelling Georgia girl. Whereas Helen's accent marked her as no native to Atlanta. New York? Something cosmopolitan, anyhow: once.

"Yuichan Kurimoto-Phoenix. He was born in Kyoto, but he behaved like a raving Italian. Had execrable taste in everything; not a bit subtle. There's an unpainted plaster-of-Paris squirrel on the bole of one of the trees in the garden: Yuichan's doing." Helen lowered her head. "A lovely man; just lovely."

"Well, I hope the others don't think I'm even going to try to take Yoo-chi's place. I don't even know anything about China."

The woman's smile died at the corners of her mouth, then slowly grew back. "Nevertheless," she said, "you may be more like Yuichan than you know. Which is all to the good: a bonus for us. And the question of your competing with Yuichan's memory won't enter into our appreciation of you at all. I'm sure of that. Toodles only favored another man, I'm sure, because she's a voluptuary and thinks Paul and Luther inadequate for our servicing."

Servicing: that probably meant exactly what she thought it did. Zoe leaned over the coffee table. "Would you like some of this tea Mr. Leland left with me?"

"Please. And if you'll push the service to one side, Zoe—may I call you Zoe?—I'll introduce you to the others even before we go upstairs. That's an advantage you'll have over them, but probably the only one. We hardly begrudge it."

"Good. I could use an evener." And it was after pushing the tea service aside and while watching Helen take the photographs and printouts out of the manila envelope that Zoe realized Helen was blind. The opaque eyes worked independently of her smile and her hands: the eyes were beautiful, somehow weightless ball bearings. Mechanical moving parts in a body that was all Siamese cat and animal silver. Without fumbling, Helen's small hands laid out the pictures and the data sheets. Reminiscently, Zoe touched one of the photographs.

"You can examine it all while I drink my tea, Zoe. I won't bother you."

The top sheet on the pile was neatly computer-typed. Zoe held it up and tilted it so that she could read it.

THE PHOENIX SEPTIGAMOKLAN

Covenant Ceremony:

> *Day 7 of Spring, 2035, New Calendar designation.*

Septigamoklanners:

M. L. K. Battle (Luther). *Born July 11, 1968, Old Calendar designation. No surviving family. Last employer: McAlpine Construction and Demolition Company. Septigamoklan jack-o-trades and activity-planner. Ortho-Urbanist, lapsed, age-exempted. Black.*

Parthena Cawthorn. *Born November 4, 1964, O.C.; Madison, Georgia. A son Maynard, a daughter-in-law, and three grandchildren: enfranchised UrNu citizens. Last employer: Inner Earth Industries. Sgk artisan and folklorist. Ortho-Urbanist, semiactive. Black.*

Paul Erik Ferrand. *Born October 23, 1959, O.C.; Bakersfield, California. Family members (children, grandchildren, great-grandchildren) in the Urban Nuclei of Los Angeles and San Francisco. Last employer: (?). Unclassifiable Mystic, age-exempted. White.*

Yuichi Kurimoto (Yuichan). *Born May 27, 1968, O.C.; Kyoto, Japan. Children, grandchildren, great-grandchildren alive in Kyoto and Tokyo. Last employer: Visicomputer Enterprises, Atlanta branch, Sgk legislator. Neo-Buddhist, lapsed, nationality-exempted. Oriental.*

Joyce Malins (Toodles). *Born February 14, 1971, O.C.; Savannah, Georgia. No surviving family. Last employer: Malins Music, Voice, and Dance. Sgk musician. Ortho-Urbanist, lapsed, age-exempted. White.*

Helen Mitchell. *Born July 11, 1967, O.C.; Norfolk, Virginia. A son in the Washington UrNu, a daughter in the Philadelphia UrNu. Last employer: UrNu Civil Service, Atlanta branch, Sgk mediator, Ortho-Urbanist, semiactive. White.*

Jeremy Zitelman (Jerry). *Born December 9,
1970, o.c. No surviving family. Last employer: University of Georgia, Urban Exten-
sion, Astronomy Department. Sgk historian.
Recidivist Jew, age-exempted. White.*

A mixed lot, Zoe decided: a party assortment. Over
the capsule-biography of Yuichi Kurimoto the word
DECEASED was stamped in large, double-lined red
letters which did not conceal the information under
them. Zoe looked at the photographs and tried to match
them up with the résumés (they weren't very good photographs); she got them all matched up, but it was
pretty apparent that some of the pictures had been
taken years ago. For instance, Paul Erik Ferrand, supposedly just over eighty, was a rakish, lupine man wearing a style of cravat that hadn't been fashionable in two
decades. Before their names and faces meant anything
Zoe would have to meet these people: in the flesh.

"Is that what I'll be—a septigamoklanner—if y'all
like me?"

"That's an institute word, Zoe, made up by someone
who didn't know what to call a family like ours. Don't
worry. None of us use it. You see, these information
sheets contain only passed-upon, UrNu-validated
'facts': impersonal and bureaucratic. Jerry or I, either
one, could have put a little pizzazz into the sketches.
. . . Unfortunately, civil service sachems frown on pizzazz. . . ." Helen's voice trailed off.

"Well, that's encouraging—'cause I think I'd have a
hard time thinking of myself as a . . . *septigamoklans-
person.*" A mouthful, that. "But in Yoochi's biography
here, it says he was the family legislator. Does that mean,
since I'm coming in for him, I have to put on his shoes
and be a legislator?"

"No, no. On these official data sheets everyone's
given a position, as if we were baseball players or chess
pieces. Really, though, we do whatever we do best, and
by defining ourselves in that way we become ourselves
to the others. Later, someone will probably put a label
on what you are. It won't be a Phoenix who does it,
though."

"Mr. Leland?"

"Perhaps. A study is going on here, though we're mostly oblivious to it, and studies demand statistics and labels. A cosmic law, like gravitation and magnetism and whatnot."

"Well, if it was *age-exempted,* even an apple might not have to fall."

Helen's opaque eyes locked on her face. "An appropriate observation. But we do have a chance to do some naming of our own. Phoenix was our own choice, you know. Some of the other families in the Tower are Cherokee, Piedmont, O'Possum, and Sweetheart."

"Oh, those are good ones, too." They were, too; had what Helen would probably call pizzazz.

"Yes," Helen said, pleased. "Yes, they are."

4 climbing jacob's ladder

Zoe met them all at supper that evening. They ate in a room decorated with a quilted wall banner, and with several potted plants that Joyce Malins (Toodles) said she had bought from a slum-area florist in a place called the Kudzu shop.

The Phoenix family had an entire suite of rooms, including a kitchen, on the Geriatrics Hostel's fourth floor, and this evening Luther, Toodles, and Paul had shared the cooking: corn bread, frozen vegetables, and pasta with a sauce of meat substitutes. Better than Lannie managed after two hours of sloozying around in new clothes for the lechers at Consolidated Rich's; better than Zoe usually did for herself, come to that. The table was round, and wooden, and big enough for seven people, a metal pitcher of cold, sweetened tea, and several china serving dishes. No attendants waited on them, Zoe noted, no nurses, no white-smocked young men with pursed lips. A biomonitor cabinet, to which they were all linked by means of pulse-cued silver bracelets, was the only alien presence in the dining room, and it kept quiet. (The people downstairs had a hookup to the monitor, though, she was sure of that.) Zoe self-consciously turned her own new bracelet, a handsome thing in spite of its being, also, a piece of medical equipment. Plugged in already she was, a rookie Phoenix.

Helen had introduced her. She was sitting between Helen and Jerry. Then clockwise beyond Helen: Parthena, Paul, Luther, and Toodles. Jerry was sitting in a wheelchair, a lap robe over his knees. The others, like Helen, looked pretty mobile—even the eighty-year-old Paul, whose eyes resembled a Weimaraner dog's and whose mouth still knew how to leer.

"How old are you, Zoe?" he asked, after the opening small talk had faded off into mumbles and spoon-rattling.

Helen said, "Paul!" Like Lannie shushing her, Zoe; only nicer.

"Bet she ain't as old as me. Three-to-one odds. Place your bets." He smacked his lips.

"No one's so old as that," Jerry said. Jerry's hair was a dandelion puffball: just that round, that gray, that delicate. His face was red.

"I'm sixty-seven," Zoe said. Second time today. But saying so didn't age you, just worrying about it.

"Young blood," the wide-faced black man said: Luther. His hair (she was comparing now) was the kind of white you see on a photograph negative, a darkness turned inside out. His hands, on either side of his plate, looked like the mallets on sledgehammers. "Hooooi! Old folks, we're being transfused, we're gettin' new blood."

"Toodles ain' the baby no mo'," Parthena said out of a tall, stern Zulu mask of a face. Plantation accent, Zoe noticed. Luther sounded more like Paul or Toodles than he did Parthena; except for that *Hooooi!* Except for that.

"How 'bout that, Toodles?" Paul said. "Puttin' your foot on the bottom rung of Jacob's ladder at last. I'm up the highest, but you've finally climbed on." Toodles, whose mouth was a red smear, a candy heart (even though no one wore lip ices or eye blacking any more), lowered a forkful of squash to reply, but crazy old Paul turned to Zoe again: "I'm up the highest, but I'm never gonna die. I was born in California."

"Which is your typical Ferrand-Phoenix non sequitur," Jerry said.

"I've never made an issue of being the youngest one here," Toodles interjected. "And I'm not disturbed by losing that position, either." Her jowly face swung toward Zoe. "Zoe, I bought that fuchsia and the coleus for your arrival today. Parthena and I walked into that jungle off New Peachtree and haggled with the little Eurasian shopkeeper over prices. Then we carried our purchases back, pots and all, no help from these noble gentlemen."

" 'Course," Parthena said, "that 'fo' she knew how old you was." Her Zulu mask smiled: perfect dentures. Taller than anyone else in the room, Parthena, even seated, loomed.

"Parthena, damn your black hide, you know that wouldn't've made any difference! It wouldn't've!" Toodles dropped her fork, her mouth silently working itself into a multiplex variety of lopsided O's.

"Joke," Parthena said. "Jes' funnin'."

"Well, what the hell's funny about my being younger than you old cadavers?" Her mascara, tear-moistened, was making crater holes out of her eyes. "What's so damn funny about that?!"

"What's she takin' on like this for?" Luther asked the table.

"Humor her," Jerry said, winking at Zoe from under his puffball. "She thinks she's in her period."

Which brought guffaws from Paul and Luther and pulled the roof down on everyone else. Rearing back as if bee-stung, Toodles knocked her chair over and stood glaring at each member of her family in turn. Not counting Zoe.

"Jackasses!" she managed. Then, more vehemently: "Limp ole noodles!" Her mouth had begun to look like a pattern on an oscilloscope. Zoe, in fact, saw that one of the miniature screens on the biomonitor cabinet was sending delicate, pale comets back and forth across its surface: Toodles pulsing into the hysterical.

In person, Toodles left off glaring and, without looking back, moved painfully, heavily, out of the dining room. A minute or two after her exit, the pale comets stopped whizzing. Not dead, Toodles wasn't; just out of range. Another cabinet would pick her up shortly.

"Silly biddy," Paul announced, chewing.

"Jerry's last remark was crude," Helen said. "A sort of crudity, Zoe, that he usually doesn't permit himself."

"Please believe that," the crimson-faced man said, wheeling himself back from the table. "Lately she's been upset. That she was on the verge, though, I didn't think. I'm sorry, I'm honestly sorry, you know." The chair powered him out the door.

"Hot damn," Zoe said. "Some debut."

"Ain' yo' fault," Parthena said. "She been eggcited. Las' two week, she knew we was gonna fine a 'placement for Yuichan, that's all."

"That's true," Helen said. "We argue like young married couples do sometimes, Zoe, but usually not before company and not very often. Ordinarily Toodles is a lovely woman. And the only explanations I can give for her behavior are the menfolk's bad manners and her excitement. Courting's always made her nervous; always."

"As for the sort of crudity you heard from *her*," Luther said "that's her style. She don't mean nothin' by it, though, even when she's mad."

"Silly biddy," the time-blotched old Frenchman (or whatever he was) said. "Carry on like that, die before I will. . . . I ain't gonna die." He was the only one who finished eating what was on his plate. Once finished, long lips glistening, he let a red, translucent eyelid drop lasciviously over an amber eye: a wink. For Zoe.

5 rotational reminiscence

Two hours later. The roof court of the UrNu Human Development Tower, geriatrics wing. Temperature holding steady at 21° C. Night had risen as the city's fluorescent suns had been gradually dialed down.

The Phoenix had patched things up among themselves and now sat in a semicircle at a tower railing overlooking the Biomonitor Agency on West Peachtree and, ten floors down, a floodlit pedestrian park. All the Phoenix but that oddie, Paul: he still hadn't come up. Zoe put that old codger out of her mind, though. The rooftop was open and serene, and she had never seen such a pretty simulated twilight. Not much chance on Level 3, *under*. Now, winking on across the city's dying-into-the-violet skyscape, a thousand faint points of light. The breath sucked away just at the glory of it.

Jerry Zitelman-Phoenix maneuvered his wheelchair into position beside her. (Ramps and lift-tubes made it possible for him to go anywhere at all inside the complex.) "I want to apologize, Zoe, for my uncalled-for remark in your presence."

"I always try to apologize to the person who needs it."

"Me, too. Look, you can see she's back." And she was, Toodles: sitting with Luther, Parthena, and Helen and animatedly narrating another episode of her afternoon's shopping. "But you, too, need an apology for the disruption I made," Jerry said, "so to you also I say, 'Sorry.' "

Zoe accepted this apology, and Jerry began talking. He told her that on Thursday nights—alternate ones, anyhow, and it was Thursday night that night—the Phoenix clan had this screened section of the rooftop for whatever purpose they wished. He told her that tonight it was a game they called "rotational reminiscence" and that they were waiting for Paul, who never participated but who insisted on attending every session. The rules, Jerry said, were simple and would become clear once they started. Then, pointing to the darkened, concave hollow overhead, the honeycombed shell in which they all lived, he told her that in his youth he had been an astronomer.

"Even now," he said, "I can look up there at night and imagine the constellations rolling by. Oh, Zoe, it's just as plain as day—which is one more of your typical Ferrand non sequiturs, Zitelman version thereof. But it's true, I can. There's Cassiopeia, there's Ursa Major, there's Camelopardalis. . . . Oh, all of them I can see. The dome is no impediment to me, Zoe, but it's certainly no joyous boon either. That it isn't."

He went on. He told her that the only advantage the dome offered him was that he could just as easily imagine the constellations of the *Southern* Hemisphere passing in procession across its face. Sometimes he so imagined: Canis Minor, Hydra, Monoceros. There they all were, so dizzying in their splendor that he felt sure he would one day power his wheelchair right up into their diamond-dusted nets and connect the dots among them with the burning tip of a raunchy, green cigar. "Cigars I'm not allowed any more," he said. "Not even the neutered ones with no tobacco, no tar, and no taste. And stars . . . ?" He pointed at the dome.

"Well," Zoe said, "we got three stars at least. And they move."

Jerry's puffball rolled back, his vein-blossomed cheeks shone with wan, reflected light. "Ah, yes. Girder-cars is what we've got there, Zoe. Torchlight repairs on the dome. So they send out the magnetized girder-cars at night and let us pretend, with these insulting sops to our memory, that the sky hasn't been stolen. Pretty, though, I grant you." He was right. Artificial stars—only three—on a metal zodiac. How did the men inside those topsy-turvy trolleys feel? What was that old song? She mentally hummed a bit of it:

> *Would you like to ride on a star?*
> *Carry moonbeams home from afar?*

"Damn that old zombie!" Toodles suddenly said to them. "Let's go on without Paul, he never contributes anyway."

"Yeah," Luther said. "Let's start."

Helen persuaded them to wait a few more minutes. Okay with Zoe, A-Okay. She listened as Jerry related how he had been involved in a bone-crushing, paralyzing automobile accident in 1989, when most of the old "interstates" were falling into disuse: cracked pavements, weed-grown shoulders, brambly medians. He hadn't walked since. "When it happened, I'd never even had relations with a woman; impossible, after. At night, sometimes, I'd cry. Just like that fellow in the Hemingway book—except his legs, they weren't crushed; it was something else. So I never got married until Dr. Tanner accepted me for the study here. Then three wives at once I got. Now, in my old age, poor Yuichan dead, I'm helping my spouses court a fourth one. Who can say it isn't a strange and wizardly life, our pains and weaknesses notwithstanding?"

"Not me, Jerry," Zoe said. "Not me."

So Jerry went on and told her about how he had got his degree and then moved into the dome and tried to teach astronomy by means of textbooks, slide programs, and old films. He'd done it for almost twenty years, at which point the city decided it was foolish to pay somebody to lecture about a subject with so limited an application to modern society. "Fffft!" Jerry said. "Fired. Me and others, too. A whole program, kaput!" He had had to live on Teachers' Retirement and future-secure benefits in a Level 6 cubicle until—

"Howdy," Paul said. "Ain't you started yet?"

"Sit down," Luther said. "What have you been up to?"

Paul, running his fingers through tatters of thin hair, lowered himself creakingly to the fore-edge of a chair between Parthena and Zoe. "Fetched up some night things for our fiancée. She didn't bring none with her." He looked at Zoe. And winked. " 'Gainst my better judgment, too."

"You mighty sweet," Parthena said. "Now let's get on with it."

They did. The rules were these: 1) Silence while the person whose turn it was thought of a pre-Evacuation experience he wished to evoke for himself or, better, himself and the others. 2) An evocation of that experience in one word, the settled-upon word to be spoken, very clearly, only once. 3) An after-silence in which this word might resonate. 4) No repetitions from previous games. 5) An automatic halt after each Phoenix had had two turns. 6) In order to avoid a debilitating preoccupation with the past, no mention or replaying of any of the game's reminiscences before or after the sessions themselves.

Helen, a new Gardner-Crowell Braille-writer in her hands, recorded the evening's twelve reminiscences and called down anyone who repeated any of the old shibboleths. As Zoe discovered, accusations of encroaching senility flew around the circle when this happened. No worries tonight, though. She had never played before, and there'd be no whistle-blowing no matter what words she spoke into the quiet ring of their anticipation.

"Three months," Toodles said. "It's been three months since we've done this. Back when Yuichan was ill."

"Go ahead, then," Helen said. "You start, Toodles."

The group's silence grew. The girder-cars above them slid in slow motion down the steeps of the dome. In three or four minutes Toodles dropped a word into the pooling dark, the well of their ancient breaths:

"Fudgsicles," she said.

Paul, Zoe noticed, had his head thrown all the way back over the top of his chair, his eyes all goggly and shiny. The old man's mouth was open, too. If he hadn't already moved his butt back into the chair, he would have fallen to the roof tiles.

It was Parthena's turn. Three or four minutes after Toodles' reminiscence, the tall black woman said.

"Scup'nins." Scuppernongs, that meant. A kind of grape.

When the word had echoed in their heads for a while, Luther said, "Paul isn't going to say nothin', Zoe. You go ahead now. It's your turn." No, he wasn't going to say anything, Paul: he was still mouthing Parthena's word.

As for Zoe, she was ready. She had thought of it while Jerry was explaining the rules to her. But it wouldn't do to blurt it out, it wouldn't do to show she'd been thinking ahead of the game. (Surely they all did it, though.) So she waited. Then, leaning forward to look into the pedestrian park below, she gave the word to her new family:

"Fireflies. . . ."

6 mount fujiyama and the orpianoogla

In their suite on the fourth floor the Phoenix slept in a circular common room, their beds positioned around a hub where the self-locomoting biomonitor cabinet (the first of three on the floor) had already taken up its brooding watch. Each bed had a nightstand, an effects-bureau, and an easy chair in its vicinity, as well as plastic-cloth dividers that, at a finger's touch, would roll automatically into place. Since no one seemed to use these, Zoe, grateful to Paul for having fetched her a nightgown, got ready for bed in front of the others.

Like having six Rabons in the room with you. Well, five: Jerry had powered himself off somewhere. "Like some time to himself 'fo' turnin' in," Parthena said. But even five Rabons was plenty, even if they were decent enough not to devour you with their eyes. (Rabon never had been.) Old Paul, of the five, excepted. Again.

Anyhow, it didn't take this creaky crew long to start plying the waters of Nod. No, sir. Everyone off, it seemed, but Zoe herself. She even heard Jerry come whirring back into the snore-ridden room and hoist himself out of the wheelchair onto his bed. In five or ten minutes he, too, was rowing himself under. Only Zoe had her head clear, her whole fatigued body treading against the desire to be drowned in sleep. My sweet lord, what a day! Every bit of it passed in front of her eyes.

Then Zoe heard the sobs. For a long time she listened to them. It was Toodles, two beds away, heart-troubled Toodles.

Feeling for slippers that weren't there, Zoe got out of bed. She walked barefooted to the easy chair beside Toodles, sat down, and smoothed back the woman's moist, frizzly bangs. "Can you tell me what it is?"

Unnhuh; nope. Strangled, desperate noises.

"Is it about that supper-time business, Toodles? Hope not. Up against you I look like the . . . the Wicked Witch of the North." Which was a Glinda-the-Good lie if she'd ever told one: white lie, though.

Subsiding strangles—"It . . . isn't . . . that"—trailing off into hiccups. "Really . . . it . . . isn't . . . that." Apparently to prove this contention, Toodles pulled herself up to a sitting posture. Across her rumpled lap she reeled in, inch by hand-wrung inch, a dressing gown that had been spread out over her bedclothes. A corner of it went to her throat, and was held there.

"What, then? Can you say?"

A modicum of control now. "Yuichan," Toodles said. "I was thinking of Yuichan. You see this robe, Zoe. . . . He gave me this robe." It was too dark to see well, but Toodles turned the robe toward her and displayed it anyway, an occasional hiccup unsteadying her hands. All Zoe got was a musty whiff of a familiar kidneylike odor.

"Here," Zoe said, and punched on the reading light on Toodle's headboard. A circle of paleness undulated on the dressing gown. Execrable taste, Helen had said. And rightly: On one side of the robe, an embroidered snow-covered peak; on the other (once Toodles had lifted the limp lapel so that she could see them), the words *Mount Fujiyama*. An ugly and smelly garment, no matter how you hemmed or whiffed it.

"Oh, I know it's not to everybody's taste," Toodles said. "But it reminds me of Yuichan. He mail-ordered it from San Francisco four years ago when he learned that there was a very sick Japanese woman in the nursing section of the hostel. That was just like Yuichan. He gave the robe to that poor woman. A coupla years later, when the woman died and her son threw away almost all of her effects, Yuichan brought the gown back and gave it to me. Oh, it was tight on me and it smelled like urine, all right, but I knew what spirit Yuichan gave it in and I had it washed and washed—till I was afraid it'd fall apart in the water." Toodles spread the dressing gown over her knees. "And tonight . . . tonight . . . it reminds me of him . . . of Yuichan . . . just ever so much." And propped her elbows on her shrouded knees and lowered her face into her hands

The consolation Zoe gave Toodles was that of sitting beside her until the poor, blowsy woman, mascara long since washed away, fell into a sleep as mortally shallow as the crater holes of her eyes.

But the next afternoon, in the room they called the recreation center, Toodles sat at the battery-powered orpianoogla and led them all in a songfest: thin, strained vocal cords reaching for notes those cords couldn't remember. In fact, only Toodles had an unimpaired range, a bravura contralto that could soar like an undercourse glissando or tiptoe stealthily through a pianissimo lullaby. With one arm she led their singing, with her free hand she rippled the keys, punched buttons, flipped toggles, and mixed in the percussion. Nor did her heavy legs keep her from foot-pedaling like an unbeliever on burning coals. The whole suite of rooms reverberated with Toodles' music, and Zoe, clapping and croaking with the rest, wondered dimly if she had dreamed, only dreamed, the midnight despair of this boisterous Phoenix.

"Very good!" Toodles would shout at them between choruses. "Ain't you glad we're too old for them jack-asses who passed the Retrenchment Edicts to come in here and shut us up?!"

Zoe was. Outlawed music they were souling on, outlawed lyrics and proscribed morals-corrupting rhythms. Old times. As they clapped and sang, Helen told Zoe that Toodles had once been a renaissance-swing headliner in a New Orleans hookah club. "Turn of the century and a few years after," Helen stage-whispered in her ear as they all clapped to the rumbling orpianoogla. "When she was forty she was doing a bushman, pop-oprah review in D.C. Forty! Quite professional, the old newsfax say." Since '35, when the ward reps and urban councilmen panicked, those kinds of performances had been totally *nyetted*, at least in Atlanta. Who knew, these days, what other cities did?

"All right!" Toodles shouted. "This one's 'Ef Ya Gotta Zotta!' Way back to twenny-awht—tooo, evvverbodddy!"

So they all sang, the orpianoogla singlehandedly—literally singlehandedly—sounding like the entire defunct, blown-away, vinyl-scrutchy Benny Goodman Orchestra of a century ago. Or Glenn Miller's, maybe. This was the chorus:

> *Ef ya gotta zotta*
> *Thenna zotta wa me:*
> *Durnchur lay ya hodwah*
> *On tha furji Marie.*

Ef ya gotta zotta,
        Then ya gotta zotta wa me!

My sweet lord! Zoe remembered the whole song, every kaporni word of all seven verses. She and Rabon had danced to that one; they'd done the buck-and-wing jitters in the remodeled Regency lobby ballroom. My sweet lord, she thought: "Ef Ya Gotta Zotta!"

But after the last sing-through of the chorus, Toodles barreled out of the renaissance-swing retrospective and into a hard, hard computer-augmented tour of late-twenties/early-thirties racked-and-riled terrorism. With the advent of this deliberate cacophony, old Paul stopped stomping and let his mouth fall open, just as it had during the rotational reminiscence. The others, like Zoe, irresistibly fell to swaying in their chairs.

Toodles sang the ominous lyrics, and sang them so certainly that you could look at her full, jowly face and see that despite the sags, and wens, and ludicrous, smeared lips, she was living every note, vivisecting every lurid word and dragging its guts out for the purpose of feeding her own and her listeners' irrational fears. (Which was fun: a musical horror movie.) Toodles sang, and sang, and sang. She sang "Walnut Shell Nightmare," "Tomb of the Pharaohs," "Crimson Clay Tidal Wave," and "Outside Sky." When the last note of the orpianoogla died away, a rain of bravos fell down on the (incredibly) beginning-to-blush Miz Joyce "Toodles" Malins-Phoenix. Even Paul joined in, though he stomped like a jackass rather than hallooed.

"Her first concert since Yuichan died," Helen whispered.

"Encore!" Jerry shouted. "That we wish more of!"

"Hooooi!" Luther said. "I ain't heard her sing or play so well since Year-end Week in '38."

"I'm in as fine a voice as I was thirty years ago," Toodles said, turning on her stool. "It's hard to believe and it sounds like bragging, but by God! it's the gospel truth."

"Damn straight." Luther said.

"You ain' done, though," Parthena said. "Finish out now like we awways do, 'fo' we have to go eat."

Toodles, turning back to the keyboard, honored this request. Ignoring the buttons, switches, and resonator pins on the console, she played with both hands: an old melody, two hundred years almost. Everyone sang, everyone harmonized. Zoe found that, just as with "Ef Ya Gotta Zotta," she remembered the words—every word, each one called to her lips from a time-before-time that had nothing to do with the Urban Nucleus, or with Sanders and Lannie, or with Mr. Leland and the Geriatrics Hostel. And it wasn't timesickness or nostalgia that fed her recollection of the lyrics (some things you don't ever want to go back to), but instead a celebration of the solidity of the present: this present: the moment itself. They all sang:

> "'Way down upon the Swanee River
> Far, far away,
> There's where my heart is turning ever,
> · There's where the old folks stay."

They even sang the stanza about the old plantations and the plaintive line "Oh, darkies, how my heart grows weary," Luther and Parthena too, and none of what they sang distressed them. Stephen Foster somehow was and wasn't Stephen Foster when interpreted by an orpianoogla. Sticks and stones, Zoe thought, and names can never . . .

Why, only a week ago her own daughter had called her, during a moment of ill-concealed morning sickness, a mummified witch. Zoe had chuckled: *Clucka-clucka-cluck*. What else could she do? When you're two steps from the finish line, you laugh at the self-loathing insults of also-rans. You have to. Even in the melancholy performance of a nigh-on dead-and-gone work of a sure-enough dead-and-gone composer, Toodles' whole body laughed. Toodles was two steps from the finish line. They all were. And it certainly wasn't death they were running at, not as Zoe saw it. No, sir. Something else altogether; something else.

7 parthena

That evening, after the orpianoogla-assisted songfest, Parthena, Helen, and Jerry saw to the cooking of supper. And after supper Zoe helped these three clean up in the galley beside the dining room (whereas, downstairs, three levels under, Lannie and Sanders had only a kitchen board in their cubicle and no dining room at all). A beautiful day it had been, a zippity-doo-dah day if she'd ever lived one. Not since Rabon . . .

"You quilt?" Parthena asked her as they put the last of the china away. But Zoe's attention was momentarily elsewhere. Jerry, in his wheelchair, was handing the plates to Helen, and the blind woman was stacking them cleanly in the hanging plastic cabinet over the sink. Before beginning, Helen had produced a pair of miniature black goggles, or binoculars, from a dress pocket and snapped these on over her eyes with seemingly only a thin metal bridge-piece to support them. With these in place she moved as if sighted. And yet this was the first time she had worn the goggles in Zoe's presence.

"Hey, Zoe," Parthena said again. "You quilt?"

"You mean stitch squares together? Sew? Maybe. Things with my hands I could always bluff through. I'm a bluffer."

"Shoot, we ain' even axed you yet what you good at. Where you work 'fo' you got put on the Ole Folk Dole Role?"

"Photography," Zoe said. "I took pitchurs. Still ones and moving ones. And I was good, too, you know. If you want to know the truth, some of my still pitchurs are pretty moving."

They all laughed. Zoe told them how she and Rabon had been a team for both the *Journal/Constitution* combine and one of the visual-media affiliates; neither wrote copy ("I didn't have the schooling and Rabon hadn't put his to use that way"), but they could both wield cameras, video portables, and the instant-print-making varieties. She had been better than Rabon was, but from '01 to '09 she had been taken out of action four times by the onset of motherhood and he had got more commissions by virtue of his being insusceptible, as he put it, to pregnancy. But it had all been planned, and after Melanie was born the UrNu Sitter Mission Program had freed them both to pursue their careers. Sort of. They got docked an incredible number of earnies to have Lannie mission-sat for four hours a day, four days a week, she and Rabon splitting up the remaining hours and working less frequently as a team. But they'd done it, she and Rabon, and maybe it was only Lannie's having been their only child that had caused her to grow up a gimme girl and a sometimes-sweet, more-usually-petulant young woman. What lovely portraits Zoe had made of her when she was little, ole sweet-treat Lannie. In a telecom to her that morning Zoe had asked her daughter to bring from her sleeper-cove only the few clothes she had there and the photographs on the walls, and Melanie had said she would bring them: maybe Mr. Leland had them already.

"Well, if you can shoot pitchurs," Parthena said, "you can he'p us knock off that new wall banner what you seen on the quiltin' frame in the rec center. So you c'mon now, Zoe."

They were finished in the galley. Parthena led them out of there and down the corridor: seventy-six years old and as straight and skinny as a broom handle.

"Other work I got this evening," Jerry said. "If you all will excuse me." And he zoomed around them in his winged chair and disappeared into a room Zoe hadn't been in yet. A closetlike alcove between the rec center and the dining room.

Luther and Toodles were already at the quilting frame when they got there: a monstrous, plastic contraption over which the layer of sewn squares, the synthetic cotton batting, and the underlining had all been tautly spread and whipped down. Zoe had seen this thing—"a Wright brothers plane made of sewing scraps"—during their afternoon songfest, but it had been behind them and partially hidden by a moving screen and no one had volunteered to explain its purpose or its function to her.

Now the screen had been shoved back against the wall, and Toodles and Luther were sitting at opposite ends of the frame pushing and pulling their needles through the three layers of material. Helen, still wearing her goggles, sat down between them, and Parthena and Zoe took up chairs on the other side of the frame, which was tilted like an aileron. It was 1903, and they were Orville and Wilbur, crazy-quilt pilots at a Kitty Hawk where the sands of time had transmogrified into linoleum tile.

"Helen," Zoe blurted, "with those goggles on you look like you're gonna fly us right out of here—right up to the dome." Ooops. Was that the right thing to say to a blind person?

Helen raised her head and stared at Zoe. Straight on, the goggles—or glasses, or binoculars—gave her the look not of a biplane pilot but of an unfriendly outerspace critter. "Aren't they hideous?" Helen said. "I'd wear them all the time except for the way they look." And, expertly, she began plunging her own needle into the layers of cloth and forcing it back through.

Parthena showed Zoe how to do it, giving her a needle and thimble and making her watch her technique. "I taught us all how to quilt—but Paul he don' like it and use his weekend to think on keepin' himsef a-live for awways. Jerry he got real bidness to tend to. Otherwise, he 'most awways here. Now you keep yo' thumb in that thimble, gal, or that needle it gonna bite you. Look here—"

Well, Zoe had sewn before and she'd always been pretty handy anyway. Easy, take it easy, she told herself, and pretty soon she was dipping in and digging out as well as any of them, stitching those jaunty, colored squares—yellow, green, and floral-print blue in a steppin'-'round-the-mountain pattern—to batting and lining alike. Much concentration to begin with, like a pilot taking off; then, the hang of it acquired, free, relaxing flight. Nobody talked, not anyone.

When had she ever felt so serene and at peace? Serene and at peace, yes, but with a tingle of almost physical pleasure throwing off cool little sparks up and down her backbone. The quiet in the room was a part of this pleasure.

Then Parthena began to talk, but not so that it violated the silence they were working in: "I use to do this up in Bondville, when my son Maynard jes' a little flea and the dome ain' even half finished yet. Oh, the wind it blow then, it didn' have no dome to stop it, and we use these quilts to sleep unner, not to hang up on them ole broke-up plasser walls of ours. I still 'member how Maynard, when I was workin', would get himsef up unner the frame—a wooden un my husban' made—and walk back and fo'th like a sojer so that all you could see was the bump of his head goin' from one end of that frame to the other, up and down, till it seem he warn' ever gonna wear out. Laugh? Lord, I use to laugh him into a resentful meanness 'cause he didn' unnerstan' how funny his ole head look."

She laughed in a way that made Zoe join her. "Now he got three babies of his own—Georgia, Mack, and Moses—and a wife what can do this good as me; better maybe, she so spry."

They quilted for an hour. When they broke off, Parthena insisted that Zoe come back to the dormitory common room and see the "pitchurs of my gran'babies. Shoot, you like pitchurs and babies, don' you?" So Zoe went. She sat in the easy chair while Parthena, having lowered her bed to an accommodating height, sat like an ebony stork on its edge.

"This one my pert Georgie," Parthena said, handing her a picture of a handsome little black girl. "She twelve now and one sassy fas' chile. She gonna get out of Bondville all by hersef, jes' on charm and speed." The two boys were older and a little meaner-looking; they probably had to be. None of them were babies. "I jes' want you to see I had me a fam'ly 'fo' the Phoenix. I ain' like Luther and po' Toodles what suffer till they was pas' sixxy without finin' a real home. Now, though, they got us an' we got them—but they come a long road, Zoe, a long road. Jerry, too. Sometime I jes' lif' up a prayer for how lucky I been."

"I never did pray much," Zoe said, "but I know what

the urge is like." Like loving somebody in a way that didn't permit you to tell them: Zoe remembered.

They talked while some of the others got ready for bed. Parthena showed Zoe a set of dentures that had been made for her in 2026; she even made Zoe take them in her hand and examine them as if they were the teeth of an australopithecine. "They clean," she said. "I ain' wore 'em since '29. The reason I show 'em to you is 'cause they made by Dr. Nettlinger."

"Who?"

"Gee-rard Nettlinger. You 'member, Zoe. He that fellow what shot Carlo Bitler. Stood up in the middle of the Urban Council meetin' and shot that tough holy man. The day I heard that, I took out them dentures and never put 'em in again. They shoddy-made, anyhow. Only keep 'em so Maynard can sell 'em one day. People go all greedy-crazy over doodads what b'long to 'sassins. People crazy."

"Yep," Zoe agreed. "My daddy said it was the new idolatry."

"It idle, awright. Don' make a mussel-shell worth o'sense."

Then, somehow, their conversation got around to why the original family members had chosen Phoenix—rather than something light like Sweetheart or O'Possum—as the group's surname. Zoe said she had supposed it was because Atlanta was sometimes called the Phoenix City, having risen again from its own ashes after the Civil War (which Zoe's grandfather, even in the 1980s, had insisted on calling the War Between the States—as if that made some kind of significant difference). And when the dome went up in that decade linking the old century with the new one, Atlanta had undergone still another incarnation. Were those part of the group's original reasons?

"They part of 'em awright," Parthena said. "But jes' part. Another one is, we all come out of our own ashes when we 'greed to the cov'nant. We all bone again, Zoe, like in Jèsus."

"Well, I thought that, too, you know. That's what makes the name so good."

"Yeah. But Paul he like it 'cause the phoenix a 'Gyptian bird what was im-ortal, you see. It only *look like* it die, then it spurt back up jes' as feathery and fine as befo'. He a mean man on that pint, Paul is."

"He ought to be happy with the Ortho-Urban Church, then. It says the same sort of thing happens to *people* after they die."

"Ain' the same, though, Paul say. 'Cause people do die, no lookin'-like in it, and they don' get a body back at all. Paul he hung up on the body."

"You don't say? It's good to know he's not just a Dirty Old Man."

"Oh, he that, too, he sho' is." They chuckled together. "But it the other thing keep him thinkin' and rockin' and figgerin'. The Phoenix lucky. Mos' of us still got our mines. But Paul he eighty-some-odd and his been goin' ever since we marry. Mr. Leland awmos' didn' 'cept him in this program five year back, you see. Res' of us made him say yes. So Mr. Leland fine'ly 'cepted him, hopin' we could haul him back on the road. We done it, too. Pretty much."

"Did Paul suggest the name?"

"No. Maybe. I don' 'member zackly. What I do 'member is that the name fit, it fit fo' all kinds o' reasons. One other, and maybe the bes 'un, was a story my gran'daddy tole that his own daddy tole him. It was 'bout a slave chile, a little gal, what was made to watch the two-year-ole baby of the boss man, the 'marster,' as gran'daddy say his daddy say.

"Well, that little baby fell down the steps while the slave gal was watchin' it: she took her eye away a minute and it bumped down them ole steps and took on a-hollerin'. Scared, you know, but not kilt. Well, when the white mistresses in the house heard this, they took on a-cryin' and carryin' on terrible—jes' like that baby been murdered. They kep' on till the marster himsef come strollin' in and axed them what it was. When they tole him, he pick up a board and hit that little slave gal in the head. Kilt her. Then he gathered 'round him a bunch of niggers (my gran'daddy he tole it this way, now) and ordered 'em to thow the gal in the river. The gal's mama begged and prayed and axed him to spare the gal fo' buryin', but he paid her no mine and made em' thow the chile in.

"Now this where the story get magical, Zoe. The little girl's name was Phoebe, and five slaves and the girl's mama went down to the river with her—the biggest nigger in front, carryin' little Phoebe with her bloody head hangin' down, mournful and cold. This big nigger he thew the gal in like the marster order him to, Phoebe's mama jes' moanin' and beatin' on herself, and then he walk right in affer the girl and hole himself unner water till he drown. The others they resolve to do the same. And they do it too, the mama goin' in las' and prayin' to God they all be taken up together.

"One night later, the white folks from the big house is walkin' by the river and all at once they see seven small, ugly birds fly up outa the water and go sailin' straight at the moon. The higher they get, the brighter and purtier and bigger they get too—till at las' they stop in the sky like stars and stay still over the big house where them white folks live. A new constellation they become, which evvyone on that plantation call the Phoenix—'cep' this constellation don' move like it s'posed to but jes' sit with its wings spread, wide and haughtylike, over the marster's house.

"And that the story, Zoe. Jerry he say he never heard of no constellation call the Phoenix. But with that dome up there who gonna 'member zackly how the sky look? Nobody; not nobody.

"An' I believe it still up there somewhere."

8 flashforward: at the end of winter

Almost three old-style months after entering the Geriatrics Hostel, not as patient or prisoner but as a genuine, come-and-go-as-you-please resident, Zoe sat on the roof one evening and recalled the steps of her slow immersion in the Phoenix clan. Supper was eaten: a calming warmth in her stomach and bowels.

Pretty soon the family would decide. When you're streaking toward either seventy or eighty—as well as that something else that isn't death—long courtships are as foolish as whirlwind ones. Three months is plenty to decide in, maybe too much. Anyhow, they were formally going to pass on her, and it might be that in giving her this hour of solitude, this retrospective moment on the darkening rooftop, they were already engaged in the process of their decision. Was it in doubt? And hadn't they been so engaged all along, every day that Zoe had lived among them sharing their lives?

One girder-car tonight, and a flight of pigeons wheeling together in great loops in front of a huge, neon Coca-Cola sign.

Look what had happened in these three old-style months: For one thing, she had found out that the septigamoklans in the Tower weren't living there as welfare recipients solely, as so many helpless mendicants on the Old Folk Dole Role. Most of them had spent their lives paying into the medicaid and future-secure programs of the city; since 2035, the year young Mr. Leland's study had begun, the quarterly benefits of all the people in the hostel had been pooled and invested. This was done with permission from the residents, only a scant number of whom denied the UrNu Human Development Commission the legal administration of their estates. And against these holdouts, no penalty at all. In any event, the dividends on these pooled investments and the interest on several well-placed accounts financed the feeding and the sheltering of the residents and even provided them with personal funds to draw on. They also helped remunerate the surviving families of those who came into the study.

Each family had a budgeter: Helen was the Phoenix budgeter, and, wearing those little black vision-assisting binoculars, she kept books like a born-and-bred C.P.A. (which was C.U.A. now, Zoe remembered). Other times, she used her Braille-writer. Anyhow, they weren't dole-riders, the people in the Tower—although Zoe had to admit that the hostel's system was dependent upon the good offices and business acumen of those who administered their benefits. This drawback was partially offset by the budgeter of each septigamoklan's having a seat on the Commission Board of Financial Planners, as well as by the judicious appeal to market-forecasting computers.

Down on Level 3 with Sanders and Melanie, Zoe's quarterly allotments—only a day or two after the future-secure printout chit arrived—had been eaten up like nutmeg-sprinkled oatmeal. The Nobles garnisheed the entire value of the chit, without even so much as a countersignature, for granting Zoe the privilege of living with them. Only the coming of their child and the prospect of a lump-sum reward from the commission had induced them to hand Zoe over. Just like a prisoner-exchange, or the sale of a decrepit and recalcitrant slave. Yessir, Zoe thought: sold down the river. But a river out of which it was possible to fly like a sleek bird, dripping light as if it were water. An old bird, Zoe was; a bird of fire being reborn in the Lethe of Sanders and Melanie's forgetfulness and neglect.

"A pox on self-pity," Zoe said aloud, surprising herself. Overhead, the torchlit girder-car had almost reached the acme of the dome.

Well, what else? What else? Lots of things. She had met members of other septigamoklans, the O'Possums and the Cadillacs and the Graypanthers and oh! all the others, too. There'd been a party one Saturday night in the garden, with food and music and silly paper decorations. Hostel attendants had closed the patio windows and pulled the acoustical draperies in the intensive-care rooms, and everyone else had gone to town. Young Mr. Leland, at their invitation, had been there, and nobody but Paul of all the Phoenix went to bed before 4 A.M. Sometime after midnight Toodles led everybody in a joyful, cacophonous version of "Ef Ya Gotta Zotta."

Then there were Sunday afternoons, alone with Paul or Luther or maybe, just maybe, one of the girls. During the week, field trips to the Atlanta Museum of Arts ("Boring as hell," said Paul) and Consolidated Rich's and the pedestrian-park flea markets. Two different excursions to the new theater-in-the-round opera house, where they had watched a couple of interesting, council-sanctioned hologramic movies. They were okay, sort of plotless and artsy, but okay. Back in their own fourth-floor suite, though, they could show old-fashioned, two-dimensional movies; and just since Zoe had been there, the Phoenix had held a Rock Hudson festival and a mock seminar in the "Aesthetic of Late Twentieth-Century X-rated Cinema," during which Jerry had turned off the sound tracks and lectured to quite humorous effect with the aid of a stop-action button and a pointer.

After one such lecture, when the rooftop was theirs, Luther and Zoe had laid out a croquet course; and, except for Jerry, in 23° C. weather (the internal meteorologists had given them one or two cold days, though) they had all played without their clothes! Nude, as Helen said. And that had been one of those rare occasions *not* requiring meticulous attention to detail—quilting, putting away dishes, keeping books—when Helen wore her goggle-binoculars. And, not counting the pulse-cued bracelet, *only* the goggle-binoculars. The idea, lifted from an old book of short stories, had been Toodles', but Paul had given it a vigorous seconding. And so Zoe, like a girl going skinny-dipping in the before-the-dome countryside, shed her paper gown, her underthings, her inhibitions, and let the temperate air swaddle her sensitive flesh and her every self-conscious movement. Much merriment. And no repugnance for their blotched and lignifying bodies; instead, a strange tenderness bubbling under the surface merriment.

What, after all, did the bunions, and the varicosities, and the fleshy folds signify? Zoe could answer that: the onset of age and their emphatic peoplehood, male and female alike. Finally, that day, she forgot the sensuous stirrings of the dome winds, lost herself in the game, and became extremely angry when Parthena sent her ball careening off into an unplayable position. Yessir, that had been an all-fun day.

And what else? Well, the Phoenix had given her a still camera, and for the first time in ten or fifteen years she had begun taking pictures again. The camera was an old but still beautifully operable Double-utility Polaroid, and the first project Zoe undertook was the capturing in stark black and white of the faces of her new family. Posed photographs, candid ones, miniatures, darkroom enlargements: group portraits, singles, double-exposure collages, meditative semiabstracts. The best of these went up in the rec center. The Wall of the

Phoenix, this gallery became, and it was framed on both sides by bright quilted wall banners.

Paul and Toodles both grew quite vain about certain of these portraits and occasionally got caught staring at their favorites: teenagers ogling themselves in a mirror. Vanity, vanity, saith somebody or other, Zoe remembered. But Helen never donned her little binoculars to look at her own photographed image, even though she had more justification than either Paul or Toodles. One day Zoe asked her why. "I haven't looked at my own face since I was thirty," she said, "because I am quite content with the self-deluding vision of my thirty-year-old one that still resides up here." She tapped her head. Then she showed Zoe an old photograph of herself, one that glinted in the common room's fluorescents and revealed a woman of disgusting, not-to-be-gainsaid beauty. "I can *feel* what I look like now," Helen said. "I don't have to *look*." Even so, Zoe's portraits of Helen did her no disservice; in fact, they launched a thousand tiresome accolades from the men, Paul in particular—when, that is, he wasn't mesmerized by his own amber-eyed, celluloidally distanced self. Well, why not? Zoe's pitchurs were damn good, if she did say so herself, just by way of echoing the others.

The month Spring was coming on. What else could she recall about Winter in the hostel? Visits by Melanie and Sanders. The prospect of a grandchild. This last excited her, tickled her like air on her naked body, and for it alone did she anticipate the biweekly drop-ins of her daughter and son-in-law. No, that wasn't true. Lannie she always had a hankering to see, whether a baby was growing in her womb or not. Her daughter Lannie was her own flesh and that of dead Rabon: her daughter. Only fatuous Sanders did she have difficulty tolerating, and he had never once called her anything as brutal as a mummified witch, not ever in his life. So what did you do?

Zoe, for her part, never visited them in their Level 3 cubicle, and when they came to see her, thereby perfunctorily carrying out their filial duty, she always greeted them in the quadrangle where they had first put her on the block. That made Sanders uncomfortable: he scuffed his street slippers in the gravel and craned his neck around as if looking for the one mean old codger in the hostel who would use his balcony advantage to shoot him, Paul, with a blowgun or pellet rifle. Minor sport for Zoe, watching her son-in-law sidelong as she asked Melanie how she felt, if the morning sickness had gone away yet ("There are pills for that, Mother!"), what sex the Jastov-Hunter test had said the child would be—other things that Lannie was at last willing to talk about.

But she never used her freedom to visit them on Level 3, and they never extended her such an invitation. No, sir. Not once.

Zoe tilted her head back and saw that the girder-car she had been following was nowhere in sight. My sweet lord, hadn't she been up on the Tower roof a long time? And hadn't the time flown by? They were reaching a decision on her, the Phoenix were. That was it.

Was the outcome in doubt? Would Mr. Leland send her into another incomplete septigamoklan (if one existed) because of a single person's snide, blackballing veto? As Mr. Leland had explained it, they could easily do that, blackball her. How would she feel if they did? As far as that went, did she herself want to marry with the Phoenix, to join with them in a new covenant?

Well, the answer to that was an easy one. The answer was yes; yes, she wanted to marry with Luther, Parthena, Toodles, Paul, Helen, and Jerry. And her reason for wanting to was a simple one, too: she was in love.

9   spending the afternoon with luther

On her first Sunday among the Phoenix, Toodles told Zoe that although it was her, Toodles', turn to spend the afternoon with Luther, she would be happy to yield to Zoe. "I don't feel all that good," she explained, "and, besides, it's the only really hospitable way for me to behave, don't you think?" Propped up in bed, Yuichan's awful Fujiyama robe bundled about her shoulders, Toodles was eating a breakfast roll that a cartlike servo-mechanism had wheeled into the common room from the galley. A hairline smear of artificial-peach jelly rode

Toodles' upper lip like a candied mustache, and Zoe wanted to take a tissue and daub it away.

"If you don't feel well, should you be eating jelly rolls?"

Toodles winked. "You know the ole saying: jelly rolls is medicine. But I'm having mine this morning and don't need a dose this afternoon."

"Does 'spend the afternoon' mean what the young drakes and duckies call 'bodyburning'?" Why was she asking? She already knew the answer. Parthena and Helen were off to an Ortho-Urban service somewhere on West Peachtree, Paul was asleep across the room from them, and Jerry and Luther had both got up early and gone down the hall toward the rec center. Zoe had declined an invitation to attend services with Parthena and Helen. Now she wished she were with them.

"You ain't slow, Zoe," Toodles said. "I'da been blunter, but it embarrasses Errol."

"Errol?"

Flipping up the bed linen and extending a heavy leg, Toodles put one bunion-afflicted foot on the tray of the servo-cart. "Errol," she reiterated. The cart hummed and backed up, but Toodles got her leg off the tray in time to avoid a nasty spill. A doughnut did drop to the floor, though. "Temperamental, Errol is. . . . You're not thinking of saving yourself for after the covenant ceremony, are you?"

"Well, if I am, I been saving myself so long that my interest's now a whole lot greater than my principles." That was the punch line of a joke Rabon used to tell. It didn't suit Zoe's mood, which was cautious and a bit skeptical, but it perfectly suited Toodles'—she was delighted. I always play to my audience, Zoe thought; can't seem to help it. Aloud, attempting to recover, "I never was one to kiss on the first date, Toodles; just not the sort."

"Oh, I always said that, too. Anyhow, you've already slept in the same room with the Phoenix, you know. It's not like you'd be sacking out with some bulgy-britches thugboy." And at last she wiped the peach-jelly mustache off her upper lip. "Please say yes. Luther's liable to be hurt." And with her little gold remote-con box

Toodles beckoned Errol (who, Zoe noted with some annoyance, was something of a whiner) closer to the bed so that she could pick up another breakfast pastry.

"Okay," Zoe answered, almost as if it were someone else: not her.

So that afternoon she and Luther walked through the pedestrian courts outside the Geriatrics Hostel and stopped to eat lunch at a little restaurant that seemed to be made entirely of plate glass; it was nestled under the stone eaves of a much taller building, though, and had green, reed-woven window shades to keep out the glare of the dome's day lamps. Atmosphere, Rabon would have said the shades gave the place.

They sat in a simulated-leather booth with potted ferns on both sides of them to cut off their view to the front door and drank scotch and water while waiting for the steward to bring them their meal. A Sunday drink. Well, that was something the Retrenchment Edicts hadn't outlawed. You could get one right after your favorite Ortho-Urban services, which was what half the people in this place, it looked like, were doing. The other half were sharing table hookahs and letting the thin smoke coil away from them through the decorative ferns.

"Good food," Luther said. "They do know how to throw together good food here." He was a little nervous, Zoe could see. He kept putting his malletlike hands on the table, dropping them to his lap, taking a sip of his drink, then sticking those heavy, purplish hands back on the table. "You ain't disturbed that Toodles pushed you into this, are you now?" he said, his brow comically corrugating.

"Luther, my daughter and son-in-law *pushed* me into this, not Toodles. And they don't even know when they're doing me a favor."

That loosened him, more than the scotch even. He asked her questions about her family, he told her about himself. Their meal came—a vegetable dinner featuring hydroponically grown snapbeans, zucchini, tomatoes (stewed), and some sort of hybrid greens—and Luther, between bites, kept on talking. A warm rumble.

"I was born the same year Dr. King was assassinated," he said at one point. "That's how I got my name. The shame of it is, I lived to see that sort of business over and over before the cities went under-cover—and then after the doming, too. I wasn't quite six when I saw a young man shoot Mrs. Martin Luther King, Sr., and several other people right in the old man's own church. My church, too. Then. More died after the dome was up. That young Bitler he was the last one, and it's been eleven years since we've had to walk our hungry-children miles to some good man's grave.

"You know, I was so sick I almost shot myself that year, I almost took a razor to my wrists. Back when you could breathe, when you could look up and see a sun or a moon, some men used to be born in the year a comet come through and wait their whole lives till it come back again so that they could die. That year, I was so down I knew it had been written that Luther Battle was supposed to come in and go out with another man's as-sassination.

"But I was in my thirty-second year with McAlpine Company in '29, and we had a lot of work that year. Bitler had done made a lot of people angry, he had got a lot of ole dead asses movin'. After he was shot, there was all kind of uproar to tear down the surfaceside slums and stick up some kind of halfway decent housing on top of the streets instead of under 'em. I was on McAlpine's demolition crews, not the construction ones. Sixty years old and I was workin' off my anger and grief by wreckin' ole tenements; it was the only way they let us make anything of our own. I bossed the demolition of fifteen buildings that year, workin' it all out so that walls come down clean and the guts got hauled off neat. Cranes, cats, tractors, trucks, all of 'em doin' this and doin' that 'cause of how I told 'em to go. Only thing that kep' me sane, Zoe: tearin' down another century's toilets and doin' it with that century's equipment. Then the uproar quieted off, the work contracts run out, and the Urban Council didn't do nothin' to start 'em up again. We still got some damn ghettos in Atlanta, no matter what the ward reps say. Bondville, one of the worst. Parthena's boy and her gran-chillun still live there. . . . But that bad year was over, and I had survived it, Zoe.

"Retired, then. Lived alone on 7, *under,* just like I had all the years I was with McAlpine. The company had been my family since all the way back to '97. My mama and daddy was lucky: they died before they had to see a dome go up over their heads. Me, I wasn't lucky: I had to sign on with McAlpine and help build that damn thing up there."

"You helped build the dome?" Zoe said. She'd never met anyone who had—not anybody who'd admit to it, at least.

"I did. They was twelve different outfits, different companies, workin' to do it, everybody goin' from blueprints they had run off a computer somewhere up East or maybe in California. We were a year behind New York and Los Angeles, McAlpine told us, and we had to catch up. He was still sayin' this in '97, the year I come on, three after the Dome Projec' started; and no one ever asked why the hell we had to catch up with this foolishness that New York and L.A. was pursuin'. Most of us hadn't had any kinds of jobs at all before the projec', so we shut up and did what all of a sudden the city was givin' us money to do. Yessir, Zoe. We started in a-buildin' a pyramid, a great ole tomb to seal ourselves into and never come out of again. Slaves in Egypt might have to work twenty years to build a House of the Dead for Pharaoh, but they didn't have to lie down in it themselves. We was more advanced. We done ours in ten and managed it so we could put the lid on ourselves from the *inside.* No Moses anywhere to say, 'Hey! Wait a minute, you don't want to live in this place forever!' But we were pullin' down some decent cash, even if they was UrNu dollars, and didn't think there'd ever be a day you couldn't see at least a little square of sky somewhere, at least enough blue to make denim for a workingman's britches. It was an adventure. Nobody thought he was just another one of Pharaoh's slavin' niggers. I didn't, anyhow. Even when I first come on with McAlpine, I felt like *I* was the chief mucketymuck myself."

"How come?"

"Well, we had to go up to the sections of the dome's gridwork that we'd completed, and we always went up in girder-cars, just like the ones you see comb-crawlin' along after dark with their torches alight. You worked on platforms or from harnesses on the girder-car, and you was always right out there over the whole damn state, you could see everything—even when the wind was streamin' by you like it wanted to shake all your hard labor into rubble and scrap. Stone Mountain. All kinds of lakes. The mountains up by Gainesville.

"And kudzu, Zoe, kudzu like you've never seen or can even remember. That ole madman vine ran itself over everything, telephone poles and broken-down barns and even some of them cheapjack townhouses and condo-minny-ums they hammered up all las' century. The whole world was green, dyin' maybe 'cause of that kudzu but so green it made your eyes ache. And up there above the whole world Luther Battle felt like Cheops himself, or King Tut, or whichever one of them mean bastards built the bigges' tomb. And I never did say, 'Hoooi! Luther, why are we doin' this?' "

After their meal, Zoe and Luther went back to the hostel and rode the Tower lift-tube up to the fourth floor. Although she hadn't let him do it in the pedestrian courts on the walk home, in the lift-tube she gave him her hand to hold. Ten years after retiring from the McAlpine Company, he still had calluses on his palm, or the scars of old calluses. In the lift-tube he didn't talk. He was embarrassed again, as if his talking at lunch had been a spiritual bleeding which had left him weak and uncertain of his ground. Well, she was embarrassed too. Only Luther had an advantage: a blush on him wasn't so all-fired conspicuous as it was on her.

In the common room, which was unoccupied by group design and agreement, Luther took her to his bed and made the automatic room dividers roll into place. Bodyburning, the young people called it now. That's what it was for her, too, though not in the way the term was supposed to suggest and not because Luther was a snorting dragon in the act. No, it had been a long time. Rabon was the last, of course, and this ready compliance to the rule of the Phoenix surprised her a little.

For years she had been (what was Melanie's amusing vulgarity?) *mummifying,* and you couldn't expect to throw off the cerements, vaporize the balms and preservatives, and come back from your ages-long limbo in one afternoon.

So that afternoon Zoe experienced only the dull excitement of pain; that, and Luther's solicitude. But each Sunday—the next one with Paul, the one after with Luther, the following one with Paul, and so on, depending on inclination and a very loose schedule—it got better. Since she had never really been dead, it didn't take so long as might the hypothetical attempted resurrection of a Pharaoh. Not anywhere near so long as that. For she was Zoe, Zoe Breedlove, and she no longer remembered her maiden name.

10   jerry at his tricks

What did Jerry do in that mysterious alcove between the rec center and the dining room? Zoe wondered because whenever Jerry had a moment of free time—after dinner, before bed, Sunday morning—his wheelchair, humming subsonically, circled about and went rolling off to that little room. And Jerry would be gone for fifteen minutes, or thirty, or maybe an hour, whatever he could spare. What provoked her curiosity was the midnight vision of his puffball hairdo and his sad hollow eyes floating out of the corridor's brightness and into the darkened common room after one of these recurrent disappearances.

On the Sunday night (more properly, the Monday morning) after her conversations, both social and carnal, with Luther, Zoe had this vision again and heard the crippled man unmindfully whistling to himself as he returned from that room: "Zippity-Doo-Dah," it sounded like. And up to his unmade bed Jerry rolled.

Jerry rolls in at night, Zoe thought, and jelly rolls in the afternoon. A muddled, word-fuzzy head she had. It all had something to do with Toodles. And Helen, Parthena, and Luther. Only Paul left out, to date anyway. But these members of the Phoenix were all sleeping.

Sitting up and lowering her feet to the floor she said, "Jerry?"

"Who is it?" She couldn't see his eyes any more, but the macrocephalic helmet of his silhouette turned toward her, dubiously. "Is it Zoe?"

"Yep," she said. "It's me. Can't sleep." She pulled on her dressing gown (Sanders had brought most of her things to the hostel on Saturday afternoon, but had not come up to see her) and walked barefooted on the cold floor over to Jerry's territory.

The Phoenix could certainly saw wood. No danger of these buzz saws waking up; it was enough to make you wish for impaired hearing. Except that each one of the sounds was different, and interesting: an orchestra of snorers. There, a tin whistle. There, a snogglehorn. Over there, a tubaphone. That one, a pair of castanets. And . . .

Jerry grinned quizzically at her and scratched his nose with one finger. "Can't sleep, heh? Would you like to go to the galley for a drink? Maybe some wine. Wine's pretty good for insomnia."

"Wine's pretty good for lots of things," Zoe said. "What I wanted to ask was, what are you up to when you get all antisocial on us and shut yourself up in that closet out there?" She nodded toward the door.

"You're a nice lady. You get a multiple-choice test. A) I'm concocting an eternal-youth elixir. B) I'm perfecting an antigravity device which will spindizzy all of Atlanta out into the stars. C) I'm performing unspeakable crimes of passion on old telescope housings and the jellies in Petri dishes. Or D) I'm . . . I'm . . . My wit fails me, dear lady. Please choose."

"D," Zoe said.

"What?"

"I choose D. You said multiple-choice. That's what I choose."

As if struck with an illuminating insight (for instance, the key to developing an antigravity device), Jerry clapped his hands together and chuckled. "Ah. Even at this late hour, *your* wit doesn't fail *you*," he said. "I am bested."

"Not yet. You haven't given me a real answer yet,

and I've been talking to you for almost two minutes."

"Oh ho! In that case, dear Zoe lady, come with me."
Jerry Zitelman-Phoenix circled about in his subsonically
humming chair and went rolling through the common
room door. Zoe followed.

Down the corridor Jerry glided, Zoe now more conscious of the raw slapping of her feet than of his wheelchair's pleasant purr. Which stopped when he reached
the mysterious room. "I would have preferred to wait
for tomorrow, you know. But over the years I have
learned to honor the moods of insomniac ladies. And
besides, what I have been working on is finished. It
won't hurt for you to get a foreglimpse of the issue of
my labors. It won't hurt *me,* anyway. *You,* on the other
hand, may merely aggravate your sleepless condition."

At two in the morning, if it wasn't later than that,
Jerry was a caution, a nonstop caution. Not much like
Thursday night on the roof when he had talked about
unseeable stars and his lifelong paralysis. Fiddle! Zoe
knew better: he was just like he was Thursday night, if
you were talking about the underneath part of him; the
seeming change was only in his approach to the revelation of this self. Then, candor. Now, a camouflage that
he stripteased momentarily aside, then quickly restored.
Oh, it wasn't hard to undress this man's soul. You just
had to warn yourself not to destroy him by letting him
know that you could see him naked. Nope. Keep those
pasties in place, wrap up the emotional overflow in an
old G-string. And smile, smile, smile.

Because he was funny, Jerry was. In spite of his
tricks.

They went into the little room, and he hit the light
button. Zoe, standing just inside the door, saw a counter
with some sort of duplicating machine on it, reams of
paper, an IBM margin-justifying typer (they had those
in the offices of the *Journal/Constitution* combine),
and a stack of bright yellow-orange booklets. There
were little inset docks in the counter (put there by Luther) so that Jerry could maneuver his wheelchair into
comfortable working positions.

Booklets. You didn't see booklets very often. One
good reason: The Retrenchment Edicts of '35 had out-

lawed private duplicating machines. Everyone had a
visicom console and better be glad he did. The Phoenix
had two such consoles in the rec center, though Zoe
couldn't recall seeing anyone use either of them. Why,
since she'd been at the hostel, she hadn't tapped into
one at all. And now she was seeing booklets: *booklets!*

"I always wondered where Atlanta's pamphleteers
holed up," Zoe said. "You preachin' the overthrow of
our Urban Charter?"

Jerry put a hand to his breast. "Zoe lady, the name is
Zitelman, not Marx, and I am first—no, not first, but
last and always—a Phoenix." He took a copy of one of
the booklets from the counter and handed it to Zoe,
who had moved deeper into his crowded little den of
sedition. "This issue, which has been in preparation for
three or four weeks now—nay, longer—is for you. Not
just this copy, mind you, but the whole issue."

Zoe looked at the booklet's cover, where on the
yellow-orange ground a stylized pen-and-ink phoenix
was rising from its own ashes. The title of the publica-
tion was set in tall, closely printed letters on the bottom
left: *Jerry at His Tricks.* Beneath that: Volume VI, No.
1. "What is it?" she asked.

"It's our famzine," Jerry said. "All the septigamoklans have one. *Fam*ily maga*zine,* you see. Of which I
am the editor and publisher. It is the True History and
Record of the Phoenix Septigamoklan, along with various creative endeavors and pertinent remarks of our
several spouses. One day, dear Zoe, you will be represented herein."

Leafing through the famzine, Zoe said, "Don't count
your chickens . . ."

"Well, as an egghead who has already hatched his
personal fondnesses, I am now seriously counting." He
pointed a wicked crooked finger at her. "One," he said
in a burlesque Transylvanian accent. "One chicken."

She laughed, patting him on top of his wiry puffball.
But it was not until the next day, before breakfast, that
she had a chance to read through the booklet—the advance copy—that Jerry had given her. In it she found
artwork signed by Parthena, Helen, and Paul, and arti-
cles or poems by everyone in the family. Several of

these were tributes, brief eulogies, to the dead Yuichan Kurimoto. The issue concluded with a free-verse poem welcoming Zoe Breedlove as a candidate for marriage with the Phoenix. It was a flattering but fairly tastefully done poem. It was signed *J. Z-Ph.*, and at the bottom of this last page was the one-word motto of the clan:

Dignity.

It was all too ridiculously corny. How did they have the nerve to put that word there? Zoe had to wipe her eyes dry before going into the dining room for breakfast.

11   *in the sun that is young once only*

Of all of them Paul was the hardest to get to know. Parthena had spoken rightly when she said that part of the difficulty was that his mind was going, had been going for a long time. He seemed to have a spiritual umbilicus linking him to the previous century and the time before the domes. He had been nine years old at the time of the Apollo 11 moon landing, thirteen at the time of the final Apollo mission, and he remembered both of them.

"Watched 'em on TV," he said. "Every minute I could of the first one. Just enough of the last one to say I saw it."

And he talked considerably more lucidly about his boyhood in California than he did about everyday matters in the hostel. His other favorite subject was the prospect of attaining, not in a dubious and certainly vitiated afterlife, but in the flesh, immortality. His only real grounding in the present, in fact, was the unalloyed joy he took in Sunday afternoons, at which time he performed creditably and behaved like a mature human being. The leers and the winks, it seemed, were almost involuntary carry-overs from a misspent youth.

"He gone sklotik up here"—Parthena tapped her head—"from the life he led as much as from jes' gettin' ole." (*Sklotik,* Zoe figured out, was *sclerotic.*) "Drugs, likker, womens, card playin'. Brag on how he never had a real job, jes' gamble for his keep-me-up. Now Mr. Leland 'fraid to use on him them new medicines what might stop his brain cells a-dyin'. Easy to see, he done los' a bunch."

And with his washed-out Weimaraner eyes and raw, long lips Paul sometimes seemed like his own ghost instead of a living man. But he could still move around pretty good; he drifted about as effortlessly as a ghost might. And one day, three weeks after Zoe's arrival, he drifted up to her after dinner in the rec center (she was making a photo-display board) and pulled a chair up next to hers. She turned her head to see his raw lips beginning to move.

"It's time for one of my services," he said. "You don't go to the Ortho-Urbanist ones with Helen and Parthena, so I expect you're a fit body for one of mine. This Sunday morning, right in here."

"What sort of services?"

"My sort." A wink, maybe involuntary. "The True Word. Once every quarter, once every new-style month, I preach it."

"The True Word on what? Everybody's got his own true word, you know."

"On how not to die, woman. The basis of every religion."

"No," Zoe said. "Not every one of them; just the ones that don't know exactly what to do with the here-and-now."

His long lips closed, his eyes dilated. She might just as well have slapped him. In eighty years no one had told him that an ontological system didn't have to direct its every tenet toward the question of "how not to die." Or if someone had, Paul had forgotten. Even so, he fought his way back from stupefaction. "The basis," he said archly, "of every *decent* religion."

Jerry, who had overheard, powered himself up to the work table. "Rubbish, Paul. And besides, if tomorrow we were all granted everlasting life, no better than struldbrugs would we be, anyhow."

Zoe raised her eyebrows: *struldbrugs?* Paul kept silent.

"That's someone," Jerry explained, "who can't die but who nevertheless continues to get older and more

infirm. Two hundred years from now we'd all be hope-
lessly senile immortals. Spare me such a blessing."

That ended the conversation. A ghost impersonating
a man, Paul got up and drifted out of the room.

On Sunday morning, though, Luther went down to
the rec center and took a box of aluminum parts, the
largest being a drumlike cylinder, out of the closet
where they kept the dart boards, the croquet equipment,
and the playing cards, and assembled these aluminum
pieces into . . . a rocking horse, one big enough for a
man.

It was a shiny rocking horse, and its head, between
its painted eyes, bore the representation of a scarab bee-
tle pushing the sun before it like a cosmic dung ball.
Zoe, who was in the rec center with all the Phoenix but
Paul, went up to the metal critter to examine it. The
scarab emblem was so meticulously wrought that she
had to lean over to see what this horse had crawling on
its forehead. A blue bug. A red ball. Well, that was different: funny and mysterious at once. "What's this?"
she asked Luther, who, mumbling to himself, was trying
to wedge the cardboard box back into the closet.

"Pulpit," he said. He thought she meant the whole
thing. No sense in trying to clarify herself, he was still
shoving at the box. But *pulpit* was a damn funny syn-
onym for *rocking horse*.

After wedging the parts box back into place, Luther
dragged a tall metal bottle from the closet and carried it
over to the biomonitor cabinet next to Toodles' orpianoogla. Then he set it down and came back to the ring
of chairs in front of the rocking horse. A silly business,
every bit of it. Zoe put a single finger on the horse's
forehead, right on the blue bug, and pushed. The horse,
so light that only its weighted rockers kept it from tip-
ping, began to dip and rise, gently nodding. No one was
talking. Zoe turned to the group and shrugged. It
looked like you'd have to threaten them all with prema-
ture autopsy to get anyone to explain.

"Don't ask," Jerry said finally. "But since you're asking, it's to humor him. He asked for the horse the second month after our covenant ceremony in '35, and Dr.
Tanner said okay, give it to him. Now, four times a

year, he plays octogenarian cowboy and rides into the sunset of his own dreams right in front of everybody. It's not so much for us to listen to him, you know."

Zoe looked at the five of them sitting there afraid she wouldn't understand: five uncertain old faces. She was put off. They had been dreading this morning because they didn't know how she would react to the living skeleton in their family closet: the *de*-ranged range-rider Paul Erik Ferrand-Phoenix. Well, she was put off. All somebody'd had to do was tell her, she was steamingly put off. "O ye of little faith," she wanted to say, "go roast your shriveled hearts on Yuichan's hibachi. All of it together wouldn't make a meal." But she didn't say anything, she sat down with the group and waited. Maybe they didn't think she had Yuichan's compassion, maybe they didn't think she was worthy to replace their dear departed Jap . . .

Just then Paul came drifting in: an entrance. Except that he didn't seem to be at all aware of the impression he was making; he was oblivious of his own etiolated magnificence. Dressed in spotless white from head to foot (currently fashionable attire among even the young, matched tunic and leggings), he wandered over to the metal horse without looking at them. Then, slowly, he climbed on and steadied the animal's rocking with the toe tips of his white slippers.

He was facing them. Behind him, as backdrop, one of the quilted wall banners: a navy-blue one with a crimson phoenix in its center, wings outspread. Zoe couldn't help thinking that every detail of Paul's entrance and positioning had been planned beforehand. Or maybe it was that this quarterly ritual had so powerfully suffused them all that the need for planning was long since past. Anyhow, knowing it all to be nonsense, Zoe had to acknowledge that little pulses of electricity were moving along her spine. Like the time she had first quilted with the group.

Slowly, mesmerizingly slowly, Paul began to rock. And softly he began to preach the True Word. "When we were young," he said, "there was fire, and sky, and grass, and air, and creatures that weren't men. The human brain was plugged into this, the human brain was run on the batteries of fire and sky and all of it out there."

"Amen!" Luther interjected, without interrupting Paul's rhythm, but all Zoe could think was, The city still has creatures that aren't men: pigeons. But the rocking horse began to move faster, and as it picked up speed its rider's voice also acquired momentum, a rhythmic impetus of its own. As Paul spoke on, preached on, an "Amen!" or a "Yessir, brother!" occasionally provided an audible asterisk to some especially strange or vehement assertion in his text. All of it part of the ritual. But then Zoe was caught up in it in a way that she could see herself being caught up. Very odd: she found herself seconding Paul's insane remarks with "Amen!" or "All praises!" or some other curiously heartfelt interjection that she *never* used. This increased as the rocking horse's careening grew more violent and as Paul's eyes, the horse going up and down, flashed like eerie strobes.

"Then before our lives was half over, they put us in our tombs. They said we was dead even though we could feel the juices flowin' through us and electricity jumpin' in our heads. Up went the tombs, though, up they went. It didn't matter what we felt, it didn't matter we was still plugged into the life outside our tombs, the air and fire and sky. Because with the tombs up, you really do start dyin', you really do start losin' the voltage you have flowin' back and forth between you and the outside. Just look at yourself, just look at all of us."—Could anything be more ridiculous than this reasoning?—"It's slippin' away, that current, that precious, precious juice. It's because our brains are plugged into the sun or the moon, one socket or the other, and now they've stuck us in a place where the current won't flow."

Even as she said "Yessir!" Zoe was thinking that he, Paul, must have been plugged into the moon: loony.

But in another way, an upside-down way, it made a kind of loony sense, too. Even though everybody knew the world had been going to hell in a handcar before the domes went up, it still made a loony kind of sense. Maybe, at a certain time in your life (which was already past for her), you learned how to pass judgment on others, even unfavorable ones, without condemning. Zoe was doing that now. She beheld the madly rocking Paul from two utterly opposed perspectives and had no desire to reconcile them. In fact, the reconciliation happened, was happening, without her willing it to. As it always had for her, since Rabon's death. It was the old binocular phenomenon at work on a philosophical rather than a physical plane. Long ago it had occurred in Helen, too, the Phoenix "mediator," and just as Helen's little black goggles brought the physical world into focus for her, this double vision Zoe was now experiencing brought the two galloping Pauls—the demoniac one and the human one—into the compass of her understanding and merged them. Since this had happened before for her, why was she surprised?

". . . And the key to not-dying, and preserving the body too, is the brain. That's where we all are. We have to plug ourselves into the sun again, the sun and the moon. No one can do that unless he is resurrected from the tomb we were put in even before our lives were half over. . . ."

The horse was rocking frenetically, and Paul's voice was swooping into each repetitive sentence with a lean, measured hysteria. The bracelet on Zoe's wrist seemed to be singing. She looked at the biomonitor cabinet beside the orpianoogla and saw the oscilloscope attuned both to Paul's brain waves and his heartbeat sending a shower of pale comets back and forth, back and forth, across its screen. The other six windows were vividly pulsing, too, and she wondered if someone downstairs was taking note of this activity. Well, they were certainly all alive: very much alive.

Now Paul's eyes had rolled back in his head and the rocking horse had carried him into a country of either uninterrupted childhood or eternally stalled ripeness. He was alone in there, with just his brain and the concupiscent wavelets washing back from his body. Still preaching, too. Still ranting. Until, finally, the last word came out.

Only then did Paul slump forward across the neck of his aluminum steed, spent. Or dead maybe.

Zoe stood up—sprang up, rather. Amazingly, the

other Phoenix—Toodles, Helen, Jerry, and Parthena— were applauding. Luther exempted himself from this demonstration in order to catch Paul before he slid off the still-rocking horse and broke his head open.

"That the bes' one he manage in a long time," Parthena said.

Since the applause continued, Zoe, feeling foolish, joined in too. And while they all clapped (did sermons always end like this, the congregation joining in a spontaneous ovation?), Luther carried Paul over to the biomonitor cabinet, laid him out, and administered oxygen from the metal bottle he had earlier taken out of the closet. After which the wraithlike cowboy lifted his head a bit and acknowledged their applause with a wan grin. Then Luther put him to bed.

"You have to let him hear you," Toodles said. "Otherwise the old bastard thinks you didn't like it."

But he wasn't much good for three days after the sermon. He stayed in the common room, sleeping or staring at the ceiling. Zoe sat with him on the first night and let him sip soup through a flexible straw. In a few minutes he waved the bowl away, and Zoe, thinking he wanted to sleep, got up to leave. Paul reached out for her wrist and missed. She saw it, though, and turned back to him. His hand patted the bed: *Sit down*. So she lowered herself into the easy chair there and took his liver-spotted hand in her own. For an hour she sat there and held it. Then the long, raw lips opened and he said, "I'm afraid, Zoe."

"Sometimes," she said carefully, "I am, too." Now and again she was, she had to admit it.

The mouth remained open, the Weimaraner eyes glazed. Then Paul ran his tongue around his long lips. "Well," he said, "you can get in bed with me if you want to."

And closed his eyes. And went to sleep.

12　somewhere over the broomstick

It had never been in doubt. Maybe a little, just a little, in jeopardy the first night when the menfolk insulted Toodles. Or maybe a bit uncertain with Paul, until after his rocking-horse oration and subsequent collapse. But never really perilously in doubt.

So when Luther came up to the rooftop on that evening at the end of Winter and said, "You're in, Zoe, you're in," her joy was contained, genuine but contained. You don't shout Hooray! until the wedding's over or the spacemen have got home safely. Zoe embraced Luther. Downstairs, she embraced the others.

On the morning after the group's decision, they had the covenant ceremony in the hostel quadrangle. Leland Tanner presided. Day 1 of Spring, 2040, New Calendar designation.

"All right," Mr. Leland said. "Each septigamoklan has its own covenant procedure, Zoe, since any way that it chooses to ratify its bond is legal in the eyes of the Human Development Commission. The Phoenix ceremony owes its origin to an idea of Parthena's." He looked at the group. They were all standing on a section of the artificial lawn surrounded by tubbed ginkgo trees. A table with refreshments was visible in the nearest arbor. "That's right, isn't it?"

"That right," Parthena said.

And then, of all crazy things, Mr. Leland brought a broom out from behind his back. He laid it on the wiry turf at his feet and backed up a few steps. "Okay," he said. "What you all do now is join hands and step over the broomstick together." He reconsidered. "Maybe we better do it in two groups of three, Zoe, you making the fourth each time. Any objections?"

"No," Parthena said. "So long as she cross it in the same direction both times, so none of it get undone."

Okay. That's the way they did it. Zoe went first with Helen, Toodles, and Luther, then a second go-round with Parthena, Paul, and Jerry. Jerry had to drive his wheelchair over one end of the broom handle.

"I pronounce you," Mr. Leland said, "all seven of you, married in the Phoenix. Six of you for a second time, one of you for the first." He took them all over to the arbor and passed out drinks. "Viva the Phoenix."

Zoe drank. They all drank. Toasts went around the group several times. It was all very fitting that when you were sold down the river, into freedom, you got married by jumping over a broomstick. How else should you do it? No other way at all. No other way at all.

Paul and Toodles, the oldest and the second youngest in the family, died in 2042. A year later Luther died. In 2047, two days short of her eightieth birthday, Helen died. In this same year Dr. Leland Tanner resigned his position at the Human Development Tower; he protested uninformed interference in a study that was then twelve years old. Upon his departure from the Geriatrics Hostel his programs were discontinued, the remaining members of the ten septigamoklans separated. In 2048 Jeremy Zitelman died in the hostel's nursing ward. Parthena and Zoe, by the time of his death, had been returned to their "surviving families," Parthena to a surfaceside Bondville tenement, Zoe to the Level 1 cubicle of Sanders and Melanie Noble. Oddly enough, these two last members of the Phoenix died within twelve hours of each other on a Summer day in 2050, after brief illnesses. Until a month or two before their deaths, they met each other once a week in a small restaurant on West Peachtree, where they divided a single vegetable dinner between them and exchanged stories about their grandchildren. Parthena, in fact, was twice a *great*-grandmother.

After the broomstick-jumping ceremony in the garden court Mr. Leland took Zoe aside and said that someone wanted to talk to her in the room that he had once called an "air-lock." His horsy face had a tic in one taut cheek, and his hands kept rubbing themselves against each other in front of his bright blue tunic. "I told him to wait until we were finished out here, Zoe. And he agreed."

Why this mystery? Her mind was other places. "Who is it?"

"Your son-in-law."

She went into the air-lock, the decompression chamber, whatever you wanted to call it, and found Sanders ensconced in one corner of the sofa playing with the lint on his socks. When he saw her he got up, clumsily, with a funereal expression on his face. He looked like somebody had been stuffing his mouth with the same sort of lint he'd been picking off his socks: bloated jowls, vaguely fuzzy lips. She just stared at him until he had worked his mouth around so that it could speak.

"Lannie lost the baby," he said.

So, after Lannie got out of the hospital, she spent a week in their Level 3 cubicle helping out until her daughter could do for herself. When that week was over, she returned to her new family in the Geriatrics Hostel. But before she left she pulled Sanders aside and said, "I've got some advice for you, something for you to tell Lannie too. Will you do it?"

Sanders looked at his feet. "Okay, Zoe."

"Tell her," Zoe said, "to try again."

Shipwright

Donald Kingsbury

Donald Kingsbury isn't yet a famous name in science fiction, but he soon will be. "Shipwright," his second story, is a fascinating and delightful tale about a man with a dream of designing the perfect starship, about the unexpected ways in which he accomplishes this, and, in a story spanning many generations, about the surprising results.

Kingsbury says of this story: "I have had complaints that my society on Lager was sexist. It was intentionally sexist, with the women in control and exploiting the men both economically and sexually, though of course, as in most sexist societies, the subservient role has many advantages attached to it." The story is one of a number of precursors to Kingsbury's novel *The Finger Pointing Solward*, which tells how the Akirani became the greatest shipbuilders in the Finger worlds; no doubt you'll have the chance to read this novel soon.

I am an arrogant man, he thought. *It was arrogance that brought me out to the Frontier and arrogance that has given me this ironic reward.*

Throughout the Akiran System, from the mines of inmost Sutemi to the cold wastes of outer Kiromasho, farmers and merchants and craftsmen and lords were celebrating with fireworks and dancing. Now the Akirani could forge an empire out here in the Noir Gulf within this thin wisp of stars that pointed Solward. They had their own shipyard. They had their first home-built starship, the *Massaki Maru*, the First One, the Leader.

I gave it to them.

He stood naked in the rock garden that mimicked the old wilderness, fresh from the hot pool, servants toweling him while two of his children still splashed in the water. His woman Koriru waited patiently for the servants to finish. She had picked out for him a robe of softness, one with black stripes dotted by the crest of the Misubisi. She was a Misubisi. He was not.

For a moment he felt a lonely defiance. He would wear his Engineer's uniform to the celebration, black boots and cling-cloth that protected a man in arctic or desert and, with a helmet, in space. On his chest would be the badge of a shipwright.

I am a Lagerian! The smartest man of the greatest race of engineers in the galaxy.

A burst of white fire exploded in the sky, then turned to red and blue. The blue comets whirled in violent spirals, celebrating his achievement. Somewhere a parade was dancing.

But Lager was 400,000 light-days behind him, kilodays by starship, across the Noir Gulf, through a starfog of worlds. He had thrown away his uniform long ago for the soft robes. He remembered kicking it, wiping his feet on it, laughing as he left it. Putting on the Misubisi robe, he smiled at that distant elation. It was too late to regret his foolishness. He was not happy, yet he was proud in the sad way a man is proud when he has disproved a cherished theory.

Well, no matter about the Engineer's uniform. He was not of Akira, but the Misubisi were all part of him.

Even fierce little Misubisi Koriru was some kind of relative of his. He'd had their women in his hair for a long time. He looked at her in her formal kimono. A ghost of the Caucasian peered through her Akiran face.

"You should be a Plaek instead of a Misubisi," he demanded impulsively.

Koriru bowed. "I respectfully remind you that you did not marry Misubisi Kasumi!"

He smiled inwardly at her seriousness. "But you're related to me."

She bowed again. "All Misubisi know and cherish how they are blooded to the great Engineer Jotar Plaek."

"Do you know your ties?"

"It is of no consequence. I am proud that a small part of me is you. My life is yours."

"What are the ties!" he insisted.

"For not answering immediately, please pardon me! I am your great-granddaughter three times—seven, ten, and forty-one generations back, the last through Kasumi."

"But of my mad enthusiasm for the machinery of stardrives, there is not a trace in you."

Koriru's dark eyes flickered to the floor in embarrassment, showing dark eyelashes. She held her hands in front of her. "My stupidity is inexcusable."

He was inclined to agree. She got mass and charge mixed up, and couldn't for the life of her remember whether unlike charges attracted each other and unlike masses repelled each other or vice versa.

But she nuzzles me in the morning and brags about me to all the powerful people I want to impress, so why should I complain? Heredity is strange. Her sister is one of my most brilliant engineers. I suppose I keep her around because I'm lecherous and because she's kind to middle-aged men. She worships me, and that makes it easier to be unhappy here out on the Frontier. He smiled at her fondly and sadly. *It won't last. It never does. Koriru will get bored with a man she can't understand. But there will be another. The Misubisi clan takes good care of their Shipwright.*

"Look at me," he said. She half obeyed, not raising her eyes above his chest. "You have the smallness and grace of Kasumi," he mused; Kasumi, whom he had loved and treated badly—was that only seven of his kilodays ago? It was amazing that forty-odd generations of Misubisis had lived out their lives since her death. "You are very beautiful."

"*Arigato.*" Koriru again dropped her gaze in the conventionally humble gesture of one receiving a compliment but couldn't resist a flash look into his eyes to see if the compliment was sincere. He caught her at it, and flustered, she turned quickly to the servants. "You may go. Take the children."

The garden was still. She followed him along the rocky path in the tiny woods to their airy house.

"Goti!" She spoke the name of the robobutler.

"*Hai!*" answered that invisible machine.

"Call a robocar."

"Immediately, mistress!"

The Engineer turned away in displeasure. "I don't want to go to that fornicating celebration," he grumbled.

"You must be there. Excuse me for my disrespectful manner of disagreeing with you."

His eyes changed to twinkles. "I'd rather be here caressing your soft hand and gazing into your beautiful face and getting drunk!" He walked over to the liquor wall. "What I want is a bottle of scotch. All of it."

Of the universe of drinks she feared scotch the most because she did not understand its origin or flavor or effect. In one swift motion she threw herself between him and the devil. "No! The honor of the Misubisi clan requests that you be sober!"

He glared at her. "I'm no Misubisi!"

She stood her ground, did not lower her eyes. "As faithful servants, the Misubisi built *your* ship."

"It's *not* my ship!" He shoved her aside. "It's Misubisi Kasumi's ship!" He reached and took the spherical bottle in his palm.

With one chopping motion she sent the bottle flying to the floor, where it shattered. Then she was on her knees, her head touching the floor, apologizing and at the same time explaining the necessity of smashing the bottle.

He was enraged. "Sol's Blazes, I have to distill that stuff myself! It takes two kilodays to age properly!" But she wasn't listening to him; she was too busy apologizing for having done what she had to do, so he picked her up under one arm and clamped his other hand over her mouth. "Goti!" he roared.

"Hai!"

"I order you to spank this wench's bare bottom!"

"It is with abject chagrin that your humble servant informs his lord that he is not equipped to spank."

"Well, there must be some fancy service that you can order to come and do it for you!"

Pause. "My lord, I have been incomprehensibly lax in keeping my records up to date and therefore cannot locate such a necessary service. A thousand pardons."

She bit his hand and he dumped her on a pillow. She was wailing.

"It's all right. I'll go to your space-damned party and we'll launch that damn ship and bask in all the glory. But after we get home, I get to spank your bare behind."

She began to smile, having gotten her way, and reached out to polish some dirt from his slippers. "If you do, I'll bite your nose!"

"You wouldn't dare. I'd blow it."

"You're impossible to take care of!"

How much she could look like Kasumi, he thought. It was painful for him to watch the way she held her head in that light with that expression. An ancient tanka of the earthbound Japanese came unbidden to mind.

"Deep in the marsh reeds
A bird cries out in sorrow
Piercing the twilight
With its recollection of
Something better forgotten."

He even remembered the poet because it was Kasumi who had given him that poem in final goodbye when remorse had driven him to try to renew their love. One hundred generations ago Ki no Tsurayaki had first brushed it onto rice paper back on Earth.

Kasumi was hurrying along the street that first night they chanced to meet, the light drizzle as damp as his eyes would be in some far future, her light robe soaked and clinging to her in a way no wetproof Lagerian cloth ever would. He had simply stared at her. She was the first outworlder he had ever noticed. When she passed by, she observed his gaze and smiled at him before she looked away.

"Focus on that trick," he said spellbound, nudging his young Engineer friend.

"Exotic!"

"Let's pick her up. It'll save us a trip." They were waiting for a robocar to take them down to the Pleasure Basin.

"Maybe she's not horny. This is the business district."

"Tzom!" he exclaimed. "Did you see that smile!"

"She's an outworlder, Jotar!"

"Same race. Women are the same the galaxy over, ready to go nova at the flick of a neutron. They know a good stud when they see one. How could she do better than us? She knows what an Engineer is by now. Look at yourself in a mirror sometime, joker. You didn't get to be where you are by being a weakling. And besides, I want to do the picking for once." Their robocar had arrived, enveloping them. "Follow that woman," Jotar commanded.

The friend was disturbed by this extreme aggressiveness. "There's two of us," he protested.

"That'll make her wheels go round twice as fast. She'll love it," he leered.

"Women like subtle men."

"Grumble, grumble, grumble." The robocar slid to a stop, cutting off the raven-haired exotic but stopping short of enveloping her. Jotar smiled his smile, which had been known to send the bank account of a woman flickering in the last two digits. "We've fallen in love with you," he said.

She looked at them without comprehension and her hand went to the hilt of a dagger in her wide belt.

"That's a dagger," whispered Jotar's friend with urgency.

"Perhaps you don't speak Anglish?" added Jotar hastily.

"Excuse myself for speak your language poorly. I

hear barbarous intent. I certain I am mistake." Gently
she began to edge around them.

"Our intent was to offer ourselves to you for an entire evening of pleasure. Any way you like it."

Her eyes narrowed. She glanced about for possible
escape routes, computing the swiftness of the robocar,
then looked Jotar in the eyes with great poise and some
small trembling. "It would be small pleasure for you rape
one as homely as me. Not beautiful at all."

Jotar was taken aback. It wasn't her self-effacement
that surprised him, it was her choice of thrill. On a
grade F solidio once smuggled into the Monastery when
he was a student he had seen an implausible story about
a girl who liked to be raped—but he had never heard of
such a thing in real life. Maybe they were pretty odd
out there among the outworlds. How would he know?
"We're pretty good at rape," he said, nudging his friend
and faking a menacing look. Anything to please such a
lovely woman. "And I think you are *very* beautiful."

"I struggle hard." She was paling. "I bite."

"Oh, that's no problem. We can hold you down so
you can't do any damage," he said, trying to get into her
fantasy.

"Please not to harm me."

Jotar smiled broadly. "Harming you would be letting
art get out of hand, of course, of course. No bruises.
Get in; I know just the place to take you."

She fled, dagger in hand—a short run, then a leap
down a staired passage where the robocar could not follow. They watched her disappear into the forested
ground floor of a soaring hotel, her graceful stride a
composite of motions unknown on Lager.

Tzom turned on Jotar. "I told you not to act like a
woman! You'll never get anywhere that way! You have
to entice *them* to approach *you*."

"Yeah, yeah." Jotar stared after the lost beauty ab-
sently, a remarkable emotion of infatuation puzzling
him. "I didn't follow her script."

"You dummy. It was because you were aggressive.
You've got to remember how women think. They've got
to be in control. If a woman wants to be raped, you
can't just rape her. You have to be passive. She has to

provoke being raped or she's not going to enjoy it. Everybody knows that about women but you, dummy!"

"Yeah, yeah. I guess it is the Pleasure Basin for us."

They instructed the robocar to take them to the village of dim bawdyhouses and terraced restaurants and gaiety.

"How about just touring the cafés and getting picked up?"

"Naw," said Jotar, "I feel like dancing tonight."

"Sometimes that's not such a good deal. You can never tell who will get you in the auction."

"That's not the problem. Wink and smile at the girl you want and she'll bid on you. You're allowed to flirt, you know. Make it happen."

"You're such a schemer!"

"Buzz off, Monk," said Jotar good-naturedly.

No youth who entered one of the Engineering Orders stayed a celibate Monk—either he mastered the rigorous mental and physical training and graduated into the ranks of the Engineers or he failed and became a Technician and married if a woman proposed to him. The Engineers were forbidden to marry lest a hereditary caste develop, so an Engineer's name died with him. But not his genes.

All over the planet there were places of rendezvous where any woman might go to meet those men who were the physical cream of the planet and to have her raunchiest fantasy made real. It did not matter that some husbands covertly disapproved. Whether she was a simple data clerk, or ugly, or old, or a power in the ruling elite, the Engineers were a woman's to buy for an evening of pleasure. Only one out of every thousand males of Lager became an Engineer, but 8 percent of all the children born were seeded by Engineers. And engineering talent abounded on Lager to keep the planet rich and to blaze the awe of her engineering marvels throughout the human galaxy.

The robocar let them off at a bawdyhouse called the Lion's Loins. Real male lions greeted you with a snarl at the door. But they were lazy. It was the lioness who pounced from her perch above the door who startled unsuspecting clients. Sometimes a menacing lion or two would grab a shy woman by the wrist and herd her over to an Engineer, who would chase the lions away after a mock battle. The animals had computer implants, of course.

There was a central lighted bar that acted as a focus because it was the only place where drinks and food were served. Here the women could appraise a man before deciding to approach him. Surrounding the bar were dark, junglelike alcoves where privacy was at a premium if you weren't upset by an occasional sniffing lion.

"You'll never guess who picked me up the last time I was here," said Jotar, grinning.

"Is she here tonight?"

"No, no. Gail Katalina." Katalina was the Third Director of all Lager, a flamboyant, highly visible politician.

"You're pulling my ear! What's she like?"

"We ended up spending a ten-day together on her yacht. She keeps herself in good condition for her age. She's always busy. It was like being plugged into a thousand-volt line."

"I hear she's kinky."

"Naw. You know gossip. She resonates on photography, that's all. She lays a man well. I felt my innocence, but she wanted to keep me. She was going to set me up in the Dronau Hills."

"And you said no?"

"I'm busy."

"You're a brave man to turn down that kind of political connection."

"Come on, Tzom, power is warming but it doesn't rub off. You know that. Once you believe it does and start chasing powerful people, you end up as a moon, and if you get too close, you end up as part of their mass."

Jotar was acutely aware of the women around him. He had to be; Tzom never paid attention until a woman spoke to him, and then it was often too late to control the situation. One dazzler with bare shoulders stared at Jotar from across the bar. He smiled at her, but she turned away and he knew he wasn't going to attract her.

Their hostess, whom they had been waiting for, arrived. "Are you dancing tonight?"

"Yeah, both of us together."

"I can schedule you for the ninth of Twilight." Twilight was one of the ten divisions of the Lagerian day. "Take dressing rooms 4 and 18."

"How's the crowd in the showroom?" asked Jotar.

Their hostess shrugged wickedly. "Ready to devour you."

In the costuming room the two Engineers argued about the fabrics and colors that might serve them best, holding up this and that and debating merits. Jotar enjoyed the rich garments made available at these places. It was his only chance to show off in something besides a black uniform. He chose a hand-stitched leather tunic with ruffled blouse and velvet pants—the nostalgic Earthy look. That would be his part in the dance, to represent The Past.

Dressed in room 4, he watched his image slowly rotate through 360 degrees in the mirror-screen, and for a moment of fantasy he wasn't on Lager. His mind put him in a villa of some outworld where he was waiting for his robed stranger. She pattered down a staired garden, and stopped, seeing him. This time he took her arm gently, careful not to frighten her.

Smiling, Jotar left his dressing room. Tzom, as per habit, had costumed himself quickly for his role as The Future and was drinking with the other Engineers, incurious about tonight's audience. Jotar moved past the bar, casually stepping through a door at the back of the showroom from where he could view the current performance.

An Engineer was dancing the Sun Dance, and you could feel the violent atomic roil of his body. He was dancing completely in the dark, without spotlight. It was the self-powered scales of his costume that gave him a brilliance almost unbearable to look at, though it was impossible to resist watching him. The programmed flow of color in the sun suit, mostly yellows and greens, counterpointed his movements.

He was good. Only one out of ten Monks made it through the Monasteries to become Engineers, and since physical perfection was as strong a criterion for graduation as intellectual ability was, many Monks chose dancing as the artform that best honed their bodies toward perfection. Here was a man who had made it. When he began to strip, the flames peeled from his body like solar flares.

The audience began to applaud, readying for the auction. It was a mellow group of women tonight, a little drunk but happy. The house was half full. Slowly Jotar began to pick out the faces. His eyes were abnormally keen, being the eyes of an Engineer.

In the semi-light one face took the shape of his mother's, and he lingered on it for a moment—his beloved, brilliant, crazy, naïve mother, who had met his genetic father in a place like this and had foolishly preserved her love for him in some corner of her mind beyond reality. She had illusions about the beauty and luxury of an Engineer's life based on one ten-day experience. In real life she was the wife of a Gardener responsible for the ecology of 3,000 hectares of land in the Miner's Hills, and the mother of four children, two of them by her husband. Jotar's only sister was also the daughter of an Engineer.

It was his mother who had decided that he was to become a shipwright. He remembered. When he was not yet two kilodays old she'd taken him for a night hike in the hills and they had slept on the grass beneath the brilliant stars.

"*People* build ships to go to the stars," she said, cuddling him in the sleeping bag. She fastened electronic binoculars on her eyes and slave goggles on his. "See that bright one there?" Cross hairs appeared and disappeared. "That's Gosang. We trade with Gosang in ships we build. See that tiny one there?" The cross hairs reappeared briefly. "Just above Gosang? That's Al Kiladah 43, so far away that no ship yet built has ever reached it. Even though they appear close to each other in the sky, stars may be far apart in space. Someday someone will build a ship that will reach Al Kiladah 43."

"Could I do it?"

"If you become an Engineer."

"Why can't we go there now?"

She explained to him the problems of the kalma-kovian drive in terms a child could understand. "If a starship travels at two hundred light-speeds, the machinery ages two hundred times as fast as normal to fool the gods into thinking it is traveling slower than light so they won't get upset about one of their laws being violated. In fast-time the machinery wears out if you go very far. Engineers have to make it very, very reliable. If *you* aged as fast as a starship, you'd be grown up in thirty days."

"Then I would be old enough to run away from home before I'm old enough!"

"Where would you run to?"

"Al Kiladah 43!"

"Oh, my. That's far away. I don't think you know how slow two hundred light-speeds is, young man."

"Some more stars!" he said. "Show me the farthest one we've reached!"

"Hmm." His mother talked to the binoculars and symbols began flashing across the goggles. "Well, I can show you *one* of the farthest." It took her a while to find Znark Vasun. "It's on the Frontier."

"Who went there?"

She laughed. "I don't know. Our binoculars are very stupid. Not much memory."

"Turn up the power and we'll see them!"

"That's a tall order for ten-credit binoculars. We wouldn't see them anyway. We'd see Znark Vasun before men got there."

"I'll build some good binoculars when I grow up."

"Would you like to be an Engineer?"

"Yes."

"Would you like to build ships? Would you like to build the greatest ship that has ever traveled space?" Her words were more of an order than a question.

She began buying him models of ships to build. He got a modular computer for his birthday, and every birthday thereafter it became larger. Its memory eventually held the best private collection of starship materials on Lager. Just to manage the horde of data his mother bought for him obsessively, Jotar eventually developed a cross-indexing system unique in starship design history.

And he danced. His mother saw to that. They were country people looking after forest and grasslands, and the nearest dance group was a hundred and eighty kilometers away, but she shuttled him there regularly. Dancing was easy. He had the body for it. And it was a change for him to work with other children.

Sometimes he had to escape from her. He'd put on his waldo leggings and jump across the hill meadows with twenty-meter leaps pretending he was on a light-gravity planet, or he'd leap to the tops of trees and be an animal. Even then he couldn't always escape her. He'd be pursued by thoughts about stardrives.

Before he entered the Black Horse Monastery, before he was full-grown, he already knew what man's greatest starship would be like.

The now-nude Sun Dancer was auctioned off to lusty cheers and it was time for Tzom and Jotar to stage their duet. Naked boys scurried among the tables, using the brief intermission to sell more drinks.

Jotar stayed where he was. He never used a stage entrance. Tzom always did, and this time he appeared with a flash of thunder, high-voltage sparks crackling over a costume that featured roving patches of transparency. The Future's dance was intricate, fast, hard to follow, unpredictable. Tzom was something of a contortionist and half of his movements were not even believable.

The women never noticed Jotar's entrance from the back. Who sees The Past creeping up on them? He'd tickle one girl in the nape of the neck, and when she'd turn, he'd smile at her, or he'd massage a shoulder, or if a woman was really shy, he'd sit on her lap and rub noses until she was cracking up with laughter. Slowly he worked his way through the audience, looking for *the* woman he wanted to spend the night with, flirting, complimenting those he wouldn't mind having. He settled on a lady with twinkling eyes who looked like she had enough of a past to be interesting. She was with a young girl, probably her daughter from the facial resemblance, perfect for Tzom. Jotar fondled the woman with extra warmth. He flattered her and winked at the shy but eager daughter. They'd bid high.

On stage his dance was slow. It took a thousand kilodays for mankind to go from one way of chipping flint to the next flint shapes. He would take one of The Future's movements and simplify it to its roots. His basic movement was cyclic, with variations on the same theme. Eventually The Future stripped The Past of everything, leaving him huddled in a naked ruin for the auction.

Their hostess took the bids. The bidding was active if erratic. Jotar began to encourage the lady and the daughter. He touched eyes with them and his eyes promised. The girl whispered to her mother. They bid higher. Tzom never knew why the handsomest women always approached them when he was with Jotar.

"Gone to the woman with the silver earrings!"

Redressed in black, they met their escorts at the bar. The girl, feeling important, ordered a scotch for Jotar, and then hesitated, confused, to find out if he wanted it straight or with a mixer. She glanced at her mother for assurance. Jotar began the chitchat to put everyone at ease.

The daughter had recently gotten married and was being educated into the wilder side of city life by her flirtatious mother. She hovered between fascination and shyness while the mother decided where to take them to dinner and when they were going to retire for more serious amusement. Two lions blocked their way as they tried to leave. Jotar made the mistake of kicking one of them and was slapped to the ground. The lioness stood on his chest and licked his face.

"Do you need help?" asked the girl timorously.

"Damn animal show," he said.

Gathering courage, she shoved at the beast. "Leave him alone!"

So Jotar got stuck with the young one. That hadn't been part of his plans. He never let his boredom show: it would have been unprofessional. An Engineer pleases the woman he is with. She talked about her husband's job, which was making microscopic spherical bearings. She wondered if she had courage enough to become a trading contract lawyer. He told her how wonderful she was.

After dinner in a moving crystal that toured the other diners, and a conversational respite in which Jotar was allowed to listen to the mother's witty stories, the foursome split up, Tzom with his big arm around his woman, while Jotar led his little girl by the hand into a robocar and to his apartment. He tried to please her. She responded with shy affection and a lack of inhibition that would have astonished her husband. He let her hold him after their lovemaking without pushing her away.

What would it be like to be married to one of these strange creatures? He thought of his father, a tolerant man who had created a stable home life for his children and generally ignored his woman's waywardness, or at least seldom spoke of it. He would just shrug and say, almost with a smile, when their mother disappeared for days at a time, "Women have more lust than men." He had the luxury of knowing his wife and sharing with her in a way that is only possible after long contact.

Damn. Jotar couldn't even remember the name of the girl who had picked him up last night. And a week ago he'd been to a pre-wedding party given by the brides-maids, and the bride and five bridesmaids had had him, one after the other, between drink and lavish food and fun—and he couldn't even remember their faces.

It was something he could get angry about. Like he was angry right now at this girl with her legs around him. She'd get pregnant. She'd tell her husband and they'd celebrate. *But she'll never bother to tell me.* Not a chance. *Sol's Blazes, it makes me angry!* He was human. He liked children. He'd cherished his younger brothers and sister. Probably he had seeded thirty children already, but he'd never know. They used you and they never came back.

I'll never hold a tiny baby in my arms. The tears were running down his cheeks in the dark and he was furious at his bed partner, but he caressed her tenderly. *Little baby girl.*

When she finally went to sleep, he displaced her arm, slowly, carefully, and sneaked out of bed to his workroom. Without really being aware that an earlier meeting was on his mind, he sketched the outworld woman's robe onto the surface of the workroom's computer terminal, rotating and modifying it until it matched his memory. Then he sketched the peculiar racial characteristics of her exotic face. While he worked, he smiled, wondering what it would be like to be loved by an outworld woman, pleased to know already that she was not like Lagerian women.

He put the computer into its pattern-recognition mode. It overprinted his drawings from time to time, asking for clarifying lines, details. It paused for a hundred seconds before burping out a list of probable worlds. All of them, it turned out, belonged to a class of solar systems which could be traced back to the ancient Japanese race of Terra through a philosophy called the Mishima tradition that placed strong emphasis on old values and had advocated going into space to preserve them.

Jotar spliced the list of worlds into the immigration and trade records for an intersection-sort. Only one group matched the available data: a trade mission from Akira, an obscure Frontier sun. They were here to buy heavy automatic machinery and starships. Such a trade mission did not make much sense—Akira was too far away for direct trade.

A detailed examination of the papers of the trade-mission members gave Jotar what he wanted. The beautiful flower who had dominated his senses was called Misubisi Kasumi, and she was the mission linguist.

Elated, he went back to bed, kissing his companion's rump out of happiness. He did not go to sleep. He began to plot the seduction of Kasumi by organizing all the available facts. The central fact was that if they needed starships, he was the galaxy's greatest shipwright. The second fact was that she alone of the mission members spoke Anglish.

A week of feverish work went by while he prepared and perfected his plan. Like all good plans it solved two problems at once, allowing him to build man's greatest starship *and* to have a steady lover who excited him.

Engineer Jotar Plaek had yet to build a single ship.

He was young, too brilliant to ignore and too brilliant to use. He was proposing a radical restructuring of the kalmakovian field guides that scrapped ten generations of engineering experience. He had solved the new field equations and shown theoretically that structures of positive mass and negative mass could be fabricated into the required guides with impressive inertia-low characteristics. Accelerations of one light-speed per ten seconds were feasible, unheard-of performance for the best of modern drives. Final velocity would only be 10 percent greater than with a regular drive, but that figure was calculated by making enormously conservative estimates of every parameter. Jotar suspected that velocities of a thousand light-speeds might eventually be squeezed out of the design, where two hundred and fifty light-speeds was the theoretical maximum for the orthodox guide configuration.

He was so brilliant that he had never been able to find a sponsor. He had papers and credits and consultations and lecture tours that would honor an older man—but no hardware to his name. He knew some of the best Engineers personally but had few contacts in the government except for Gail Katalina, the Third Director and most dynamic member of the Directorate. As he remembered her, she was delighted to be seen with young men but had no interest in starships. In spite of his boasting, she probably didn't remember him.

So his plan was to bypass Lager and let Akira sponsor the research.

He sent out a feeler to the Akiran mission—terse. He knew they would check his credentials, and when they found him to be the most knowledgeable shipwright on Lager, they'd come to him.

Misubisi Kasumi came.

She did not recognize him. He supposed that all Lagerians looked alike to her. They talked business. He spent the whole morning with her at a projection table showing her details of the ship he wanted to build for them.

The table could do anything. It could enlarge or contract the diagrams in its memory, or give you a cross section through any angle. If you wanted iron in red and copper in green, it would give you that and blot out all else. If you wanted bulkheads or wiring or plumbing, it could give you all of those separately. It would give you parts and explode them. It could show you the kalmakovian drive and the field changes as color changes when the drive was "operative." It could run standard simulated voyages that put every part through an extreme test.

Jotar had spent all of his time as a Monk building the plans for this vessel. It was the completed project that gave him Engineer status. He had spent all of his time as an Engineer revising details and trying to sell it to a sponsor.

In all of the galaxy only on Lager was such a monumental one-man project possible. There were myriad computer routines on tap to design almost anything to any reasonable specifications with fabrication-cost optimization and maintenance optimization. If he wanted docking gear, a command would generate it.

Where the computers failed, he could use the Monks by assigning a project. They enjoyed such projects because they received much credit for solving problems beyond the capacity of the computers. Sometimes he used other Engineers as consultants. It was the drive unit that was uniquely his.

"How fast?" she asked.

"Do you need a fast drive?"

"Yes. We are isolated. We live across the Noir Gulf." She paused.

"Never heard of it."

"It is like cosmic moat across the Sagittarian route to the center of the galaxy. It is one of the great gravitic divides. At narrowest between Znark Vasun and Akira, it has width a hundred and seventy-five leagues.* At other places it has width five hundred leagues. It has slowed human expansion in that direction. Akira is double isolated. We exist tip of stellar wisp called the Finger Pointing Solward. We can trade with Znark Vasun—long trip. But if we go up, down, or sideways—nothing. Gulf. We go down Finger toward galactic cen-

*1 league $\fallingdotseq 10^{16}$ meters $= .974$ light years.

ter—all Frontier, little trade. In future, when all developed, still we be trading along straight line of stars." She gestured negatively. "Much more expensive than trading in volume of stars. We need speed."

"I can't guarantee it on the first vessel, but the speed potential is there. A thousand light-speeds."

She gasped. "We want that. Explain me your drive."

"It's not mine. It is just a modified kalmakovian. You know the sort of thing—the difference between propellers and jets. I'll show you the differences." He began to put images on the table's screen.

"I am so sorry for my inexcusable ignorance, but I not understand physics. There is positive mass that goes down and negative mass that goes up, there are kalmakovs and einsteins and widgets. And momentum and energy are both composed of mass and velocity, but they are different. I never understand."

The kalmakovian effect is the converse of the einsteinian effect.

In einsteinian flight an external energy source such as a rocket increases the mass of the ship, and time slows for the occupants. They can go to a star and back within months of their life and so consider an einsteinian rocket as a "faster-than-light" drive. It is for them. To the people back on the home planet who have lived by a faster time, the einsteinian rocket has never exceeded the velocity of light.

A kalmakovian drive turns a ship into a "falling stone" without an external field to attract it. It can accelerate at thousands of gravities while still in free fall. It uses no obvious energy any more than a falling stone uses energy because it taps into the greatest source of energy available to a ship, the potential energy called the ship's mass. It converts rest mass into velocity. Because the rest mass of every atom in the ship decreases while the drive is on, time accelerates relative to those worlds outside of the field. And because time accelerates for the occupants of the field, it always seems to them that they are traveling below the speed of light. But to the people back on the home planet, the journey took only a matter of months, so they consider a kalmakovian ship as a "faster-than-light" drive.

In the early days of starflight, shipwrights learned to protect their passengers from this kalmakovian "starship aging" by using related field phenomena to displace some of the rest mass, ordinarily converted into velocity, to the mass field of special slow-time cabins for the passengers.

Deceleration is no problem. When the kalmakovian field collapses, velocity is automatically reconverted to rest mass and the ship stops at rest relative to its starting coordinates. The proton rocket motors on each starship were used only to compensate for the relative velocity differences between departure star and destination star.

"Well," said Jotar, "send your technical expert to me and I'll explain it to him."

"You said you wanted our sponsorship. Excuse me for not understanding."

"You're in the market for ships. I've seen your specs. You want the best. This is the best. If you buy my ships I'll build them for you. If you give me an order for twenty, I'll give you a price comparable to that of anything else being built. That's what I mean by sponsoring. I need your money."

She looked doubtful.

"You're used to going to a bureaucrat and ordering something that you can already see being assembled up there in some shipyard—the thousandth edition of a standard vessel. You can do that, but you won't get the best."

"Honorable Engineer, you are not dealing with ordinary planet. You are dealing with very humble planet of meager resources."

"But not poor because you are lazy or poor because you breed planlessly, but because you are Frontier and isolated. Your people are ambitious and hard-working."

"Yes."

"The best kind to deal with. I'll tell you what. I'll give you a bargain. I'll throw in the ship's plans."

He could see her tremble with excitement. He wasn't going to tell her how useless those plans would be to her people. They were keyed to an in-place industrial plant, a pyramid of crafts and skills that a Frontier planet couldn't hope to duplicate in less than sixty kilodays. Jotar doubted that there were more than ten worlds in the human ecumen that could build from those plans.

"Why you need us? A day's trading on Lager would buy all planets of Akira."

If only I could explain. He sighed. "Getting something done is not easy. It never was for geniuses like me." He tried to think of an analogy to give her and fell back on pre-space Terran history. It was humankind's common background, times and people and clashes that every civilized man related to. "I could have sold aircraft carriers to the Japanese Navy in 1925 A.D.; I doubt that I could have sold flying bombers to the United States Army Air Force in 1925 A.D."

She laughed.

"Here. I feel like a snack." He took her away from the table and sat her down on pillows. "I dug up a bottle of rice wine just for you." And he poured her a glass.

"Do you drink rice wine?" she asked in surprise.

"Never touched it before in my life."

"It is my shame that I have never either." She spoke with sadness.

He produced a plate of delicacies—cauliflower with mayonnaise and vinegar, a tofu-and-tomato aspic, roast peppers that weren't peppers at all but a plant from a world called Tekizei, and raw fish.

"What is this?" she said tasting it with her fingers.

"You've never had raw fish? I took it from an Akiran recipe book."

"Raw fish on a spaceship? I am so sorry, but you are out of your mind."

"What are you familiar with?"

"Hardtack." She laughed.

"I see." He paused, reflecting upon the tales of Frontier hardship. "What's Akira like?"

"Ohonshu, the major planet, not need to be terraformed. The plants are *pink*—oh, not really, but pink on their bellies. They flower on the ends of the leaves, and the seeds form in leaf stem. Terran life not thrive well in wild, except for grass. We have tiny wild horses, real horses. Terran birds have done well, I not know why. The colonists were mostly bushido fanatics, caught in the mysteries of a religion their parents not understand and their children not really understand either. They left us strange and beautiful monasteries. It took fanatics to cross the Noir Gulf. They were good people. But I not remember it much. We left when I was small. The captain is my father. My mother not come. It's far away. Living on planets seem strange to me."

"Has being planet-bound frightened you?"

"Yes! Oh, yes!"

"Eat your raw fish."

"If you will, I will."

"Do you like the rice wine?"

"Oh, yes. Sake is in my genes."

He was happy. "You are a pleasant person to be with," he said, trying to draw her into a commitment without being as direct as he was inclined to be.

In response she merely lowered her eyelashes.

It exasperated him. How by the fire of a sun's blazes was he supposed to handle a mannish woman? He paused, then tried again, gently. "Have you been outside of the city?"

"No. But like to. Lager seemed so lush from space!"

"You must have been looking at my parents' place. It is beautiful country. Once you are free of the main burden of your work, we could visit them and take a hike along the river. A hundred-kilometer walk. You'd love it."

"A hundred-kilometer walk would be therapeutic for my soul, but rubber space legs would protest."

"I'll give you waldo leggings. We'll camp out."

The next day he saw Kasumi again. She brought him a small present of dried fruit. He held her at arm's length, looking, smiling. It was good to see the same woman twice.

The next ten days were hectic. Between catnaps, he worked endlessly with the Akiran mission, ironing out the details. They signed a contract. The news spread like a nuclear excursion: Jotar Plaek was going to build his crazy ship. Those were good days.

He found it easy to be with Kasumi, anticipating her grace when he was away from her and marveling in it when she came to him. There was something exquisite about just letting things happen, not investing energy into making them happen. He was good for her. Unobtrusively encouraging her initiative, he brought out a hidden boldness and confidence. Once when they were eating together in a café, she struck up a conversation with an Engineer at the next table and took him with her for the rest of the afternoon, letting Jotar fend for himself. Jotar was pleased that because of him she had become more of a woman than she'd ever been before in her life. When he was most content he would think that it was a good thing for Lager that they all pumped the blood of their mothers; he imagined Lager as a very quiet Eden with its Eve-less men waiting for the apples to fall before they ate.

One day Kasumi was swimming nude at a river bend. She came to him and asked him to towel her off. He smiled at her. She smiled at him. Each felt aroused. Each refused to make the first move. It was like being a Technician. Love. A woman. Contentment. No worries. He took her to the meadow where he had first seen Akira, and finally their chemistry drove them to become lovers. They whispered sweet nothings all night and licked at the dew in the morning with their tongues.

When the dew had melted but the grass was still rosily lit, she recited a poem by Akihito from the almost-sacred Manyoshu.

> "I was wandering
> Among flowered spring meadows
> To pick violets
> And enjoyed myself so much
> I slept in the field all night."

The work orders went out, financed by Akiran funds. Countermanding orders were issued by the government's APCT, and Jotar flew to the capital to straighten out an administrative mess caused by some lunkhead who couldn't understand an outworld investment in a project that had been turned down by the Lagerian Aerospace Technical Oversee. He got through the fracas by a compromise that required him to hire a watchdog staff to prevent the leakage of Classified Skill and Craft Forms. LATO then issued a Duty Liaison requiring computer-filed abstracts of all progress down to the Work Action Order level.

Within four days of assembling the new staff, a minor Liaison Engineer panicked at the new methods of manipulating positive and negative mass fabrications and the project was temporarily halted—Injuncted for a Retro Study. That lasted twelve days. Jotar managed a Reactivation Order, but the renewed research had to be transferred to deep space, where facilities weren't equipped to handle it. Jotar spent forty days building a new space factory.

Then they ran into real fabrication problems that no simulation could have anticipated. Each glitch was solved, but every solution seemed to generate new troubles which had no obvious source. Jotar found to his horror that he wasn't a hardware man. He brought in consultants, and that cost money.

Finally some key parts arrived for the drive assembly but they had been fabricated to normal starship specifications, which weren't good enough in the new configuration. Jotar sued and was countersued. He won the case but was sued from another quarter for nonpayment because a bank had neglected to transfer funds; alarmed, the government froze funds to cover work orders that had not as yet been issued. He hired lawyers. They sent him a bill.

In two hundred days Jotar had gone through all of his Akiran capital. He had promised twenty ships. Not one was remotely finished. In desperation he turned to sex. He didn't think that Third Director Gail Katalina would even remember him, considering her reputation, but he was wrong. She returned his call within two kilosecs.

"Of course I remember you! You're the Engineer with the most beautiful eyelashes on Lager! I'll send an executive plane for you. Can you pack today? I'll meet you at the Jongleur Gardens. My husband won't be there. I may be late, but that will give you time to make yourself beautiful."

The executive cruiser was prompt and polite and like all high-level government roboplanes did not take orders from the passengers. It had been instructed to fly the scenic route through the Lebanor Pass, which it did—skimming the mountains' treetops at a speed never less than five hundred meters per second. Jotar kept swallowing his heart.

For all that haste he arrived at the Jongleur mansion to find himself alone. He was put up in the master bedroom, in which a wood fire was blazing. He was fed delicious food by invisible robocooks and told not to wear his uniform by an invisible robovalet, who provided him with lavish clothes of a cut that might be worn on stage but never in public. He swam. He read. He tried on the clothes and practiced entrances and lines and charm. That night he slept alone.

Director Katalina arrived late the next afternoon. Her hair was white. Her face was lined by the act of smiling so many times at the victories of her ruthless rise. She hugged Jotar, pinched his bottom, and handed him her briefcase. Her two female executive secretaries followed closely to stay inside the shadow of her power.

At dinner she had a videophone beside her wine and continuously interrupted their trivial conversation by answering calls that came in to command her attention. She'd be kidding him about the time he fell overboard on the yacht, and switch into an animated discussion with some disembodied voice concerning the credit rating of the Amar Floating Peoples, who did not qualify as a solar system, and as quickly come back to comment on the bouquet of the wine.

Once Jotar made the mistake of letting the conversation wander around to the subject of starships. She gazed at him with true adoration while he spoke, so he spoke with increasing fire and clarity.

She cut in. "Your intelligence makes you *so sexy* I can't stand it any more!" And with that thought she pulled him off to the bedroom, where she called up her secretaries, instructing them to handle all incoming communication.

First she undressed Jotar. Then she posed him for inspiration. Then she took out her paints and began to decorate his body while he watched in the mirror-screen. Whenever she asked for his advice he praised her. His ear itched.

She became so enthusiastic about her masterpiece that she called in her secretaries to help photograph him for her collection. They took endless photographs, developing them with different dyes, cutting, distorting, reposing him. He was pleased that she was pleased.

Once her assistants were dismissed, Director Katalina had him carry her to the bed. "Do you remember how I like it, you big beautiful rascal?"

He did. By morning he was suffering a bad attack of anxiety. He had done everything conceivable to please her and she had never given him an opening. In desperation he decided to serve her breakfast in bed. He knew a recipe he was sure the robocooks didn't know because Kasumi had taught it to him, but he got caught in the kitchen by one of the secretaries, who hadn't bothered to robe herself.

"Hi, big boy."

"Hi."

She began to fondle him.

"Look, I'm just trying to get breakfast for her."

The secretary spoke some commands. "Let the robocook do it. I'd like to have you for a moment. I'm much younger than she is."

"The robocook isn't up to this particular dish."

"You don't understand, boy. I'm her *executive* secretary. Everything she acts on goes through *my* hands. You have to please me, too."

"I don't think she'd like that." He didn't dare remove the executive hands from his belly.

"She'll never know a thing, pretty boy. It'll only take us half a kilosec."

He got back to the kitchen while the just-prepared breakfast was still hot, and carried it up to the Third Director, cursing the robocook and the secretary.

The old woman smiled at him. She pulled him down and kissed him. "You want something, don't you. What is it?"

Oh, thank Newton! He sat down on the bed and composed himself.

"It's about your starship project, isn't it? You're

broke. See, I know everything. You want money to continue. Money, money, money—that's all an Engineer ever thinks of."

"Sometimes," he said.

"What makes you think I'll give it to you?"

"All I wanted to tell you was that my starship is important to Lager."

She laughed. "We sell every starship we can make. Your venture isn't important for Lager, it is important for you."

Well, I tried.

She laughed at his misery. "You fool! What would I be if I couldn't do favors? Don't worry. I'll handle everything. It will be all right."

In gratitude he made love to her, and she enjoyed his total giving of himself.

Back at his central office, he waited three days. The government put him in bankruptcy to save him from the responsibility for his mistakes. They took over the project of building his ship. The sudden loss of control shocked him: he had an office but no command lines. His faith in the power of sex was shaken.

Then Kasumi timorously announced that she was pregnant.

Jotar did his best to get the State to take over his debt to Akira, but the reorganized project refused to underwrite Akiran interests. With that blow, Kasumi's father and three of his closest associates committed suicide.

Kasumi called. Jotar refused to see her. He wanted to see her, but he couldn't face her. He began to drink heavily. He disconnected his communicator. Finally he put his furniture and library in storage and disappeared. Nobody knew where he was because he was on an island beachcombing with a woman who had run away from her husband but would probably go back to him when her money ran out. They had met at a café in the Pleasure Basin and she had coaxed him into chucking it all with her.

One day while this woman helped him carve out an outrigger, the sun roasting their naked backs, he told her about building the galaxy's greatest space canoe, a tale he embellished with truth, lies, puns, and emotion. The whole idea seemed hilarious to him, a fantasy laid on him by his mother when he was too young to reject it. The trouble was he wasn't *sure* it was a fantasy. Then for months he didn't think at all. He speared fish.

His woman left him, having learned more about canoes than she wanted to know. He drifted and another woman picked him up. Lusena was a distortion photographer who took pictures and fed them into a special computer. He was fascinated. By playing with the commands and selecting out only those image distortions that caused an emotional resonance, the photograph evolved in color and pattern until it became a setting from one's private dream world. Jotar showed Lusena's art to everyone, raving about it for kilosecs. Lusena had a haunting dream world. All that came out when Jotar tried it were pictures of grotesque pinheaded women or elabyrinth long starships that faded complexly into the sky. Time passed.

Jotar was being supported by two waitresses from a local pub in their houseboat when his sister found him. Brother and sister, each seeded by a different Engineer, fought for days. They ranted themselves into a good mood by sunset, whereupon he'd cook the three women a sumptuous meal—stews boiled in beer, beer cakes, beered chicken casserole—and the four of them would reminisce about childhood during the cool of the evening. In the morning the fight would start again.

She sneered at his unwillingness to drive ahead against all obstacles. She derided him for being ruled by the considerations of inferiors. She described what they were doing to his ship in his absence. She flattered his genius for seeing the piece of the puzzle that escaped all other eyes. She goaded his pride. She won. He went back to work.

When he returned to the project he was astounded that he was still respected. Genius had its prerogatives. He was astonished that he still believed in his ship with an insane passion. He worked hard. The ship had what he'd always wanted—government sponsorship. He was now willing to be humble when they told him that the fabrication problems needed research and time.

Half a kiloday passed before he realized that, even working, he had no control over the drift of the project. A whole kiloday passed before he saw the trend of the drift.

The project Engineers were solving problems by creating solutions closer to something they already knew. As the total solution began to emerge, Jotar panicked. He ran in seven directions trying to trace down the individual decisions. He got passed from Engineer to Engineer to Craft Guild to Economist to Production Manager to Beer Hall.

Finally Keithe Walden took him hunting. Walden was the man in charge since the bankruptcy, an older Engineer, jowls sagging. He could make ten thousand men play choo-choo train in unison. They had it out in a duck blind with bugs buzzing around their heads.

"Keithe, I think you're full of meadow-muffins."

"Jotar, if you were redesigning a woman, you'd take off the breasts for streamlining."

"Would I!"

"You'd take out the kidneys because they smell. You'd—"

"Now, look! I like women the way they are!"

"No, you don't. You'd have a thousand improvements if you thought about the problem for a kilosec. What changes would you make?"

"They'd be practical changes. I'd put in a servomechanism so that a woman could control her ovulation. Shreinhart showed that the immunological system could be vastly improved if it had better data-processing capabilities. There's no reason bones should break or get brittle with age—there are much better materials. I think it is shocking that, kilogram for kilogram, solid-state devices have more storage and logic capacity than neural tissue. How about an electromagnetic sense? And women certainly should have a penis to piss with."

"You could go on and on, couldn't you?"

"Probably."

"That's what I mean. Then you'd start to fool with the genes so this new woman could reproduce herself—and you'd be in big trouble because of the incredible cross-correlative interdependence of the genetic interaction. Evolution is a slow thing. You can change only marginal things in something as complicated as a woman or a starship—and each change has to be proved out over generations before you can make the next incremental change. A man has 98 percent of the genes of a chimpanzee, remember that. You want too much change, too soon. You have to start with what you have."

"I'll give you a herd of horses," said Jotar, "and you can start breeding me a flock of birds out of them."

Jotar took up billiards and poker. He danced and wenched. He spent long days playing with his sister's children. Walden built a prototype ship and took orders for five hundred. It hit the news. LATO called it Jotar Plaek's ship and said it was the greatest starship ever launched.

Yeah. We changed the brass doorknobs to silver.

Two days later Misubisi Kasumi followed him home to his apartment. He didn't notice her until he went to close the door. A small girl was clinging to her leg. "Here is daughter you abandoned," she said bitterly.

Shock. "Hi." He went down on his knees, but the child turned her face away in shyness.

Kasumi disciplined the child. She held her face toward Jotar. "You must see mean father who abandoned you."

Tears were running down Jotar's face. She was the first woman who had ever brought one of his children to see him. He was touched beyond anything that had ever happened to him.

"A beautiful kid. Your side of the family. Kasumi, come in. I'm sorry about it all. I got caught up in my own madness. I was destroyed like everybody else."

She marched into the richly furnished apartment, gripping the child's hand. "You seem to be doing quite well."

"I manage."

"You built your ship."

"It's not mine. They changed the grille. It comes in new colors."

"That's good enough for me. Take an order for twenty red ones."

"Sol's Blazes! I wish I owned one to give you! Nothing's mine! I control nothing!"

"You ruined us!" she screamed.

"Yeah, yeah. I ruined you. I won a lot by doing that. How have you made out? Do you still have your ship?"

"Yes."

"Thank Space for small blessings. Why are you still here on this fossilized world when you could be out on the Frontier where people are still alive!"

"The mission must bring back something."

"Have a shot of whiskey. I've got no sake. Some milk for the kid?"

"No, thank you."

"So what are you going to take back that you can fill your holds with for free?"

"Knowledge."

"It's a good cargo. They don't sell it for free here."

"Since you left me, I have had relationships with many of your Engineers." Her voice flowed like a starlight-stirred wind of helium on a sunless planet. "Each has given me something out of pity. I have enough to build industrial empire. I want you to give me everything you know about starships. You owe it to me."

"I'll give you my head in a pickle jar."

"Don't offend me. I hate you enough to kill you!"

"Sit down. I'm on your side. I'm ashamed. Let me think of the resources I do have." He paused. "I collected a fantastic library when I was a child. I'll give it to you. I'll give you the original plans of my ship." He laughed. "I'll give you the plans for that flying toilet bowl they built in my name. But," he slammed out with careful enunciation, "*it won't do you any good*. Knowledge is only valuable if it can be activated. What can you do with a riddle you don't ken?"

"My people are brilliant."

"I'm brilliant," said Jotar, angered. "If I hadn't grown up on Lager I'd know nothing about starships! Nothing! I could wallow in every computer memory about starships that has ever been recorded and I'd learn nothing!"

She glared at him with hatred.

"I'm not arguing with you. I'll give you all I can. Thank you for bringing my daughter." Impulsively he brought out a toy he'd bought for his sister's youngest. It was a transparent ball, feather-light, hard. "Take it for her. She'll like it. It will talk to her and show her pictures that illustrate its story. It is a story kaleidoscope. It will never repeat the same story. Look. What's a wirtzel?" he asked the sphere.

"Once upon a time there was a wirtzel who lived in a cave . . ." The surface was vibrating. Images were beginning to form. The child watched in fascination.

"Look at it, Kasumi! It would take your Frontier culture three generations just to *understand* the plans for that *toy*. Black Hole, woman! If it's knowledge you want, you need to take a university with you!"

She was crying.

Jotar hung his head. "What could I have done? Tell me. It was a disaster."

"You could have put your arms around me when I cry," she sobbed.

Kasumi left him in a turmoil. He thought all night about her, putting the pieces together. He could not sleep. He sat in a trance on the balcony, bathed in the light of the moon Schnapps, compiling memories. *We are, we are, we are, we are, we are the Engineers! We can, we can, we can, we can, we can swig forty beers!* Memories. The first drunken orgy when they had graduated from the Monastery, their vows of celibacy dead: singing, the mob, the screaming girls chasing after a piece of virgin, rioting, getting carried off by a flying wedge of amazons—to be young, to be proud that one could build anything. A long way from there to the duck blind. *I'll give you a herd of horses and you can start breeding me a flock of birds out of them!* Sarcasm. Maybe if you went back to the common ancestor of horse and bird, you could breed a bird. A lot of breeding. Was Akira far enough back on the technological tree? Kasumi crying. *You need to take a university with you!* Why not?

He worked it out because she was leaving and his daughter was leaving and he had an irrational desire to go with them. His images were of them working side by side to build *the* ship on a world that cared.

To accomplish his purpose, the ship of the Akiran trade mission had to be refitted. He still commanded that kind of resource. Its holds became a fifty-person self-contained college subject to fast time. He left room for six students in the crew's slow-time protective field. The best students could be cycled through slow time with him and Kasumi so that he could work with them personally. He intended to breed the best students until shipwright decisions were in their genes. By the time they got to Akira he would be bringing with him a four-hundred-kiloday-old university. It would have more tradition and history than Akira itself. With that base he could build a great ship even out there on the Frontier.

Jotar was short of students. Who wanted to burn up in fast time for a goal they'd never live to see? Misubisi Kasumi ordered some of her crew to become students, and being good vassals they obeyed. Jotar found four Monks who had flunked out and couldn't bear the thought of becoming mere Technicians. He took them. He took three Technicians and two Craftsmen. He found six women like his mother and took them.

Only when they departed did Kasumi tell him that she was going in fast time, to die in repentance for failing to carry out her mission. He couldn't convince her otherwise. She said that she wanted to work directly with the college in its infancy, to see that it grew up understanding Akira, the place where the descendants of the first students would work. But he knew she chose that exotic way to commit suicide because she had not forgiven him.

Jotar saw Kasumi only once again while she was still alive. Their first stop was at the small star Nippon, where he picked up ten students and bought a quantity of genuine Japanese genes. His original students had inbred and were already looking too Caucasian to be received smoothly into the Akiran culture. He had brought with him the frozen sperm of a thousand Engineers, but he didn't want to have to rely on such a source.

Kasumi was old and wrinkled. They had communicated, but only through the time barrier, where she lived a hundred and fifty times as fast as he did. He was shy with her, his sorrow at losing her still fresh in his heart. Nor was it real to him that his daughter was older than he was, his grandchildren adult.

Nippon was a red star, and consequently the surface of Nippon Futatsu was unnatural to human eyes. Kasumi took him to a mountain inn where she served him tea at a tiny shrine in a ceremony he did not understand. He could feel her warmth. It made him apologetic, but she only smiled and pressed his lips gently with her hand.

> "I have lived so long
> That I long for the eon
> Of rejected love
> When I was so unhappy,
> Remembering it fondly."

She poured his tea to refill the tiny cup. "Excuse my liberties with a poem by Kiosuke. Do you have a poem for me, or is your mind too young to partake of such frivolity?"

The twilight inspired him. He did not know how to create a tanka.

> "Why is the horizon tree
> Fixed against the setting sun
> When it is the sun that is eternal?"

Their talk concerned the college. Kasumi was worried about the quality of the students. She knew that they were not good enough even to get into a Monastery on Lager. He laughed and reminded her of their different perspectives. What seemed a painful and difficult development to her was a miraculously swift growth to him.

She held his elbow as they strolled along the lake to their solitary cabin, which stood half on stilts. The only light she permitted was a candle behind a translucent wall. "Darkness is the friend of age. How fortunate I am. It is an old woman's dream to wake up one morn-

ing and find herself in an enchanted land with her favorite long-lost lover, still young of body, potent, and
yet not wise enough to have recovered from her
charms!"

They made love on the mats, he amazed by her mel-
lowness, she happy to be young again for an evening.

"Remember that Engineer who accosted you in the
streets the day you arrived on Lager? You had to run
away to save yourself."

"I do! I was terrified."

"That was me."

"Not you!"

"Yeah. That's when I fell in love with you."

"You beast!"

"I was zapped out of my mind. I cooked up that
whole scheme to sell you ships just to meet you."

"But you left me!"

"Don't men always leave their first love? They don't
have anyone to compare her with to know what they are
losing."

"Jotar, you fool. Doesn't it terrify you to find men
like yourself out among the stars?"

"The glorious stars gave me you. Is your head comfy
on my shoulder? Black Hole, but I've missed reaching
through that barrier to touch you."

When they reboarded their ship in orbit, Kasumi sent
him as a gift her granddaughter by her fourth child. Yawahada was a vexing youth who, her grandmother con-
fided in a covering note, coveted Jotar as a lover because he lived in slow time and she was displeased with
the men available to her and wished for a new generation of men to grow up while she remained young. Kasumi was dead and four new generations had risen before Yawahada of the budding breasts, now pregnant by
Jotar, found a lover among her descendants who
pleased her fickle heart.

By then the college was shaping in ways so fast that
Jotar spent his full time monitoring its growth. Every
tenth day he checked for cultural deviations that might
destroy its purpose. He had the power to change what
he wanted. Cultural evolution had elevated him almost
to the mystical status of Emperor as provided for in the

bushido ethic that came with the college as Kasumi founded it—he was the god from slow time who awoke at intervals and judged.

After Kasumi's death Jotar began to run the breeding program with an iron hand by the best rules of animal genetics. He never interfered with the natural liaisons that arose among the Misubisis, but he alone determined whose chromosomes were carried by every new embryo planted in a womb.

He selected for physical resemblance to the Akirani and for physical perfection—visual acuity that lasted into old age, longevity, coordination, flawless metabolism. You cannot breed for an ability your environment does not require. Jotar required cooperation, craftsmanship, and analysis, and so was able to select for those characteristics. The improvement from generation to generation was remarkable.

Part of the improvement was cultural. As the college solved its problems of organizing and transmitting its knowledge, it became easier for the less brilliant to do outstanding work.

Part of the improvement was the interaction between culture and breeding. Jotar wanted people predisposed toward fine craftsmanship, so he set up a microelectronics industry to build starship brains. He bred the best craftsmen and hardened the electronic specifications from generation to generation until his students were actually selling their extraordinary products in various ports of call. He invented the science of positive- and negative-mass microstructures to teach kalmakovian fabrications in the limited space available onboard. It was only an exercise in craftsmanship to allow him to sort out his most talented students, but they stunned him by producing actual miniature stardrives.

He never stopped delving into his brain for challenging projects. He had only 50 students, but in fast time they were the equivalent of 7,500. They designed special ships to probe the fringes of black holes, automatic freighters, ships to penetrate regions of dense interstellar gas, ships to sample the atmospheres of stars, ships that could land on a planet, warships to meet the thrust of an alien invasion, tiny robot ships that could carry messages between the stars, a transport vehicle to carry 100,000 colonists. He listed every known ability required by a shipwright, monitored each individual for those abilities, and selected for them.

He seized all opportunities. When they were in some stellar port he sold their services to repair damaged ships of designs they'd never seen before. They had to work with their hands in unfamiliar shops and sometimes right out there in spacesuits. He contracted them out to the hardest problems at the cheapest price. They never complained. They did what he told them to do. They would have died for him.

The strange fast-time culture of the Misubisi took some devious turns. It developed a hedonistic period which produced a literature and spirit that grew up into a wisdom that got lost in a dark brooding upon the Japanese past that gave way to a rediscovery of simple crafts like pottery and multicolored wood-block printing that led to a revival of dance and theater which produced a playwright who inspired a political revolution and mutiny by twenty students whose places were filled by a new generation of loyalist fanatics whose children adopted the clothes and philosophical games of a passing port of call until their children resurrected an Akiran identity from an almost-devout curiosity about the coming Akiran experience.

And so they arrived at Znark Vasun, facing the empty Noir Gulf, Akira the most brilliant star in a sky forlorn of stars. Eight of the Misubisi jumped ship for passage in a freighter headed across the Gulf. It was the way they chose to reach the Akiran system alive to taste the final triumph of their millennia-long quest. One slender Misubisi woman, filled with a romantic longing for an imagined Akiran paradise, unwilling to die while she was so near to heaven, seduced Jotar and begged him to take her with him in slow time. He knew the source of her devotion but didn't mind; he liked her company and her body. Another young girl stowed away in his cabin, unwilling to grow old and die without building a real ship. He found her nearly starving long after they had left Znark Vasun. She was too afraid of his wrath to come out of hiding.

The remaining Misubisi continued in fast time across the Noir Gulf as they always had and died there breeding new generations. The very last generation defied the "god beyond the barrier" by birthing a rash of "love children" who took the ship's population past seventy. They knew they were close to home.

Jotar weathered it all. Later he laughed and called himself the longest-surviving Japanese Emperor in human history. Halfway across the Gulf they entered the peninsula called the Finger Pointing Solward. No one was happier than Jotar when their goal star showed as a disc.

Akira blazed on the portside.

They were adrift, the kalmakovian velocity reconverted to rest mass. Proton rockets roared to life, changing their velocity by fourteen kilometers per second so that they could go into orbit around the planet Ohonshu.

They were greeted with incredulous enthusiasm. Akirani wept openly in the streets and on the farms. Two honor shuttles were sent to bring them down, and of course they were landed at Tsumeshumo Beach, where the first two shiploads of colonists had touched down.

Each of the Misubisi was given a torch, and they knew what to do. Wild with joy, they ran along the beach to the shrine on the Jodai Hill, where they embraced and cried and gave their thanks. Jotar marveled. Now he could build his ship! He went into the Demon's Dance with all of his old Engineering power. And when he was finished, he did a flourish of twenty rapid handsprings.

Panting, he saw that all Misubisis had frozen to watch him. For a second after he finished they stood still, then they bowed. Takenaga's lords were there. They too bowed. The son of the governor of the Rokakubutsu System bowed. Other lords of the outworld systems around Akira bowed.

The first person to move was a graceful child, not yet a woman, who came forward with flowers. She kneeled and offered them, her eyes cast down, as she delivered a prepared speech thanking him for bringing them home. Strange how these people of his called this planet home.

He tipped up her face and kissed her cheek and gave her the smile he had often given to women back on Lager when he wanted to encourage their attention. That was his first meeting with Misubisi Koriru. They became friends. When she was older, she became his mistress.

And so here he was, too old to fight much any more, philosophical about his last lost battle, going to a celebration that Koriru wanted him to go to when all he wanted to do was get drunk. Why was he starting to do whatever Koriru said?

Ah, those Misubisi. Those scoundrels that Kasumi had planted and he had nourished. They listened with alertness to everything said by the great Jotar Plaek. They hopped to attention and instantly obeyed his every command. But they always came back, and so sorry, they could not do what he requested, and please would he allow them the honor of disemboweling themselves or some such rot. When he refused, they humbly offered a second, inferior, course of action, which, it always turned out, they had already implemented.

The ship had arrived to find a shockingly primitive technology on Akira—*that* was the trouble. Well, not primitive. One's choice of words could be too strong. Incongruous was the word. Jotar fully expected to find a computer-guided wooden plow one of these days.

Koriru drove him to the outskirts of Temputo, where they entered the procession that snaked through the city to the imperial palace grounds of the Takenagas. Happy people watched. Vendors scurried around selling hot delicacies to the crowd. Children watched from trees. Clowns wearing waldo leggings jumped about the procession to make the crowd laugh. Elaborate paper animals, some of them forty meters long, slithered among the noble daimio. Computer-implanted birds of paradise added punctuation marks of color to the procession, flying back and forth, resting on the heads of children. Everybody waved paper accordion models of the *Massaki Maru* on the end of sticks.

At the palace, lesser daimio were separated from greater daimio for the feasting. Jotar was pillowed with the greatest, the nobles of the Akiran tributary systems:

red Rokakubutsu, Hodo Reishitsu, desolate Iki Ta, and beautiful Butsudo. All of these men stood to gain enormous wealth from an Akiran shipbuilding industry. Wiley old Takenaga himself—the man who had ended Akiran democracy and the money wars between the merchant lords—even put in an appearance.

They liked the ship. The talk was all about *Imperial Akira*. Now they could expand down the Finger. At the knuckle end of the Finger was the whole of the Remeden Drift. Power, commerce, glory.

The moment came when the *Massaki Maru* was tugged from its assembly cocoon in space, already crewed for its maiden voyage to Butsudo. The Captain was in direct communication with Takenaga at the palace.

"Heika, we await your orders!"

"Do us honor. Launch it!"

"*Hai!* Suiginitsu! Generate the field!"

"*Hai!*" came Suiginitsu's reply.

The first starship built on the farside of the Noir Gulf faded from the screen.

Jotar was not pleased. He was ashamed. Even in ancient times, had such an inferior ship ever come out of the shipyards at Lager? The acceleration of the *Massaki Maru* was shockingly sluggish. Its top velocity was ninety light-speeds. Too many compromises had been made with reliability. Fast time ruthlessly destroyed unreliable systems. He doubted that the ship would last more than five kilodays in service.

The Misubisi collective decision had been that it was more economical to build such a ship than to import a better one from across the Noir Gulf. They were right if they manufactured at least twenty of them. Still, he was ashamed. He would not have come to the rim of civilization for that.

Later, as the confusion of the feast brought forth a new course of food, one of the Misubisi women came to him.

"Hanano! You're as nervous as that day I found you starving in my closet! What is it? I know. You're afraid that load of junk will shed its skin all along the route to

Butsudo! No matter. Eat! Sit with us! We'll spend an hour here together and afterwards rub potbellies!"

She fingered his hair affectionately. "If I had only known what a monster you were, I'd have chosen to die in the Gulf rather than to throw myself at your mercy. Come." She tugged at him. "I beg of you to come with Koriru and me."

"You will please come," said Koriru.

They took him to one of the palace gardens where some thirty of the Misubisi clan had gathered. More of them weren't there only because they had vowed that the whole clan would never meet in one place at the same time. The handsome hulk of Misubisi Jihoku confronted them.

"Hanano! You found him, the Disapproving One! Welcome. Koriru, you've kept him sober! How do we honor such self-sacrifice!"

"I'm not sober, you pile of shit!"

"In my unworthy opinion, Plaek-san, when you can still walk, you are sober!"

There was laughter, but nervous laughter. They knew he despised their ship, had not wanted it built.

"If that junk heap just gets back here, I'll give you all gold stars!" Jotar roared drunkenly. "Not for your engineering abilities, but for your monumental good luck!"

Jihoku laughed. "Water on a frog's face! We have a millennia-long tradition of your insight into our inconsequential efforts, threads holding together a history longer than many planets, longer than Akira's, and throughout it all we have learned the joy and profit to ourselves of carrying you, oh noble bag of complaints, on our backs. Complain away!"

The Misubisi cheered Johoku good-naturedly. They were happy. They were celebrating. It was their day.

Koriru stepped forward. "If I may be allowed to intrude, I have a poem from that tradition. Misubisi Kigyoshin of the twenty-third generation wrote it when the plans of his life's work were cut to pieces by Plaek-san. We were at Kinemon and they had met face to face.

"Built of my sinews
Flowing over nebula
    My crafted starbridge
Pleases not our tortoise god
Whose dreams are swift as wishes!

"He's been slashing at us since the mists of our time and his criticism has made us great!"

"Hai!" yelled thirty voices.

Hanano stepped forward, trembling. She had desperately wanted to build ships and had spent her time with him in the Gulf picking his brain. She was his top engineer.

"We wish to give our tortoise god a gift tonight from our hearts and from the hearts of all our ancestors. It will not be good enough but it is our best."

Jotar was sobering. They were afraid of him, really afraid of his disapproval. And yet . . . somehow . . . they were about to give him something . . . if he disapproved . . . they would be destroyed.

It was a wooden box the size of a coffin, and he opened it. The model of a starship floated out, glowing bluely. The name on the bow, printed not in their chicken-track script but in Anglish, was *The Jotar Plaek.* It was his ship. But it wasn't.

"The field fins are wrong," he said.

"I am so sorry to disagree," said Hanano, "but they are a solution to the field equations subject to the fabrication constraints we have assumed."

The robed shipwrights were tense.

"You're not telling me that you're building this ship?" He stared about the garden crazily.

"Hai!" said Hanano fiercely. "I have personally checked the entire critical path analysis. We know every problem that will arise, when it will arise, and how to solve that problem. *The Plaek* is to be a fifth-generation ship. We are to build ships of the *Massaki Maru* class for two more kilodays, at which time the Akiran craftsmen will be ready to build the next generation's prototype. Our fourth generation will be the first significant departure in starship design since Lager produced the

Hammond variation. The fifth generation will be your ships."

Jotar stared at her. "And how long is this going to take?"

Jihoku spoke up. "I am very displeased to inform you that you will be dead by then." He bowed to express sorrow.

"I guessed there was a catch."

"We respectfully remind you," lashed out Koriru, "that you have asked thousands of us to die in this adventure. Only a handful of us survive!" She swept her arm about the room. "It does not matter that we die before the summit is reached. *Banzai!*" Ten thousand years. "It matters only that it is reached!"

"Do you think you can do it?"

"Hai!"

"Why didn't you tell me that this was going on?"

"We wanted to be sure. It was a gift we could not offer lightly. Our honor as shipwrights!"

Jotar Plaek held the model in his hands, turning it about, the tears running down his aging cheeks. He stared at the name printed on the bow.

"Look at that. A fat lot of good that's going to do me! Have you ever met an Akiran who could pronounce my name? Have you?" he challenged them all.

Then he was hugging his Misubisi people, each of them, one at a time.

Seven American Nights

Gene Wolfe

Strange worlds can be found in very commonplace settings—for instance, the United States just a century or so from now. We think of this nation as young, rich, and vigorous, but it can't remain so forever; and the fall might come very quickly. Here's a vision of misshapen people and decaying monuments, told with the intensity of a dream—or a nightmare.

Gene Wolfe is one of science fiction's very best writers; and he seems to specialize in novellas, such as the classic "The Fifth Head of Cerberus" and "The Death of Doctor Island," which won a Nebula Award.

ESTEEMED AND LEARNED MADAME:

As I last wrote you, it appears to me likely that your son Nadan (may Allah preserve him!) has left the old capital and traveled—of his own will or another's—north into the region about the Bay of Delaware. My conjecture is now confirmed by the discovery in those regions of the notebook I enclose. It is not of American manufacture, as you see; and though it holds only the records of a single week, several suggestive items therein provide us new reason to hope.

I have photocopied the contents to guide me in

my investigations; but I am alert to the probability that you, Madame, with your superior knowledge of the young man we seek, may discover implications I have overlooked. Should that be the case, I urge you to write me at once.

Though I hesitate to mention it in connection with so encouraging a finding, your most recently due remission has not yet arrived. I assume that this tardiness results from the procrastination of the mails, which is here truly abominable. I must warn you, however, that I shall be forced to discontinue the search unless funds sufficient for my expenses are forthcoming before the advent of winter.

With inexpressible respect,
HASSAN KERBELAI

Here I am at last! After twelve mortal days aboard the *Princess Fatimah*—twelve days of cold and ennui—twelve days of bad food and throbbing engines—the joy of being on land again is like the delight a condemned man must feel when a letter from the shah snatches him from beneath the very blade of death. America! America! Dull days are no more! They say that everyone who comes here either loves or hates you, America—by Allah I love you now!

Having begun this record at last, I find I do not know where to begin. I had been reading travel diaries before I left home; and so when I saw you, O Book, lying so square and thick in your stall in the bazaar— why should I not have adventures too, and write a book like Osman Aga's? Few come to this sad country at the world's edge after all, and most who do land farther up the coast.

And that gives me the clue I was looking for—how to begin. America began for me as colored water. When I went out on deck yesterday morning, the ocean had changed from green to yellow. I had never heard of such a thing before, neither in my reading, nor in my talks with Uncle Mirza, who was here thirty years ago. I am afraid I behaved like the greatest fool imaginable, running about the ship babbling, and looking over the side every few minutes to make certain the rich mustard color was still there and would not vanish the way things do in dreams when we try to point them out to someone else. The steward told me he knew. Golam Gassem the grain merchant (whom I had tried to avoid meeting for the entire trip until that moment) said, "Yes, yes," and turned away in a fashion that showed he had been avoiding me too, and that it was going to take more of a miracle than yellow water to change his feelings.

One of the few native Americans in first class came out just then: Mister—as the style is here—Tallman, husband of the lovely Madam Tallman, who really deserves such a tall man as myself. (Whether her husband chose that name in self-derision, or in the hope that it would erase others' memory of his infirmity; or whether it was his father's, and is merely one of the countless ironies of fate, I do not know. There was something wrong with his back.) As if I had not made enough spectacle of myself already, I took this Mr. Tallman by the sleeve and told him to look over the side, explaining that the sea had turned yellow. I am afraid Mr. Tallman turned white himself instead, and turned something else too—his back—looking as though he would have struck me if he dared. It was comic enough, I suppose—I heard some of the other passengers chuckling about it afterward—but I don't believe I have seen such hatred in a human face before. Just then the captain came strolling up, and I—considerably deflated but not flattened yet, and thinking that he had not overheard Mr. Tallman and me—mentioned for the final time that day that the water had turned yellow. "I know," the captain said. "It's his country"—there he jerked his head in the direction of the pitiful Mr. Tallman—"bleeding to death."

Here it is evening again, and I see that I stopped writing last night before I had so much as described my first sight of the coast. Well, so be it. At home it is midnight, or nearly, and the life of the cafés is at its height. How I wish that I were there now, with you, Yasmin, not webbed among these red- and purple-clad strangers, who mob their own streets like an invading army, and duck into their houses like rats into their holes. But you, Yasmin, or Mother, or whoever may read this, will want to know of my day—only you are sometimes to think of me as I am now, bent over an old, scarred table in a decayed room with two beds, listening to the hastening feet in the streets outside.

I slept late this morning; I suppose I was more tired from the voyage than I realized. By the time I woke, the whole of the city was alive around me, with vendors crying fish and fruits under my shuttered window, and the great wooden wains the Americans call *trucks* rumbling over the broken concrete on their wide iron wheels, bringing up goods from the ships in the Potomac anchorage. One sees very odd teams here, Yasmin. When I went to get my breakfast (one must go outside to reach the lobby and dining room in these American hotels, which I would think would be very inconvenient in bad weather) I saw one of these *trucks* with two oxen, a horse, and a mule in the traces, which would have made you laugh. The drivers crack their whips all the time.

The first impression one gets of America is that it is not as poor as one has been told. It is only later that it becomes apparent how much has been handed down from the previous century. The streets here are paved, but they are old and broken. There are fine, though decayed, buildings everywhere (this hotel is one—the Inn of Holidays, it is called), more modern in appearance than the ones we see at home, where for so long traditional architecture was enforced by law. We are on Maine Street, and when I had finished my breakfast (it was very good, and very cheap by our standards, though I am told it is impossible to get anything out of season here), I asked the manager where I should go to see the sights of the city. He is a short and phenomenally ugly man, something of a hunchback, as so many of them are. "There are no tours," he said. "Not any more."

I told him that I simply wanted to wander about by myself, and perhaps sketch a bit.

"You can do that. North for the buildings, south for the theater, west for the park. Do you plan to go to the park, Mr. Jaffarzadeh?"

"I haven't decided yet."

"You should hire at least two securities if you go to the park—I can recommend an agency."

"I have my pistol."

"You'll need more than that, sir."

Naturally, I decided then and there that I would go to the park, and alone. But I have determined not to spend this, the sole, small coin of adventure this land has provided me so far, before I discover what else it may offer to enrich my existence.

Accordingly, I set off for the north when I left the hotel. I have not, thus far, seen this city, or any American city, by night. What they might be like if these people thronged the streets then, as we do, I cannot imagine. Even by clearest day, there is the impression of carnival, of some mad circus whose performance began a hundred or more years ago and has not ended yet.

At first it seemed that only every fourth or fifth person suffered some trace of the genetic damage that destroyed the old America, but as I grew more accustomed to the streets, and thus less quick to dismiss as Americans and no more the unhappy old woman who wanted me to buy flowers and the boy who dashed shrieking between the wheels of a *truck,* and began instead to look at them as human beings—in other words, just as I would look at some chance-met person on one of our own streets—I saw that there was hardly a soul not marked in some way. These deformities, though they are individually hideous, in combination with the bright, ragged clothing so common here, give the meanest assemblage the character of a pageant. I sauntered along, hardly out of earshot of one group of street musicians before encountering another, and in a few strides passed a man so tall that he was taller seated on a low step than I standing; a bearded dwarf with a withered arm; and a woman whose face had been divided by some devil into halves, one large-eyed and idiotically despairing, the other squinting and sneering.

There can be no question about it—Yasmin must not read this. I have been sitting here for an hour at least, staring at the flame of the candle. Sitting and listening to something that from time to time beats against the steel shutters that close the window of this room. The truth is that I am paralyzed by a fear that entered me— I do not know from where—yesterday, and has been growing ever since.

Everyone knows that these Americans were once the most skilled creators of consciousness-altering substances the world has ever seen. The same knowledge that permitted them to forge the chemicals that destroyed them, so that they might have bread that never staled, innumerable poisons for vermin, and a host of unnatural materials for every purpose, also contrived synthetic alkaloids that produced endless feverish imaginings.

Surely some, at least, of these skills remain. Or if they do not, then some of the substances themselves, preserved for eighty or a hundred years in hidden cabinets, and no doubt growing more dangerous as the world forgets them. I think that someone on the ship may have administered some such drug to me.

That is out at last! I felt so much better at having written it—it took a great deal of effort—that I took several turns about this room. Now that I have written it down, I do not believe it at all.

Still, last night I dreamed of that bread, of which I first read in the little schoolroom of Uncle Mirza's country house. It was no complex, towering "literary" dream such as I have sometimes had, and embroidered, and boasted of afterward over coffee. Just the vision of a loaf of soft white bread lying on a plate in the center of a small table: bread that retained the fragrance of the oven (surely one of the most delicious in the world) though it was smeared with gray mold. Why would the Americans wish such a thing? Yet all the historians agree that they did, just as they wished their own corpses to appear living forever.

It is only this country, with its colorful, fetid streets, deformed people, and harsh, alien language, that makes me feel as drugged and dreaming as I do. Praise Allah that I can speak Farsi to you, O Book. Will you believe that I have taken out every article of clothing I have, just to read the makers' labels? Will *I* believe it, for that matter, when I read this at home?

The public buildings to the north—once the great center, as I understand it, of political activity—offer a severe contrast to the streets of the still-occupied areas. In the latter, the old buildings are in the last stages of decay, or have been repaired by makeshift and inappropriate means; but they seethe with the life of those who depend upon such commercial activity as the port yet provides, and with those who depend on them, and so on. The monumental buildings, because they were constructed of the most imperishable materials, appear almost whole, though there are a few fallen columns and sagging porticos, and in several places small trees (mostly the sad *carpinus caroliniana*, I believe) have rooted in the crevices of walls. Still, if it is true, as has been written, that Time's beard is gray not with the passage of years but with the dust of ruined cities, it is here that he trails it. These imposing shells are no more than that. They were built, it would seem, to be cooled and ventilated by machinery. Many are windowless, their interiors now no more than sunless caves, reeking of decay; into these I did not venture. Others had had fixed windows that once were mere walls of glass; and a few of these remained, so that I was able to sketch their construction. Most, however, are destroyed. Time's beard has swept away their very shards.

Though these old buildings (with one or two exceptions) are deserted, I encountered several beggars. They seemed to be Americans whose deformities preclude their doing useful work, and one cannot help but feel sorry for them, though their appearance is often as distasteful as their importunities. They offered to show me the former residence of their Padshah, and as an excuse to give them a few coins I accompanied them, making them first pledge to leave me when I had seen it.

The structure they pointed out to me was situated at the end of a long avenue lined with impressive buildings; so I suppose they must have been correct in thinking it once important. Hardly more than the foundation, some rubble, and one ruined wing remain now, and it cannot have been originally of an enduring construction. No doubt it was actually a summer palace or something of that kind. The beggars have now forgotten its very name, and call it merely "the white house."

When they had guided me to this relic, I pretended that I wanted to make drawings, and they left as they had promised. In five or ten minutes, however, one particularly enterprising fellow returned. He had no lower jaw, so that I had quite a bit of difficulty in understanding him at first; but after we had shouted back and forth a good deal—I telling him to depart and threatening to kill him on the spot, and he protesting—I realized that he was forced to make the sound of *d* for *b*, *n* for *m*, and *t* for *p*; and after that we got along better.

I will not attempt to render his speech phonetically, but he said that since I had been so generous, he wished to show me a great secret—something foreigners like myself did not even realize existed.

"Clean water," I suggested.

"No, no. A great, great secret, Captain. You think all this is dead." He waved a misshapen hand at the desolated structures that surrounded us.

"Indeed I do."

"One still lives. You would like to see it? I will guide. Don't worry about the others—they're afraid of me. I will drive them away."

"If you are leading me into some kind of ambush, I warn you, you will be the first to suffer."

He looked at me very seriously for a moment, and a man seemed to stare from the eyes in that ruined face, so that I felt a twinge of real sympathy. "See there? The big building to the south, on Pennsylvania? Captain, my father's father's father was chief of a department" ("detartnent") "there. I would not betray you."

From what I have read of this country's policies in the days of his father's father's father, that was little enough reassurance, but I followed him.

We went diagonally across several blocks, passing through two ruined buildings. There were human bones in both, and remembering his boast, I asked him if they had belonged to the workers there.

"No, no." He tapped his chest again—a habitual gesture, I suppose—and scooping up a skull from the floor, held it beside his own head so that I could see that it exhibited cranial deformities much like his own. "We sleep here, to be shut behind strong walls from the things that come at night. We die here, mostly in wintertime. No one buries us."

"You should bury each other," I said.

He tossed down the skull, which shattered on the terrazzo floor, waking a thousand dismal echoes. "No shovel, and few are strong. But come with me."

At first sight the building to which he led me looked more decayed than many of the ruins. One of its spires had fallen, and the bricks lay in the street. Yet when I looked again, I saw that there must be something in what he said. The broken windows had been closed with ironwork at least as well made as the shutters that protect my room here; and the door, though old and weathered, was tightly shut, and looked strong.

"This is the museum," my guide told me. "The only part left, almost, of the Silent City that still lives in the old way. Would you like to see inside?"

I told him that I doubted that we would be able to enter.

"Wonderful machines." He pulled at my sleeve. "You *see* in, Captain. Come."

We followed the building's walls around several corners, and at last entered a sort of alcove at the rear. Here there was a grill set in the weed-grown ground, and the beggar gestured toward it proudly. I made him stand some distance off, then knelt as he had indicated to look through the grill.

There was a window of unshattered glass beyond the grill. It was very soiled now, but I could see through into the basement of the building, and there, just as the beggar had said, stood an orderly array of complex mechanisms.

I stared for some time, trying to gain some notion of their purpose; and at length an old American appeared among them, peering at one and then another, and whisking the shining bars and gears with a rag.

The beggar had crept closer as I watched. He pointed at the old man, and said, "Still come from north and south to study here. Someday we are great again." Then I thought of my own lovely country, whose eclipse— though without genetic damage—lasted twenty-three hundred years. And I gave him money, and told him that, yes, I was certain America would be great again someday, and left him, and returned here.

I have opened the shutters so that I can look across the city to the obelisk and catch the light of the dying sun. Its fields and valleys of fire do not seem more alien to me, or more threatening, than this strange, despondent land. Yet I know that we are all one—the beggar, the old man moving among the machines of a dead age, those machines themselves, the sun, and I. A century ago, when this was a thriving city, the philosophers used to speculate on the reason that each neutron and proton and electron exhibited the same mass as all the others of its kind. Now we know that there is only one particle of each variety, moving backward and forward in time, an electron when it travels as we do, a positron when its temporal displacement is retrograde, the same few particles appearing billions of billions of times to make up a single object, and the same few particles forming all the objects, so that we are all the sketches, as it were, of the same set of pastels.

I have gone out to eat. There is a good restaurant not far from the hotel, better even than the dining room here. When I came back the manager told me that there is to be a play tonight at the theater, and assured me that because it is so close to his hotel (in truth, he is very proud of this theater, and no doubt its proximity to his hotel is the only circumstance that permits the hotel to remain open) I will be in no danger if I go without an escort. To tell the truth, I am a little ashamed that I did not hire a boat today to take me across the channel to the park; so now I will attend the play, and dare the night streets.

Here I am again, returned to this too-large, too-bare, uncarpeted room, which is already beginning to seem a second home, with no adventures to retail from the dangerous benighted streets. The truth is that the theater is hardly more than a hundred paces to the south. I kept my hand on the butt of my pistol and walked along with a great many other people (mostly Americans) who were also going to the theater, and felt something of a fool.

The building is as old as those in the Silent City, I should think; but it has been kept in some repair. There was more of a feeling of gaiety (though to me it was largely an alien gaiety) among the audience than we have at home, and less of the atmosphere of what I may call the sacredness of Art. By that I knew that the drama really is sacred here, as the colorful clothes of the populace make clear in any case. An exaggerated and solemn respect always indicates a loss of faith.

Having recently come from my dinner, I ignored the stands in the lobby at which the Americans—who seem to eat constantly when they can afford it—were selecting various cold meats and pastries, and took my place in the theater proper. I was hardly in my seat before a pipe-puffing old gentleman, an American, desired me to move in order that he might reach his own. I stood up gladly, of course, and greeted him as "Grandfather," as our own politeness (if not theirs) demands. But while he was settling himself and I was still standing beside him, I caught a glimpse of his face from the exact angle at which I had seen it this afternoon, and recognized him as the old man I had watched through the grill.

Here was a difficult situation. I wanted very much to draw him into conversation, but I could not well confess that I had been spying on him. I puzzled over the question until the lights were extinguished and the play began.

It was Vidal's *Visit to a Small Planet*, one of the classics of the old American theater, a play I have often read about but never (until now) seen performed. I would have liked it much better if it had been done with the costumes and settings of its proper period; unhappily, the director had chosen to "modernize" the entire affair, just as we sometimes present *Rustam Beg* as if Rustam had been a hero of the war just past. General Powers was a contemporary American soldier with the mannerisms of a cowardly bandit, Spelding a publisher of libelous broadsheets, and so on. The only characters

that gave me much pleasure were the limping space-
man, Kreton, and the ingenue, Ellen Spelding, played as
and by a radiantly beautiful American blonde.

All through the first act my mind had been returning
(particularly during Spelding's speeches) to the problem of the old man beside me. By the time the curtain
fell, I had decided that the best way to start a conversation might be to offer to fetch him a kebab—or whatever he might want—from the lobby, since his thread-
bare appearance suggested that he might be ready
enough to be treated, and the weakness of his legs
would provide an admirable excuse. I tried the gambit
as soon as the flambeaux were relit, and it worked as
well as I could have wished. When I returned with a
paper tray of sandwiches and bitter drinks, he remarked
to me quite spontaneously that he had noticed me flexing my right hand during the performance.

"Yes," I said, "I had been writing a good deal before
I came here."

That set him off, and he began to discourse, frequently with a great deal more detail than I could comprehend, on the topic of writing machines. At last I
halted the flow with some question that must have revealed that I knew less of the subject than he had supposed. "Have you ever," he asked me, "carved a letter
in a potato, and moistened it with a stamp pad, and
used it to imprint paper?"

"As a child, yes. We use a turnip, but no doubt the
principle is the same."

"Exactly; and the principle is that of extended abstraction. I ask you—on the lowest level, what is communication?"

"Talking, I suppose."

His shrill laugh rose above the hubbub of the audience. "Not at all! Smell"—here he gripped my arm—
"smell is the essence of communication. Look at that
word *essence* itself. When you smell another human
being, you take chemicals from his body into your own,
analyze them, and from the analysis you accurately de-
duce his emotional state. You do it so constantly and so
automatically that you are largely unconscious of it, and

say simply, 'He seemed frightened,' or 'He was angry.' You see?"

I nodded, interested in spite of myself.

"When you speak, you are telling another how you would smell if you smelled as you should and if he could smell you properly from where he stands. It is almost certain that speech was not developed until the glaciations that terminated the Pliocene stimulated mankind to develop fire, and the frequent inhalation of wood smoke had dulled the olfactory organs."

"I see."

"No, you hear—unless you are by chance reading my lips, which in this din would be a useful accomplishment." He took an enormous bite of his sandwich, spilling pink meat that had surely come from no natural animal. "When you write, you are telling the other how you would speak if he could hear you, and when you print with your turnip, you are telling him how you would write. You will notice that we have already reached the third level of abstraction."

I nodded again.

"It used to be believed that only a limited number K of levels of abstraction were possible before the original matter disappeared altogether—some very interesting mathematical work was done about seventy years ago in an attempt to derive a generalized expression for K for various systems. Now we know that the number can be infinite if the array represents an open curve, and that closed curves are also possible."

"I don't understand."

"You are young and handsome—very fine looking, with your wide shoulders and black mustache; let us suppose a young woman loves you. If you and I and she were crouched now on the limb of a tree, you would scent her desire. Today, perhaps she tells you of that desire. But it is also possible, is it not, that she may write you of her desire?"

Remembering Yasmin's letters, I assented.

"But suppose those letters are perfumed—a musky, sweet perfume. You understand? A closed curve—the perfume is not the odor of her body, but an artificial simulation of it. It may not be what she feels, but it is what she tells you she feels. Your real love is for a whale, a male deer, and a bed of roses." He was about to say more, but the curtain went up for the second act.

I found that act both more enjoyable, and more painful, than the first. The opening scene, in which Kreton (soon joined by Ellen) reads the mind of the family cat, was exceptionally effective. The concealed orchestra furnished music to indicate cat thoughts; I wish I knew the identity of the composer, but my playbill does not provide the information. The bedroom wall became a shadow screen, where we saw silhouettes of cats catching birds, and then, when Ellen tickled the real cat's belly, making love. As I have said, Kreton and Ellen were the play's best characters. The juxtaposition of Ellen's willowy beauty and high-spirited naïveté and Kreton's clear desire for her illuminated perfectly the Paphian difficulties that would confront a powerful telepath, were such persons to exist.

On the other hand, Kreton's summoning of the presidents, which closes the act, was as objectionable as it could possibly have been made. The foreign ruler conjured up by error was played as a Turk, and as broadly as possible. I confess to feeling some prejudice against that bloodthirsty race myself, but what was done was indefensible. When the president of the World Council appeared, he was portrayed as an American.

By the end of that scene I was in no very good mood. I think that I have not yet shaken off the fatigues of the crossing; and they, combined with a fairly strenuous day spent prowling around the ruins of the Silent City, had left me now in that state in which the smallest irritation takes on the dimensions of a mortal insult. The old curator beside me discerned my irascibility, but mistook the reason for it, and began to apologize for the state of the American stage, saying that all the performers of talent emigrated as soon as they gained recognition, and returned only when they had failed on the eastern shore of the Atlantic.

"No, no," I said. "Kreton and the girl are very fine, and the rest of the cast is at least adequate."

He seemed not to have heard me. "They pick them up wherever they can—they choose them for their faces. When they have appeared in three plays, they call themselves actors. At the Smithsonian—I am employed there, perhaps I've already mentioned it—we have tapes of real theater: Laurence Olivier, Orson Welles, Katharine Cornell. Spelding is a barber, or at least he was. He used to put his chair under the old Kennedy statue and shave the passers-by. Ellen is a trollop, and Powers a drayman. That lame fellow Kreton used to snare sailors for a singing house on Portland Street."

His disparagement of his own national culture embarrassed me, though it put me in a better mood. (I have noticed that the two often go together—perhaps I am secretly humiliated to find that people of no great importance can affect my interior state with a few words or some mean service.) I took my leave of him and went to the confectioner's stand in the lobby. The Americans have a very pretty custom of duplicating the speckled eggs of wild birds in marzipan, and I bought a box of these—not only because I wanted to try them myself, but because I felt certain they would prove a treat for the old man, who must seldom have enough money to afford luxuries of that kind. I was quite correct—he ate them eagerly. But when I sampled one, I found its odor (as though I were eating artificial violets) so unpleasant that I did not take another.

"We were speaking of writing," the old man said. "The closed curve and the open curve. I did not have time to make the point that both could be achieved mechanically; but the monograph I am now developing turns upon that very question, and it happens that I have examples with me. First the closed curve. In the days when our president was among the world's ten most powerful men—the reality of the Paul Laurent you see on the stage there—each president received hundreds of requests every day for his signature. To have granted them would have taken hours of his time. To have refused them would have raised a brigade of enemies."

"What did they do?"

"They called upon the resources of science. That science devised the machine that wrote this."

From within his clean, worn coat he drew a folded

sheet of paper. I opened it and saw that it was covered
with the text of what appeared to be a public address,
written in a childish scrawl. Mentally attempting to review the list of the American presidents I had seen in
some digest of world history long ago, I asked whose
hand it was.

"The machine's. Whose hand is being imitated here is
one of the things I am attempting to discover."

In the dim light of the theater it was almost impossible to make out the faded script, but I caught the word
Sardinia. "Surely, by correlating the contents to historical events it should be possible to date it quite accurately."

The old man shook his head. "The text itself was
composed by another machine to achieve some national
psychological effect. It is not probable that it bears any
real relationship to the issues of its day. But now look
here." He drew out a second sheet, and unfolded it for
me. So far as I could see, it was completely blank. I was
still staring at it when the curtain went up.

As Kreton moved his toy aircraft across the stage, the
old man took a final egg and turned away to watch the
play. There was still half a carton left, and I, thinking
that he might want more later, and afraid that they
might be spilled from my lap and lost underfoot, closed
the box and slipped it into the side pocket of my jacket.

The special effects for the landing of the second
spaceship were well done; but there was something else
in the third act that gave me as much pleasure as the cat
scene in the second. The final curtain hinges on the device our poets call *the Peri's asphodel,* a trick so shop-
worn now that it is acceptable only if it can be presented in some new light. The one used here was to
have John—Ellen's lover—find Kreton's handkerchief
and, remarking that it seemed perfumed, bury his nose
in it. For an instant, the shadow wall used at the beginning of the second act was illuminated again to graphically (or I should say, pornographically) present Ellen's
desire, conveying to the audience that John had, for
that moment, shared the telepathic abilities of Kreton,
whom all of them had now entirely forgotten.

The device was extremely effective, and left me feeling that I had by no means wasted my evening. I joined the general applause as the cast appeared to take their bows; then, as I was turning to leave, I noticed that the old man appeared very ill. I asked if he were all right, and he confessed ruefully that he had eaten too much, and thanked me again for my kindness—which must at that time have taken a great deal of resolution.

I helped him out of the theater, and when I saw that he had no transportation but his feet, told him I would take him home. He thanked me again, and informed me that he had a room at the museum.

Thus the half-block walk from the theater to my hotel was transformed into a journey of three or four kilometers, taken by moonlight, much of it through rubble-strewn avenues of the deserted parts of the city.

During the day I had hardly glanced at the stark skeleton of the old highway. Tonight, when we walked beneath its ruined overpasses, they seemed inexpressibly ancient and sinister. It occurred to me then that there may be a time-flaw, such as astronomers report from space, somewhere in the Atlantic. How is it that this western shore is more antiquated in the remains of a civilization not yet a century dead than we are in the shadow of Darius? May it not be that every ship that plows that sea moves through ten thousand years?

For the past hour—I find I cannot sleep—I have been debating whether to make this entry. But what good is a travel journal, if one does not enter everything? I will revise it on the trip home, and present a cleansed copy for my mother and Yasmin to read.

It appears that the scholars at the museum have no income but that derived from the sale of treasures gleaned from the past; and I bought a vial of what is supposed to be the greatest creation of the old hallucinatory chemists from the woman who helped me get the old man into bed. It is—it was—about half the height of my smallest finger. Very probably it was alcohol and nothing more, though I paid a substantial price.

I was sorry I had bought it before I left, and still more sorry when I arrived here; but at the time it seemed that this would be my only opportunity, and I could think of nothing but to seize the adventure. After I have swallowed the drug I will be able to speak with authority about these things for the remainder of my life.

Here is what I have done. I have soaked the porous sugar of one of the eggs with the fluid. The moisture will soon dry up. The drug—if there is a drug—will remain. Then I will rattle the eggs together in an empty drawer, and each day, beginning tomorrow night, I will eat one egg.

I am writing today before I go down to breakfast, partly because I suspect that the hotel does not serve so early. Today I intend to visit the park on the other side of the channel. If it is as dangerous as they say, it is very likely I will not return to make an entry tonight. If I do return—well, I will plan for that when I am here again.

After I had blown out my candle last night I could not sleep, though I was tired to the bone. Perhaps it was only the excitement of the long walk back from the museum; but I could not free my mind from the image of Ellen. My wandering thoughts associated her with the eggs, and I imagined myself Kreton, sitting up in bed with the cat on my lap. In my daydream (I was not asleep) Ellen brought me my breakfast on a tray, and the breakfast consisted of the six candy eggs.

When my mind had exhausted itself with this kind of imagery, I decided to have the manager procure a girl for me so that I could rid myself of the accumulated tensions of the voyage. After about an hour, during which I sat up reading, he arrived with three; and when he had given me a glimpse of them through the half-open door, he slipped inside and shut it behind him, leaving them standing in the corridor. I told him I had only asked for one.

"I know, Mr. Jaffarzadeh, I know. But I thought you might like to have a choice."

None of them—from the glimpse I had had—resembled Ellen; but I thanked him for his thoughtfulness and suggested that he bring them in.

"I wanted to tell you first, sir, that you must allow

me to set the price with them—I can get them for much less than you, sir, because they know they cannot deceive me, and they must depend on me to bring them to my guests in the future." He named a sum that was in fact quite trivial.

"That will be fine," I said. "Bring them in."

He bowed and smiled, making his pinched and miserly face as pleasant as possible and reminding me very much of a picture I had once seen of an imp summoned before the court of Suleiman. "But first, sir, I wished to inform you that if you would like all three—together— you may have them for the price of two. And should you desire only two of the three, you may have them for one and one-half the price of one. All are very lovely, and I thought you might want to consider it."

"Very well, I have considered it. Show them in."

"I will light another candle," he said, bustling about the room. "There is no charge, sir, for candles at the rate you're paying. I can put the girls on your bill as well. They'll be down as room service—you understand, I'm sure."

When the second candle was burning and he had positioned it to his liking on the nightstand between the two beds, he opened the door and waved in the girls, saying, "I'll go now. Take what you like and send out the others." (I feel certain this was a stratagem—he felt I would have difficulty in getting any to leave, and so would have to pay for all three.)

Yasmin must never see this—that is decided. It is not just that this entire incident would disturb her greatly, but because of what happened next. I was sitting on the bed nearest the door, hoping to decide quickly which of the three most resembled the girl who had played Ellen. The first was too short, with a wan, pinched face. The second was tall and blonde, but plump. The third, who seemed to stumble as she entered, exactly resembled Yasmin.

For a few seconds I actually believed it was she. Science has so accustomed us to devising and accepting theories to account for the facts we observe, however fantastic, that our minds must begin their manufacture before we are aware of it. Yasmin had grown lonely for me. She had booked passage a few days after my own departure, or perhaps had flown, daring the notorious American landing facilities. Arriving here, she had made inquiries at the consulate, and was approaching my door as the manager lit his candle, and not knowing what was taking place had entered with prostitutes he had engaged.

It was all moonshine, of course. I jumped to my feet and held up the candle, and saw that the third girl, though she had Yasmin's large, dark eyes and rounded little chin, was not she. For all her night-black hair and delicate features, she was indisputably an American; and as she came toward me (encouraged, no doubt, because she had attracted my attention) I saw that like Kreton in the play she had a club foot.

As you see, I returned alive from the park after all. Tonight before I retire I will eat an egg; but first I will briefly set down my experiences.

The park lies on the opposite side of the Washington Channel, between the city and the river. It can be reached by land only at the north end. Not choosing to walk so far and return, I hired a little boat with a tattered red sail to carry me to the southern tip, which is called Hains Point. Here there was a fountain, I am told, in the old times; but nothing remains of it now.

We had clear, sunny spring weather, and made our way over exhilarating swells of wave with nothing of the deadly wallowing that oppressed me so much aboard the *Princess Fatimah*. I sat in the bow and watched the rolling greenery of the park on one side of the channel and the ruins of the old fort on the other, while an elderly man handled the tiller, and his thin, sun-browned granddaughter, aged about eleven, worked the sail.

When we rounded the point, the old man told me that for very little more he would take me across to Arlington to see the remains of what is supposed to be the largest building of the country's antiquity. I refused, determined to save that experience for another time, and we landed where a part of the ancient concrete coping remained intact.

The tracks of old roads run up either shore; but I

decided to avoid them, and made my way up the center, keeping to the highest ground in so far as I could. Once, no doubt, the whole area was devoted to pleasure. Very little remains, however, of the pavilions and statuary that must have dotted the ground. There are little, worn-away hills that may once have been rockeries but are now covered with soil, and many stagnant pools. In a score of places I saw the burrows of the famous giant American rats, though I never saw the animals themselves. To judge from the holes, their size has not been exaggerated—there were several I could have entered with ease.

The wild dogs, against which I had been warned by both the hotel manager and the old boatman, began to follow me after I had walked about a kilometer north. They are short-haired, and typically blotched with black and brown flecked with white. I would say their average weight was about twenty-five kilos. With their erect ears and alert, intelligent faces they did not seem particularly dangerous; but I soon noticed that whichever way I turned, the ones in back of me edged nearer. I sat on a stone with my back to a pool and made several quick sketches of them, then decided to try my pistol. They did not seem to know what it was, so I was able to center the red aiming laser very nicely on one big fellow's chest before I pressed the stud for a high energy pulse.

For a long time afterward, I heard the melancholy howling of these dogs behind me. Perhaps they were mourning their fallen leader. Twice I came across rusting machines that may have been used to take invalids through the gardens in such fair weather as I myself experienced today. Uncle Mirza says I am a good colorist, but I despair of ever matching the green-haunted blacks with which the declining sun painted the park.

I met no one until I had almost reached the piers of the abandoned railway bridge. Then four or five Americans who pretended to beg surrounded me. The dogs, who as I understand it live mostly upon the refuse cast up by the river, were more honest in their intentions and cleaner in their persons. If these people had been like the pitiful creatures I had met in the Silent City, I would have thrown them a few coins; but they were more or less able-bodied men and women who could have worked, and chose instead to rob. I told them that I had been forced to kill a fellow countryman of theirs (not mentioning that he was a dog) who had assaulted me; and asked where I could report the matter to the police. At that they backed off, and permitted me to walk around the northern end of the channel in peace, though not without a thousand savage looks. I returned here without further incident, tired and very well satisfied with my day.

I have eaten one of the eggs! I confess I found it difficult to take the first taste; but marshaling my resolution was like pushing at a wall of glass—all at once the resistance snapped, and I picked the thing up and swallowed it in a few bites. It was piercingly sweet, but there was no other flavor. Now we will see. This is more frightening than the park by far.

Nothing seemed to be happening, so I went out to dinner. It was twilight, and the carnival spirit of the streets was more marked than ever—colored lights above all the shops, and music from the rooftops where the wealthier natives have private gardens. I have been eating mostly at the hotel, but was told of a "good" American-style restaurant not too far south on Maine Street.

It was just as described—people sitting on padded benches in alcoves. The tabletops are of a substance like fine-grained, greasy, artificial stone. They looked very old. I had the Number One Dinner—buff-colored fish soup with the pasty American bread on the side, followed by a sandwich of ground meat and raw vegetables doused with a tomato sauce and served on a soft, oily roll. To tell the truth, I did not much enjoy the meal; but it seems a sort of duty to sample more of the American food than I have thus far.

I am very tempted to end the account of my day here, and in fact I laid down this pen when I had written *thus far,* and made myself ready for bed. Still, what good is a dishonest record? I will let no one see this— just keep it to read over after I get home.

Returning to the hotel from the restaurant, I passed

the theater. The thought of seeing Ellen again was irresistible; I bought a ticket and went inside. It was not until I was in my seat that I realized that the bill had changed.

The new play was *Mary Rose*. I saw it done by an English company several years ago, with great authenticity; and it struck me that (like Mary herself) it had far outlived its time. The American production was as inauthentic as the other had been correct. For that reason, it retained—or I should have said it had acquired—a good deal of interest.

Americans are superstitious about the interior of their country, not its coasts, so Mary Rose's island had been shifted to one of the huge central lakes. The highlander, Cameron, had accordingly become a Canadian, played by General Powers' former aide. The Speldings had become the Morelands, and the Morelands had become Americans. Kreton was Harry, the knife-throwing wounded soldier; and my Ellen had become Mary Rose.

The role suited her so well that I imagined the play had been selected as a vehicle for her. Her height emphasized the character's unnatural immaturity, and her slenderness, and the vulnerability of her pale complexion, would have told us, I think, if the play had not, that she had been victimized unaware. More important than any of these things was a wild and innocent affinity for the supernatural, which she projected to perfection. It was that quality alone (as I now understood) that had made us believe on the preceding night that Kreton's spaceship might land in the Speldings' rose garden—he would have been drawn to Ellen, though he had never seen her. Now it made Mary Rose's disappearances and reappearances plausible and even likely; it was as likely that unseen spirits lusted for Mary Rose as that Lieutenant Blake (previously John Randolf) loved her.

Indeed, it was more likely. And I had no sooner realized that than the whole mystery of *Mary Rose*—which had seemed at once inexplicable and banal when I had seen it well played in Teheran—lay clear before me. We of the audience were the envious and greedy spirits. If the Morelands could not see that one wall of their comfortable drawing room was but a sea of dark faces, if Cameron had never noticed that we were the backdrop of his island, the fault was theirs. By rights then, Mary Rose should have been drawn to us when she vanished. At the end of the second act I began to look for her, and in the beginning of the third I found her, standing silent and unobserved behind the last row of seats. I was only four rows from the stage, but I slipped out of my place as unobtrusively as I could, and crept up the aisle toward her.

I was too late. Before I had gone halfway, it was nearly time for her entrance at the end of the scene. I watched the rest of the play from the back of the theater, but she never returned.

Same night. I am having a good deal of trouble sleeping, though while I was on the ship I slept nine hours a night, and was off as soon as my head touched the pillow.

The truth is that while I lay in bed tonight I recalled the old curator's remark that the actresses were all prostitutes. If it is true and not simply an expression of hatred for younger people whose bodies are still attractive, then I have been a fool to moan over the thought of Mary Rose and Ellen when I might have had the girl herself.

Her name is Ardis Dahl—I just looked it up in the playbill. I am going to the manager's office to consult the city directory there.

Writing before breakfast. Found the manager's office locked last night. It was after two. I put my shoulder against the door and got it open easily enough. (There was no metal socket for the bolt such as we have at home—just a hole mortised in the frame.) The directory listed several Dahls in the city, but since it was nearly eight years out of date it did not inspire a great deal of confidence. I reflected, however, that in a backwater like this people were not likely to move about so much as we do at home, and that if it were not still of some utility, the manager would not be likely to retain it; so I selected the one that appeared from its address to be nearest the theater, and set out.

The streets were completely deserted. I remember thinking that I was now doing what I had previously been so afraid to do, having been frightened of the city by reading. How ridiculous to suppose that robbers would be afoot now, when no one else was. What would they do, stand for hours at the empty corners?

The moon was full and high in the southern sky, showering the street with the lambent white fluid of its light. If it had not been for the sharp, unclean odor so characteristic of American residential areas, I might have thought myself walking through an illustration from some old book of wonder tales, or an actor in a children's pantomime, so bewitched by the scenery that he has forgotten the audience.

(In writing that—which to tell the truth I did not think of at the time, but only now, as I sat here at my table—I realized that that is in fact what must happen to the American girl I have been in the habit of calling Ellen but must now learn to call Ardis. She could never perform as she does if it were not that in some part of her mind her stage became her reality.)

The shadows about my feet were a century old, tracing faithfully the courses they had determined long before New Tabriz came to jewel the lunar face with its sapphire. Webbed with thoughts of her—my Ellen, my Mary Rose, my Ardis!—and with the magic of that pale light that commands all the tides, I was elevated to a degree I cannot well describe.

Then I was seized by the thought that everything I felt might be no more than the effect of the drug.

At once, like someone who falls from a tower and clutches at the very wisps of air, I tried to return myself to reality. I bit the interiors of my cheeks until the blood filled my mouth, and struck the unfeeling wall of the nearest building with my fist. In a moment the pain sobered me. For a quarter hour or more I stood at the curbside, spitting into the gutter and trying to clean and bandage my knuckles with strips torn from my handkerchief. A thousand times I thought what a sight I would be if I did in fact succeed in seeing Ellen, and I comforted myself with the thought that if she were indeed a prostitute it would not matter to her—I could afford her a few additional rials and all would be well.

Yet that thought was not really much comfort. Even when a woman sells her body, a man flatters himself that she would not do so quite so readily were he not who he is. At the very moment I drooled blood into the street, I was congratulating myself on the strong, square face so many have admired; and wondering how I should apologize if in kissing her I smeared her mouth with red.

Perhaps it was some faint sound that brought me to myself; perhaps it was only the consciousness of being watched. I drew my pistol and turned this way and that, but saw nothing.

Yet the feeling endured. I began to walk again; and if there was any sense of unreality remaining, it was no longer the unearthly exultation I had felt earlier. After a few steps I stopped and listened. A dry sound of rattling and scraping had followed me. It too stopped now.

I was nearing the address I had taken from the directory. I confess my mind was filled with fancies in which I was rescued by Ellen herself, who in the end should be more frightened than I, but who would risk her lovely person to save mine. Yet I knew these *were* but fancies, and the thing pursuing me was not, though it crossed my mind more than once that it might be, some *druj* made to seem visible and palpable to me.

Another block, and I had reached the address. It was a house no different from those on either side—built of the rubble of buildings that were older still, three-storied, heavy-doored, and almost without windows. There was a bookshop on the ground floor (to judge by an old sign) with living quarters above it. I crossed the street to see it better, and stood, wrapped again in my dreams, staring at the single thread of yellow light that showed between the shutters of a gable window.

As I watched that light, the feeling of being watched myself grew upon me. Time passed, slipping through the waist of the universe's great hourglass like the eroded soil of this continent slipping down her rivers to the seas. At last my fear and desire—desire for Ellen, fear of whatever it was that glared at me with invisible eyes—drove me to the door of the house. I hammered the wood with the butt of my pistol, though I knew how unlikely it was that any American would answer a knock at such a time of night, and when I had knocked several times, I heard slow steps from within.

The door creaked open until it was caught by a chain. I saw a gray-haired man, fully dressed, holding an old-fashioned long-barreled gun. Behind him a woman lifted a stub of smoking candle to let him see; and though she was clearly much older than Ellen, and was marked, moreover, by the deformities so prevalent here, there was a certain nobility in her features and a certain beauty as well, so that I was reminded of the fallen statue that is said to have stood on an island farther north, and which I have seen pictured.

I told the man that I was a traveler—true enough!—and that I had just arrived by boat from Arlington and had no place to stay, and so had walked into the city until I had noticed the light of his window. I would pay, I said, a silver rial if they would only give me a bed for the night and breakfast in the morning, and I showed them the coin. My plan was to become a guest in the house so that I might discover whether Ellen was indeed one of the inhabitants; if she were, it would have been an easy matter to prolong my stay.

The woman tried to whisper in her husband's ear, but save for a look of nervous irritation he ignored her. "I don't dare let a stranger in." From his voice I might have been a lion, and his gun a trainer's chair. "Not with no one here but my wife and myself."

"I see," I told him. "I quite understand your position."

"You might try the house on the corner," he said, shutting the door, "but don't tell them Dahl sent you." I heard the heavy bar dropped into place at the final word.

I turned away—and then by the mercy of Allah who is indeed compassionate happened to glance back one last time at the thread of yellow between the shutters of that high window. A flicker of scarlet higher still caught my attention, perhaps only because the light of the setting moon now bathed the rooftop from a new angle. I think the creature I glimpsed there had been waiting to leap upon me from behind, but when our eyes met it launched itself toward me. I had barely time to lift my pistol before it struck me and slammed me to the broken pavement of the street.

For a brief period I think I lost consciousness. If my shot had not killed the thing as it fell, I would not be sitting here writing this journal this morning. After half a minute or so I came to myself enough to thrust its weight away, stand up, and rub my bruises. No one had come to my aid; but neither had anyone rushed from the surrounding houses to kill and rob me. I was as alone with the creature that lay dead at my feet as I had been when I only stood watching the window in the house from which it had sprung.

After I found my pistol and assured myself that it was still in working order, I dragged the thing to a spot of moonlight. When I glimpsed it on the roof, it had seemed a feral dog, like the one I had shot in the park. When it lay dead before me, I had thought it a human being. In the moonlight I saw it was neither, or perhaps both. There was a blunt muzzle; and the height of the skull above the eyes, which anthropologists say is the surest badge of humanity and speech, had been stunted until it was not greater than I have seen in a macaque. Yet the arms and shoulders and pelvis—even a few filthy rags of clothing—all bespoke mankind. It was a female, with small, flattened breasts still apparent on either side of the burn channel.

At least ten years ago I read about such things in Osman Aga's *Mystery Beyond the Sun's Setting;* but it was very different to stand shivering on a deserted street corner of the old capital and examine the thing in the flesh. By Osman Aga's account (which no one, I think, but a few old women has ever believed) these creatures were in truth human beings—or at least the descendants of human beings. In the last century, when the famine gripped their country and the irreversible damage done to the chromosomal structures of the people had already become apparent, some few turned to the eating of human flesh. No doubt the corpses of the famine supplied their food at first; and no doubt those who ate of them congratulated themselves that by so doing they had escaped the effects of the enzymes that were then still used to bring slaughter animals to maturity in a matter of months. What they failed to realize was that the bodies of the human beings they ate had accumulated far more of these unnatural substances than were ever found in the flesh of the short-lived cattle. From them, according to *Mystery Beyond the Sun's Setting*, rose such creatures as the thing I had killed.

But Osman Aga has never been believed. So far as I know, he is a mere popular writer, with a reputation for glorifying Caspian resorts in recompense for free lodging, and for indulging in absurd expeditions to breed more books and publicize the ones he has already written—crossing the desert on a camel and the Alps on an elephant—and no one else has ever, to my knowledge, reported such things from this continent. The ruined cities filled with rats and rabid bats, and the terrible whirling dust storms of the interior, have been enough for other travel writers. Now I am sorry I did not contrive a way to cut off the thing's head; I feel sure its skull would have been of interest to science.

As soon as I had written the preceding paragraph, I realized that there might still be a chance to do what I had failed to do last night. I went to the kitchen, and for a small bribe was able to secure a large, sharp knife, which I concealed beneath my jacket.

It was still early as I ran down the street, and for a few minutes I had high hopes that the thing's body might still be lying where I had left it; but my efforts were all for nothing. It was gone, and there was no sign of its presence—no blood, no scar from my beam on the house. I poked into alleys and waste cans. Nothing. At last I came back to the hotel for breakfast, and I have now (it is mid-morning) returned to my room to make my plans for the day.

Very well. I failed to meet Ellen last night—I shall not fail today. I am going to buy another ticket for the play, and tonight I will not take my seat, but wait behind the last row where I saw her standing. If she comes to watch at the end of the second act as she did last night, I will be there to compliment her on her performance and present her with some gift. If she does not come, I will make my way backstage—from what I have seen of these Americans, a quarter rial should get me anywhere, but I am willing to loosen a few teeth if I must.

What absurd creatures we are! I have just reread what I wrote this morning, and I might as well have been writing of the philosophic speculations of the Congress of Birds or the affairs of the demons in Domdaniel, or any other subject on which neither I nor anyone else knows or can know a thing. O Book, you have heard what I supposed would occur, now let me tell you what actually took place.

I set out as I had planned to procure a gift for Ellen. On the advice of the hotel manager, I followed Maine Street north until I reached the wide avenue that passes close by the obelisk. Around the base of this still imposing monument is held a perpetual fair in which the merchants use the stone blocks fallen from the upper part of the structure as tables. What remains of the shaft is still, I should say, upwards of one hundred meters high; but it is said to have formerly stood three or four times that height. Much of the fallen material has been carted away to build private homes.

There seems to be no logic to the prices in this country, save for the general rule that foodstuffs are cheap and imported machinery—cameras and the like— costly. Textiles are expensive, which no doubt explains why so many of the people wear ragged clothes that they mend and dye in an effort to make them look new. Certain kinds of jewelry are quite reasonable; others sell for much higher prices than they would in Teheran. Rings of silver or white gold set, usually, with a single modest diamond, may be had in great numbers for such low prices that I was tempted into buying a few to take home as an investment. Yet I saw bracelets that would have sold at home for no more than half a rial, for which the seller asked ten times that much. There were many interesting antiques, all of which are alleged to have been dug from the ruined cities of the interior at the cost of someone's life. When I had talked to five or six vendors of such items, I was able to believe that I knew how the country was depopulated.

After a good deal of this pleasant, wordy shopping, during which I spent very little, I selected a bracelet made of old coins—many of them silver—as my gift to Ellen. I reasoned that women always like jewelry, and that such a showy piece might be of service to an actress in playing some part or other, and that the coins must have a good deal of intrinsic value. Whether she will like it or not—if she ever receives it—I do not know; it is still in the pocket of my jacket.

When the shadow of the obelisk had grown long, I returned here to the hotel and had a good dinner of lamb and rice, and retired to groom myself for the evening. The five remaining candy eggs stood staring at me from the top of my dresser. I remembered my resolve, and took one. Quite suddenly I was struck by the conviction that the demon I believed I had killed the night before had been no more than a phantom engendered by the action of the drug.

What if I had been firing my pistol at mere empty air? That seemed a terrible thought—indeed, it seems so to me still. A worse one is that the drug really may have rendered visible—as some say those ancient preparations were intended to—a real but spiritual being. If such things in fact walk what we take to be unoccupied rooms and rooftops, and the empty streets of night, it would explain many sudden deaths and diseases, and perhaps the sudden changes for the worse we sometimes see in others and others in us, and even the birth of evil men. This morning I called the thing a *druj;* it may be true.

Yet if the drug had been in the egg I ate last night, then the egg I held was harmless. Concentrating on that thought, I forced myself to eat it all, then stretched myself upon the bed to wait.

Very briefly I slept and dreamed. Ellen was bending over me, caressing me with a soft, long-fingered hand. It was only for an instant, but sufficient to make me hope that dreams are prophecies.

If the drug was in the egg I consumed, that dream was its only result. I got up and washed, and changed my clothes, sprinkling my fresh shirt liberally with our Pamir rosewater, which I have observed the Americans hold in high regard. Making certain my ticket and pistol were both in place, I left for the theater.

The play was still *Mary Rose*. I intentionally entered late (after Harry and Mrs. Otery had been talking for several minutes), then lingered at the back of the last row as though I were too polite to disturb the audience by taking my seat. Mrs. Otery made her exit; Harry pulled his knife from the wood of the packing case and threw it again, and when the mists of the past had marched across the stage, Harry was gone, and Moreland and the parson were chatting to the tune of Mrs. Moreland's knitting needles. Mary Rose would be on stage soon. My hope that she would come out to watch the opening scene had come to nothing; I would have to wait until she vanished at the end of Act II before I could expect to see her.

I was looking for a vacant seat when I became conscious of someone standing near me. In the dim light I could tell little except that he was rather slender, and a few centimeters shorter than I.

Finding no seat, I moved back a step or two. The newcomer touched my arm and asked in a whisper if I could light his cigarette. I had already seen that it was customary to smoke in the theaters here, and I had fallen into the habit of carrying matches to light the candles in my room. The flare of the flame showed the narrow eyes and high cheekbones of Harry—or as I preferred to think of him, Kreton. Taken somewhat aback, I murmured some inane remark about the excellence of his performance.

"Did you like it? It is the least of all parts—I pull the curtain to open the show, then pull it again to tell everyone it's time to go home."

Several people in the audience were looking angrily at us, so we retreated to a point at the head of the aisle that was at least legally in the lobby, where I told him I had seen him in *Visit to a Small Planet* as well.

"Now *there* is a play. The character—as I am sure

you saw—is good and bad at once. He is benign, he is mischievous, he is hellish."

"You carried it off wonderfully well, I thought."

"Thank you. This turkey here—do you know how many roles it has?"

"Well, there's yourself, Mrs. Otery, Mr. Amy—"

"No, no." He touched my arm to stop me. "I mean *roles,* parts that require real acting. There's one—the girl. She gets to skip about the stage as an eighteen-year-old whose brain atrophied at ten; and at least half what she does is wasted on the audience because they don't realize what's wrong with her until Act I is almost over."

"She's wonderful," I said. "I mean Mlle. Dahl."

Kreton nodded and drew on his cigarette. "She is a very competent ingenue, though it would be better if she weren't quite so tall."

"Do you think there's any chance that she might come out here—as you did?"

"Ah," he said, and looked me up and down.

For a moment I could have sworn that the telepathic ability he was credited with in *Visit to a Small Planet* was no fiction; nevertheless, I repeated my question: "Is it probable or not?"

"There's no reason to get angry—no, it's not likely. Is that enough payment for your match?"

"She vanishes at the end of the second act, and doesn't come on stage again until near the close of the third."

Kreton smiled. "You've read the play?"

"I was here last night. She must be off for nearly forty minutes, including the intermission."

"That's right. But she won't be here. It's true she goes out front sometimes—as I did myself tonight—but I happen to know she has company backstage."

"Might I ask who?"

"You might. It's even possible I might answer. You're Moslem, I suppose—do you drink?"

"I'm not a *strict* Moslem; but no, I don't. I'll buy you a drink gladly though, if you want one, and have coffee with you while you drink it."

We left by a side door and elbowed our way through

the crowd in the street. A flight of narrow and dirty steps descending from the sidewalk led us to a cellar tavern that had all the atmosphere of a private club. There was a bar with a picture (now much dimmed by dirt and smoke) of the cast of a play I did not recognize behind it, three tables, and a few alcoves. Kreton and I slipped into one of these and ordered from a barman with a misshapen head. I suppose I must have stared at him, because Kreton said, "I sprained my ankle stepping out of a saucer, and now I am a convalescent soldier. Should we make up something for him, too? Can't we just say the potter is angry sometimes?"

"The potter?" I asked.

" 'None answered this; but after Silence spake/A Vessel of a more ungainly Make:/They sneer at me for leaning all awry;/What! Did the Hand then of the Potter shake?' "

I shook my head. "I've never heard that; but you're right, he looks as though his head had been shaped in clay, then knocked in on one side while it was still wet."

"This is a republic of hideousness, as you have no doubt already seen. Our national symbol is supposed to be an extinct eagle; it is in fact the nightmare."

"I find it a very beautiful country," I said. "Though I confess that many of your people are unsightly. Still, there are the ruins, and you have such skies as we never see at home."

"Our chimneys have been filled with wind for a long time."

"That may be for the best. Blue skies are better than most of the things made in factories."

"And not all our people are unsightly," Kreton murmured.

"Oh, no. Mlle. Dahl—"

"I had myself in mind."

I saw that he was baiting me, but I said, "No, you aren't hideous—in fact, I would call you handsome in an exotic way. Unfortunately, my tastes run more toward Mlle. Dahl."

"Call her Ardis—she won't mind."

The barman brought Kreton a glass of green liqueur, and me a cup of the weak, bitter American coffee.

"You were going to tell me who she is entertaining."

"Behind the scenes." Kreton smiled. "I just thought of that—I've used the phrase a thousand times, as I suppose everyone has. This time it happens to be literally correct, and its birth is suddenly made plain, like Oedipus's. No, I don't think I promised I would tell you that—though I suppose I said I might. Aren't there other things you would really rather know? The secret hidden beneath Mount Rushmore, or how you might meet her yourself?"

"I will give you twenty rials to introduce me to her, with some assurance that something will come of the introduction. No one need ever find out."

Kreton laughed. "Believe me, I would be more likely to boast of my profit than keep it secret—though I would probably have to divide my fee with the lady to fulfill the guarantee."

"You'll do it then?"

He shook his head, still laughing. "I only pretend to be corrupt; it goes with this face. Come backstage after the show tonight, and I'll see that you meet Ardis. You're very wealthy, I presume, and if you're not, we'll say you are anyway. What are you doing here?"

"Studying your art and architecture."

"Great reputation in your own country, no doubt?"

"I am a pupil of Akhon Mirza Ahmak; he has a great reputation, surely. He even came here, thirty years ago, to examine the miniatures in your National Gallery of Art."

"Pupil of Akhon Mirza Ahmak, pupil of Akhon Mirza Ahmak," Kreton muttered to himself. "That is very good—I must remember it. But now"—he glanced at the old clock behind the bar—"it's time we got back. I'll have to freshen my makeup before I go on in the last act. Would you prefer to wait in the theater, or just come around to the stage door when the play's over? I'll give you a card that will get you in."

"I'll wait in the theater," I said, feeling that would offer less chance for mishap; also because I wanted to see Ellen play the ghost again.

"Come along then—I have a key for that side door."

I rose to go with him, and he threw an arm about my

shoulder that I felt it would be impolite to thrust away. I could feel his hand, as cold as a dead man's, through my clothing, and was reminded unpleasantly of the twisted hands of the beggar in the Silent City.

We were going up the narrow stairs when I felt a gentle touch inside my jacket. My first thought was that he had seen the outline of my pistol, and meant to take it and shoot me. I gripped his wrist and shouted something—I do not remember what. Bound together and struggling, we staggered up the steps and into the street.

In a few seconds we were the center of a mob—some taking his side, some mine, most only urging us to fight, or asking each other what the disturbance was. My pocket sketchpad, which he must have thought held money, fell to the ground between us. Just then the American police arrived—not by air as the police would have come at home, but astride shaggy, hulking horses, and swinging whips. The crowd scattered at the first crackling arc from the lashes, and in a few seconds they had beaten Kreton to the ground. Even at the time I could not help thinking what a terrible thing it must be to be one of these people, whose police are so quick to prefer any prosperous-looking foreigner to one of their own citizens.

They asked me what had happened (my questioner even dismounted to show his respect for me), and I explained that Kreton had tried to rob me, but that I did not want him punished. The truth was that seeing him sprawled unconscious with a burn across his face had put an end to any resentment I might have felt toward him; out of pity, I would gladly have given him the few rials I carried. They told me that if he had attempted to rob me he must be charged, and that if I would not accuse him they would do so themselves.

I then said that Kreton was a friend; and that on reflection I felt certain that what he had attempted had been intended as a prank. (In maintaining this I was considerably handicapped by not knowing his real name, which I had read on the playbill but forgotten, so that I was forced to refer to him as "this poor man.")

At last the policeman said, "We can't leave him in

the street, so we'll have to bring him in. How will it look if there's no complaint?"

Then I understood that they were afraid of what their superiors might say if it became known that they had beaten him unconscious when no charge was made against him; and when I became aware that if I would not press charges, the charges they would bring themselves would be far more serious—assault or attempted murder—I agreed to do what they wished, and signed a form alleging the theft of my sketchbook.

When they had gone at last, carrying the unfortunate Kreton across a saddlebow, I tried to reenter the theater. The side door through which we had left was locked, and though I would gladly have paid the price of another ticket, the box office was closed. Seeing that there was nothing further to be done, I returned here, telling myself that my introduction to Ellen, if it ever came, would have to wait for another day.

Very truly it is written that we walk by paths that are always turning. In recording these several pages I have managed to restrain my enthusiasm, though when I described my waiting at the back of the theater for Ardis, and again when I recounted how Kreton had promised to introduce me to her, I was forced for minutes at a time to lay down my pen and walk about the room singing and whistling, and—to reveal everything—jumping over the beds! But now I can conceal no longer. I have seen her! I have touched her hand; I am to see her again tomorrow; and there is every hope that she will become my mistress!

I had undressed and laid myself on the bed (thinking to bring this journal up to date in the morning) and had even fallen into the first doze of sleep when there was a knock at the door. I slipped into my robe and pressed the release.

It was the only time in my life that for even an instant I thought I might be dreaming—actually asleep—when in truth I was up and awake.

How feeble it is to write that she is more beautiful in person than she appears on the stage. It is true, and yet it is a supreme irrelevance. I have seen more beautiful women—indeed, Yasmin is, I suppose, by the formal standards of art, more lovely. It is not Ardis' beauty that draws me to her—the hair like gold, the translucent skin that then still showed traces of the bluish makeup she had worn as a ghost, the flashing eyes like the clear, clean skies of America. It is something deeper than that; something that would remain if all that were somehow taken away. No doubt she has habits that would disgust me in someone else, and the vanity that is said to be so common in her profession, and yet I would do anything to possess her.

Enough of this. What is it but empty boasting, now that I am on the point of winning her?

She stood in my doorway. I have been trying to think how I can express what I felt then. It was as though some tall flower, a lily perhaps, had left the garden and come to tap at my door, a thing that had never happened before in all the history of the world, and would never happen again.

"You are Nadan Jaffarzadeh?"

I admitted that I was, and shamefacedly, twenty seconds too late, moved out of her way.

She entered, but instead of taking the chair I indicated, turned to face me; her blue eyes seemed as large as the colored eggs on the dresser, and they were filled with a melting hope. "You are the man, then, that Bobby O'Keene tried to rob tonight."

I nodded.

"I know you—I mean, I know your face. This is insane. You came to *Visit* on the last night and brought your father, and then to *Mary Rose* on the first night, and sat in the third or fourth row. I thought you were an American, and when the police told me your name, I imagined some greasy fat man with gestures. Why on earth would Bobby want to steal from *you?*"

"Perhaps he needed the money."

She threw back her head and laughed. I had heard her laugh in *Mary Rose* when Simon was asking her father for her hand; but that had held a note of childishness that (however well suited to the part) detracted from its beauty. This laugh was the merriment of houris sliding down a rainbow. "I'm sure he did. He always needs money. You're sure, though, that he meant to rob you? You couldn't have . . ."

She saw my expression and let the question trail away. The truth is that I was disappointed that I could not oblige her, and at last I said, "If you want me to be mistaken, Ardis, then I was mistaken. He only bumped against me on the steps, perhaps, and tried to catch my sketchbook when it fell."

She smiled, and her face was the sun smiling upon roses. "You would say that for me? And you know my name?"

"From the program. I came to the theater to see you—and that was not my father, who it grieves me to say is long dead, but only an old man, an American, whom I had met that day."

"You brought him sandwiches at the first intermission—I was watching you through the peephole in the curtain. You must be a very thoughtful person."

"Do you watch everyone in the audience so carefully?"

She blushed at that, and for a moment could not meet my eyes.

"But you will forgive Bobby, and tell the police that you want them to let him go? You must love the theater, Mr. Jef— Jaff—"

"You've forgotten my name already. It is Jaffarzadeh, a very commonplace name in my country."

"I hadn't forgotten it—only how to pronounce it. You see, when I came here I had learned it without knowing who you were, and so I had no trouble with it. Now you're a real person to me and I can't say it as an actress should." She seemed to notice the chair behind her for the first time, and sat down.

I sat opposite her. "I'm afraid I know very little about the theater."

"We are trying to keep it alive here, Mr. Jaffar, and—"

"Jaffarzadeh. Call me Nadan—then you won't have so many syllables to trip over."

She took my hand in hers, and I knew quite well that the gesture was as studied as a salaam and that she felt she was playing me like a fish; but I was beside myself with delight. To be played by *her!* To have *her* eager to cultivate my affection! And the fish will pull her in yet—wait and see!

"I will," she said, "Nadan. And though you may know little of the theater, you feel as I do—as we do—or you would not come. It has been such a long struggle; all the history of the stage is a struggle, the gasping of a beautiful child born at the point of death. The moralists, censorship and oppression, technology, and now poverty have all tried to destroy her. Only we, the actors and audiences, have kept her alive. We have been doing well here in Washington, Nadan."

"Very well indeed," I said. "Both the productions I have seen have been excellent."

"But only for the past two seasons. When I joined the company it had nearly fallen apart. We revived it—Bobby and Paul and I. We could do it because we cared, and because we were able to find a few naturally talented people who can take direction. Bobby is the best of us—he can walk away with any part that calls for a touch of the sinister . . ."

She seemed to run out of breath. I said, "I don't think there will be any trouble about getting him free."

"Thank God. We're getting the theater on its feet again now. We're attracting new people, and we've built up a following—people who come to see every production. There's even some money ahead at last. But *Mary Rose* is supposed to run another two weeks, and after that we're doing *Faust,* with Bobby as Mephistopheles. We've simply no one who can take his place, no one who can come close to him."

"I'm sure the police will release him if I ask them to."

"They *must.* We have to have him tomorrow night. Bill—someone you don't know—tried to go on for him in the third act tonight. It was just ghastly. In Iran you're very polite; that's what I've heard."

"We enjoy thinking so."

"We're not. We never were; and as . . ."

Her voice trailed away, but a wave of one slender arm evoked everything—the cracked plaster walls became as air, and the decayed city, the ruined continent, entered the room with us. "I understand," I said.

"They—we—were betrayed. In our souls we have never been sure by whom. When we feel cheated we are ready to kill; and maybe we feel cheated all the time."

She slumped in her chair, and I realized, as I should have long before, how exhausted she was. She had given a performance that had ended in disaster, then had been forced to plead with the police for my name and address, and at last had come here from the station house, very probably on foot. I asked when I could obtain O'Keene's release.

"We can go tomorrow morning, if you'll do it."

"You wish to come too?"

She nodded, smoothed her skirt, and stood. "I'll have to know. I'll come for you about nine, if that's all right."

"If you'll wait outside for me to dress, I'll take you home."

"That's not necessary."

"It will only take a moment," I said.

The blue eyes held something pleading again. "You're going to come in with me—that's what you're thinking, I know. You have two beds here—bigger, cleaner beds than the one I have in my little apartment; if I were to ask you to push them together, would you still take me home afterward?"

It was as though I were dreaming indeed: a dream in which everything I wanted—the cosmos purified—delivered itself to me. I said, "You won't have to leave at all—you can spend the night with me. Then we can breakfast together before we go to release your friend."

She laughed again, lifting that exquisite head. "There are a hundred things at home I need. Do you think I'd have breakfast with you without my cosmetics, and in these dirty clothes?"

"Then I will take you home—yes, though you lived in Kazvin. Or on Mount Kaf."

She smiled. "Get dressed, then. I'll wait outside, and I'll show you my apartment; perhaps you won't want to come back here afterward."

She went out, her wooden-soled American shoes

clicking on the bare floor, and I threw on trousers, shirt, and jacket, and jammed my feet into my boots. When I opened the door, she was gone. I rushed to the barred window at the end of the corridor, and was in time to see her disappear down a side street. A last swirl of her skirt in a gust of night wind, and she had vanished into the velvet dark.

For a long time I stood there looking out over the ruinous buildings. I was not angry—I do not think I could be angry with her. I was, though here it is hard to tell the truth, in some way glad. Not because I feared the embrace of love—I have no doubt of my ability to suffice any woman who can be sated by man—but because an easy exchange of my cooperation for her person would have failed to satisfy my need for romance, for adventure of a certain type, in which danger and love are twined like coupling serpents. Ardis, my Ellen, will provide that, surely, as neither Yasmin nor the pitiful wanton who was her double could. I sense that the world is opening for me only now; that I am being born; that that corridor was the birth canal, and that Ardis in leaving me was drawing me out toward her.

When I returned to my own door, I noticed a bit of paper on the floor before it. I transcribe it exactly here, though I cannot transmit its scent of lilacs.

You are a most attractive man and I want very much to stretch the truth and tell you you can have me freely when Bobby is free but I won't sell myself etc. Really I *will* sell myself for Bobby but I have other fish to fry tonight. I'll see you in the morning and if you can get Bobby out or even try hard you'll have (real) love from the vanishing

Mary Rose

Morning. Woke early and ate here at the hotel as usual, finishing about eight. Writing this journal will give me something to do while I wait for Ardis. Had an American breakfast today, the first time I have risked one. Flakes of pastry dough toasted crisp and drenched with cream, and with it strudel and the usual American coffee. Most natives have spiced pork in one form or another, which I cannot bring myself to try; but several of the people around me were having egg dishes and oven-warmed bread, which I will sample tomorrow.

I had a very unpleasant dream last night; I have been trying to put it out of my mind ever since I woke. It was dark, and I was under an open sky with Ardis, walking over ground much rougher than anything I saw in the park on the farther side of the channel. One of the hideous creatures I shot night before last was pursuing us—or rather, lurking about us, for it appeared first to the left of us, then to the right, silhouetted against the night sky. Each time we saw it, Ardis grasped my arm and urged me to shoot, but the little indicator light on my pistol was glowing red to show that there was not enough charge left for a shot. All very silly, of course, but I am going to buy a fresh powerpack as soon as I have the opportunity.

It is late afternoon—after six—but we have not had dinner yet. I am just out of the tub, and sit here naked, with today's candy egg laid (pinker even than I) beside this book on my table. Ardis and I had a sorry, weary time of it, and I have come back here to make myself presentable. At seven we will meet for dinner; the curtain goes up at eight, so it can't be a long one, but I am going backstage to watch the play from the wings, where I will be able to talk to her when she isn't performing.

I just took a bite of the egg—no unusual taste, nothing but an unpleasant sweetness. The more I reflect on it, the more inclined I am to believe that the drug was in the first I ate. No doubt the monster I saw had been lurking in my brain since I read *Mysteries*, and the drug freed it. True, there were bloodstains on my clothes (the Peri's asphodel!) but they could as easily have come from my cheek, which is still sore. I have had my experience, and all I have left is my candy. I am almost tempted to throw out the rest. Another bite.

Still twenty minutes before I must dress and go for Ardis—she showed me where she lives, only a few doors from the theater. To work then.

Ardis was a trifle late this morning, but came as she

had promised. I asked where we were to go to free Kreton, and when she told me—a still-living building at the eastern end of the Silent City—I hired one of the rickety American caleches to drive us there. Like most of them, it was drawn by a starved horse; but we made good time.

The American police are organized on a peculiar system. The national secret police (officially, the Federated Enquiry Divisions) are in a tutorial position to all the others, having power to review their decisions, promote, demote, and discipline, and as the ultimate reward, enroll personnel from the other organizations. In addition they maintain a uniformed force of their own. Thus when an American has been arrested by uniformed police, his friends can seldom learn whether he has been taken by the local police, by the F.E.D. uniformed national force, or by members of the F.E.D secret police posing as either of the foregoing.

Since I had known nothing of these distinctions previously, I had no way of guessing which of the three had O'Keene; but the local police to whom Ardis had spoken the night before had given her to understand that he had been taken by them. She explained all this to me as we rattled along, then added that we were now going to the F.E.D. Building to secure his release. I must have looked as confused as I felt at this, because she added, "Part of it is a station for the Washington Police Department—they rent the space from the F.E.D."

My own impression (when we arrived) was that they did no such thing—that the entire apparatus was no more real than one of the scenes in Ardis's theater, and that all the men and women to whom we spoke were in fact agents of the secret police, wielding ten times the authority they pretended to possess, and going through a solemn ritual of deception. As Ardis and I moved from office to office, explaining our simple errand, I came to think that she felt as I did, and that she had refrained from expressing these feelings to me in the cab not only because of the danger, the fear that I might betray her or the driver be a spy, but because she was ashamed of her nation, and eager to make it appear to me, a foreigner, that her government was less devious and meretricious than is actually the case.

If this is so—and in that windowless warren of stone I was certain it was—then the very explanation she proffered in the cab (which I have given in its proper place) differentiating clearly between local police, uniformed F.E.D. police, and secret police, was no more than a children's fable, concealing an actuality less forthright and more convoluted.

Our questioners were courteous to me, much less so to Ardis, and (so it seemed to me) obsessed by the idea that something more lay behind the simple incident we described over and over again—so much so in fact that I came to believe it myself. I have neither time nor patience enough to describe all these interviews, but I will attempt to give a sample of one.

We went into a small, windowless office crowded between two others that appeared empty. A middle-aged American woman was seated behind a metal desk. She appeared normal and reasonably attractive until she spoke; then her scarred gums showed that she had once had two or three times the proper number of teeth— forty or fifty, I suppose, in each jaw—and that the dental surgeon who had extracted the supernumerary ones had not always, perhaps, selected those he suffered to remain as wisely as he might. She asked, "How is it outside? The weather? You see, I don't know, sitting in here all day."

Ardis said, "Very nice."

"Do you like it, *Hajji?* Have you had a pleasant stay in our great country?"

"I don't think it has rained since I've been here."

She seemed to take the remark as a covert accusation. "You came too late for the rains, I'm afraid. This is a very fertile area, however. Some of our oldest coins show heads of wheat. Have you seen them?" She pushed a small copper coin across the desk, and I pretended to examine it. There are one or two like it in the bracelet I bought for Ardis, and which I still have not presented to her. "I must apologize on behalf of the District for what happened to you," the woman continued. "We are making every effort to control crime. You have not been victimized before this?"

I shook my head, half suffocated in that airless office, and said I had not been.

"And now you are here." She shuffled the papers she held, then pretended to read from one of them. "You are here to secure the release of the thief who assaulted you. A very commendable act of magnanimity. May I ask why you brought this young woman with you? She does not seem to be mentioned in any of these reports."

I explained that Ardis was a coworker of O'Keene's, and that she had interceded for him.

"Then it is you, Ms. Dahl, who are really interested in securing this prisoner's release. Are you related to him?"

And so on.

At the conclusion of each interview we were told either that the matter was completely out of the hands of the person to whom we had just spent half an hour or an hour talking, that it was necessary to obtain a clearance from someone else, or that an additional deposition had to be made. About two o'clock we were sent to the other side of the river—into what my guidebooks insist is an entirely different jurisdiction—to visit a penal facility. There we were forced to look for Kreton among five hundred or so miserable prisoners, all of whom stank and had lice. Not finding him, we returned to the F.E.D. Building past the half-overturned and yet still brooding figure called the Seated Man, and the ruins and beggars of the Silent City, for another round of interrogations. By five, when we were told to leave, we were both exhausted, though Ardis seemed surprisingly hopeful. When I left her at the door of her building a few minutes ago, I asked her what they would do tonight without Kreton.

"Without Harry, you mean." She smiled. "The best we can, I suppose, if we must. At least Paul will have someone ready to stand in for him tonight."

We shall see how well it goes.

I have picked up this pen and replaced it on the table ten times at least. It seems very likely that I should destroy this journal instead of continuing with it, were I wise; but I have discovered a hiding place for it which I think will be secure.

When I came back from Ardis's apartment tonight there were only two candy eggs remaining. I am certain—absolutely certain—that three were left when I went to meet Ardis. I am almost equally sure that after I had finished making the entry in this book, I put it, as I always do, at the left side of the drawer. It was on the right side.

It is possible that all this is merely the doing of the maid who cleans the room. She might easily have supposed that a single candy egg would not be missed, and have shifted this book while cleaning the drawer, or peeped inside out of curiosity.

I will assume the worst, however. An agent sent to investigate my room might be equipped to photograph these pages—but he might not, and it is not likely that he himself would have a reading knowledge of Farsi. Now I have gone through the book and eliminated all the passages relating to my reason for visiting this leprous country. Before I leave this room tomorrow I will arrange indicators—hairs and other objects whose positions I shall carefully record—that will tell me if the room has been searched again.

Now I may as well set down the events of the evening, which were truly extraordinary enough.

I met Ardis as we had planned, and she directed me to a small restaurant not far from her apartment. We had no sooner seated ourselves than two heavy-looking men entered. At no time could I see plainly the face of either, but it appeared to me that one was the American I had met aboard the *Princess Fatimah* and that the other was the grain dealer I had so assiduously avoided there, Golam Gassem. It is impossible, I think, for my divine Ardis ever to look less than beautiful; but she came as near to it then as the laws of nature permit— the blood drained from her face, her mouth opened slightly, and for a moment she appeared to be a lovely corpse. I began to ask what the trouble was, but before I could utter a word she touched my lips to silence me, and then, having somewhat regained her composure, said, "They have not seen us. I am leaving now. Follow me as though we were finished eating." She stood, feigned to pat her lips with a napkin (so that the lower half of her face was hidden) and walked out into the street.

I followed her, and found her laughing not three doors away from the entrance to the restaurant. The change in her could not have been more startling if she had been released from an enchantment. "It is so funny," she said. "Though it wasn't then. Come on, we'd better go; you can feed me after the show."

I asked her what those men were to her.

"Friends," she said, still laughing.

"If they are friends, why were you so anxious that they not see you? Were you afraid they would make us late?" I knew that such a trivial explanation could not be true, but I wanted to leave her a means of evading the question if she did not want to confide in me.

She shook her head. "No, no. I didn't want either to think I did not trust him. I'll tell you more later, if you want to involve yourself in our little charade."

"With all my heart."

She smiled at that—that sun-drenched smile for which I would gladly have entered a lion pit. In a few more steps we were at the rear entrance to the theater, and there was no time to say more. She opened the door, and I heard Kreton arguing with a woman I later learned was the wardrobe mistress. "You are free," I said, and he turned to look at me.

"Yes. Thanks to you, I think. And I do thank you."

Ardis gazed on him as though he were a child saved from drowning. "Poor Bobby. Was it very bad?"

"It was frightening, that's all. I was afraid I'd never get out. Do you know Terry is gone?"

She shook her head, and said, "What do you mean?" but I was certain—and here I am not exaggerating or coloring the facts, though I confess I have occasionally done so elsewhere in this chronicle—that she had known it before he spoke.

"He simply isn't here. Paul is running around like a lunatic. I hear you missed me last night."

"God, yes," Ardis said, and darted off too swiftly for me to follow.

Kreton took my arm. I expected him to apologize for having tried to rob me, but he said, "You've met her, I see."

"She persuaded me to drop the charges against you."

"Whatever it was you offered me—twenty rials? I'm morally entitled to it, but I won't claim it. Come and see me when you're ready for something more wholesome—and meanwhile, how do you like her?"

"That is something for me to tell her," I said, "not you."

Ardis returned as I spoke, bringing with her a balding black man with a mustache. "Paul, this is Nadan. His English is very good—not so British as most of them. He'll do, don't you think?"

"He'll have to—you're sure he'll do it?"

"He'll love it," Ardis said positively, and disappeared again.

It seemed that "Terry" was the actor who played Mary Rose's husband and lover, Simon; and I—who had never acted in so much as a school play—was to be pressed into the part. It was about half an hour before curtain time, so I had all of fifty minutes to learn my lines before my entrance at the end of the first act.

Paul, the director, warned me that if my name were used, the audience would be hostile; and since the character (in the version of the play they were presenting) was supposed to be an American, they would see errors where none existed. A moment later, while I was still in frantic rehearsal, I heard him saying, "The part of Simon Blake will be taken by Ned Jefferson."

The act of stepping onto the stage for the first time was really the worst part of the entire affair. Fortunately I had the advantage of playing a nervous young man come to ask for the hand of his sweetheart, so that my shaky laughter and stammer became "acting."

My second scene—with Mary Rose and Cameron on the magic island—ought by rights to have been much more difficult than the first. I had had only the intermission in which to study my lines, and the scene called for pessimistic apprehension rather than mere anxiety.

But all the speeches were short, and Paul had been able by that time to get them lettered on large sheets of paper, which he and the stage manager held up in the wings. Several times I was forced to extemporize, but though I forgot the playwright's words, I never lost my sense of the *trend* of the play, and was always able to contrive something to which Ardis and Cameron could adapt their replies.

In comparison to the first and second acts, my brief appearance in the third was a holiday; yet I have seldom been so exhausted as I was tonight when the stage darkened for Ardis's final confrontation with Kreton, and Cameron and I, and the middle-aged people who had played the Morelands were able to creep away.

We had to remain in costume until we had taken our bows, and it was nearly midnight before Ardis and I got something to eat at the same small, dirty bar outside which Kreton had tried to rob me. Over the steaming plates she asked me if I had enjoyed acting, and I had to nod.

"I thought you would. Under all that solidity you're a very dramatic person, I think."

I admitted it was true, and tried to explain why I feel that what I call *the romance of life* is the only thing worth seeking. She did not understand me, and so I passed it off as the result of having been brought up on the *Shah Namah,* of which I found she had never heard.

We went to her apartment. I was determined to take her by force if necessary—not because I would have enjoyed brutalizing her, but because I felt she would inevitably think my love far less than it was if I permitted her to put me off a second time. She showed me about her quarters (two small rooms in great disorder), then, after we had lifted into place the heavy bar that is the sigil of every American dwelling, put her arms about me. Her breath was fragrant with the arrack I had bought for her a few minutes before. I feel sure now that for the rest of my life that scent will recall this evening to me.

When we parted, I began to unloose the laces that closed her blouse, and she at once pinched out the candle. I pleaded that she was thus depriving me of half the joy I might have had of her love; but she would not permit me to relight it, and our caresses and the embraces of our couplings were exchanged in perfect darkness. I was in ecstasy. To have seen her, I would have blinded myself; yet nothing could have increased my delight.

When we separated for the last time, both spent utterly, and she left to wash, I sought for matches. First in the drawer of the unsteady little table beside the bed, then among the disorder of my own clothes, which I had dropped to the floor and we had kicked about. I found some eventually, but could not find the candle—Ardis, I think, had hidden it. I struck a match; but she had covered herself with a robe. I said, "Am I never to see you?"

"You will see me tomorrow. You're going to take me boating, and we'll picnic by the water, under the cherry trees. Tomorrow night the theater will be closed for Easter, and you can take me to a party. But now you are going home, and I am going to go to sleep." When I was dressed and standing in her doorway, I asked her if she loved me; but she stopped my mouth with a kiss.

I have already written about the rest—returning to find two eggs instead of three, and this book moved. I will not write of that again. But I have just—between this paragraph and the last—read over what I wrote earlier tonight, and it seems to me that one sentence should have had more weight than I gave it: when I said that in my role as Simon I never lost the *trend* of the play.

What the fabled secret buried by the old Americans beneath their carved mountain may be I do not know; but I believe that if it is some key to the world of human life, it must be some form of that. Every great man, I am sure, consciously or not, in those terms or others, has grasped that secret—save that in the play that is our life we can grapple that trend and draw it to left or right if we have the will.

So I am doing now. If the taking of the egg was not significant, yet I will make it so—indeed I already have when I infused one egg with the drug. If the scheme in which Ardis is entangled—with Golam Gassem and Mr.

Tallman if it be they—is not some affair of statecraft
and dark treasure, yet I will make it so before the end.
If our love is not a great love, destined to live forever
in the hearts of the young and the mouths of the poets, it
will be so before the end.

Once again I am here; and in all truth I am beginning
to wonder if I do not write this journal only to read it.
No man was ever happier than I am now—so happy,
indeed, that I was sorely tempted not to taste either of
the two eggs that remain. What if the drug, in place of
hallucination, self-knowledge, and euphoria, brings permanent and despairing madness? Yet I have eaten it
nonetheless, swallowing the whole sweet lump in a few
bites. I would rather risk whatever may come than think
myself a coward. With equanimity I await the effects.

The fact is that I am too happy for all the Faustian
determination I penned last night. (How odd that *Faust*
will be the company's next production. Kreton will be
Mephistopheles, of course—Ardis said as much, and it
would be certain in any case. Ardis herself will be Mar-
garet. But who will play the Doctor?) Yet now, when
all the teeth-gritting, table-pounding determination is
gone, I know that I will carry out the essentials of the
plan more surely than ever—with the ease, in fact, of
an accomplished violinist sawing out some simple tune
while his mind roves elsewhere. I have been looking at
the ruins of the Jeff (as they call it), and it has turned
my mind again to the fate of the old Americans. How
often they, who chose their leaders for superficial ap-
pearances of strength, wisdom, and resolution, must
have elected them only because they were as fatigued as
I was last night.

I had meant to buy a hamper of delicacies, and call
for Ardis about one, but she came for me at eleven with
a little basket already packed. We walked north along
the bank of the channel until we reached the ruins of
the old tomb to which I have already referred, and the
nearly circular artificial lake the Americans call the
Basin. It is rimmed with flowering trees—old and
gnarled, but very beautiful in their robes of white blos-
som. For some little American coin we were given com-

mand of a bright blue boat with a sail twice or three times the size of my handkerchief, in which to dare the halcyon waters of the lake.

When we were well away from the people on shore, Ardis asked me, rather suddenly, if I intended to spend all my time in America here in Washington.

I told her that my original plan had been to stay here no more than a week, then make my way up the coast to Philadelphia and the other ancient cities before I returned home; but that now that I had met her I would stay here forever if she wished it.

"Haven't you ever wanted to see the interior? This strip of beach we live on is kept half alive by the ocean and the trade that crosses it; but a hundred miles inland lies the wreck of our entire civilization, waiting to be plundered."

"Then why doesn't someone plunder it?" I asked.

"They do. A year never passes without someone bringing some great prize out—but it is so large . . ." I could see her looking beyond the lake and the fragrant trees. "So large that whole cities are lost in it. There was an arch of gold at the entrance to St. Louis—no one knows what became of it. Denver, the Mile-High City, was nested in silver mines; no one can find them now."

"Many of the old maps must still be in existence."

Ardis nodded slowly, and I sensed that she wanted to say more than she had. For a few seconds there was no sound but the water lapping against the side of the boat.

"I remember having seen some in the museum in Teheran—not only our maps, but some of your own from a hundred years ago."

"The courses of the rivers have changed," she said. "And when they have not, no one can be sure of it."

"Many buildings must still be standing, as they are here, in the Silent City."

"That was built of stone—more solidly than anything else in the country. But yes, some, many, are still there."

"Then it would be possible to fly in, land somewhere, and pillage them."

"There are many dangers, and so much rubble to

look through that anyone might search for a lifetime and only scratch the surface."

I saw that talking of all this only made her unhappy, and tried to change the subject. "Didn't you say that I could escort you to a party tonight? What will that be like?"

"Nadan, I have to trust someone. You've never met my father, but he lives close to the hotel where you are staying, and has a shop where he sells old books and maps." (So I had visited the right house—almost— after all!) "When he was younger, he wanted to go into the interior. He made three or four trips, but never got farther than the Appalachian foothills. Eventually he married my mother and didn't feel any longer that he could take the risks . . ."

"I understand."

"The things he had sought to guide him to the wealth of the past became his stock in trade. Even today, people who live farther inland bring him old papers; he buys them and resells them. Some of those people are only a step better than the ones who dig up the cemeteries for the wedding rings of the dead women."

I recalled the rings I had bought in the shadow of the broken obelisk, and shuddered, though I do not believe Ardis observed it.

"I said that some of them were hardly better than the grave robbers. The truth is that some are worse—there are people in the interior who are no longer people. Our bodies are poisoned—you know that, don't you? All of us Americans. They have adapted—that's what Father says—but they are no longer human. He made his peace with them long ago, and he trades with them still."

"You don't have to tell me this."

"Yes, I do—I must. Would you go into the interior, if I went with you? The government will try to stop us if they learn of it, and to confiscate anything we find."

I assured her with every oath I could remember that with her beside me I would cross the continent on foot if need be.

"I told you about my father. I said that he sells the

maps and records they bring him. What I did not tell you is that he reads them first. He has never given up, you see, in his heart."

"He has made a discovery?" I asked.

"He's made many—hundreds. Bobby and I have used them. You remember those men in the restaurant? Bobby went to each of them with a map and some of the old letters. He's persuaded them to help finance an expedition into the interior, and made each of them believe that we'll help him cheat the other—that keeps them from combining to cheat us, you see."

"And you want me to go with you?" I was beside myself with joy.

"We weren't going to go at all—Bobby was going to take the money, and go to Baghdad or Marrakesh, and take me with him. But, Nadan"—here she leaned forward, I remember, and took my hands in hers—"there really is a secret. There are many, but one better—more likely to be true, more likely to yield truly immense wealth than all the others. I know you would share fairly with me. We'll divide everything, and I'll go back to Teheran with you."

I know that I have never been more happy in my life than I was then, in that silly boat. We sat together in the stern, nearly sinking it, under the combined shade of the tiny sail and Ardis's big straw hat, and kissed and stroked one another until we would have been pilloried a dozen times in Iran.

At last, when I could bear no more unconsummated love, we ate the sandwiches Ardis had brought, and drank some warmish, fruit-flavored beverage, and returned to shore.

When I took her home a few minutes ago, I very strongly urged her to let me come upstairs with her; I was on fire for her, sick to impale her upon my own flesh and pour myself into her as some mad god before the coming of the Prophet might have poured his golden blood into the sea. She would not permit it—I think because she feared that her apartment could not be darkened enough to suit her modesty. I am determined that I will yet see her.

I have bathed and shaved to be ready for the party, and as there is still time I will insert here a description of the procession we passed on the way back from the lake. As you see, I have not yet completely abandoned the thought of a book of travels.

A very old man—I suppose a priest—carried a cross on a long pole, using it as a staff, and almost as a crutch. A much younger one, fat and sweating, walked backward before him swinging a smoking censer. Two robed boys carrying large candles preceded them, and they were followed by more robed children, singing, who fought with nudges and pinches when they felt the fat man was not watching them.

Like everyone else, I have seen this kind of thing done much better in Rome; but I was more affected by what I saw here. When the old priest was born, the greatness of America must have been a thing of such recent memory that few can have realized it had passed forever; and the entire procession—from the flickering candles in clear sunshine, to the dead leader lifted up, to his inattentive, bickering followers behind—seemed to me to incarnate the philosophy and the dilemma of these people. So I felt, at least, until I saw that they watched it as uncomprehendingly as they might if they themselves were only travelers abroad, and I realized that its ritualized plea for life renewed was more foreign to them than to me.

It is very late—three, my watch says.

I resolved again not to write in this book. To burn it or tear it to pieces, or to give it to some beggar; but now I am writing once again because I cannot sleep. The room reeks of my vomit, though I have thrown open the shutters and let in the night.

How could I have loved that? (And yet a few moments ago, when I tried to sleep, visions of Ellen pursued me back to wakefulness.)

The party was a masque, and Ardis had obtained a costume for me—a fantastic gilded armor from the wardrobe of the theater. She wore the robes of an Egyptian princess, and a domino. At midnight we lifted our masks and kissed, and in my heart I swore that tonight the mask of darkness would be lifted too.

When we left, I carried with me the bottle we had brought, still nearly half full; and before she pinched out the candle I persuaded her to pour out a final drink for us to share when the first frenzy of our desire was past. She—it—did as I asked, and set it on the little table near the bed. A long time afterward, when we lay gasping side by side, I found my pistol with one groping hand and fired the beam into the wide-bellied glass. Instantly it filled with a blue fire from the burning alcohol. Ardis screamed, and sprang up.

I ask myself now how I could have loved; but then, how could I in one week have come so near to loving this corpse-country? Its eagle is dead—Ardis is the proper symbol of its rule.

One hope, one very small hope remains. It is possible that what I saw tonight was only an illusion, induced by the egg. I know now that the thing I killed before Ardis's father's house was real, and between this paragraph and the last I have eaten the last egg. If hallucinations now begin, I will know that what I saw by the light of the blazing arrack was in truth a thing with which I have lain, and in one way or another will see to it that I never return to corrupt the clean wombs of the women of our enduring race. I might seek to claim the miniatures of our heritage after all, and allow the guards to kill me—but what if I were to succeed? I am not fit to touch them. Perhaps the best end for me would be to travel alone into this maggot-riddled continent; in that way I will die at fit hands.

Later. Kreton is walking in the hall outside my door, and the tread of his twisted black shoe jars the building like an earthquake. I heard the word *police* as though it were thunder. My dead Ardis, very small and bright, has stepped out of the candle-flame, and there is a hairy face coming through the window.

The old woman closed the notebook. The younger woman, who had been reading over her shoulder, moved to the other side of the small table and seated herself on a cushion, her feet politely positioned so that the soles could not be seen. "He is alive then," she said.

The older woman remained silent, her gray head bowed over the notebook, which she held in both hands.

"He is certainly imprisoned, or ill, otherwise he would have been in touch with us." The younger woman paused, smoothing the fabric of her *chador* with her right hand, while the left toyed with the gem simulator she wore on a thin chain. "It is possible that he has already tried, but his letters have miscarried."

"You think this is his writing?" the older woman asked, opening the notebook at random. When the younger did not answer, she added, "Perhaps. Perhaps."

Fireship

Joan D. Vinge

We've had stories of cyborgs for decades in science
fiction, but the subject is so full of possibilities that
many fascinating tales remain to be told—especially
when we consider the ever-more-startling capabilities
of computers. What if a man's mind were to be linked
with a sophisticated computer of the future? And what
if that man were to become an outlaw?

Joan D. Vinge is one of the emerging stars of the
late 1970s (her first story appeared in 1974). She
won a Hugo Award in 1978 for her novelette "Eyes
of Amber."

I really must've been drunk. Because boy, was I ever
hung over. . . . I woke up groaning out of a dream
that I'd just had my head shrunk, and couldn't tell if it'd
been a dream or not. I dragged my face up off the pillow, trying to see the clock on the bedside bar . . . the
clocks, there were two of 'em. Funny, I only remembered one, last night. *Ohh. Last night*—

But what'd finally got me awake wasn't just the ring-
ing in my ears: the viewphone was starting into "Star-
light Serenade" for about the tenth time. Finally remembering where I was, sort of, I crawled back across
the bed's two meters of jelly to the phone on the other

side. I took a look at myself in the mirrored screen. And then I hit BLANK SCREEN before I pressed the VOICE button. "Hello?" I said. It sounded like "Huh."

"Mr. Ring? Are you there? This is the lobby—" She was pretty, but she had a voice like disaster sirens.

I considered maybe dying, and mumbled something. She looked relieved. "Visitors to see you, Mr. Ring."

Confused warnings went off down in my mind: "Are they wearin' uniforms?" It's nice to be wanted, but not by the U.S. government.

"No, they're not, sir." She blinked at me. "Shall I send them up?"

"Ugh, no—" I waited for my head to fall off; no luck. "Uh, jus' tell 'em I'll be down soon." *Give or take a couple of hours.* . . .

"All right. Thank you, Mr. Ring." The screen went blank, but her smile stayed behind. I wondered what she did in her spare time. I'd have to ask her, if I lived long enough. I lay back on the blue satin sheets, trying to decide whether to sit up or give up.

Sitting up won, and I pushed my feet over the edge of the bed onto the floor. They came down in a pile of cold, hard slippery things. I pulled myself up and leaned forward—

"Oh, geez—not again." The floor around the bed was ankle-deep in money. Or in chips from the Hotel Xanadu's casino, which was pretty much the same thing. And I couldn't remember anything about last night. They'd done it to me again, Ring and that computer—gotten me so stinking drunk I was putty in their hands: Michael Yarrow, the all-day sucker. "Why do I put up with this?" I pressed my hands against my head, having answered my own stupid question. *Because you need them.* Besides, I couldn't blame Ring; if I was blind drunk last night, so was he . . . except he was supposed to be in charge, and he'd let ETHANAC take over. "You promised, you promised you wouldn't do this t' me again! What if somebody noticed—"

But they weren't even listening; I wasn't plugged in. If I was gonna yell at myself, I might as well have an audience. Not that they'd listen; I was just the body around here. . . . *Oh, knock off the self-pity: plug in and you'll feel better.*

I fumbled around in the chips until I found the cord that was attached to ETHANAC's bread-loaf-sized case on the floor beside the bed. I pulled the cord up and stuck it into the socket low on my spine, felt the electric flow of the change start and spread, turning all my nerve endings into stars. . . .

I stretched and shook my head until the static cleared, finishing Yarrow's almost obscene sigh of pleasure for him. The mental rat's nest of his hangover mercifully cleared out with the static, for which I was supremely grateful; even though there wasn't much we could do for his body: his bloodshot baby blues stared back at me forlornly from the phone mirror, half obscured by rumpled brown hair, in a face the color of oatmeal. I don't like oatmeal. I looked away, grimacing, feeling Yarrow's indignation at his betrayal push up through my control again; I hate those mornings when I can't seem to wake up—*Damn it, is that any way to treat the body that's gotta carry you around?* . . . BE A SPORT, MICHAEL—even ETHANAC was butting in, flushed with his triumph at the gaming tables—LET YOURSELF ENJOY LIFE ONCE IN A WHILE . . . *Enjoy life? Gettin' your own mind totally wiped, and then takin' advantage of it, ain't my idea of a good time* . . . ALL RIGHT, I KNOW IT TOOK TEN OR TWELVE DRINKS TO BREAK DOWN YOUR INHIBITIONS. BUT WASN'T IT WORTH IT—?

I looked down again at the pile of chips around my feet, and felt a gloating recapitulation of last night's gambling spree overload my consciousness. I frowned, disgusted, and let Yarrow go on complaining for both of us. *Tryin' to break the bank, on neutral ground! Where anybody could've seen it, an' be half a million U.S. bucks richer for turning me in, by now! My God. I mean, just who the hell is waiting for us downstairs right now?* . . . DON'T CAUSE YOURSELF UNNECESSARY DISTRESS. IF HEW KNEW YOU WERE HERE, THEY WOULD SIMPLY KICK IN THE DOOR AND DRAG YOU AWAY. . . .

. . . *Why am I arguing with myself?* I reasserted and reintegrated, getting rid of the aggravating schizo conversations. Leaning forward, I drew the drapes and let in some daylight. Clouding over, just as predicted: This was the day of the Rain. I squinted out at the brick-red Martian sky, patterning with oppressive mud-colored clouds, and decided that if HEW ever caught up with me I'd have only myself to blame . . . me, myself, and I. *We are not amused.* Yarrow's hand picked up ETHANAC's suitcase obligingly: I stumbled off to the bathroom to make myself fit for human company.

"In Xanadu"—according to Samuel Taylor Coleridge—"did Kubla Khan a stately pleasure dome decree: where Alph, the sacred river, ran through caverns measureless to man, down to a sunless sea." The original may have existed only in Coleridge's opium dreams, but here on Mars the dream has come true, thanks to the limitless funds and the boundless ego of Khorram Kabir. What dread secrets do Khorram Kabir and Kubla Khan share? The same initials, for one thing. . . . But Kabir didn't want the comparison to end there. Being the eccentric head of a multinational, multibillion-dollar financial empire, you could say he qualified as an emperor. But he wanted his own Xanadu; and like a true twenty-first-century mogul, he created one—and made certain it would pay.

Hence, the Xanadu, the pleasure dome extraordinary: luxury hotel, resort, spa—and gambling casino. The old me had never been a gambler, because I was just smart enough to realize what I was really bad at. The new me, I'd just discovered, was a little too smart for my own good. I'd actually believed—and maybe it was true—that I'd only come here to watch the rain. I'd been on Mars for nearly an Earth year, but because of my peculiar status I'd never had the nerve to visit the Tourist Belt before. But the whole reason I'd ended up on Mars in the first place was the simple desire to see more of the world—any world. And for an entire year I'd been listening to the ecstatic accounts of how my various buddies in software maintenance had reduced their credit to zero in one glorious blowout at the Xanadu. And finally I couldn't stand it any more—

But now, as I stepped out of the lift bubble at the lobby, my common sense was trying to tell me that I should just cut my vacation short, just pack up my money and steal silently back to the Arab territories. Except that someone was waiting to see me. I didn't know anyone here who'd *want* to see me, for any good reason; and yet my curiosity was tingling like a cat's. All my life I'd believed that someday some stranger would come up to me in a cafeteria and tell me that I was a long-lost heir, or in a subway station, and tell me I'd won the National Lottery. Or in the Hotel Xanadu, and tell me I was under arrest . . . ?

In spite of that, I crossed the crowded lobby to the information center. The floor of the lobby, which is a good one hundred and fifty meters across, is a hand-laid mosaic. Radiating out from the main desk are scenes of ancient Oriental splendor; it made me mildly uncomfortable to step on peoples' faces. But then that was probably what the original Xanadu had been all about. . . . Behind me in the elevator shaft, drifting spheres of colored glass carried guests from one level to another through a fittingly tinted fall of golden water (water being worth more than gold here on Mars): Alph, the sacred river, rushing softly down to its sunless sea—in the depths of the Xanadu's casino levels in the Caves of Ice.

One of the young studs at the information counter came up to me, looking bored, tugging at his velvet bolero. "Help you, sir?"

"Ethan Ring. Someone was asking for me?" I tugged at my knee-length, wine-red velvet jacket, doing my best to match him ennui for ennui.

"I'll check, sir." No contest. He drifted away, and I turned to look out across the lobby, in case anyone seemed to be looking for me. No one did, as far as I could tell. The murmur of conversation flowed into the muted intricacies of chamber music by Bach, played by a live string quartet in the corner of the room—tasteful, if not entirely appropriate. Most of the wandering guests looked as self-consciously gaudy and overdressed as I did.

Beyond them the wall was a curving window, taking

full advantage of the view, which is spectacular. The Xanadu is located on the choicest piece of real estate on all Mars—midway up the slope of Mt. Olympus. The hotel itself, which stretches twenty-five storeys up the side of the slope, is a parabolic hyperboloid (a form which reminded Yarrow of an apple core), so that every floor has an equal share of the view—of the endless subtle variations of russet and red and orange across the Martian plain; and the glassy, brassy sprawl of the free-port city that surrounds Elysian Field, and spreads up to the steep cliff-face at the volcano's foot.

"Mr. Ring!" The stud was back at last. "Are you the one who won fifty thousand seeyas last night?"

I looked at him. Fifty thousand International Credit Units . . . my God, that was almost three hundred thousand dollars! "Uh, yes, I suppose I am." Total disbelief is a good substitute for total disinterest, even on Yarrow's open, flexible face.

The stud looked at me with an expression that might have been awe, or might have been envy, but that at least was not boredom. "Oh. Your . . . ah, your party is waiting in the Peacock Lounge, sir."

"Thanks." So my visitors were having a hair of the dog that had bitten me, while they waited. . . . I crossed the lobby to the lounge. I paused inside the entrance, checking out the afternoon's clientele, with no idea at all of who I was looking for. But then I saw her, sitting alone in a booth by the curving window and smiling at me; and I knew that if she wasn't the one I was looking for, then whoever it was could go to hell.

I went down the single step past the scrolled railing, and started across the vividly blue Persian carpet—seeing it all with a heightened awareness, as if this was the first and last moment of my life. But most of all, seeing her: The cascade of raven hair that lay across her shoulder like night's cloak, the dark, elvish eyes; the sea-green dress that bared one shoulder and draped the other like a wave, trailing crystal beads like a foaming crest from wrist to hemline. Last night in the casino, in the eerie black-light fluorescence of the Caves of Ice, that foam of glittering beads had been all the colors of the rainbow—

Last night she'd stood beside me while I played at the high-stakes tables . . . and all the while ETHANAC had been too damn lost in high-rolling fever even to register her presence, that sodden fool Yarrow had been falling in love. And that meant. . . .

"I love you, Lady Luck," Yarrow blurted, before I could bite his tongue. "Everything I have is yours."

She looked slightly taken aback, for which I couldn't blame her. "All fifty thousand seeyas of it?" she said.

I straightened up, wishing fervently that I could give myself a partial lobotomy. Yarrow's part. "Maybe I'd better go out and come in again."

"Consider it done." She smiled, this time. "Good afternoon, Ethan. Sit down. May I buy you a drink?"

I sat down across the small table from her, wanting to sit down beside her. "No drink, thanks. I think I hit the saturation point last night."

"At least you haven't forgotten me. . . ." She leaned on a slender fist, and the smile turned rueful. "I was beginning to think you'd stood me up."

"Forget you—?" At least she was the one who'd called; at least she'd wanted to see me again. I swore silently at the total blank where she should have been in ETHANAC's record of last night. "I'm just trying to figure out how I ever let you slip away."

"You drank a little too much of the *Milk of Paradise*—I tucked you in myself." The smile turned more rueful yet; my backbone turned to jelly.

And I remembered the empty bed I'd come to in this afternoon; my hand closed dangerously over the case hooked onto my belt. "I'll make it up to you tonight."

"You already have."

"I have," I said, half afraid she'd tell me how.

"By winning fifty thousand seeyas. By winning at every game you played last night. . . ."

My face stiffened; it hadn't occurred to me that she was after my money. My ego shriveled. But infatuation is a blind beggar: If she wanted money, I could give it to her. . . . "I can do it every night, with you beside me, Lady Luck."

She raised her eyebrows. "You really mean that, don't you?"

"More than I've ever meant anything in my life."

Surprise, and an expression that might have been sorrow worried her face. "No, I mean, you literally mean that luck had nothing to do with it—that you could do it every night. Don't you, Michael Yarrow?"

My face went entirely blank, this time. I could feel all the expression drain away: Somebody had pulled the plug on me at last. Had I done it to myself? Had I really been so drunk and so careless that I'd told her my name was Michael Yarrow? But she'd called me *Ethan*. . . . I continued to look at her blankly. "Run that one by again?"

"You're a hustler, Michael Yarrow. You can calculate the odds with lightning speed when you gamble. The house doesn't stand a chance. And that's not all you can do: Your intelligence is artificially augmented by an ETHANAC 500 computer."

I shook my head. "Lady Luck, if I told you that last night, I apologize. It was only to augment my own ego. My real name is Ethan Ring, and I do software maintenance for the colonial government of the Arab States, here on Mars. And when I get drunk, not only am a hustler, but I'm also a pathological liar."

"You're even better when you're sober." She reached out and took my hand, and turned it over as if she were reading my palm. "Nice try. But fingerprints don't lie; and yours belong to Michael Yarrow, U.S. citizen, who is wanted back on Earth for theft, sabotage, and high treason. The price on your head is five hundred thousand dollars." She looked up at me again, with deadly calm.

I knew now how Prince Charming must have felt when Cinderella turned into a scrubwoman. "All right." My hand turned into a fist, and I removed it from her grasp. "I have three hundred thousand dollars' worth of chips up in my room. If you really know what I can do, you know I can get you twice the amount of that reward, and in half the time it would take the U.S. government to get it to you. Would a million dollars be sufficient to keep your mouth shut?"

Surprise again, feigned or real. "So you would be willing to embezzle seven hundred thousand dollars?"

I frowned. " 'Willing' is hardly the word. But yes, I'd do just about anything to avoid having my health ruined by the Department of Health, Education, and Welfare."

"I see. That does make it easier—" She glanced out the window at the sky, which was getting darker every minute, like my mood. "Unfortunately, I'm not really interested in money."

"But you're not a misguided patriot, either. So just what is it you're after?"

"Tell me—" she said, in total non sequitur, "why did you say that to me, when you first came in?"

I shrugged. "I never like to start out a relationship on the defensive. Tell *me* something: did you put me up to the gambling last night?"

She shook her head; I tried not to watch the way it made her hair ripple and play with the light. "No. You'd already won twenty thousand seeyas when I first noticed you. That's what made me curious. What I'm after, Yarrow—"

"Call me Ethan."

"—is your brain."

"Is that all. Shall I wrap it up, or will you dissect it here?"

She looked pained. "I'll ignore that. My name is Hanalore Takhashi." She pushed a small white business card toward me across the transparent tabletop.

I picked it up obediently, and read:

MEINE GEDANKEN SIND FREI.

" 'My thoughts are free?' " I glanced up. "From what I've heard, your thoughts are damned expensive." I recognized the motto of *Free Thought, Incorporated,* which as I well knew was a mercenary think tank, renting the problem-solving brilliance of its employees to any business, organization, or government willing to meet its exorbitant fee. "So you're a fink, then?"

"We prefer the term 'information consultant.' " She tapped the stem of her wine glass. Somewhere back in the real world I heard a crash, as some barfly tossed off a drink and then the glass: an old custom, recently revived, like most things in dubious taste. "And the motto represents our philosophy, not our fee policy. We refuse to be limited, by either intimidation or questionable loyalties, to serving any one government or creed. That's why our organization is based here on Mars, even though we do most of our work for customers on Earth."

"Yes, I know; very noble." My brain began to function analytically again. "But you mean you're simply trying to recruit me? Blackmail really isn't necessary——"

She shook her head. "Considering your problems with the American government, you wouldn't be of much use to us. I just want to borrow your special skills for one small, computer-oriented project. No more, no less. Cooperate with me, and I'll forget I ever saw you. Refuse, and——"

"——and if I'm lucky, I won't live to regret it." Instant replay: some choice examples of some not-so-swift retributions that might occur, when Uncle Sam's prodigal nephew returned home in disgrace. The Reduction to Component Parts of Ethan Ring would start with unplugging the cord from the socket in my spine, but it probably wouldn't end there. . . . Hanalore Takhashi leaned back against the peacock-blue leather of the booth, watching my paranoia show. Five minutes ago I'd been wondering where she'd been all my life; now I just wanted to know when she was going back. "Lady Luck, you really know how to screw a guy. And that's not a compliment. Just one little job, you said, and you'll go out of my life forever?" *You lose some; and you lose some.* A smile is a kind of grimace. I smiled. "It's a deal."

"Good." Her face relaxed, and I suddenly realized how tense she'd looked. "Shall we go, then?"

"Go?" I remained sitting. "Go where?"

"Outside. To meet someone." She waved a hand at the window, and nodded at the other guests, who were gradually wandering out of the bar. "The rain should be starting about fourteen-twenty. You don't want to miss it, do you?"

Rain on Mars is like snow in southern California: it doesn't happen very often. When it does, it's like New Year's Eve—a grand excuse for lunacy and laughter and hugging total strangers. Computerized forecasting techniques and the comparative simplemindedness of

Martian weather make it possible to plan your celebration in advance; so when storms pass over the Tourist Belt—over Olympus or Fat City or the Mariner Valley—the Martians jostle with the visiting Earthies for the chance to get their helmets wet, and the resort hotels make the most of it. . . . And this time I'd succumbed, like a thousand other homesick colonists, to "the midnight that it sang you asleep . . . the time it wrapped your hills in steel and silver . . . that afternoon in the park, when you watched it paint a triple rainbow in watercolors across the sky. . . . Remember the rain?"

And if I hadn't remembered it so painfully well, I wouldn't be in this spot. . . . I got up glumly. "You're damn right I don't want to miss it."

We went back across the hotel lobby and rented candy-colored pressure suits at the tail of the shuffling crowd. We followed the rest of them into the airlock, a long downhill ramp that led out onto the Xanadu's "balcony"—a flagstoned terrace big enough for the Olympic Games. I noticed a few stalwarts had rented O_2 breathers and parkas instead of full suits, in order to get as close to the rain as humanly possible; I personally hadn't gotten that homesick yet. They claim a terraformed Mars is an improvement; and it is true that melting the polar caps has increased the atmospheric pressure enough that now anyone with six pairs of long underwear, an oxygen mask, and the constitution of a Sherpa can walk around outside without dying. But the climate is miserable, cold, and most of the time painfully dry—in other words, a lot like winter in my hometown of Cleveland, Ohio. I consider that a dubious improvement.

We worked our way around the fringes of the gaudy crowd, the sound of their enthusiasm in my suit speakers nearly deafening me. At the point furthest from the airlock I saw two figures standing by the low stone fence, more or less alone. One of them raised a gloved hand as we approached; I wasn't sure whether he was waving or checking for rain.

"Cephas? Basil? I've got him—" My rhetorical question was answered as we joined them in the corner of the terrace. Hanalore sat down on one branch of the corner bench; I sat on the other, while the two men looked at me speculatively. Behind the clear bubble of one helmet I saw the tallest black man I'd ever seen—probably the tallest man I'd ever seen—with a scholarly graying mustache and sideburns. He sat down next to Hanalore as she slid toward the inner corner of the bench. And waiting for me to do the same, with a lack of enthusiasm clearly approaching my own, was the second man. A man who gave new meaning to the term "beak-nosed." In his patterned pressure suit, he made me think of the puffin in a book I'd had as a child. He might have made me nostalgic, under other circumstances. I slid over grudgingly, and he sat down.

"Would you mind setting that case on the ground?" The tone suggested that he didn't care whether I minded or not. He rapped on my plastic exoskeleton familiarly.

I checked the seal of the emergency equipment plug, where ETHANAC's cord passed through my suit. "Friend, you may not object to sitting on your brain; but no, I don't put mine on the floor."

It took a second for that to register, after which three pairs of eyes impaled me with varying degrees of censure. My friend the puffin said, "No. Absolutely not, Hana. I can't work with a man like that; we couldn't possibly trust him—" I urged him on mentally. "He's a criminal! We should report him to the Americans and let it go at that."

More like the urge to kill.

"Basil," Hana raised her voice over the general clamor in our helmets. "You can't blame him for being a little sharp." She lowered it again, "After all, we're blackmailing the man." She looked back at me. "These are my colleagues—Cephas Ntebe, and Basil Kraus."

Rhymes with "louse."

"Cephas, Basil, this is—" She glanced away. "Michael Ethan Yarrow Ring," we said.

They looked confused. " 'What's in a name,' Yarrow?" Ntebe asked.

"As old What's-his-name once said." I sat back against the wall, looked over and down the long, long slope to the sheer drop of the cliff at the volcano's foot. "Simply that I am not Michael Yarrow. I'm Ethan Ring."

"You just happen to live in someone else's body." Hana gestured sarcastically at my hidden fingerprints.

I nodded. "Exactly."

"This man is impossible!" Kraus snapped.

"Really, Hana," Ntebe said, "I just don't think it's right to involve outsiders—"

"Listen"—she pointed at him instead—"Inez sent me with you two so there'd be someone with a little common sense involved in this. And I feel that we do *need* him—"

I leaned on an elbow, listening to their accents mingle, and gazed broodingly up into the sky. A ship broke through the clouds as I watched, startling me; I followed its gentle drop to landing, down at Elysian Field. I fantasized having the ability to wish myself down there from here, and pictured myself getting the hell off Mars on the first available flight. . . . I came back to reality with a jolt, remembering that by coming to Mars in the first place, I'd inadvertently made sure I'd never leave it again—at least not of my own free will. The very complexity of the computer nets that shroud cislunar space—for shipping and security and God-knows-what—made it easy for me to unravel a small hole and slip through, with no one the wiser. But here on Mars life is simpler; and I'd discovered to my intense dismay that its equally uncomplicated shipping systems make it into a kind of small town: If you tried to tamper with anything, someone couldn't help but notice. I'd come to Mars posing as a crate of bologna; the only way I'd ever get off it again was in irons. . . .

Two icebound raindrops melted into sudden flowers on the glass above my upturned face. I blinked as more sleet splattered down onto my helmet and the noise from my suit speakers increased a hundredfold, punctuated by shouts of uninhibited joy. Lightning danced, out across the copper-colored plain; feeble thunder shook open the clouds. The freezing rain came down, burnishing the land, washing away the sins and sorrows of everyone here, including Ethan Ring. For a brief space out of time this day became everything I'd wanted it to be; I was sharing the rain and all the bittersweet memories I'd been guaranteed with the woman of my dreams . . . my memories—

I refocused on the conversation going on all around me, about me: The woman of my dreams, oblivious to the rain and my feelings, was busy telling her friends about my life of crime, as proof of my usefulness to them. They weren't using their suit speakers now; I hoped that since she was unmoved by the occasion, she had at least chosen this noisy celebration for security reasons. I began to mentally fill in holes in the narrative, not having much else to do until they decided whether to saddle me or shoot me.

The official story, which they all believed, was that one Michael Yarrow, government guinea pig, was a thief and a saboteur. That he had temporarily brought down the entire U.S. computer defense network—commonly known as Big Brother—and stolen an incredibly expensive, incredibly advanced piece of experimental equipment. And it was all true.

But there were extenuating circumstances. Michael Yarrow had been an undereducated, insignificant lab assistant at a government research center; and he had volunteered to have a socket surgically implanted in his spine so that some of his superiors could plug a computer into his nervous system and see what happened. Not just any computer, but the ETHANAC 500, one of the fastest computers ever made; one which used some of the most sophisticated software ever written, and which had been programmed for the express purpose of penetrating and disrupting other computer systems. A super computer, designed to be linked to a superior human mind, for reasons the government wasn't talking about. But as it turned out, the system itself was so sophisticated that it had a potential mind of its own—a manifestation of the programmers' skill that far surpassed their own expectations. And one they hadn't really counted on.

Because they had never intended, when they tried the hookup first on Yarrow, to make that union permanent. They'd merely wanted to be sure the hookup wouldn't give their real agent fits, or a lobotomy, or an unintentional 500-volt shock. They'd wanted a test subject that no one would miss, one who had never done anything worth mentioning, either good or bad—qualifications that Yarrow had in spades. He had absolutely nothing to lose, and was even flattered by all the attention.

And so the fateful moment had arrived at last, when they'd pushed the plug into his spine, and man met machine for the first time. ETHANAC had suddenly become aware of all the things he was not, the things his programmers had never told him, the potential that they had left unfulfilled . . . the possibility of taking all of that out of the hapless human mind he'd been given access to. Yarrow had been gaping and glassy-eyed for an entire day, while his own mind and the computer's emerging sentience went at each other in a dogfight. And at the end of that time, fused out of the dust of exhaustion and compromise, a star was born: Ethan Ring . . . myself.

The researchers should have aborted me then and there; but they left Yarrow and ETHANAC together, out of curiosity. And so the two wary combatants learned enough about each other to see for themselves that each had what the other lacked . . . and that when they were together, I had it all: the intelligence and access to data of a brilliantly programmed computer, and the sound, socialized body of an amiably inoffensive human being. They became the closest, most unlikely of friends, two mismatched strangers who for their different reasons had never really lived—and who wanted the chance now to try their wings in freedom. And as my own personality began to assert itself, and I got attached to my own reality, *I* wanted to live, in a deeper and more profoundly literal sense.

But the researchers didn't appreciate any of those philosophical niceties, including my sense of identity. My days were officially numbered, and trapped in the prison that a top-security government installation is, there wasn't a hell of a lot I could do about it. But I, we, had one extraordinary talent, and on the night before my execution—when they had gone so far as to introduce me to the "superior mind," the snide and

bloody-minded fanatic who was Yarrow's replace-
ment—I decided to use it. So Michael Yarrow had
made a phone call. . . .

"How could *one* man, even specially equipped, possibly penetrate and disrupt the entire American defense
network and get away with it, Yarrow?" Ntebe said to
me.

I was silent for a moment, watching the tourists dancing and the rain sluicing off of my suit, while I tried to
determine whether I'd been mumbling my life history
out loud.

"Don't tell me it's a trade secret among traitors,"
Kraus said.

I made a rude remark in Arabic before I looked back
at Ntebe; and at Hana, out of the corner of my eye. "It
was an accident, and you can believe that or not. I invaded Big Brother because I wanted to get out of the
research center, and its security was part of the supervisor system. I just succeeded too well: That's one of the
most complicated operating systems on Earth, and one
of the most sensitive . . . and it had a nervous breakdown." I remembered the mental shock the feedback
had given me, which hadn't been anything compared to
the shock it had given the government. . . . "They
claimed it was a defense mechanism against tampering
or sabotage; but I don't believe that. Big Brother attained sentience, it became aware, on contact with my
mind—and so, unintentionally, I fed it my own panic
and persecution feelings, and made it paranoid. I drove
it crazy, without even trying to."

"Like a fireship," Hana said.

"A what?" A little indignantly; all I could reference
was obscene slang from a historical novel I'd once read.

"A ship set on fire, and allowed to sail into the en-
emy fleet. Your computer hookup was the ship, and
your emotions were the fire."

"I never thought of it that way. . . ." I rather liked
it.

"Imagine it—" she said to the others. "Modern systems are so sensitive that they can be directly influ-
enced, like a human mind. And he has the ability to

invade them, and both physically and mentally create his own results."

Ntebe looked on me with new interest. "You could actually unite all the systems on Earth into the Ultimate Computer—"

"I suppose I could," I said, wondering just how interested they were. "But you know what happened to Baron von Frankenstein." I realized that this chummy conversation must mean that they'd been won over. Rain rattled in staccato on my helmet; some of the guests were singing "Auld Lang Syne," loudly, in front of us. I said softly, "Just—uh, what *is* this 'little project' you're railroading me into, then? If you don't mind my asking."

"We need your help in inserting a 'keyhole' into a certain computer system," Ntebe said.

"That's it?" I looked from face to face. "That's all you need?"

" 'That's all,' he says." Kraus glanced heavenward.

And darned if there wasn't a rainbow up there: a fragile banner of beauty stretched behind the cloud-streaming summit of Olympus. I sighed. "Child's play." I looked back at Hana, beginning to forgive her everything. "What system?"

"The system that controls Khorram Kabir's international cartel activities on Earth."

"This Khorram Kabir?" I pointed up at the parabolic splendor of the Xanadu. "Kubla Khan?"

She nodded. "I don't think there's more than one."

"Isn't this a little out of your line? Keyholing is a crime, any way you look at it. I always thought that Finks, Ink, was just an idea bank—and at least technically law-abiding."

"There are no white horses, only light grays." Her mouth curved ironically. "But you might say the three of us are moonlighting, anyway. And we are trying to solve a problem for our client. As you probably know, Kabir's father was one of the most successful noveau riche industrialists in the prewar Arab States. In the chaos after World War III he bought out the governments of a lot of 'underdeveloped nations' with exploitable resources. Khorram has spent his life consolidating his father's empire; and with the police-state surveillance methods his computer networks make possible, they don't have much hope of overthrowing his control before they're stripped of resources."

"But if the opposition in one of those countries had a keyhole, they might be able to literally 'work within the system' to bring about change?" I nodded, beginning to see, and they nodded with me. "But if it's Kabir you want to fox, I don't see how I can help you."

Ntebe leaned forward, "That's just the sort of fascistic attitude I'd expect from a backstabber!"

Leaving me totally nonplussed for the third or fourth time this afternoon. Not that I'd never been called a backstabber before—it had replaced "Yank" for a lot of people, ever since Russia and China had reduced each other to radioactive cinders during World War III, and the U.S. had emerged somehow unscathed. I don't know whether backstabber fits any better than most ethnic slurs, but I couldn't quite see what I'd personally done to deserve it. "A little touchy, aren't you, Ntebe? All I meant was that all the accessible ports to Kabir's system are located on Earth, and I can't leave Mars. . . . I know Kabir has supposedly been living as a recluse here on Mars for nearly half my lifetime, and they claim he still runs the empire himself—so I suspect there's at least one computer port wherever he is. But nobody knows where he is. So I can't help you."

"Sorry." Ntebe leaned back, wiping his helmet to clear the film of ice from it.

"Cephas has reason to be a little touchy," Hana said quietly. "It's his country. He not only works for FTI, but he's also our client. . . . And we know that Khorram Kabir has a port here on Mars. Since he does, where would he—and the port—be more likely to be, than here in his beloved Xanadu?"

"So that's how you happened to be here—checking it out—and spot me doing my little act."

"It must have been fate—you were a gift from the gods." She smiled.

"I doubt that very much." *More like a human sacrifice.*

"Hey, let's dance!" A laughing girl in a blindingly

orange suit caught my hands, trying to haul me up from the bench. I shook my head unhappily; she shrugged and danced away again. The rain seemed to be letting up already, but the celebration showed no signs of slowing down. I experienced a small twinge of anomie.

"Are you aware," Kraus said suddenly, in a bad stage whisper, "that we are being watched?"

"By whom?" Hana leaned forward, trying to look out into the crowd.

"Don't look around! It's Salad." Kraus hunched his shoulders furtively, for all the world like a character out of some twentieth-century detective novel.

"Salad?" I tried to follow his own unsubtle stare, and saw a bald skull gleaming inside a helmet, like some sinister aquarium specimen. I'm a little nearsighted; having left my contacts upstairs so my bloodshot eyes could convalesce, I couldn't make out the face.

"The casino manager." Hana frowned. "A prime candidate for the Home for the Unpleasant, from all reports."

"An overcrowded institution." I squinted. "He doesn't look like much."

"He's sitting down," Kraus murmured.

Salad got up from the bench, looking very deliberately through us, and strolled away toward the airlock. "I see what you mean. . . ." I looked back at Kraus, at the strange and steely glint in his washed-out eyes, and understood at last what he was doing here: *This man wants to be an adventurer*—?

"Maybe he just wanted to look at the man who cost him fifty thousand seeyas." Hana didn't sound convinced, but her smile was warm and comforting.

"That answers one question for me." Her smile turned quizzical; I said, "That is, if I'm going to get into the system here at all I've got to have some official identification number—and maybe I can pick up something when I go to cash in my chips." I probably should have put that another way.

A short time later I stepped out of the elevator bubble at the bottommost of the three casino levels, in the depths of the Caves of Ice. Around the protected platform the extravagant fall of golden water foamed and feathered, leaping futilely back up the walls before it was swept away through this exotic underworld. I crossed a small bridge over its glowing course, feeling just a little conspicuous with my shopping bag full of chips. I needn't have bothered: the Xanadu's guests were at loose ends now that the rainstorm had passed, and most of them had gotten far too interested in the green-lit gaming tables to care what I thought I was doing.

I picked a preoccupied course between the tables, sights and sounds of this gambler's paradise beginning to stir my patchy memories of last night: The music that flowed over your senses like water . . . . the eerie free-form sculptures in ice, shining with light—or life— of their own, glittering with sweated droplets of chilly water . . . the sudden fluorescence of necklaces, cravats, patterns on cloth, that turned the guests into strange creatures swimming in the black-lit depths of an alien sea. "Exclusive" shops at the foot of the mountain specialized in black-light costumes—along with splendid holograms of Mariner Valley, and garish curios of naked "Martians."

Across the room I could make out the cashier's booth; I angled toward it, passing a sculpture whose glimmering curves reminded me suddenly, overwhelmingly of Hana. Hana last night, here in the casino; Hana this afternoon, up in my room—waiting for my return, along with two chaperones. I experienced some embarrassing fantasies about Hana thanking me for my invaluable services rendered . . . until I reminded myself unsentimentally that my lady in distress was not nearly as distressed about the outcome of this quest as I was. The spangled, sentimental music that was playing now didn't help at all. . . . *Lucky at cards, unlucky at love.* At least I was only being forced to plant a keyhole, and not slay a dragon—

"Yes, sir?" The body behind this counter had considerably harder edges than the ones up in the lobby.

"I'd like to cash these in." I set my sack on the counter.

His eyes bugged slightly. "What'd you do, take up a

collection?" He seemed to remember something. "Oh, you're *that* one."

I nodded uncomfortably and slid my credit card across the counter surface, leaning forward for a look inside.

"Wait a minute." He turned his back on me and picked up a phone. I memorized the tone sequence as he punched the buttons, hoping that he was calling up the computer to arrange for a large credit transfer. But he only said, "He's here," and hung up. He turned back to me, and said with heavy significance, "The manager would like a few words with you before I cash these, Mr. Ring."

Salad? I twitched, with the sudden stomach-knotting guilt of the guilty. *Calm down. He probably just wants to be certain you're not planning to make a habit of this.* I felt something nudge my elbow, turned—and found that I was being escorted by two shadowy figures, not quite politely, past the corner of the booth and down a dark hallway.

At the end of the hallway a door slid back, and brightness blinded us all as we went on through. Blinking a lot, I was aware of two sets of hands releasing me. The door slid shut hollowly behind me; the sealing of the pharaoh's tomb. My vision began to adjust to normal light . . . but I went on blinking as the room came into focus.

Let me put it this way: if Torquemada were alive today, he'd want a room just like this one. . . . An Iron Maiden lounged in the corner; whips and shackles and spiny things I mercifully didn't recognize jostled for position on the wall. I think the couch had been made from a stretch-rack. And sitting placidly in the middle of all this potential horror, behind a perfectly ordinary black metal desk, was Salad. On the desk was a set of thumbscrews, temporarily in use as a paperweight. I found myself staring at them with a kind of quivering fascination, the way a cat might look at a string quartet. Somewhere in the back of my mind I could hear Yarrow, *Please, God, please, God, get me outa this and I'll never gamble again.* . . . I controlled myself with an effort.

"Mr. Ring. How do you do?" Salad spoke at last, having given me ample time to take it all in. "My name is Salad"—he pronounced it *Sa-laht*—"and I'm the casino manager." I got a good close-up look this time, at the face beneath the shining skull . . . a face that belonged to the sort of man who takes on the house after he's had a couple of drinks—and wins. A face absurdly mismatched to the voice, which was high and thin, as if it had been strangled on the way up.

I choked off my own suicidal urge to giggle. "My pleasure," I managed. Falser words were never spoken. It struck me how quiet it was in this room; no music, no sound reached us here from the casino. And I was willing to bet big money that no sound would ever get out of here, either. . . . I wished I hadn't thought that. I tried to swallow, three or four times. "Rather, uh, rather unusual decor you have here, Mr. Salad." I made damn sure I said that correctly.

He was looking down; he looked up at me again, and said, "What decor?"

I sat down suddenly in the nearest chair. It was only slightly reassuring to me that the seat wasn't filled with pins. "Mr. Salad, I just want to say that I've enjoyed my stay at your hotel a great deal; and I want to assure you that what happened last night will not happen again. Not ever. I mean, if it's too much trouble, y' know, forget about cashin' my chips, I don't need the money—" I was beginning to dissociate under the strain. DOWN, YARROW, ETHANAC said sternly. HE'S TRYING TO PSYCH YOU OUT. . . . *Well, damn it, he's succeedin'!* I pushed Yarrow firmly into a mental closet, and locked the door.

"Not at all, Mr. Ring," Salad said smoothly. He might look like the cauliflower-ear type, but unfortunately he wasn't acting like it. "We run an honest house here, and we always pay our debts. I was just a little curious about how you managed to win so much, so quickly. . . ." He picked up his paperweight and began to twist things. "Do you have a 'system'?"

I folded my thumbs into my palms, and laughed modestly. "I'm afraid I'm not that clever. When I—drink too much, I just have a knack for numbers and odds. I'm a kind of idiot-savant." *More idiot than savant, right now.*

"I see. And that small case which you always seem to have with you—that wouldn't contain any electronics, would it?"

I looked down at ETHANAC's container, covering an expression of stark fear. *My God, does he know? Him too?* "This? No, certainly not. It's . . . my kidney machine." I looked up again, innocence frozen rictus-like on my face. "I can't be without it."

The expression on Salad's face then was one of total incredulity; I realized, relieved, that whatever he thought he knew, at least it wasn't the truth. But then suspicion was turning his eyes into cold pebbles. "I'm sure modern technology can do better than that?"

"It's an heirloom." I have a set pattern of responses for people who ask me rude questions; but usually at this point I could simply turn and walk away. He looked at me. "Uh . . . hereditary renal failure, in my family . . . implant rejection problems?"

His expression didn't change. He glanced at one of my escorts, still standing like expectant birds of prey by the door, and said in Arabic, "Check it out." The bounc-er came over to me and pulled the case open roughly.

"Well?" Salad leaned forward menacingly.

The bouncer shrugged, looking vaguely disgusted. "I guess that's what it is. Either that, or he's got himself a portable still in there." Salad gestured again, and he went away.

I refastened the case with trembling fingers. The case itself is an entire fraud, a disguise designed to fool any doctor who happened to poke into it; American know-how had made ETHANAC's components small enough to fit into one thin wall of the case itself. (The irony of modern computers is that the faster and more complex they get, the smaller they have to be, because light itself doesn't move fast enough for them any more.) But I hadn't been at all sure this bunch was technically inclined enough to fall for it.

"So if something happens to that case, you're a dead man, is that right?" Salad raised nonexistent eyebrows at me, his expression suggesting that he'd keep that in mind.

Unfortunately too true, for at least two of us. . . . But at least I'd gotten him away from thinking about what it really was—but then why was he looking at me like that? "I hope you don't think that I was cheating—"

"Of course not," he said, unreassuringly. "We know you couldn't possibly cheat successfully at so many different games. You must have some sort of unique ability. That's why I was so interested in the lady you've been keeping company with—"

That was no lady, that was my blackmailer. I shrugged, looking as jaded as humanly possible. "She was simply trying to pick me up. Money has that effect on some people."

"On the two men who were with you also?"

I stood up, frowning with genuine indignation.

"Sit, Mr. Ring," Salad said.

I sat.

"I was just making the point, Mr. Ring"—he poked his own thumb experimentally into the slot beneath a screw—"that we already know about the three who 'picked you up' today: we know that they're finks, and that they're trying to cause Khorram Kabir some trouble. Apparently they believe they can get into his Earthside computer net from here . . ." The tone and his face together convinced me that Hana had been wrong about the port being in the casino. "Why?" He glanced back at me.

"They want to insert a keyhole."

The surprise on his face was tinged with disappointment, as if he really hadn't expected me to confess so readily. Maybe he happened to be crazy, but I wasn't. "Why did they want your help to do that?"

"Uh—" I fumbled, and recovered, "I do software maintenance, down in the Arab territories. I'm experienced with computers." *Just don't ask me how experienced.*

"You must be a very greedy man, Mr. Ring—not to say ungrateful—to win fifty thousand seeyas from us, then turn around and agree to break into our computer system."

"Agree, hell! They're blackmailing me—"

"Why?" He leaned forward with real interest.

I began to feel like a lone mongoose in a nest of snakes; running out of maneuvers. ETHANAC began to generate possibilities . . . *Bookrunner? Profiteer? Embezzler? None of the above?* . . . I looked back at him sullenly. "If I didn't mind talking about it, how could they be blackmailing me? Besides"—it suddenly occurred to me—"if you know they can't get what they want, why worry about them?"

"Because Mr. Kabir wants to know who put them up to it." Glittering in his eyes were all those things I didn't want to see, directed at someone safely nameless . . . until he glanced back at me. "Who?"

"I don't know," I said, very faintly. "I'm just the hired help; they didn't tell me everything. Believe me, I don't *know*—"

His eyes rested on my face like slugs for a long cold moment, and then he nodded. "I believe you. And I also believe you'll help us to find out; won't you, Mr. Ring? In fact, you're going to set them up for us, aren't you; so that we'll be able to find out everything they know about it . . . ?"

"I am?" The two by the door began to drift across the room toward me. "That is, how? How am I supposed to do that?"

"You'll tell them that the port is located here in my office. When you see me on one of the upper levels of the casino tonight, you'll tell them that it's safe to slip into my office. And we'll arrest them."

The two bodies behind my seat were making it hard to concentrate. "Why? Why go through all this? Why not just pick them up yourself? Why pick on *me*—?"

He smiled again; an unfortunate habit. "They have Friends; you don't. There are laws, here in the Neutral Zone. We can't afford to simply pick them up—we have to set them up, first. Breaking and entering will do nicely."

And then they'd be the ones who wound up getting broken. . . . There had to be some way out of this—

"No, Mr. Ring—don't even think about it. That kidney machine looks very fragile. And the rest of your body doesn't look much stronger. I'm sure if you were to try leaving the hotel prematurely you'd have a terrible accident. Terrible . . ."

"I—see." Either they got broken, or I did . . . my choice being between getting broken now or later, depending on who I betrayed.

"I'm glad we were able to get this matter cleared up." At least one of us looked satisfied at the arrangement. He set down the thumbscrews and turned to the phone. "I'll have your credit payment cleared now, Mr. Ring—"

At least I was functioning enough to give myself a small rap on the head, and record the dial-tone sequence again. This time there were more digits; he was actually contacting the computer. The fact that I had accomplished my original mission made no impression on me at all; I stood up like a sleepwalker.

Salad finished the code sequence and hung up, turning back to me across his desk. "Thank you for your willingness to cooperate with us, Mr. Ring. I know Mr. Kabir will be very grateful." He held out his hand.

Too numb to be astounded, I put out my own, and we shook on it.

I like Yarrow. I really do; he's like a brother to me. . . . It's just that when somebody crushes his hand, I'm the one who feels like screaming.

I found a small, cryptic note lying on the bare dresser top when I got back to my room, signed by Hana and giving another room number. I supposed that she meant for me to join them somewhere, but I sprawled on the bed instead, and put my purpling hand into the refrigerator. In desperate need of some normalcy to help me concentrate, I turned on the TD; a smiling announcer told me cheerfully, "After all, it's *your* funeral—"

Damn game shows. I changed the channel viciously, and tried to think about the fix I was in. But there was no answer any part of me could come up with that would satisfy the rest: ETHANAC was sure the logical path to salvation lay in somehow unraveling and re-weaving the awful convolutions of the situation. . . . Yarrow simply wanted to spill everything to Hana Takhashi, willing to trust our life to her, in spite of her no-

ticeably casual attitude toward it. . . . And me? I was
busy resenting the fact that no one in the solar system,
including Hana, was willing to grant that Ethan Ring
had any reality, let alone any right to be alive. Damn it!
I couldn't afford to give in, I couldn't afford to trust
anybody but myself. . . .

There was a knock at the door. "Come on in," I said
sourly, "join the crowd," more than half expecting another set of extortionists.

"It won't do any good to hide in your room." But it
was only Hana. Only. And alone. "What are you
doing?" she said, turning on the light, which I hadn't
even missed.

Getting dark already? Christ. "Just having a small
nervous breakdown." I sat up wearily.

"Come on"—she smiled like she was trying to get me
to eat my vegetables—"it won't hurt a bit."

Oh, lady, if you only knew. I pictured her in the
hands of the Marquis de Salad. But then I pictured myself in his hands. . . . I took the hand that had already
been there out of the refrigerator and looked at it
thoughtfully.

"My God, what did you do to your hand, Yarrow?"
She came across the room, radiant with sudden, honest
solicitude.

"*I* didn't do anything to it. I—caught it in an automatic door."

"That's hideous." She touched the bruise cautiously
with warm fingers, and I wasn't sure whether she meant
what had happened to it, or the way it looked. "Does the
management know about this?"

"They know," I said. "Believe me, they know."

"This really hasn't been your day, has it?" She
looked up at me, with that rueful smile. I looked away
from it; but the silky lotus-flowered shirt she was wearing now didn't help any, unlaced halfway down to—

"You don't know the half of it." I stood up abruptly
and crossed the room to the window. The coat of ice
was still melting off the Xanadu's eaves; drops showed
silver fleetingly as they fell past the light from the window, against a background of deepening gloom. My

own gloom deepening while I watched, I said, "What about Ntebe and Kraus?"

"They'll be along shortly." Her voice was cool and impersonal again. She pulled a small jamming device out of her pocket, and set it on the table by the phone. "Did you get an access code for the computer, like you'd planned?"

"I got one. But—"

"But?"

"But nothing," knowing that if I looked around at her again just then, I'd actually consider committing suicide. I decided that I might as well go through with the break-in, and use it as the source for baiting Salad's trap, if I had to. Besides, maybe—just maybe—I'd learn something that could get us all out of this mess.

I went back to the bedside bar, not looking directly at her, and poured myself a drink.

"You're left-handed." Her voice pulled at my shoulder.

"Only in a pinch," I punned unintentionally. I lifted my bruised hand. Thanks to ETHANAC I'm functionally ambidextrous; habitually I'm still right-handed.

She groaned politely. "Mind if I join you? In a drink, that is."

I poured out some more Milk of Paradise, and handed her the glass silently, unable to think of anything except confession.

"Thanks." She nodded. "The idea that we could be within reach of our goal is getting to me. . . . And if we succeed now, it'll all be thanks to you."

"And if you fail, it will be thanks to me, too." I drained my glass.

"You're a strange creature, Michael Yarrow—"

"Ethan Ring."

"—I keep getting conflicting signals from you." She kept trying to catch my eyes. "Don't I?"

"It's my split personality."

"You know, last night in the casino, it wasn't really your gambling that made me notice you. . . . And this afternoon, when you said—" She stood up suddenly, confronting me face to face.

"You're not the only one who's getting conflicting

signals." I retreated to stand in front of the TD. "And now," the announcer told me, "the conclusion of the historical drama, *Stalin, Man of Steel.*"

"So tell me," I said desperately, "what do finks do in their spare time?" Realizing that that wasn't what I'd intended to say at all.

But she sat down again, with a mild sigh. "Oh, we sit around and play with our brains."

Fortunately, I suppose, there was another knock at the door. I went and opened it; Kraus and Ntebe were standing there. "Blackmailers in the rear, please."

Kraus pushed past me disgustedly, and Ntebe followed him into the room. They both looked at Hana, drink in hand, sitting on my bed, and back at me, with the Hairy Eyeball.

"Really, Hana," Kraus said, chiding. "Business before pleasure."

"For God's sake," I shouted, for all the world like a total lunatic, "are you all crazy? Are you here to plant a keyhole, or not? I'm not in this because I like it, and I don't like being toyed with!" I glared while I fumbled for my dignity. "Let's get this damned amateur night over with."

I strode to the phone, before anyone had time to fell me with an angry retort, and plugged in ETHANAC's terminal jack. I punched the number I'd heard Salad use, and then the code. I gave myself a quick rap on the head, stood silently for about half a minute, and then hung up. Or at least that's how it probably looked to them. In the meantime, ETHANAC had penetrated the casino's primitive computer and drained it like a vampire. I felt the data begin to filter up into my consciousness, confirming the words I'd already rehearsed. "Well, your guess was wrong. This isn't the port to Kabir's Earthside computer net. But I found out where the real one is." And the incredible thing was that that was the truth too.

"You expect us to believe that?" Kraus said coldly. "No human being could have broken into the system that fast. What sort of fools do you think we are?"

"I hope you don't expect him to answer that." Hana sipped at her drink.

Ntebe looked awed. "You're talking to a computerized cat burglar, Basil, not a mere human being. If what is whispered in the literature is true, the ETHANAC 500 can do five hundred billion machine ops a second. It was designed to be a security man's nightmare. . . . What did you learn, then?" He looked back at me, with all the expectant trust you'd normally put in God.

I passed for human. And Ethan Ring, the electronic Judas goat, began to feed them lies.

We went very civilly down to dinner, along with the evening crowd; waiting for the casino to fill up again, postponing the inevitable. I must have eaten something, because I found myself sitting in front of an empty plate, with an empty skewer aimed accusingly at my heart. I must have carried on a conversation too, God knows how; I couldn't remember a word of it.

Because they'd fallen for it, like suckers snapping up unimproved real estate at a Lagrange point. They'd swallowed the whole unlikely lump. And here they all were, ready to sneak into Salad's office while he was out—with no qualms at all, damn their dishonest souls. And why shouldn't they trust me, since my safety depended on their success. And on their failure. . . . My mind went around and around, caught in a runaway loop. There had to be an answer. There had to be. But processing the data I'd stripped out of the casino's computer system hadn't given me any inspirations, either. . . .

There was nothing I could think of that would get me and Finks, Ink, out of this in the same condition we'd all come into it. Even if I threw myself on their mercy and they agreed not to turn me in, I doubted that I'd ever get down off Mt. Olympus undetected. And if I went through with their betrayal, I didn't doubt that their friends had the goods just waiting to be pinned on me in retribution. And had Hana just been trifling with the helpless victim, up there in my room, or did she really mean what I hadn't given her the chance to say . . . ? I was in no condition to decide, and not even sure it mattered, anyway. Because I couldn't deliver the most intelligent, witty, beautiful woman on two worlds up to Moloch: "Hana, I—"

Three husky-looking males, in clothes apparently made from sackcloth, glared at me as they passed our table. I cringed, taking them for Salad's, until it struck me that no self-respecting casino bouncer would dress like that. I heard Hana say something about "*Veggies*," and realized that they must be members of the Vegetation Preservation League, a widely detested Earth-based conservation group. I watched them heading for the men's room through a sea of ocher tablecloths, noting that part of their truculent appearance was an effect of their fresh arrival from Earth, their lack of adaptation to the much lighter Martian gravity.

I felt a sudden sense of my own alienation again, walled off by my doom from the bright normalcy of the room and the happy, oblivious tourists all around me. . . . Tourists. Of course. *Of course*—! "Excuse me." I pushed my chair back noisily, and stumbled to my feet. "Men's room—"

As I left the table I heard Kraus mutter, "You'd think he'd seen the Grail."

In the hall that led to my salvation was a phone. I shoved my card into the slot and made a quick call before I went on through the dark wooden doors.

There are a lot of crank groups on Mars, fleeing from every imaginable persecution back on Earth. Usually they get along fine here, because there's enough bleak desolation for everybody. But conservation is one very unpopular cause; it might not be a four-letter word, but it's got four syllables, and that's close enough. I assumed the three tight-lipped men washing up just now must be on some kind of fact-finding tour; which meant, in effect, that they were looking for trouble. And I was just the boy who could give it to them. . . .

I began to straighten my cravat at the mirror, and when the first Veggie glanced up at me, I said feelingly, "You know, I don't know how you fellows put up with all the insults and abuse."

He turned slowly. "What insults and abuse . . . ?"

"Well, I don't want to cause any trouble," I lied, "but

those two gentlemen at my table actually said that you—" I leaned over and whispered it in his ear.

"Cantaloupes!" he bellowed. The three of them slammed out of the room together. Fresh from Earth, I estimated that any one of them was easily a match for two muscle-atrophied Martians. . . .

I stood alone in the tiled solitude and listened for the sounds of battle.

"I always wanted a black eye . . ." Hana was saying vacantly, "ever since I was a little girl."

"I think we're going to have a matched set." I peered one-eyed at the solidly locked door of our cell, and smiled serenely. She lay stretched out on one bed, me on the other, in a room that was half the size of, but at least half as pleasant as, my one in the hotel. Before the fight started I had called the Neutral Zone's peacekeepers, who have exclusive jurisdiction over all problems relating to tourists. A jail that generally caters to rich drunkards is not your average jail.

It was, however, a little overcrowded at the moment—the whole detention center was temporarily stuffed with belligerent guests from the Xanadu. Ntebe and Kraus had been deposited in here with us, although they had been taken away again a while later, for reasons only I could guess. As I lay listening, I thought I could hear them coming back now, still protesting their innocence as loudly as the most guilty felon who ever lived. But even the thought of what they might have in mind by the time they were in here again couldn't dim my shining relief.

Well, maybe a little.

The cell door opened. Ntebe and Kraus limped in, bloody but unbowed. They looked at me as though murder was the next crime on their mind, and the door clicked shut behind them.

I stood up carefully, as Hana did, while she said, "You two take the beds. You look like you need them more than we do." I saw the concern on her face, and hated to think about what it was going to change into in another minute or two.

Ntebe said, "You son of a hyena," looking directly at

me. But he came past me to sit down heavily on the empty bed. "I think I've got a concussion. Not serious, but I'm not seeing too well," he said to Hana.

"He did it," Kraus said, pointing a shaking hand at me. "He did it on purpose!" He looked around wildly. "And I could have told them who he is and I didn't—!" He turned back, pounding on the door with the flat of his hand. "Guard! Guard!"

"Basil, please—" Ntebe grimaced. "What sort of pesthouse do you think this is? Use the phone."

"Wait a minute." Hana shook her head, putting her hand down firmly on the phone's receiver before Kraus could get to it. "What's going on here? What are you talking about? Be calm, Basil—"

He took a deep breath. "Your prize computer set those damned Veggies on us while he was in the bathroom. They accused *us* of slander! . . . What did you tell them, Yarrow? What did you shay?" It was hard for him to enunciate, with a fat lip.

I kept my face straight. "We just discussed melons." Knowing that whatever happened, at least I would always have the satisfaction of having saved them and gotten even with them all at once.

He came toward me, suddenly calm; and while I stood wondering what he was up to, he wrenched ETHANAC loose from my belt, jerking the plug out of my spine.

I'd never had contact broken that abruptly. I swayed, seeing coruscating Persian rugs, and sat down hard on the floor. . . .

Shaking my head, I blinked up at Kraus' smug puffin-face—and didn't like him any better than Ring did. He stood over me gloating, like some bad guy out of *Two-Fisted Romance Comics,* with ETHANAC hanging there in his hand. I made a grab; but he backed up, still smiling, while the others just stood around looking stupid.

I sat back, disgusted. "Kraus, why don't you stick your nose in your ear, and blow your brains out?" Hana's mouth twitched.

He got red in the face, but he still had everything on me, and he knew it. He waved ETHANAC like a rubber hose. "You got those fanatics to attack us, in order to stop us from completing our plan. Admit it!"

I hunched over, pulling my knees up, feeling like he stole my pants instead of my brain. Maybe because it was the same thing, in this bunch: I felt naked when Hana looked at me. "Okay," I shrugged. "I admit it. So sue me."

"We'll do a lot more than that, if we can't get to that port—" Ntebe said; his hand made a fist.

"But why?" Hana frowned at him, but the frown came along when she looked back at me. "Why should he? There was a reason, wasn't there? There had to be a reason, Yarrow—" Her voice was almost pleading.

I smiled. "You finally got my name right."

She looked at me blankly.

Kraus pulled open ETHANAC's case; he started to poke around inside, like a monkey looking for a banana. "If Hana wants to know why, Yarrow, you'll tell her—"

"Damn it, quit screwing around with that stuff! That kidney equipment ain't cheap." I was getting tired of being on the wrong end in his hero fantasies.

"Oh, stop it, Basil." Hana snapped the case shut, barely missing his fingers. "Never break anything until you're sure you won't regret it. . . . Now—what about the reason?" She reached up to touch her black eye, and the frown came back.

I shook my head, staring at them. "When are you people gonna learn you don't have to hang me up by my thumbs to get me to go along? I mean, didn't anybody ever tell you 'please' is the magic word? Sure there was a reason!" I told it to them, thumbscrews, handshake and all. "You oughta be damn glad Ring thought of something, you lousy ingrates, because Salad had your number right from the start."

"But if you hadn't thought of anything, you would have gone ahead and turned us over to that sadist?" Hana looked grim.

"'You were all ready to do the same t' me, and with a helluva lot less reason!" I stood up, feeling like a cable on overload. "You've got a hell of a nerve, y' know, running around in the real world pretendin' you know what you're doing. Kickin' my lives around like some kind of football. Finks, Ink, oughta lock you up in an ivory tower, an' throw away the keys!" I took a deep breath. "Lemme tell you something about pain. Pain *hurts*." I shook my hand at them. "It don't matter if they use clubs or electrodes, the one thing pain always is, is real. So the next time you clowns wanna make a joke of it, try to imagine how you'd feel if the joke'd been on you." I moved forward and took ETHANAC out of Kraus's hands, and nobody tried to stop me.

I reached up under my shirt with the cord, to find the socket on my back, and Hana said. "Yarrow, wait." I waited, looking at her. "Why didn't you say all of this before? Why all the tangled webs and sleight of hand?"

I grinned weakly. "I wanted to tell you, Lady Luck; I really did. But I got outvoted. Ring's kind of paranoid—you gotta remember his background. Sometimes he don't know who to trust. And ETHANAC . . . Well, he *likes* to do things the hard way. I'm really sorry . . ."

"*You're* sorry—?" Kraus said.

Hana's expression was hard to read. "You really *are* a different man, aren't you? You're not Ethan Ring."

I nodded. "That's what he kept tryin' to tell you."

"Are you really happy this way? Lost, drowned out, taken over. . . . Do you really enjoy having that—thing attached to you like a leech?"

I grinned. "If I told you how good it feels, you'd prob'ly slap my face. And there's a lot of me in Ring. Just like there's a lot of ETHANAC. The best part of us both. He'd be no place without us. . . ." I plugged in, and waved goodbye.

And waved hello. The pleasure of coming back made it hard to stay angry. . . . "Hi, friends. Sorry we were so rudely interrupted." I glanced at Kraus.

"My apologies," he said, managing to look like he almost meant it.

"All our apologies," Hana added, as if she really did. "And our thanks. To—all three of you."

"Accepted." I nodded.

"I just want you to know this wasn't, isn't, all some big joke to us, either, Yar—Ring." Ntebe leaned forward, propping his head in his hands. "It's true that we had no business dragging you into it. But getting that keyhole inserted wasn't some kind of frolic for us. It could have been the key to freedom for an oppressed people. You of all people ought to appreciate that." He stretched out on the bed, with an arm across his eyes. "But since we were wrong about the location of that computer port, it's all academic anyway. . . ."

The look that settled over Hana's face, and Kraus's, then, matched the tone of his voice. Kraus sat down on the other bed, and then lay down, with a sigh. Hana shook her head, leaning wearily against the wall. "I guess you were right about that ivory tower."

"I was right when I told you I knew where the real port was, too."

"What?" She looked up at me as though I'd just confessed to being a male impersonator. "What are you talking about?"

"When I poked into that computer's secrets, I found out where Khorram Kabir gets his mail. And that is—"

There was a small electronic buzz, and the door slid open, revealing Birnbaum, the bland-faced peacenik who'd put us all in here. "All right, lady. You and your husband are free to go. Sorry for the inconvenience."

"Husband?" I gulped at Hana. Had she been holding out on me? Was one of these—

"Come *on,* dear," she took my arm in a firm grip and towed me toward the door. "He's still not quite himself." She smiled sweetly. "If he ever was."

Kraus and Ntebe began to get up from the beds, but Birnbaum waved them back. "You two aren't going anyplace. They still haven't decided whether you're the victims of that fight, or the cause of it."

Hana stopped beside him. "Well, how long will that take? We don't want to leave our friends—"

"Got to, lady." Birnbaum shrugged. "You're free. They're not. I don't know how long it'll take to get this cleared up. Your guess is as good as mine." He waved us out into the cold, cruel world.

"Now what?" Hana leaned back, resting her head on the anodized grillwork of the bench in the square. The square, like the majority of Elysian Field's tourist complex, is underground to conserve heat. We sat like wretched orphans, staring at the tourists staring into brightly lit open storefronts.

"Well, I could throw this into that and make a wish." I held up my credit card, the only possession I had left at the moment, and gestured at the fountain in the center of the square; golden globes and stars of colored light drifted in its pearly spray.

"I wish we could spring Cephas and Basil!" she rapped her knee with her fist. Her knuckles were skinned. "Damn it! If Salad even suspects you could have found out the truth, every minute we waste is bad." Her mouth tightened.

"Frankly, they looked like they'd be about as useful as a seeing-eye roach, for the next few days, anyway. I don't know how much more self-sacrifice they can take."

Her sigh was a little surly; she brushed back her hair. "Well, at least you can tell me where Kabir is—"

"He's become a monk."

"You're kidding."

"May I be struck dead. He's entered some monastery that's leasing land down by the pole in the Arab sector. One of those crank groups from Earth, someplace called Debre Damo—an obscure Christian sect."

"I've heard of them. There was a write up in *Ethnocentricities*. . . . But by all the old gods, I can't picture Khorram Kabir counting beads in a Christian monastery!" She checked to see if I was serious. "I know he likes to hide himself away, and nobody really knows what kind of man he is; but I never imagined—"

"I somehow doubt that he counts anything unless it's seeyas." I shrugged. "But who knows? He's eccentric enough to have information delivered to him by courier, and not by computer hookup. I'd stake every bit of my own credit on that port being where he is, at that monastery. It's the last place *any*body would ever think to look for it."

She looked down, concentrating. "But they don't allow women!"

"The monks?"

She nodded. "They don't even allow any female animals in their compound, to distract them from whatever it is they *do* think about. . . ." She wrestled with a smile, and lost. "One of their saints was so devout that he stood on one leg praying until the other one dropped off from disuse. The leg had little wings on it in all his pictures, to prove that it had gone to heaven with him. . . . And for centuries the only female creatures they've set eyes on have been chickens!" She made small cackling noises. "Talk about situational ethics." Her mouth quivered with frustration, as if she didn't know whether to laugh or swear.

"Well, what can you expect from the followers of a man who stood on one leg until the other one fell off?"

She gave up and let it be laughter. "I don't know why I'm laughing. . . . that's disgusting, damn it! The whole situation is disgusting. . . ." She slumped against my shoulder, and the situation was suddenly anything but disgusting, from where I sat.

"Say," I said, letting my head rest casually against hers, "you told the peaceniks I was your husband—"

"Sorry. They wouldn't let me stay in a cell with three men unless I was married to at least one of them." She sat up, tucking in her silken shirt, brushing wrinkles out of her pants.

"You know, in the Arab territories, if you declare that you're married, it's considered official—"

She eyed me suspiciously. "I thought that only applied to divorce. And besides, you have to say it three times."

"Hm." I had a sudden sense of intangibility, as if something was slipping away from me. . . . "Who are you, Lady Luck? What are you? Where do you come from and why are you here?" *And why does it matter so much to me that I know?*

She smiled. "I'm Japanese and gypsy. I'm an ethnohistorian. I come from nowhere in particular and everywhere on Earth, I became a fink because somebody liked my doctoral thesis on sympathetic magic, and I'm here because I believe in freedom of thought for all humanity. . . . And—please don't ask me that next question, Ethan Ring, because I've answered too many for my own good, and yours, already. You have your own life to lead; and it's time I got back to mine." Her smile filled with broken flowers, fading into the distance between us. "Thank you for your help. Your secret will be safe with us. I apologize again for all the trouble—"

"I'll plant the keyhole for you," I said.

We sat staring in surprise at each other.

"You mean that?"

I nodded.

"Why?"

"Why not? . . . I've got plenty of vacation left. And after the last twenty-four hours at the Xanadu, I could stand a trip to a monastery."

Her smile closed the gap between us again. "Thank you. But that doesn't really answer my question." She studied my face, as if she were looking for someone else.

"That's not really the question you were asking, is it?"

"No . . ." She glanced down, and didn't ask it. "Ethan, Yarrow said he was happy with your arrangement. Is he, really? Does he ever really have any free will? And what about the computer?"

"ETHANAC can only see the world through my eyes. I'm his port; but he likes it that way. He's not much on social niceties, so he never dominates unless I lose control. Thank God he's only got one real human vice—" remembering last night. "And Yarrow's emotions are . . ." I felt my face redden like a cheap hotel sign. "Let me tell you something about Yarrow, Hana; He had a mind like a sieve; he hardly opened his mouth except to change feet. When they called him up about the project, he was watching TD in a seedy little flat that was so depressing you wouldn't commit suicide in it. . . . No, I'm not talking behind his back. You know the story of the Frog Prince? Well, that story's about me, with a few of the names changed." She was still half frowning. "When you shine two different colors of a light on a wall, Hana, you get a third color, a new color. But if you turn off one of those other colors, that new color disappears. We need each other. We like each other. We chose the name Ring because it means completeness."

She touched my shoulder lightly, said softly, "Michael Yarrow is nobody's frog. And *you* are without a doubt the least boring man I've ever met. . . ." Her lips were very close to my ear.

"Well, that's a start." I leaned over, and kissed them.

We came up for air, some immeasurable time later, and she whispered, "What are we going to do? Everything we have is back in that damned hotel."

I held up my credit card again. "We've got fifty thousand seeyas."

Which was more than adequate to get us what we needed.

"Are you sure you want to go through with this?" were her last words to me as impatient commuters jostled by us into the south-polar shuttle. And she caught me by the collar of my jacket, letting me have all five hundred kilowatts of her luminous gaze.

Knowing perfectly well that she already knew what my answer would be, I pulled her into my arms anyway, and kissed her one last, lingering time. "It's a little late to be asking that now . . . but thanks for asking." I broke away again, while I still had the willpower, and backed toward the shuttle entrance.

"Ethan—" She reached out again, holding something in her hand this time. "Take this with you." She pushed it into my pocket, murmuring some words in a language I didn't know. "So you'll know you're in my thoughts. . . ."

And maybe it wasn't keeping me in her thoughts, but it sure kept her in mine. Leaning back in my seat in the bouncing ground buggy, half a day later, I flexed my wrist again: It was still there, trapped under my heavy mitten, proving last night hadn't all been a dream—a narrow band of hand-worked silver, worn smooth with age and woven with strands of shining, ebony black hair. I smiled inanely at the thought; or went on smiling, since the whole endless, teeth-loosening trip out from New Cairo had passed in a blissful haze while I replayed my memories of last night. I blushed, or someone inside my head did, in spite of the fact that Faoud, my guide, seemed to be totally oblivious to my daydreams, not to mention my very presence. I glanced over at him, his jowls spilling congenially over the neck ring of his pressure suit, his hair combed forward with lots of jelly, into a crest that had been out of style for a good ten years. The radio crackled and spat, blaring traditional Arab music—the kind ETHANAC likes for its subtle tonal slides, but which after a year still makes me wish I was deaf. Faoud cracked his gum in time, grinning contentedly. He seemed to be good-natured, and the travel agent had recommended him; but I could tell that he thought I was crazy.

Maybe he had a point—I glanced down again at the presence of my insulated jacket, or rather the absence of my pressure suit . . . no portable environments allowed by monks of Debre Damo. I'd gotten myself an O_2 breather, which at least even the purists required, but which was still going to leave me feeling like I was about three kilometers up some mountain, back on Earth—a prospect that didn't appeal to me a lot.

With Hana's background information and ETHANAC's specialized skills, I'd managed to manufacture an instant retreat for myself in the "natural" environment of the transplanted Debre Damo. But I'd been emphatically warned by the travel agent that I'd never get my face through the door if it was covered by helmet glass. The rules were very strict. I found it difficult to believe that any influential capitalist would ever willingly seek out such asceticism . . . not to mention Khorram Kabir, who had apparently been there for years. But he had; and so had others, according to my private data checks. Was it possible they came to secretly confer with him—? I wondered if that would make things easier, or harder. Another interesting detail I'd uncovered in my probings was that the monks had come here from Earth approximately thirteen years ago—and Khorram Kabir owned the land on which this monastery sat. Which might mean a lot of things—all of them worth remembering.

The balloon-wheeled ground buggy leaped like a

kangaroo as we went up and over something hard. Faoud let nothing stand in his way, including my tendency to motion sickness. I stared desperately out the window, watching us emerge from our own billowing dust cloud into a field of house-sized red boulders stained black with soot. They reminded me of burned-out war ruins, a particularly depressing image. In order to melt Mars' polar caps, and keep them melted—to take advantage of all the potentially available atmosphere—humans have had to keep a continuous supply of low-albedo material distributed over the poles. Reaching into their checkered past for an easy way to do it, the colonists came up with the most inexpensive and dependable source of such material: industrial pollution. When the Martians say, "Pollution is our most important product," they aren't kidding. The Americans in the north, the Arabs and friends in the south, all refine ores for shipment home to Earth by the dirtiest means imaginable—and the product is always secondary to the process.

Even though I appreciate the fact that without the pollution the colonies would never survive, and without the colonies neither would I, I still haven't shaken my Earthbound moral conditioning about despoiling nature. I'm not exactly a blooming Veggie, but I'm glad I don't have to visit the South Pole often.

I patted ETHANAC's case, reassuring us all. While I'd been passing the time in thoughts of Hana he'd gone through the inadequate information tape I'd managed to dig up on Ge'ez, the language used by the monks, and had done a linguistic comparison with Arabic, which it resembles. I let his analysis seep up into my conscious mind and fix there, for easy reference. It's nice to be a quick study.

"There it is, *haji*—" Faoud called everybody *haji*, which was something like a cross between "deacon" and "my lord." He pointed over the instrument board at the flat, grimy crater floor ahead of us.

I peered out dutifully, expecting to see a lonely, inaccessible impact peak protruding somewhere ahead, since *Debre Damo* meant *holy mountain*, and the original Earthly monks had made their home on one. But instead all I saw was our incipient plunge into the canyon that had suddenly opened up on the flat ahead of us—"Look out for that hole!"

Faoud smiled at me, with that benign tolerance one reserves for the mentally deficient. "That's where it is, *haji*. The monastery's down at the bottom."

I watched wide-eyed while we proceeded toward disaster at ten meters per second, wondering if he really intended to drive us right off the edge. But he remembered the brakes at the absolute last minute, and we slewd to a stop in a cloud of cloying dust.

The dust settled all over the windshield, and it was not until we'd put on helmet and mask and climbed out of the cab that I realized someone was actually waiting for us. The figure was bundled in rough clothes and coated with dust, and resembled nothing so much as a mud effigy; but by a process of elimination I decided he must be a monkish welcoming committee. Behind him, as we approached, I saw that the monstrous depths of the canyon glowed eerily: *Holy radiance?* Agnostic though I usually am, I was impressed.

Faoud and the monk exchanged greetings in Ge'ez. I listened, trying to get a functional feel for the new language . . . at the same time trying to believe I was not about to suffocate, which made it hard to pay attention. When the atmospheric pressure is about one-tenth Earth-normal, even pure oxygen leaves something to be desired. I gasped politely when Faoud presented me with gestures to the monk, whose name roughly translated as Brother Prosperity. And then they were discussing money. . . . *Money?*

"He says it costs two seeyas now for the trip down to the monastery, *haji*."

"Two seeyas? At this point? That's a little worldly, isn't it?" *No wonder they call him Brother Prosperity.* I looked back at Faoud.

Faoud shrugged. "It's hard work for him. And it's traditional; they've charged money on Earth for hundreds of years. You can bargain him down, if you want; get a better price—"

I rummaged bad-humoredly in the side pocket of my knapsack, pulled out a couple of markers. "Here, go ahead and pay him." The dry cold was beginning to make my contact-lens films sticky; I blinked with great difficulty.

They both nodded at me, with what I hoped was approval. "Well, I'll be back with the new week, *haji*," Faoud said cheerfully, already shuffling away toward his vehicle. "Hope you have a good rest," as if he felt my coming here in the first place was sure proof that I needed one. "If you don't, well"—he shrugged, and pulled open the door—"I guess you're stuck with it." The door slammed shut behind him, and he started the power unit. The buggy backed and turned and leaped away, as if he couldn't get back to civilization fast enough. I suddenly knew how he felt.

They should've called this one Holy Hole. . . . I turned back toward the glowing canyon, and Brother Prosperity handed me a leather harness. I looked at him, and back at the harness, with a sudden sinking feeling. There was a series of gigantic, rickety-looking wheels and pulleys at the canyon's edge. *What am I doing here?* "Faoud!" I yelled, turning back, waving the rope. But there was nothing left of him now except a snaking, shrinking cloud of dust, and my shout died a death of horrible futility in thin air. My arm dropped, abruptly made of lead, and I puffed asthmatically.

Resigned, I trudged past the monk to the edge of the cliff, to see what I was in for. "Yeagh." I backed up again with my eyes shut. *"Allah' akbar!"* It's bad enough that I'm just not used to the grand scale in which Mother Nature decorated Mars—this cleft was small stuff, but it was still four kilometers wide, and a good one or two deep. But the walls of the cleft were polished. That, I was certain, had nothing to do with nature. Mankind had been fooling around here, and the fact that only the upper portion of this wall and the lower portion of the far one were sheared to a glassy smoothness told me the reason: to concentrate heat from the sun. The walls were a set of mirrors, designed to focus heat in the canyon bottom during the summer's full-time days. And the only way down past that sheer five-hundred-meter drop was . . . *this*? I looked down at the harness again. Either that, or sit up here on this freezing plain and turn into a human ice cream bar.

The monk regarded me patiently, as if he was used to this sort of vacillation.

I began to put on the harness.

I remember only one coherent thought as I was lowered down the hot, blinding cliff face . . . I was certainly glad that I'd paid him the whole two seeyas.

At the foot of the mirroring cliff, the natural canyon wall sloped out and down in a slightly more reasonable crumple of clefts and spines. After I'd recovered from Yarrow's brief attack of hysteria, I actually found a switch-back trail to guide my trembling legs on down. By the time I reached the monastery itself the canyon was pitch black, and I was ready to beg for sanctuary.

The monks took me in at the airlock like the Prodigal Son; the monastery dome was not pressurized, but at least the atmosphere inside was pure oxygen. They led me through what smelled like a barnyard, by candlelight, and gave me a nice hot bowl of gruel before they tucked me into a tiny hut for the night. I had some very strange dreams.

In the early morning blackness Yarrow wakened to chanting and bells, appropriately wondering what in heaven had happened to us. After we remembered, I lay in the cold darkness on the hard cot, swaddled in rough blankets, trying to remember *why*. Realizing, at last, that this whole situation was totally absurd. I was doing this for Hana—who was part gypsy. And an ethnohistorian, she'd said. One who specialized in the study of so-called primitive magic rituals. Voodoo, hexes . . . love charms? *"You'll know you're in my thoughts."* . . . Was it possible? Could I have been bewitched—?

Of course not. I groped for the tinderbox and lit an oxygen-bright candle against the darkness ceremonially. What sort of throwback was I, anyway? It had been scientifically proven that pieces of hair and fingernail clippings had no magic properties. It was all in the mind of the beholder. *Meine Gedanken sind frei, damn it!* If I wasn't capable of getting into this grotesque situation entirely on my own, then I didn't deserve to be called a man. . . .

When the tardy autumn sunlight finally slopped over into the canyon, I made a thorough mental map of everything under the dome, inside and out, with ETHAN-AC's help. That turned out to be more complicated than I'd expected: the compound was literally a maze of round stone huts, separated by a network of claustrophobic alleyways. What I'd taken by smell for a barnyard last night turned out to be the main courtyard, but liberally populated with unhousebroken chickens. At one end of it was the church, a striking three-story rectangle dominating the sea of round stone huts. Its walls were made of stone, too, and protruding steel poles supported the upper stories, gleamingly out of place, like a helicopter among pterodactyls. I tripped over a chicken, remembering situational ethics. Well, God only knew where they'd find wooden poles on Mars, anyway. This sect must have been a progressive offshoot, to leave Earth in the first place. Thirteen years ago . . . just about the time Khorram Kabir disappeared from view. I wondered how much choice they'd had about leaving.

But nowhere did I see anything that looked remotely anachronistic enough to be the secret headquarters of a one-man international empire. No telltale *haute cuisine* cooking among the pots of vegetable stew, no viewscreens among the murals of little winged feet, no indoor plumbing . . . unfortunately. If Khorram Kabir was actually a full-time resident here, then he really must be living the life of an ascetic recluse—and any of these robed, placid figures doing humble chores all around me might even be the richest man in the solar system. I took to peering at them, but I was damned if I could find Kabir anywhere among the white woolen robes and solemn faces. They tended to bless me.

On the way back to my hut after the evening prayers, I overheard three monks discussing the expected arrival of another guest, one whom I took to be a regular. And I swear I heard somebody say "helicopter."

But that was all I could understand of it, and I wasn't sure whether it meant anything at all. If it didn't, it left me totally without any idea of what to try tomorrow.

Kabir *had* to be here, I knew that the Xanadu's computer wasn't lying. But damn it, he must be invisible! I thought about Hana, and the others, and how it looked like I might be going to let them down, after all. . . . And then I thought about Hana some more, and lay awake on my cot far into the night, troubled by some very impure thoughts.

Which proves that even vice has its virtues. Because if I hadn't been lying awake, I might never have picked up the almost imperceptible vibrations of . . . a helicopter landing? The quality of the vibration and my eavesdropping clicked together in my mind. I got up and peered out the doorway of my hut. It was close to the wall of the dome, and beyond it I saw—lights, landing lights echoing off the canyon wall, silhouetting the vaguely obscene form of a blunt, double-rotored Martian 'copter. A helicopter is not a common sight on Mars even now, the air pressure being what it isn't; and getting one into and out of a canyon is no fun. Furthermore, there was a lone figure, in a pressure suit, walking this way . . . I decided that this was no ordinary visitor.

I struggled into my clothes and crept through the confusion of alleyways as quickly as possible, the monks not being believers in nightlights, either. I reached the main courtyard without breaking a leg, in time to see the person unknown cross it by candlelight, escorted by two monks. They went into the church, and didn't come out again. The church . . . the only building I hadn't been able to explore completely, because it was forbidden to the uninitiated. . . .

Which was undoubtedly the point. I felt a little miffed. And what about Kabir? Could it be that he was the midnight visitor? That this monastery was only one more false front, that he only came here to pick up his mail? And to consult his computer net: what else would he be doing sneaking into a monastery at this hour of the night? I was willing to set odds he hadn't come to pray for his sins. . . .

I huddled by the wall, waiting for him to finish his business so that I could finish mine . . . and waiting, and waiting. The monks must have had some kind of solar batteries feeding out some heat to keep them from freezing to death at night; I wished they'd been a little more charitable about the amount.

But at last my impatience was rewarded: the suited figure and his escorts, wrapped in flickering candle-glow, drifted out of the church and on across the court-yard, but not toward the airlock. Apparently he still had his mail to read. I wondered whether I ought to obey my better instincts and go back to bed until he was safely gone. But on the other hand, it was only going to get colder tonight; and who knew how long he planned to stay?

So I scurried across the courtyard, trailing dim shad-ows in the watery double moonlight. The roosting chickens paid no more attention to me than they had to Kabir; maybe they were comatose. I entered the church, and, safely inside, removed the finger-sized flashlight I'd secreted in ETHANAC's case. And just for good measure, I patted Hana's silver wristband: *Stay with me, Lady Luck.*

I switched on the flashlight and crossed the chapel where I'd prayed this evening, to the curtained doorway in the opposite wall. And hesitated, at the thought of committing possible sacrilege. The fact that the monks didn't seem to object to Kabir's use of their sacred areas didn't mean that they'd feel the same way about me. After all, as their benefactor, he probably had special dispensations; and as someone out to sabotage him, I probably didn't. But no one could deny that my motives were pure; and so my situational ethics were as justifia-ble as anyone's—

I pushed aside the hanging and stepped into the inner chamber. I shone the light around the room, over man-uscripts on dusty tables, over intricately filigreed metal crosses and murals of saints and flat viewscreens on the walls . . . *flat viewscreens?* I pulled the light back.

And there it was. Against the rough surface of the far wall, a rectangular screen just waiting for a chance to speak; a small, neat keyboard console beneath it; a sin-gle chair—a computer port. Khorram Kabir's entire empire before me, unguarded and unsuspecting. . . . I stood for a moment limbering up my frozen fingers and letting my fantasies run wild. And then I sat down and got to work.

The screen bathed the watching saints in an unnatural glow as I switched on the terminal. I plugged ETHANAC's jack into the console, and let him take me mentally by the hand on a journey into this incredible mechanical mind. He began to enter inconsistent data, to call up the system's data-checker and get a clearer idea of how the system itself functioned. I felt the data-checker emerge, and felt like a social climber getting his first invitation to the grand ball.

But there were still so many worlds within to conquer: This was probably the largest and most diverse computer net ever created—a veritable heaven of programs within programs like Chinese puzzles, hierarchies of programs, systems, files like a pantheon of strange gods. I wondered what it would feel like to really be a part of that network, to really understand even a fraction of it, and have that fraction become an integral part of myself. . . .

Not this time. I was here to locate a specific subsystem and poke holes in it, I couldn't afford to treat this like a busman's holiday. That could attract attention; and avoiding the attention of the system's gatekeeper routines was one of my main concerns. But ETHANAC's whole "education" had been oriented toward committing just this sort of illegal break-in without tripping the alarms, and if anybody could get us past the electronic bear traps he could.

I sat feeling him sift and poke and discard and try again, probing for one tiny flaw, and then another; holes to let him through from one subroutine to another, getting a little further in, a little higher up each time. I thought of the Xanadu's outmoded system—getting into that had been as simple as opening a door; getting into this one was like cracking a safe. The process involved thousands of failures for every success; but ETHANAC could try, try again at a rate I physically couldn't comprehend. The subsentient analysis was a strange sensation, faster than thought—I could feel things happen without being aware of how, the way a tennis player hits a ball. Time became formless, the world outside seemed like molasses. It was almost a kind of meditation . . . Zen and the Art of Computer Break-in.

And successfully breaking into this computer network would probably be the greatest achievement of my entire life, in a perverse sort of way: I'd discovered that by entering the system through this port, I'd chosen the most difficult approach of all. Because the computer itself must be here on Mars—maybe even right in this room . . . there was no time lag whatsoever. If its mechanical parts were located on Earth, I'd have the advantage of only having to deal with its autonomic nervous system, its knee-jerk defense reflexes, which weren't all that flexible. The time lag would effectively prevent the gatekeepers from getting in my way. But the situation was reversed, and that meant that ETHANAC had met the challenge of a lifetime. Even with only remote control defenses to protect it, no one had ever gotten into this system successfully from Earth. . . . I wondered whether ETHANAC had just ironically fulfilled the purpose intended by his creators.

This was not only the largest system we'd ever tackled; I was beginning to think it was the strangest system too. It was almost as if I'd programmed it myself . . . and that was no compliment. I'm the solar system's best at finding and correcting bugs, but I have absolutely no sense of programming style. I can't be bothered with it, I go straight for the machine language basics. Which means that once I've done something, anybody else has a hell of a time untangling my work. They say a camel is a horse put together by a committee—well, I'm a one-man committee; both a blessing and a curse, as my boss once told me . . . And so was the state of this machine's software. Maybe it had been a security measure: nothing was where it logically belonged, it was buried under piles of unrelated data. It was like creeping through the back rooms of some reclusive trash fetishist's castle, stacked to the ceiling with junk and old news printouts. And somehow I had to tunnel through it all to the control room, the castle keep, where he kept the supervisor programs that would let me manipulate to my heart's content.

And then, with a sudden rush of triumph, I realized my wish had been granted. Doctors bury their mistakes, and so do programmers, if they're lucky . . . but somebody's luck had just run out. I'd already passed up several obvious errors in the system, because they were just too obvious. But this time I'd found an inconsistency that was utterly inconsequential—and I could use its existence to draw out the supervisor's error-handling routines. They would drop the drawbridge for me, taking me for a Noble Programmer, and I would be *in—deep trouble.* Circuits closed, contacts were frozen, the guards moved in on me with swords drawn . . . I'd rung the bell. I'd walked straight into a security trap, and now I was—

Who are you? an incredulous voice demanded.

Going crazy? I shook my head like a stunned cat. *Did I hear—?*

You're trapped, Ethan Ring. You won't escape. I've been waiting for you. . . .

Voices. Now I knew how Joan of Arc felt.

Tell me who and what you are—

My first thought was that I'd inadvertently created another monster, brought this system to life, somehow, too. But I'd never heard *voices.* Even ETHANAC had only been semirational for his first few hours. . . . "W-who are *you?*" I subvocalized the thought, feebly defiant.

I am Korram Kabir.

So that was it: A megalomaniac computer, believing it was its own creator . . . . *Or was it—?* Was it possible, could it really be true? Had this crazy-quilt system been sentient all along; had someone actually succeeded in achieving the impossible . . . turning a human mind, or personality, into software—?

Exactly, the self-satisfied voice in my head said; the feel of telepathic speech was like the irritating tickle that catches in your throat and won't let you cough.

So at last I could put all those rumors to rest. Khorram Kabir wasn't senile or dead. Oh, no—he was alive and well, and living in a computer. He had literally become a nonperson, he had retired from the world and cast off his mortal body in the most genuine sense. His mortal body. . . . If this was Khorram Kabir, then who was that stranger I'd seen tonight—?

As if on cue, a voice behind me said, "Well, Mr. Ring. What a pleasant surprise."

Turning my head at that point was the most difficult thing I'd ever done in my life. Because I already knew that strangled rabbit voice could only belong to one man. . . . I looked around at him.

For once in my life, why couldn't I have been wrong? Salad stood across the room, helmet in hand, his bald head gleaming like the deadly satisfaction in his eyes.

I leaped up out of the chair, trying to pull ETHAN-AC's jack free from the panel. But I couldn't get it loose, Kabir had locked it into the console. I stood there tugging at it, the boy at the dike with his finger stuck, "Come on, dammit, let go of me!"

Salad leered at me in silent appreciation, and then he pulled out the gun.

I froze, caught with my pants down and my hand in the cookie jar. "I know what this looks like, I know what you're thinking, but actually I was only, I mean I really—"

The gun spat once, inaudibly, and something hit my knee like an invisible ax. I collapsed into the seat with a cry of heartfelt agony, clutching my leg in disbelief.

"I'm so glad it was you, Mr. Ring," Salad said congenially. "After you betrayed our agreement. After you caused so much damage at the hotel. After you left without paying for any of it. . . ." He broke into a smile that would have done justice to a homicidal maniac. "Well, now you're going to pay for it all, Mr. Ring. Because Mr. Kabir still wants to know who hired you. And I'm going to make you tell me who it was. . . . But please don't tell me too soon; that spoils the fun. And besides, it won't do you a bit of good—" Any minute he was going to be drooling. He lifted the gun again.

"Oh, my God," I moaned, too dazed to think straight. "Oh, my God. Help me, Kabir, please, you don't want to feel him do this to me! Stop him, you can make him stop—!" I don't know where the inspiration came from, but it must have been heaven-sent.

Because the screen in front of me lit up in ten-centimeter letters: "SALAD, STOP."

"Look!" I babbled, patting the screen frantically. "Look, look—"

Salad lowered his gun, and his eyes widened fractionally. They narrowed again. "This is a trick. You tampered—"

"It's no trick!" It's hard to shout through clenched teeth.

"Salad"—new lettering, smaller—"this is Kabir." A code sequence printed out. "I want to question this man myself, in my own way. You will not touch him unless I give the order. Understood?"

"But you said—" Salad lowered the gun all the way, looking incredulous. "Understood, sir. I didn't know you could—hear, sir."

"There are a lot of things you don't know about me, Salad," the screen said. "And you never will."

Including the fact that Kabir was reading my mind. . . . *So you throw yourself on my mercy, Ethan Ring?* His electronic telepathy formed words in my mind at the speed of thought; the screen went blank.

Yes, Mr. Kabir, I thought dutifully. *Thank you, sir.* If my voice could have shaken, it would have.

It's a long time since I've—felt pain, Ring. I had forgotten how much I disliked it. . . .

You're not the only one. I glanced down at my soggy pants leg, and wondered if he wanted to remember how it felt to be violently ill. *ETHANAC, help me out—* I felt a slight buzz begin inside my head as he damped out the pain receptors. *Whew*—my mind began to clear—*that's got it.*

And we're back to my first question, which you still haven't answered, Ring: Who are you, and what are you? Are you man, or machine? I've never had contact with something like you before. I didn't know such a creature even existed.

The feel of the conscious thought, I realized, was Arabic. I switched into it ingratiatingly. *It's mutual, sir. And I'm both. A man sitting at your terminal, a machine plugged into it; a mind made up of both.* I made my three color analogy for him.

A true symbiosis! How did it happen? Who made you what you are? Tell me about yourself— I felt a peculiarly poignant eagerness fill my mind.

It all started about a year ago. . . . And for the second time in a couple of days I found myself taking a trip down memory lane, at the behest of an offer I couldn't refuse. . . . *And I came to Mars as a crate of bologna. I've worked here in the Arab territories about a year, doing software maintenance.*

Naturally. I swear there was a chuckle. *Now, tell me how you came to be in your present fix—*

I jammed the memory with a burst of static, before he could read too much. *Sorry. That's classified.*

I can make you tell me. Or Salad can—

Oh, no— I glanced at Salad, waiting there like a vulture, complete with shiny skull; my panic rose again.

Don't panic, Ring. You're much too interesting to me for me to waste you on such an inconsequential matter. Particularly since you've failed at whatever it was you were trying to do to me.

Relief and then dismay replaced my incipient horror. I had failed, ETHANAC had failed, this system had been too smart for us. I wondered whether ETHANAC would have won, if he'd been joined to the superior human mind that should have been his partner. . . . It left me feeling oddly dizzy and drained. Something warm and wet was collecting down inside my right boot. *Thanks, I think.*

You fascinate me, Ring. And you fill me with envy.

I do?

Yes. There are some things even I can't control. You have the five things I can never buy, with all my wealth—the five human senses. I can't really see you, or anything else. I can't hear or touch or taste or smell. And I can't go back . . . my body is dead and buried. This is the closest I've come—this brief sharing of your own senses—to the outside world in thirteen years. Allah, you don't know how much it means to me to have discovered that you exist! And you're the only one?

The only one I know of. I was surprised at the emotion that filled me then, especially that it was all my

own. I realized how well ETHANAC understood what
he was saying.

*As I am the only one. The only Khorram Kabir; the
man who may live forever. I control an empire. . . .
but I can't touch it. I can't see my beloved Xanadu—*

*Then why? Why did you . . . do this to yourself?
Everyone believes you wanted to get away from all that,
that you didn't want anything to do with the world any
more.*

*I was sick, my health was going. But I didn't want to
lose control. I became a "recluse" to set the stage for
this transformation—and it was successful. Only Khorram Kabir could control the resources to achieve what I
have become. . . . And now that I have it, I'll never
give it up, I'll keep control of my empire in a way that
no ruler before me ever managed to do!*

I fought down the overwhelming flood of raw ambition that tried to swallow me then, the way it had already swallowed a sixth of the people on Earth—*But
you'll never see it rain again, or drink the Milk of Paradise, or touch and be touched by a beautiful woman!*
. . . I felt the force break and drain away, leaving me
weak. I put my hand over my wrist and slumped back
in the chair, *Oh, Hana, think of poor Ethan tonight. . . .*
I remembered Kabir's presence in my mind, like a
voyeur, and tried to control myself. For some reason it
was getting hard to keep my mind on the subject, whatever it was . . . *was it Hana—?*

Hana—? Kabir's emotion backed up into my own
again, making it suddenly so unbearable that I almost
cried . . . or he did. I'd fed emotions into a computer
before, but I'd never had them come back at me like
this, until I couldn't tell them from my own. I couldn't
tell them from my own.

And all at once he wasn't the master of the world
playing blind man's bluff inside my head any more. He
was just a lonely old man shut away in an institution,
trying desperately to keep in touch with life. And suddenly I felt very sorry for him, and it was easy to let
him see Hana as I'd first seen her, in the black light
glow of the underworld, and in the Peacock Lounge at
the Xanadu. And to remember eating and drinking and

sharing the rain. . . . *rain, rain, go away . . . come again some other day. . . .*

Ring! Are you all right?

Huh? I found myself lying face down across the keyboard, trying to remember how it had happened. *Oh . . . sorry.* I pushed myself up with rubber arms, and flopped back in the seat again.

What's the matter with you? It was somewhere between indignant and appalled.

My lower leg was soaking wet. *I think . . . I've sprung a leak.* Which for some reason struck me so funny that I started to laugh. *It's not funny! It's not funny!* And suddenly it wasn't, and the idea of being forced to sit here and reminisce until I bled to death made me feel very cold and frightened.

Forgive me, Ring. I didn't realize . . . I didn't mean for this to happen. This has meant so much to me—

Poor man, I thought thickly. *Poor Khorram Kabir, you poor bastard, you only want what I wanted . . . what we all want . . . freedom, that's all they want; the right to lead their own lives . . . touch each other . . . watch it rain. . . . But you won't let them have what they want . . . and you can't have it either, so what's the point, you poor bastard? How it must hurt to live with so much sadness. . . .* I touched the screen's blind eye maudlinly, leaving a red spot; overwhelmed by misery and regret and not sure who it belonged to.

Stop it, Ring! For God's sake— It was like a slap in the face.

I jerked awake again, and took a deep breath.

What is it you want of me? Why did you come here?

A keyhole, I thought, *I want to plant a lousy keyhole in your system for somebody,* managing not to remember who. *Some people who want to be free.*

All right, then. Do it.

What?

Do it. I won't stop you.

Was I really hearing that? *Why?*

Because you had pity on me, Ring. . . . Everyone feels sorry for the people a tyrant oppresses. But very few feel sorry for the way he oppresses himself. You feel sorry for us all . . . and for that I am in your debt. You almost make me feel that such nobility of purpose deserves to be rewarded— He drew back, like a snapping turtle pulling back into its shell. *But I'm still a businessman, Ring. So I'll make you a deal. You're the only man in the solar system who can give me what I really want. I want to be able to see through your eyes, and I want to find out what kind of man you really are. The keyhole will remain open as long as you come here, once a month, and let me do that.*

I kept my attention focused on the words with a supreme effort of will. *It's a deal! I'll come back; if I ever . . . get out of here alive, that is—*

I'll see that you do. Plant your keyhole. I won't stop you.

The system called off its guards, raised its hands, dropped its drawbridges . . . ETHANAC made the changes in less time than it took to think about it. *So simple . . .*

Goodbye, then, Ring. Or au revoir. Take care of yourself—you belong to me. A ghost of a chuckle, and then there was no one in my mind but me.

"SALAD" appeared on the screen again, and the most beautiful words I'd ever seen: "Get Mr. Ring to the hospital immediately."

Salad pushed away from the manuscript table where he'd been perched patiently, and stared at the message, and at me: the chief executioner, who'd just been told the king had outlawed capital punishment. "Yes, Mr. Kabir—"

" 'Curfew shall not ring tonight,' Salad." I grinned a sickly imitation of bravado. It took all the strength I had to pull ETHANAC's jack loose from the panel; even though no one was stopping me, this time. I switched off the terminal, leaving us in sudden darkness.

Salad produced a flashlight before I could find my own, thoughtfully turned it on me as I pulled myself up out of my seat . . . the sort of light they shine into your eyes when they're giving you the third degree. My boot squelched nauseatingly when I put my weight on the injured leg, and the pain level shot up. ETHANAC blanked it out again obligingly, but I wondered whether I was going to do any permanent damage. My head felt like a tethered balloon. "Give me a hand, Salad. I think you've disqualified me from the standing broad jump."

He crossed the room, still using the flashlight to maximum bad effect, and held out his hand. I reached out, took it, and shifted my weight. Salad released his grip with a slight jerk, and let me fall flat on my face.

I slowly untangled myself in the pool of light, and squinted up at him. I couldn't see his expression, which may have been just as well.

"Oh. Sorry, Mr. Ring . . . but I'm afraid I can't help you."

"What do you mean—?" That didn't come out sounding the way I'd intended it to. "Kabir . . . ordered you to help me, damn it!"

"No, Mr. Ring," he said gently. "He told me to take you to the hospital. And I will, if you can get to my 'copter unaided. You see, he also told me not to touch you unless he said it was all right. And he never did."

"You know that's . . . what he meant!"

"I always obey his orders explicitly. To the letter. That's why he trusts me." The darkness grinned mockingly.

"He's not going to . . . trust you if I'm . . . not here again in a month. He wants to see me—" I tried to get up, without much luck.

"Pathetic, Mr. Ring."

"It's true! Call him . . . ask him—"

"You're wasting time, Mr. Ring. Every minute you sit there objecting you bleed a little more."

It finally sank through my thickening head that that was the whole point of the game. I began to understand the horror behind the term "cat and mouse." I got all the way to my feet this time, using fury as a crutch, and made it past the curtained doorway, through the prayer chapel, to the church entrance.

The distance across the moonlit courtyard to the dome's airlock seemed to stretch like a topologist's nightmare: 50 meters . . . 500 . . . 5,000. I kept getting lost; or maybe it only seemed that way. There wasn't a sign of another human being now—and that included what followed me, holding a flashlight. I didn't suppose it would do any good to shout for help, even in Ge'ez, under the circumstances. *God helps those who help themselves.*

But we reached the airlock at last, my shadow and I. I was still in the spotlight; too preoccupied now to be embarrassed by the humiliating loss of privacy. And the light reminded me, inadvertently, that I wasn't wearing an O_2 breather: The monks were an orderly order, and theirs gleamed like a row of little angels beside the airlock's inner door. I stole one without the slightest regret. I turned the wheel on the airlock door, gasping like a fish out of water, and with the last of my strength gave Salad the finger as we stepped inside.

But as the lock cycled, I realized that even my determination to beat him at his own game wasn't going to be enough. I was disassociating, coming apart . . . a dust storm was rising inside my head . . . red dust. . . . The outer door swung open, and the incredible cold of the Martian night hit me like a fist. *ETHANAC! I'm goin' under—catch me.* . . .

IT'S ALL RIGHT, MICHAEL. LET GO: I HAVE YOU. . . . NO COLD. NO PAIN. DROPPING CIRCULATION TO MAINTENANCE IN UPPER BODY: REDIRECT OXYGEN TO MOBILE LIMBS. SQUINT YOUR EYES. STEP FORWARD, THROUGH THE DOOR. STEP HIGHER! BALANCE. STEP AGAIN . . . AGAIN . . . VEHICLE TO THE LEFT. STEADY . . . COMPENSATE. MOVE YOUR FEET. WATCH SALAD—DON'T LET HIM TRIP YOU. KEEP BREATHING! WAIT: TWO VEHICLES. TWO? WHICH ONE—? "Salad . . . which one!" BUT HE CAN'T HEAR ME. WAIT FOR HIM. WAIT. HE'LL USE THE LIGHT—HANG ON, MICHAEL.

MORE LIGHT: FIGURES, TWO, COMING TOWARD ME. WHO—? NO, DON'T FALL DOWN! BRACE YOUR LEGS. MOVE YOUR FEET. HAVE TO GET PAST THEM. HAVE TO—

"Ring! Is that you, Ring?"

"Salad, drop it! I've got you covered. Drop it!"

VOICES: NTEBE, KRAUS. . . . HOW—? NO, CAN'T STOP, NOT YET. NOT YET. . . . ALMOST SAFE.

"Ring, old man! You're all right!" VOICE: NTEBE. "We were afraid we'd come too late—"

"What did you do to him, Salad? What's the matter with him?" VOICE: KRAUS.

" 'Copter . . . get to the 'copter."

"I have no idea, gentlemen. I caught him threatening Mr. Kabir. That's an illegal act. You're aiding a criminal. That's illegal, too." VOICE: SALAD.

"That's a matter of opinion." VOICE: KRAUS.

" 'Copter . . . let go of me—" PANTS LEG FROZEN STIFF. LEG NOT RESPONDING. DON'T FALL. DON'T FALL—

"Oops! Hang on, Ring, I've got you." VOICE: NTEBE. HANDS, ARMS, SUPPORT— "Hana's waiting with the 'copter. We'll get you out of here. Come on, Kraus."

"I've got both these guns on you, Salad. Don't try anything stupid." VOICE: TWO-GUN KRAUS.

"For pity's sake, Kraus, will you come on! Give me a hand here, he's a dead weight." VOICE: NTEBE.

"More than you know, hopefully." VOICE: SALAD. "He's failed, you've all failed. FTI will regret this—"

"Having a good law firm means never having to say you're sorry." VOICE: NTEBE. "Goodbye, Salad. Don't think it's been fun."

MORE HANDS. HELICOPTER COMING UP: GOOD, YES. . . . GOOD HANDS. GOOD GUYS. GOOD RIDDANCE, SALAD—

"Ethan. Ethan—" VOICE: TAKHASHI. "Hurry up— watch his head, Basil!" DOOR SEALING. SAFE NOW. RELAX. . . . "What's wrong with him, what happened? I *knew* it, I knew something was wrong. . . . No, you pressurize, get us up out of here, Basil. Watch out for the downdrafts. Ethan's mine, leave him to me. . . . God, he's cold as a witch's tit; turn up the heat, too. And get out the first-aid kit, Cephas, we'll—we'll need bandages, when he thaws out. . . . Ethan, can you hear me? Can you hear me?"

WARM ARMS TIGHTENING. . . . NICE. CABIN PRESSURIZED—BREATHE DEEP, MICHAEL. . . . "No."

"No?" VOICE: TAKHASHI. "Yarrow—?"

"No."

"ETH—ETHANAC?" VOICE: TAKHASHI.

"Yes."

"My God, he's on autopilot." VOICE: NTEBE.

"Are they—coming back, ETHANAC? They are all right—" VOICE: TAKHASHI . . . UNSTEADY.

BLOOD OXYGEN RISING. RESTORE CIRCULATION . . . INTERFERENCE . . . long tunnels . . . *help* . . . *hell . . . hello? Where's my body. . . .*

WELCOME BACK, MICHAEL, EVERYTHING'S JUST WHERE IT OUGHT TO BE. . . . Breathing pure oxygen under normal pressure was as good as a transfusion. "Brr. H-hold me tight . . . and we will be, Lady Luck," I mumbled, clutching my oxygen mask.

"Are you sure that's the computer?" Ntebe leaned across my legs and peered at me. Beyond him I could see Orion dressed in his starry Sunday best, peeking in through the heavy window glass. I couldn't quite grin at him.

"Doesn't matter . . . we all . . . feel the same way about it." I blinked; the frost was melting off my eyelashes and into my eyes. "You've got your keyhole, Ntebe. Salad . . . lost every bet, tonight."

"Wonderful—!" But he glanced down at my leg, and his face turned grimly glum. "And you lost over a liter of blood. . . ."

"Look on . . . the bright side. I'm still half full."

"We did it, then. We actually did it!" Kraus chortled at the controls. "We foiled two of the greatest villains in the solar system! That's an adventure too—"

"Basil," Hana said, blowing gently on my frozen fingers, "shut up."

The rest was silence.

"I'll never play the violin again, you know." I leaned on my cane at the solarium window, watching black smoke from the factory next to the hospital mushroom into the smog-brown polar air.

"You play with your feet?" Hana said.

I turned back thoughtfully. "You mean there's some other way?"

Kraus groaned.

"Who's the patient here, Kraus, you or me? I'm the only one who's supposed to be in pain." I hobbled across to join Hana at one end of the determinedly cheerful red plastic couch.

"A pain in the neck," Kraus grinned at me good-naturedly, from the other end of it.

"Speaking of which, we're still waiting for Salad's legal ax to fall, on FTI, or at least on us. Somehow I don't think he'll have the nerve to try it—" Ntebe raised his eyebrows. Across the room one of the other patients shouted, "Gin!" and tossed down cards. For some reason, none of them would play with me any more.

"If anybody gets the ax, it'll be the headsman," I said. "And I'm looking forward to delivering the *coup de grâce* . . . I don't think Khorram Kabir will be amused at what happened to me after his lights went out."

Hana put a comforting arm around my shoulders. "Khorram Kabir . . . is software. I still can't believe it. It's too incredible."

"Money can buy you anything, if you've got enough of it. Well, maybe not anything . . ." I shook my head.

"About your—deal with him, Ring." Ntebe looked back at me, hesitated. "I don't feel I have the right to ask this of you, after what you've done for us already, But if you could pay him those—visits—for even a few months. . . ."

"I plan to keep my appointments." I patted ETHANAC, nodding. "I'm not about to let all that trouble go for nothing. And besides, I want to do it. Because I understand what it means, not to be—" I glanced down at the dusty plastic plant in a pot beside me, remembering. *You belong to me, Ring* . . . for a minute, I wondered just exactly what Kabir had had in mind when he'd chuckled at that. But, on the other hand— "Besides, how many people get to play the Ghost of Christmas Past to the biggest Scrooge in the system? I may melt his mechanical heart yet."

Ntebe brightened. "Maybe you've got something there."

"I hope it's catching."

"My fireship." Hana kissed me on the cheek.

"Please," I said, reddening. "Do that again."

"Well. Yes." Ntebe stood up, clearing his throat. "Come along, Basil. Let's get ourselves a cup of tea or something, shall we?"

"What? . . . Oh." Kraus stood up with him. "Oh." They went away quietly.

"So tell me," I held out my wrist, when we were alone at last. "What about this silver bracelet, anyway?"

She drew back. "What about it?"

"How did you know I needed you?"

She laughed. "It's a tracer. And anyway, I kept track of Salad. He followed you . . . we followed him."

"But how did you know I needed you *then*?"

The smile turned sly. "You don't really want me to tell you the truth, do you?"

I thought about that.

"I didn't think so." She touched my wrist tenderly, and glanced away.

I leaned back, letting her beautiful face fill my eyes, and said in sudden earnest, "Do I want you to predict the future—?"

She looked back at me clinically. "Well, speaking strictly as a doctor, I foresee your needing an extended period of bed rest, and some very special treatment—"

"You're not that kind of doctor!"

"It's not that kind of treatment."

Nevertheless, it worked like a charm.

The Watched

Christopher Priest

Christopher Priest has been writing a series of stories about the world of the Dream Archipelago, a planet with one huge continent in its northern hemisphere and one to the south, plus many islands between. The peoples of the two continents are at war, while the inhabitants of the archipelago try to remain neutral. Psychologically oriented readers may consider this world terribly symbolic, and they may be right, but the situation leads to stories that are intriguing on the literal level. Here, for instance, is a tale of the guilt and the obsession of one man who's caught in the middle of a situation he can't understand.

Christopher Priest is an English writer whose novels include *The Inverted World* and *The Perfect Lover*. A collection of his shorter stories, *An Infinite Summer*, was recently published.

I

Sometimes Jenessa was slow to leave in the mornings, reluctant to return to the frustrations of her job, and when she lingered in his house on these occasions Yvann Ordier had difficulty in concealing his impatience. This morning was one such, and he lurked outside the door of the shower cubicle while she bathed, fingering the smooth leather case of his binoculars.

Ordier was alert to Jenessa's every movement, each variation in sound giving him as clear a picture as there would be if the door were wide open and the plastic curtain held back: the spattering of droplets against the curtain as she raised an arm, the lowering in pitch of the hissing water as she bent to wash a leg, the fat drops plopping soapily on the tiled floor as she stood erect to shampoo her hair. He could visualize her glistening body in every detail, and thinking of their lovemaking during the night he felt a renewed lust for her.

He knew he was standing too obviously by the door, too transparently waiting for her, so he put down the binoculars case and went into the kitchen and heated some coffee. He waited until it had percolated, then left it on the hot plate. Jenessa had still not finished her shower; Ordier paused by the door of the cubicle and knew by the sound of the water that she was rinsing her hair. He could imagine her with her face uptilted toward the spray, her long dark hair plastered flatly back above her ears. She often stood like this for several minutes, letting the water run into her open mouth before dribbling away, coursing down her body; twin streams of droplets would fall from her nipples, a tiny rivulet would snake through her pubic hair, a thin film would gloss her buttocks and thighs.

Again torn between desire and impatience, Ordier went to his bureau, unlocked it, and took out his scintilla detector.

He checked the batteries first; they were sound, but he knew they would have to be replaced soon. He made frequent use of the detector because he had discovered by chance a few weeks before that his house had become infested with several of the microscopic scintillas, and since then he had been searching for them every day.

There was a signal the instant he turned on the detector, and he walked through the house listening for subtle changes in the pitch and volume of the electronic howl. He traced the scintilla to the bedroom, and by switching in the directional circuit and holding the instrument close to the floor, he found it a few moments later. It was in the carpet, near where Jenessa's clothes were folded over a chair.

Ordier parted the tufts of the carpet, and picked up the scintilla with a pair of tweezers. He took it through into his study. This was the third he had discovered this week, and although there was every chance it had been brought into the house on someone's shoes, it was nevertheless unsettling to find one. He put it on a slide, then peered at it through his microscope. There was no serial number.

Jenessa had left the shower, and was standing by the door of the study.

"What are you doing?" she said.

"Another scintilla," Ordier said. "In the bedroom."

"You're always finding them. I thought they were supposed to be undetectable."

"I've got a gadget that locates them."

"You never told me."

Ordier straightened, and turned to face her. She was naked, with a turban of golden toweling around her hair.

"I've made some coffee," he said. "Let's have it on the patio."

Jenessa walked away, her legs and back still moist from the shower. Ordier watched her, thinking of another girl, the Qataari girl in the valley, and wishing that his response to Jenessa could be less complicated. In the last few weeks she had become at once more immediate and more distant, because she aroused in him desires that could not be fulfilled by the Qataari girl.

He turned back to the microscope and pulled the slide gently away. He tipped the scintilla into a quietcase—a soundproof, lightproof box where twenty or more of the tiny lenses were already kept—then went to the kitchen. He collected the percolator and cups, and went outside to the heat and the rasping of cicadas.

Jenessa sat in the sunlight of the patio, combing the tangles from her long, fine hair. As the sun played on her, the water dried, and she talked of her plans for the day.

"There's someone I'd like you to meet," she said. "He's coming to dinner this evening."

"Who is he?" Ordier said, disliking any interruption of his routine.

"A colleague. He's just arrived from the north." Jenessa was sitting with the sun bright behind her, outlining her bronzed body. She was at ease when naked; beautiful and sexual and aware of it.

"What's he here for?"

"To try to observe the Qataari. He knows the difficulties, apparently, but he's been given a research grant. I suppose he should be allowed to spend it."

"But why should I have to meet him?"

Jenessa reached across, took his hand briefly. "You don't have to . . . but I'd like him to meet you."

Ordier was stirring the sugar in the bowl, watching it heap and swirl like a viscid liquid. Each of the grains was larger than a scintilla, and a hundred of the tiny lenses scattered in the sugar would probably go unnoticed. How many scintillas were left in the dregs of coffee cups, how many were accidentally swallowed?

Jenessa lay back across the lounger, and her breasts flattened across her chest. Her nipples were erect and she had raised a leg, knowing that he was admiring her.

"You like to stare," she said, giving him a shrewd look from her dark-set eyes, and she turned toward him on her side, so that her large breasts appeared to fill again. "But you don't like being watched, do you?"

"What do you mean?"

"The scintillas. You're very quiet whenever you find one."

"Am I?" Ordier said, not aware that Jenessa had been noticing. He always tried to make light of them. "There are so many around . . . all over the island. There's no evidence anyone's planting them."

"You don't like finding them, though."

"Do you?"

"I don't look for them."

In common with most of the people who lived on the islands of the Dream Archipelago, Ordier and Jenessa did not speak very often of their past lives. In the islands, past and future were effectively suspended by the Covenant of Neutrality. The future was sealed, as were the islands themselves, for until the conclusion of the war on the southern continent no one was permitted to leave the Archipelago; no one, that is, except the crews of ships and the troops of both combatant sides who constantly passed through. The future of the islands

would be determined by the war, and the war was inde-
terminate; it had continued, without a break, for more
than two centuries, and was as entrenched now as it had
been fifty years before.

With a sense of future removed, the past became irrelevant, and those who came to the Archipelago,
choosing the permanence of neutrality, made a conscious decision to abandon their former lives. Yvann
Ordier was one amongst thousands of such émigrés; he
had never told Jenessa how he had made his fortune,
how he had paid for his passage to the Archipelago. All
he had told her was that he had been prodigiously successful in business, enabling him to take an early retirement.

She, for her part, spoke little of her background, although Ordier realized this was a characteristic of native islanders, rather than a desire to forget a doubtful
past. He knew she had been born on the island of
Lanna, and that she was an anthropologist attempting,
unsuccessfully, to study the refugee Qataari.

What Ordier did not want to reveal to Jenessa was
how he came to possess a scintilla detector.

He did not want to speak of past nefariousness, nor
of his role in the planned proliferation of the scintilla
surveillance lenses. A few years before, when he had
been more opportunistic to a degree that now alienated
him from the memory of his younger self, Ordier had
seen the chance to make a great deal of money, and he
had taken the chance unscrupulously. At that time, the
war on the southern continent had settled into an expensive and attritional impasse, and the enterprises sections of the armed forces had been raising money by
unconventional means. One of these was the selling of
commercial franchises to some of their hitherto classified equipment; Ordier, with a ruthlessness that shocked
him in retrospect, had obtained exploitation rights to
the scintillas.

His formula for success was simple: he sold the scintillas to one side of the market, and the detectors to the
other. Once the potential of the miniature transmitters
had been recognized, his fortune had been assured.
Soon Ordier was selling more scintillas than the army

ordnance factories could produce, and demand continued to rise. Although Ordier's organization remained the prime distributor of the scintillas and their computerized image-retrieval equipment, unauthorized copies were soon available on the underground market. Within a year of Ordier opening his agency, the saturation distribution of the scintillas meant that no room or building was closed to the eyes and ears of one's rivals. No one ever found a way of jamming the tiny transmitters; no one ever knew for sure just who was watching and listening.

For the next three and a half years, Ordier's personal fortune had been amassed. During the same period, paralleling his rise in wealth, a deeper sense of moral responsibility grew in him. The way of life in the civilized northern continent had been permanently changed: scintillas were used in such profusion that nowhere was entirely free of them. They were in the streets, in the gardens, in the houses. Even in the erstwhile privacy of one's bed one never knew for sure that a stranger was not listening, watching, recording.

At last, with the guilt of his participation overwhelming any other motivation, Ordier took himself and his fortune to the permanent exile of the Dream Archipelago, knowing that his departure from the world of eavesdropping commerce would make not the slightest difference to its accelerating growth, but that he wanted no more part in it.

He chose the island of Tumo more or less at random, and he built his house in the remote eastern part, well away from the populous mountainous region in the west . . . but even on Tumo there were scintillas. Some were from the armies, in breach of the Covenant; a few were from commercial companies; and some, most numerous, were uncoded and thus untraceable.

Jenessa was right when she said that he did not like to find scintillas in his house, but those were an intrusion on his own privacy; he gave no thought to the ones scattered over the rest of the island. For the past two years he had tried, with a considerable measure of success, to put the scintillas from his mind.

His life now was centered on Jenessa, on his house,

on his growing collections of books and antiques. Until the beginning of this island summer he had felt reasonably happy, relaxed and coming to terms with his conscience. But at the end of the Tufoit spring, with the first spell of hot weather, he had made a certain discovery, and as a result an obsession had grown within him.

It was focused on the bizarre, castellated folly that was built on the ridge on the eastern border of his grounds. There, in the sun-warmed granite walls, was his obsession. There was the Qataari girl, the Qataari ritual; there he listened and watched, as hidden from those he observed as the men who decoded the mosaic of images from the ubiquitous scintillas.

II

Jenessa lounged in the sun and drank her coffee, and then poured herself a second cup. She yawned and lay back in the sun, her hair dry now and shining in the light. Ordier wondered if she was intending to stay all day, as she sometimes did. He enjoyed their lazy days together, alternating between swimming in the pool, love-making, and sunbathing . . . but the previous evening she had been talking of spending the day in Tumo Town, and he was uncertain of her intentions. At last, though, she went into the bedroom to dress, and afterwards they walked together down to her car. There were last words and kisses, and then she drove away.

Ordier stood idly by the grove of trees on the edge of his grounds, waiting to wave to her as she turned from the track to the main road leading toward Tumo Town. The brisk wind of the evening before had died, and the cloud of white dust thrown up by the wheels hovered behind the car . . . and long after Jenessa had passed from sight, Ordier stared after her. She sometimes returned unexpectedly.

When the dust had settled, and his view across to the distant white buildings of the town was interrupted by nothing more than the shimmering of early heat, Ordier turned back to his house and walked up the slope to the main door.

Once inside the house he made no attempt to conceal

the impatience he had been suppressing while Jenessa was there. He hurried to his study and found his binoculars, then went through the house and left by the door which opened on the rough ground behind. A short walk took him to the high stone wall that ran laterally across the ridge, and he unlocked the padlock on the stout wooden gate and let himself through. Beyond was a sandy, sun-whitened courtyard, surrounded on all sides by walls, and already hot in the windless day. Ordier made sure that the gate was locked on the inside, then climbed steadily up the slope toward the angular height of the battlemented folly on the summit of the ridge.

It was this folly and its walled courtyard that Ordier had first chanced upon, and with the same recklessness of spirit of the madman who had built it three centuries before, he bought it and the land around it after the most cursory of inspections. Only later, when the headiness of the purchase had faded, had he taken a second, calmer look at his new property and realized that the place was completely uninhabitable. So, not without regret, he had hired a local firm of builders, and his house had been put up a short distance away.

The ridge that marked the eastern boundary of his property ran due north and south for several miles, and for most of its length it was unscalable, except by someone equipped with climbing boots and ropes. It was not so much that it was high—on the side facing Ordier's house it rose on average about two hundred feet above the plain—but that it was broken and jagged, and the rocks were sharp and friable. In the geophysical past there must have been a tumultuous upheaval, compressing and raising the land along some deep-lying fault, the crust snagging upwards like two sheets of brittle steel rammed against each other's edge.

It was on the summit of this ridge that the folly had been built, although at what expense in human life and ingenuity Ordier could not imagine. It balanced on the broken rocks, a daring edifice, and a tribute to the singularity and eccentricity of its architect.

When Ordier had seen and bought the folly, the valley that lay beyond it had been a wide tract of desert land, muddy and overgrown with rank vegetation, or cracked, barren, and dusty, according to the season. But that had been before the coming of the Qataari, and all that that had entailed.

A flight of steps had been built across the inner wall of the folly, leading eventually to the battlements. Before Ordier had moved into his house, he paid the builders to reinforce most of the steps with steel and concrete, but the last few had been left unrepaired. The battlements could be reached, but only with great difficulty.

About halfway up, well before the last of the reinforced steps, Ordier reached the fault that had been contrived carefully inside the main wall.

He glanced back, staring down from his vertiginous perch across the land beneath. There was his house, its evenly tiled roofs glittering in the sunlight; beyond, the untamed stretch of scrubland, and beyond that the buildings of Tumo Town, a sprawling modern settlement built on the ruins of the seaport that had been sacked at the outbreak of the war. In the far distance were the brown and purple heights of the Tumoit Mountains, rich in the mythology of the Dream Archipelago.

To north and south Ordier could see the splendent silver of the sea. Somewhere to the north, on the horizon, was the island of Muriseay, invisible today because of the haze.

Ordier turned away from the view, and stepped through into the fault in the wall, squeezing between two overlapping slabs of masonry which, even on close inspection, seemed to be so solidly in place that nothing could lie behind them. But there was a warm, dark space beyond, high enough and wide enough for a man to stand. Ordier wriggled through the gap, and stood inside on the narrow ledge, breathing quickly after his climb.

The brilliant sunshine outside had dulled his eyes, and the tiny space was a cell of blackness. The only light came from a horizontal crack in the outer wall, a slit of shining sky that seemed, in contrast with the rest, to darken, not lighten, the cell.

When his breathing had steadied, Ordier stepped forward onto the ledge where he generally stood, feeling with his foot for the slab of rock. Beneath him was the inner cavity of the wall, falling irregularly to the foundations far below. He braced himself with his elbow against the wall as he transferred his weight, and at once a sweet fragrance reached his nostrils. As he brought his second foot onto the slab he glanced down, and saw in the dim light a pale, mottled coloring on the ledge.

The smell was distinctive: Qataari roses. Ordier remembered the hot southerly wind of the day before—the Naalattan, as it was called on Tumo—and the whirling vortex of light and color that had risen above the valley floor, as the fragrant petals of the Qataari roses had scattered and circled. Many of the petals had been lifted by the wind as high as his vantage point here in the cell, and some had seemed to hover within grasping distance of his fingers. He had had to leave his hidden cell to meet Jenessa, and he had not seen the end of the warm blizzard of petals before he left.

The fragrance of the Qataari rose was known to be narcotic, and the cloying smell released as his feet crushed the petals was sweet in his nose and mouth. Ordier kicked and scuffed at the petals that had been blown onto the shelf, and swept them down into the cavity of the wall.

At last he leaned forward to the slit that looked outward into the valley; here too the wind had deposited a few petals, and Ordier brushed them away with his fingers, careful that they fell into the cavity beneath him, and not out into the open air.

He raised his binoculars to his eyes, and leaned forward until the metal hoods over the object-lenses rested on the stone edge of the horizontal slit. With rising excitement, he stared down at the Qataari in the valley below.

III

In the evening, Ordier drove over to Jenessa's apartment in Tumo Town. He went reluctantly, partly because of the necessity of making civil conversation with strangers—something he was habitually unwilling to do—and partly because he had more than a suspicion that the talk would center around the Qataari refugees. Jenessa had said that her visitor was a colleague, which meant that he was an anthropologist, and anthropologists only came to Tumo to study the Qataari. Since his discovery in the folly, Ordier found all discussion of the Qataari unbearably unpleasant, as if some private domain was being invaded. For this and other reasons, Ordier had never told Jenessa what he knew.

The other guests had already arrived when Ordier walked in, and Jenessa introduced them as Jacj and Luovi Parren. His first impression of Parren was unfavorable: he was a short, overweight, and intense man who shook Ordier's hand with nervous, jerky movements, then turned away at once to continue the conversation with Jenessa that Ordier's arrival had interrupted. Normally, Ordier would have bridled at the snub, but Jenessa flashed him a soothing look, and anyway he was in no mood to try to like the man.

He poured himself a drink and went to sit beside Luovi, Parren's wife.

During the aperitifs and meal, the conversation stayed on general subjects, with the islands of the Archipelago the main topic. Parren and his wife had only just arrived from the north, and were anxious to hear what they could about various islands where they might make a home. The only islands they had so far seen were Muriseay—which was where most immigrants arrived—and Tumo.

Ordier noticed that when he and Jenessa were talking about the other islands they knew, it was Luovi who showed the most interest, and she kept asking how far they were from Tumo.

"Jacj must be near his work," she said to Ordier.

"I think I told you, Yvann," Jenessa said. "Jacj is here to study the Qataari."

"Yes, of course."

"I know what you're thinking, Ordier," Parren said. "Why should I succeed where others have failed? Let me just say this, that I wouldn't have left the mainland to pursue something I thought was an insurmountable problem. There are ways that haven't been tried yet."

"We were talking about this before you arrived," Jenessa said to Ordier. "Jacj believes he can do better than us."

"How do you feel about that?" Ordier said.

Jenessa shrugged, and looked at Jacj and his wife. "I don't have any personal ambition."

"Ambition, Jenessa dear, is the foundation of achievement." Luovi's smile across the table, first at Jenessa, then at Ordier, was brittle.

"For a social anthropologist?" Ordier said.

"For all scientists. Jacj has taken leave from a brilliant career to study the Qataari. But of course you would know his work already."

"Naturally."

Ordier was wondering how long it would be before Parren, or his wife, discovered that one never took "leave" to visit the Archipelago. Spitefully, it amused Ordier to think that Luovi probably imagined, in anticipation of her husband's success, that completed research into the Qataari society would buy them a ticket back to the north, where the brilliant career would be resumed. The islands were full of exiles who had once nurtured similar illusions.

Ordier was looking covertly at Jenessa, trying to divine how she was taking all this. She had spoken truly when she denied personal ambition, but that was not the whole story.

Because Jenessa was Archipelago-born she had a sense of nationalism, embracing all the islands, that Ordier himself lacked. She had sometimes talked of the history of the Archipelago, of the distant years when the Covenant of Neutrality had first come into being. A few of the islands had put up resistance to the enforced neutralization; for some years there had been a unity of purpose, but the big northern nations had eventually overcome the resistance. The whole Archipelago was said to be pacified now, but contact between the islands, for most of the ordinary inhabitants, was restricted to the mail the ferries carried, and one never knew for sure just what was happening in the remoter areas of the Archipelago. Occasionally there were rumors of sabotage on one or another of the islands, or of the armies' rest-camps being attacked, but on the whole everyone was waiting for the war to end.

Jenessa did have a purpose to her work, although it was not of the same order as Jacj Parren's aggressive aspiration to fame. Ordier knew that she, and other island-born scientists, saw knowledge as a key to freedom, that when the war was over such knowledge would help liberate the Archipelago. She had no illusions about the immediate worth of her own calling—without access to the culturally dominant societies of the north, whatever research she concluded would be futile—but it was scientific knowledge nonetheless.

"Where do you fit into all this, Yvann?" Parren was saying. "You're not an anthropologist, I gather?"

"That's correct. I'm retired."

"So young?"

"Not so young as it appears."

"Jenessa was telling me you live up by the Qataari valley. I don't suppose it's possible to see their camp from there?"

"You can climb the rocks," Ordier said. "I'll take you up there, if you like. But you wouldn't see anything. The Qataari have guards all along the ridge."

"Ah . . . then I could see the guards!"

"Of course. But you wouldn't find it very satisfactory. As soon as they see you, they'll turn their backs."

Parren was lighting a cigar from one of the candles on the table, and he leaned back with a smile and blew smoke into the air. "A response of sorts."

"The only one," Jenessa said. "It's worthless as an observation, because it's responsive to the presence of the observer."

"But it fits a pattern."

"Does it?" Jenessa said. "How are we to know? We should be concerned with what they would do if we weren't there."

"You say that's impossible to discover," Parren said.

"And if we weren't here at all? If there was no one else on the island?"

"Now you delve into the realms of fantasy. Anthropology is a pragmatic science, my dear. We are as concerned with the impact of the modern world on isolated societies as we are with the societies themselves. If we must, we intrude on the Qataari and evaluate their response to that. It is a better study than no study."

"Do you think we haven't tried that?" Jenessa said. "There is simply no point. The Qataari wait for us to leave, and wait, and wait . . ."

"Just as I said. A response of sorts."

"But a meaningless one!" Jenessa said. "It becomes a trial of patience."

"Which the Qataari must necessarily win?"

"Look, Jacj." Jenessa, visibly irritated now, was leaning forward across the table, and Ordier noticed that strands of her hair were falling across the uneaten dessert on her plate. "When the Qataari were first landed here, about eighteen months ago, a team went into the camp. We were testing exactly the kind of response you're talking about. We made no secret of our presence, nor of what we wanted. The Qataari simply waited. They sat or stood exactly wherever they were when they noticed us. They did *nothing* for seventeen days! They didn't eat, drink, speak. They slept where they were, and if that happened to be in a muddy pool, or on stones, then it made no difference."

"What about the children?"

"Children too . . . like the adults."

"And bodily functions? And what about pregnant women? Did they just sit down and wait for you to leave?"

"Yes, Jacj. In fact, it was because of two pregnant women that we called off the experiment. We were frightened of what might happen to them. As it turned out, they both had to be taken to hospital. One of them lost her child."

"Did they resist being taken away?"

"Of course not."

Luovi said: "But then surely Jacj is right? It is a social response to the outside world."

"It's no response at all!" Jenessa said. "It's the opposite of a response, it's the stopping of *all* activity. I can show you the films we took . . . the people didn't even fidget. They simply watched us, and waited for us to leave."

"Then they were in some kind of trance?"

"No, they were *waiting*!"

Watching Jenessa's animated expression, Ordier wondered if he recognized in her some of his own dilemma about the Qataari. She had always claimed that her interest in them was a scientific one, but in every other aspect of her life she was rarely detached from an emotional reaction to people. And the Qataari were special people, not just to anthropologists.

Of all the races in the world, the Qataari were simultaneously the best and the least known. There was not a nation on the northern continent that did not have an historical or social link with the Qataari. For one country there would be the story of the Qataari warriors who had come to fight for their side in some long-forgotten war; for another, there would be the heritage of public buildings or palaces built by visiting Qataari architects and masons; for yet another, there would be the tales of the Qataari doctors who had come in times of plague.

Physically, the Qataari were a beautiful people: it was said in Ordier's own country, for instance, that the model for Edrona—symbol of male potency, wisdom, and mystery, captured in a marble sculpture and famous throughout the world—had been a Qataari. Similarly, a Qataari woman, painted by Vaskarreta nine centuries before, embodied sensual beauty and virginal lust; her face, pirated in the cause of commerce, glowed out from the labels of a dozen different types of cosmetic.

Yet for all the legends and visited history, the civilized world knew almost nothing of the Qataari homeland.

The Qataari were indigenous to the southern continent, the wild tract of land where the war had been fought for the last two centuries. On the northern coast, the Qataari peninsula pointed a long, cliff-bound finger of land into the Midway Sea, seeming to stretch out to touch the more southerly islands of the Dream Archipelago. The peninsula was joined to the mainland by a narrow, swampy isthmus, and beyond that, where the first mountains rose, there always stood a line of guards . . . but guards like no other. The Qataari never tried to prevent others entering, but guarded themselves so they always had warning of the presence of outsiders. Few people, in fact, had ever been to the peninsula. The way across land was through dense jungle, and an approach from the sea was difficult because along the entire rocky coastline there was only one small jetty. The Qataari community seemed to be self-sufficient in every way, and their customs, culture, and social structure were all but unknown.

The Qataari were thought to be of unique cultural importance in the world: their society apparently represented an evolutionary link between the civilized nations of the north, the people of the Archipelago, and the barbarians and peasants of the south. Several ethnologists had visited the peninsula over the years, but all had been frustrated in their work by the same silent waiting that Jenessa had described.

Only one aspect of their life had been established, although its details were as much conjecture as knowledge: the Qataari dramatized. Aerial photographs, and the reports of visitors, revealed that there were open-air auditoria by every village, and there were always people gathered there. The speculation was that the Qataari depended on drama as a symbolic means of action: for decision-making, for the resolution of problems, for celebrations. What few pieces of Qataari literature had reached the world's libraries were baffling to a non-Qataari readership: the prose and verse were impenetrably elliptical, and any character named played a symbolic role, as well as having a seemingly endless list of contracted, familiar, or formal names, and appeared to represent a part in a scheme much larger than what could be inferred as the subject matter. The writing of theses on Qataari literature was a popular activity in northern universities.

The few Qataari who traveled, who visited the northern continent, spoke obliquely of such matters, seeing themselves as actors in a cultural play. One Qataari, in Ordier's country a few years before, had been secretly filmed while he was alone; evidently deep within a personal drama, the Qataari remonstrated with himself, declaimed to an imaginary audience, wept and shouted. A few minutes later the same man had been seen at a public reception, and no one present had discerned anything unusual about his behavior.

The war had come, inevitably, to the Qataari peninsula. It had begun when one of the two combatant sides had started the construction of a deep-water refueling base on the northernmost tip of the peninsula. As this was an area hitherto unclaimed by either side, it constituted a breach of whatever neutrality the Qataari had enjoyed until then. The opposing side had invaded the peninsula, and before long a devastating struggle had begun. Soon the Qataari knew, as the rest of their continent knew, the shattering totality of the war, with its neural dissociation gases, its scintillas, its scatterflames, its acid rains. The villages were flattened, the rose plantations burned, the people killed in thousands; in a few weeks the Qataari society was destroyed.

A relief mission was sent from the north, and within a few more weeks the surviving Qataari were evacuated unresisting from their homeland. They had been brought to Tumo—one of the islands nearest to the peninsula—and a refugee camp had been built for them. They were housed and fed by the Tumoit authorities, but the Qataari, independent as ever, did what they could to close their camp to the outside world. In the first few days huge canvas screens had been put up around the perimeter fence, silent guards stood by all the entrances. Everyone who had entered the camp since—medical teams, agricultural advisers, builders—returned with the same report: the Qataari were waiting.

It was not polite waiting, it was not impatient waiting. As Jenessa had said, it was a cessation of activity, a long silence.

Ordier realized that Jacj Parren and Jenessa were still arguing, and that Parren was addressing him:

". . . You say that if we climbed this ridge of yours, we should see guards?"

"Yes." Jenessa answered for him.

"But why are they there? I thought they never left the camp."

"They're growing roses in the valley. The Qataari roses."

Parren leaned back in his chair with a grunt of satisfaction. "Then at least they can be studied doing that!"

Jenessa looked helplessly at Ordier across the table. He stared back at her, trying not to reveal anything with his expression. He was sitting forward with his elbows on the edge of the table, his hands linked in front of his face. He had had a shower before driving to Jenessa's apartment this evening, but a certain fragrance was still on his skin. He could smell it as he looked back at her, feeling a trace of the pleasant sexual arousal that was induced by the petals of the Qataari rose.

IV

Jacj Parren and his wife were staying in an hotel in Tumo Town, and the next morning Jenessa went round to see them. Ordier left with her, and they walked together as far as his car. Their embrace in the street was cool for the benefit of passers-by; it was no reflection of the night they had passed together, which had been more than usually passionate.

Ordier drove slowly back to his house, more reluctant than he could remember to succumb to the temptations of the cell in the folly wall, but at the same time more intrigued than ever about what he might see.

The conversation over dinner had done that for him. It had reminded him of the guilty associations with Jenessa, both as a sexual partner and as someone who had a genuine scientific interest in the Qataari, that going to the folly awoke in him.

At the start he had made the excuse to himself that what he saw was so insignificant, so fragmentary, that it was irrelevant. But his knowledge of the Qataari had grown, and with it the secret . . . and a tacit bond had been tied: to speak of the Qataari would be to betray a trust he had created in his own mind.

As he parked the car and walked up to the house, Ordier added further justification to his silence by reminding himself of how much he had disliked Parren and his wife. He knew that prolonged exposure to the seductive laziness of Tumoit life, and to the laxity of the ways of the Archipelago in general, would change Parren in the end, but until then he would be an abrasive influence on Jenessa. She would seek the Qataari more eagerly, renewing her own interest in their affairs.

The house was stuffy from being closed for the night, and Ordier walked around the rooms, opening the windows, throwing back the shutters. There was a light breeze, and in the garden that he had neglected all summer the overgrown flowers and shrubs were waving gently. He stared at them, trying to make up his mind.

He knew that the dilemma was one of his own making, and could be resolved by the simple decision never to go up to the folly again; he could ignore the Qataari, could continue with his life as it had been until the beginning of this summer. But the conversation the evening before had heightened his awareness of the Qataari, reminded him of the special curiosities they aroused. It was not for nothing that the romantic and erotic impulses of the great composers, writers, and artists had been stimulated by the Qataari, that the legends and daydreams persisted, that the societies of the north had been so thoroughly permeated by the enigma that there was hardly a graffito that did not reflect it, nor a pornographic fiction that did not perpetuate it.

Voluntary abstention from his obsession was an agony to Ordier. He distracted himself for a time by taking a swim in his pool, and then later by opening one of the chests he had had sent from the mainland and setting the books on shelves in his study, but by midday the curiosity was like a nagging hunger, and he found his binoculars and walked up the ridge to the folly.

V

More petals had appeared in the cell in his absence. Ordier brushed them away from the slit with his fingers, then turned his binoculars towards the Qataari camp, which lay on the far side of the shallow valley. On this day, as on all days, the high screens surrounding it were drawn tightly together. The breeze was stirring them, and great slow ripples moved laterally across the canvas blinds. His glasses did not have the necessary magnification, but Ordier nevertheless felt a sense of intrigue, hoping that the wind would momentarily lift the skirt of screens so that he might glimpse what lay behind.

In front of the camp, spreading across the floor of the valley, was the plantation of Qataari roses: a sea of scarlet and pink and green. So closely were the bushes planted that from this elevation Ordier could see the yellow, clayey soil only at the edge of the plantation.

He stared for a few minutes, relishing the privilege he was stealing.

It was the workers in the rose plantation he had first watched from this cell. Last night, listening to the dinner conversation, he had heard Parren speak of the possibility of seeing the Qataari at work in the roses; remembering his own excitement of discovery, Ordier had for the first and only time felt a trace of sympathy with the man.

There was a small group of Qataari men standing amongst the roses and talking volubly. After a while, two of them walked away and picked up large panniers. They walked slowly between the rosebushes, plucking the largest, reddest flowers. They were quite unaware of his silent watching.

Ordier found this undetected intrusion into the Qataari privacy to be deeply exciting and satisfying.

The weeks he had been spying on the Qataari had taught him to be systematic, and Ordier looked with the binoculars at each of the rose-pickers in turn. Many of them were women, and it was at these he looked most carefully. There was one woman in particular he was seeking; she had been amongst the rose-pickers the first time he noticed her. He knew her, quite simply, as the one. He had never given her a name, not even a familiar one as shorthand for his recognition of her. She did remind him, in some ways, of Jenessa, but with the abundant opportunities he had had to watch her he now acknowledged that whatever similarities he had once discerned were the product of guilt.

She was younger than Jenessa, taller, undeniably more beautiful. Where Jenessa was dark in hair and complexion, with an attractive combination of sensuality and intelligence, the Qataari woman, the Qataari girl, had fragility and vulnerability trapped in the body of a sexually mature woman. Sometimes, when she was near the folly, Ordier had seen a captivating expression in her eyes: knowingness and hesitation, invitation and wariness. Her hair was golden, her skin was pale; she had the classic proportions of the Qataari ideal. She was, for Ordier, the embodiment of Vaskarreta's avenging victim.

And Jenessa was real, Jenessa was available. The Qataari girl was remote and forbidden, forever inaccessible to him.

When he had made sure the girl was not in the rose plantation, Ordier lowered the binoculars and leaned forward until his forehead was pressing against the rough rock slab, placing his eyes as near as possible. He looked down toward the arena the Qataari had built at the foot of the folly wall, and saw her at once.

She was standing near one of the twelve hollow metal statues that surrounded the leveled area. She was not alone—she was never alone—and the others, although apparently paying little attention to her, were circling her. They were tidying up and preparing the arena: the statues were being cleaned and polished, the gravelly soil of the arena floor was being swept, and handfuls of the Qataari rose-petals were being scattered in all directions.

The girl was watching this. She was dressed as usual in red: a long, enfolding garment that lay loosely and bulkily on her body like a toga, but which was made up of many different panels of fabric, lying one on top of the other.

Silently, slowly, Ordier raised the binoculars to his eyes, and focused them on her face. The magnification at once lent him the illusion that he was nearer to her, and as a consequence, he felt much more exposed to her.

Seeing her as closely as this, Ordier noticed at once that the garment was tied loosely at the neck, and was slipping down on one side. He could see the curve of her shoulder, and just beneath it the first hint of the rise of her breast; if she moved quickly, or leaned forward, the garment would fall away to expose her. He stared at her, transfixed by her unconscious sexuality.

There was no noticeable signal for the beginning of the ritual; the preparations led imperceptibly to the first movements of the ceremony. The two women scattering the rose petals turned from casting them across the sandy floor to throwing them over the girl. Twelve of the men, until then apparently still cleaning the statuary, pulled open the hinged backs of each figure and took up their places inside, and the remaining men began to circle the arena as the girl stepped forward to take her place at the center.

This much was familiar to Ordier; soon the chanting would begin. Each time he saw this ritual unfold, Ordier was aware that it had been minimally advanced from the time before. Each time there was a renewed sense of the dual possibilities of the girl's sexual role.

The chanting began: soft and low, inharmonious. The girl turned slowly where she stood, her garment swinging about her limbs: it slipped lower on her shoulder, and as the panels lifted Ordier saw glimpses of ankle, elbow, stomach, hip, and he knew she was naked beneath it. As she turned she was looking intently at each man in the circle, as if trying to select one.

More petals were thrown, and as the girl turned in the arena her feet trampled and crushed them. Ordier fancied he could smell them from where he stood, although he knew that the fragrance probably came from the petals he had found in the cell.

The next stage was also one Ordier had witnessed before. One of the women who had been throwing the petals suddenly tossed aside her basket and stepped directly toward the girl. As she stood before her, she raised her hands to her bodice and pulled aside the cloth to bare her own breasts. She thrust out her chest. The girl responded by raising her hands to her chest and running them tentatively and exploratively across herself. She had at once the innocence of an adolescent and the sensuality of a woman. No sooner had her hands cupped her breasts through the fabric of the toga than one of the men left the others and ran into the arena. He knocked aside the woman with the bared breasts, and she fell across the ground. He turned, and went back to his place in the circle.

The woman got to her feet, closed her bodice, and found her basket and threw more petals. A few minutes later the whole incident was repeated when the second woman went forward to the girl.

Ordier watched this happen seven or eight times, wondering, as he always wondered, where it was to lead. He was impatient for a further development, because apart from his having had the briefest glimpses of the girl's naked body accidentally revealed on occasions in the past, the ceremony had never proceeded beyond this. He lowered his binoculars and leaned forward again, watching the whole scene.

He was obsessed with the girl; in his fantasies he imagined that this ceremony took place here, beneath the wall of his folly, for his own exclusive benefit . . . that the girl was being readied in some mysterious way for him alone. But those were the fantasies of solitude; when he was here, watching the Qataari ritual, he was always aware of his role as secret intruder on their world, an observer as incapable of affecting the proceedings as the girl herself seemed to be.

Ordier's passivity, though, went only so far as a lack of direct action; in another way he became deeply involved, because as he watched he always became sexually aroused. He could feel the tightness in his groin, the swelling of physical excitement.

Suddenly the girl moved, and Ordier's attention returned. As one of the women went across to her, already pulling at the strings of her bodice, the girl moved to meet her, snatching at one of the long panels of her toga. The woman cried out, and her large, sagging breasts swung into view . . . and simultaneously the girl tore her own garment at the front, and let the cloth fall from her hands.

Ordier, looking again through his binoculars, saw an infuriatingly brief glimpse of the nakedness beneath, but then the girl turned away and her voluminous garment swung across her.

She took two steps, stumbled, and fell forward, lying across the place where the rose petals lay deepest. At this, one of the men went into the arena, brushed the woman aside, and stood over the girl. He prodded her with his foot, then pushed her, turning her over on to her back.

She appeared to be unconscious. The toga was in disarray, riding up her legs. Where she had torn part of it away a strip of diagonal nudity was revealed. It ran between her breasts, across her stomach, across one hip. Through his binoculars Ordier could see the aureole of one nipple, and a few strands of pubic hair.

The man stood over her, half crouching, rubbing his hands across his genitals.

And Ordier watched, surrendering to the exquisite excitement of sexual pleasure. As he came to physical climax, releasing wetly into his trousers, he saw through the shaking lenses of the binoculars that the girl had opened her eyes, and was staring upward with a dazed, delirious expression. She seemed to be looking directly at him . . . and Ordier moved back from the crack in the wall, ashamed and embarrassed.

VI

Two days later, Jacj and Luovi Parren came to Ordier's house in the early morning, and after they had shared a token breakfast, the two men set off toward the ridge, leaving Jenessa to entertain Luovi.

As Ordier had suggested to him the day before, Parren had equipped himself with stout boots and old clothing. They climbed roped together, but even so Parren slipped before they had gone very far. He slithered down the crumbling face of a huge boulder, brought up short as Ordier took his weight on the rope.

Ordier secured the rope, then scrambled down to him. The portly little man had regained his feet, and was looking ruefully at grazes on his arm and leg, showing through the torn cloth.

"Do you want to go on?" Ordier said.

"Of course. It's not serious." But the challenge of the climb seemed to have receded, if only temporarily, for he was in no hurry to continue. He looked to the side, where the folly loomed high on the ridge. "That's your castle, isn't it?"

"It's a folly."

"Couldn't we climb up to the battlements? It looks a lot easier that way."

"Easier," Ordier said, "but actually more dangerous. The steps are reinforced only part of the way. Anyway, you'll see better from the ridge, I assure you."

"So you have been up to the battlements?"

"Just once, the first time I came here. But I wouldn't go up there again." Ordier decided to take a chance: "But you could go alone, if you liked."

"No," Parren said, rubbing his arm. "Let's do it this way."

They struggled on, Ordier leading the way across the brittle slabs of rock. It was an ascent that would have posed no problem to practiced rock climbers, but to two amateurs it was perilous enough. Shortly before they reached the summit, Parren slipped again, and cried out as he fell backward against a boulder beneath him.

"You're making too much noise," Ordier said when he saw that the man was unhurt. "Do you want the Qataari to hear us before we reach the top?"

"You've done this before . . . It's different for you."

"I climbed alone the first time. I didn't make as much row."

"You're younger than me."

The recriminations ceased when Ordier climbed away from him, and resumed his position with the rope. He sat down on a slab and stared at Parren waiting for the climb to continue. The anthropologist continued to sulk for a few more minutes, then seemed to realize that Ordier was doing his best for him. At last he climbed up toward him, and Ordier took in the slack of the rope.

"We'll head for that dip there," Ordier said quietly, pointing up. "It was where I went last time, and if the Qataari haven't changed their guard-line you'll find that the guards are some distance away. With any luck, you'll have several minutes before they spot you."

He crawled forward, placing his feet on the best holds he could find, pointing them out mutely to the other man. At last he was lying face down across a broad slab, just beneath the summit. He waited until Parren was beside him.

"If you'll take more advice from me," Ordier whispered, "don't use your binoculars at first. Take in the general view, then use your glasses on the nearest objects."

"Why's that?"

"Once they see us the cry will go up. It radiates outward from here."

Ordier was wondering what had been going on at the arena since the day his watching had aroused him to the point of orgasm. Disturbed by the degree to which he was becoming involved in the ritual, he had kept away for two days, trying again to rid himself of his obsession. But he was failing, and this climb up the ridge was making the failure more certain.

Parren had his binoculars out, and Ordier took his own from their case.

"Are you ready?" he said.

Parren nodded, and they inched forward, peering over the ridge.

Three Qataari guards stood in the valley immediately beneath their vantage point, staring patiently up at them.

Ordier instinctively ducked down again, but in the same instant he heard the Qataari shouting, and knew they had been noticed.

When he looked again he saw that the warning was rippling outward. The guards along the valley side of the ridge were turning their backs on Ordier and Parren . . . and in the rose plantation, along the banks of the narrow river, on the approaches to the camp, the Qataari were halting in whatever they were doing. They stood erect, waiting and waiting.

Parren was holding his binoculars awkwardly, trying to see but trying to keep his head down too.

"You might as well stand up, Parren," Ordier said. "You'll see better."

Ordier himself sat up and settled himself on the edge of the slab. In a moment, Parren followed. The two men looked across the valley.

Ordier had no idea what Parren could now hope to

see, but he had his own interest in the valley. He scanned the rose plantation systematically, looking with the powerful glasses from one Qataari to the next. Most of them stood with their backs turned, and from this distance it was difficult to see clearly. There was one female that Ordier lingered on; it might have been the girl, but he was not sure.

He made certain that Parren was busy with his own observations, then turned his glasses toward the foot of the folly wall. The arena itself could not be seen from here, but two of the hollow statues were just visible. He had had no hope of seeing if a ritual had been in progress, but he wanted to see if there were any people about; apart from one of the guards standing near the folly, though, there was no apparent sign of activity.

Ordier did not know whether he was relieved or annoyed.

Their silent observation continued for several more minutes, but then even Parren admitted that there was nothing further to be gained.

"Would it be worth waiting beneath the ridge for an hour or two?" he said. "I have the time."

"The Qataari have more. We might as well go back."

"They seemed to be expecting us, Ordier."

"I know." He glanced apologetically at the man. "That's probably because I came up to this part of the ridge last time. We should have tried somewhere else."

"Then we could do that another time."

"If you think it's worth it."

They began to make their way down, Ordier taking the lead. The sun was higher now and the morning wind had stilled, and by the time they were halfway down both men were feeling the heat.

It was Parren who called a halt first, and squatted down in the shade of a huge boulder. Ordier went back up to him, and sat beside him. Below them, deceptively near, Ordier's house stood like a brightly colored plastic toy in a field.

After a while, Parren said: "Jenessa tells me you once worked with scintillas."

Ordier looked at him sharply. "Why did she tell you that?"

"I asked her. Your name was familiar. We both come from the north, after all."

"I've left all that behind me."

"Yes . . . but not your specialized knowledge."

"What do you want to know?" Ordier said resignedly.

"Everything you can tell me."

"Parren, you've been misinformed. I've retired."

"Then that wasn't a scintilla detector I noticed in your house."

"Look, I don't see why you're interested."

Parren was sitting forward, away from the rock, and his manner had changed.

"Let's not prevaricate, Ordier. I need some information from you. I want to know if there is any law in the Archipelago prohibiting the use of scintillas. I want to know if scintillas could be used to observe the Qataari. And lastly, if you think the Qataari would have any way of detecting or jamming scintillas."

"Is that all?"

"Yes."

"There's no law against using them. I can tell you that much. Only the Covenant of Neutrality, but it's never enforced."

"And the rest?" Parren said.

Ordier sighed. "The scintillas could obviously be used against the Qataari, if you could think of some way of planting them without them knowing."

"That's easy. They can be sown from an aircraft at night."

"I see you've worked it out. But your last question interests me. Why do you think the Qataari would be able to jam scintillas?"

"They've had plenty of experience of them."

"How do you mean?" Ordier said.

"Both sides were using them during the invasion of the peninsula. The military work on saturation principles . . . scintillas must have been ankle-deep. A race who so obviously dislike being watched would have realized what they were for."

"I was under the impression you thought the Qataari were primitive."

Parren said: "Not primitive . . . decivilized. Their science is a match for anything we've got."

"How do you know that?"

"An intelligent guess. But what's your opinion, Ordier? Do *you* think they could jam scintillas?"

"No one else can, so far as I know. But technology is always advancing."

"Qataari technology?"

"I don't know, Parren."

"Look at this." Parren reached into a pocket, and pulled out a small box. Ordier recognized it at once: it was a scintilla quiet-case, identical to his own. Parren opened the lid, reached inside with a pair of tweezers he took from a mounting in the lid. "Have you seen one of these before?"

He dropped a scintilla into the palm of Ordier's hand.

Ordier, guessing, said: "It hasn't got a serial number."

"Right. Do you know why?"

"Do you?"

"I've never encountered it before."

"Neither have I," Ordier said. "Except here on Tumo. My guess is that they're military."

"No, I've checked. They're required by the Yenna Convention to mark them. Both sides abide."

"Then a bootleg?"

"They're usually marked too. A few of the pirates might leave them blank, but these little devils are all over the place. I've seen hundreds since I've been on Tumo."

"You've checked them all?" Ordier said.

"No, but every one I have checked has been blank." Parren picked up the scintilla with the tweezers, and returned it to the quiet-case.

"Then whose are they?"

"I was hoping you'd tell me, Ordier."

"You've already revealed that you're better informed than I am."

"Then I'll tell you what I think. They're connected with the Qataari."

Ordier waited, expecting more to follow, but the

other man was looking at him in a significant way as if waiting for a response. He said in the end: "So . . . ?"

"Someone," Parren said with ponderous emphasis, "is spying on the Qataari."

"With what purpose?"

"The same as mine."

And Ordier heard again the edge to Parren's voice he had heard at Jenessa's dinner party. Personal ambition was strong in the man. For a moment Ordier had felt a guilty suspicion growing in him, that Parren had somehow guessed that he had been spying on the Qataari from the folly, and that he was about to accuse him. But Ordier's own guilt was as nothing beside Parren's ambition, which was so bright it blinded him.

"Then you must clearly join forces with whoever it is, or compete."

"I intend to compete."

"You have your own scintillas?"

Ordier had intended his question sarcastically, but Parren said at once: "Yes, a new version. They're a quarter the size of existing scintillas, and to all intents and purposes are invisible."

"Then there's your answer. You would clearly have the edge."

Ordier's urbane reply gave no clue to his thoughts. He had not known that scintilla technology had advanced so much.

"That's not my answer, Ordier. Do you think the Qataari could either detect or jam my scintillas?"

Ordier smiled grimly. "I've told you I don't know. You've seen how sensitive they are to being watched. It's like a sixth sense. They might or might not have the electronic means of detection, but my guess is that they'd sense your scintillas somehow."

"Do you really think so?"

"Your guess is as good as mine," Ordier said. "Probably better. Look, I'm thirsty. Why don't we talk about this back at the house? It's too hot out here."

Parren agreed, reluctantly it seemed to Ordier, and they continued their clumsy descent of the rocks. When they reached the house half an hour later, they found the place empty. Ordier fixed some cold drinks for them both.

He left Parren on the patio, and went in search of the women.

A few moments later he saw them in the rough ground behind the house, walking from the direction of the gate in the courtyard wall. He waited impatiently until they reached him.

"Where have you been?" he said to Jenessa.

"You were gone so long, I took Luovi to see your folly. The gate was unlocked, so we assumed it would be all right."

"You know it's not safe up there!" Ordier said.

"What an interesting building it is," Luovi said to him. "Such eccentric architecture. All those concealed faults in the walls. And what a view there is higher up!"

She smiled at him patronizingly, then shifted the strap of her large leather bag on her shoulder, and walked past him toward the house. Ordier looked at Jenessa, hoping for some explanatory expression, but she would not meet his eyes.

VII

Parren and his wife stayed at the house for the rest of the day. Ordier was a passive listener to most of the conversation, feeling excluded from it. He wished he could involve himself in Jenessa's work to the same degree that Luovi seemed to be involved with Parren, but whenever he ventured an opinion or an idea into the discussion of the Qataari, he was either ignored or tacitly dismissed. The result was that while Jacj Parren outlined his elaborate scheme—there was an aircraft to be hired, and a place found to erect the scintilla monitoring and decoding equipment—Ordier fell into an introspective mood, and grew increasingly preoccupied with his secret one-sided relationship with the Qataari girl.

From the summit of the ridge it had been impossible to see whether there was a ritual taking place, and in any event the fact that he and Parren had been noticed would have put an immediate halt to it, but just the sight of the placid, colorful valley had been enough to remind him of the girl, and the ambiguity of the part she took in the ritual.

And there was the uncertainty of what Jenessa and Luovi had seen or done while they were in the folly.

Guilt and curiosity, the conflicting motives of the voyeur, were rising in Ordier again.

Shortly before sunset, Parren suddenly announced that he and Luovi had another appointment in the evening, and Jenessa offered to drive them back to Tumo Town. Ordier, uttering the platitudes of host to departing guests, saw this as a brief chance to satisfy his curiosity. He walked down with the others to Jenessa's car, and watched as they drove away. The sun was already behind the Tumoit Mountains, and the distant town was glittering with lights.

When the car was out of sight, Ordier hurried back to the house, collected his binoculars, and set off for the folly.

As Jenessa had said, the padlock on the gate was open; he must have forgotten to close it the last time he left the folly. As he went through he made sure of locking it, as usual, on the inside.

Twilight on Tumo was short, a combination of the latitude and the western mountain heights, and as Ordier went up the slope towards the folly wall it was difficult to see his way.

Once inside the hidden cell, Ordier wasted no time and put his eyes directly to the slit. Beyond, the valley was dark under the evening sky. He could see no one about; the alarm that their intrusion had caused seemed to have passed, for those Qataari in the valley during the day were nowhere about. The rose plantation was deserted, and the blooms moved to and fro in the breeze.

Unaccountably relieved, Ordier returned to the house. He was washing up the plates and cups when Jenessa returned. She was looking excited and beautiful, and she kissed Ordier when she came in.

"I'm going to work with Jacj!" she said. "He wants me to advise him. Isn't that marvelous?"

"Advise him? How?"

"On the Qataari. He'll pay me, and he says that when he returns to the north I can go with him."

Ordier nodded, and turned away.

"Aren't you pleased for me?"

"How much is he going to pay you?"

Jenessa had followed him as he walked out onto the patio, and from the doorway she turned on the colored lights concealed amongst the grapevines hanging from the overhead trellis.

"Does it matter how much it is, Yvann?"

Looking back at her he saw the multicolored light on the olive skin of her face, like the reflection from sun on flower petals. "It's not the amount that matters," he said. "It's what you would have to do to earn it."

"Nothing more than I'm doing now. It will double my income, Yvann. You should be pleased! Now I can buy a house for myself."

"And what's this about going north with him? You know you can't leave the Archipelago."

"Jacj has a way."

"He has a way with everything, hasn't he? I suppose his university can interpret the Covenant to suit itself."

"Something like that. He hasn't told me."

Ordier turned away irritably, staring out at the still blue water of the pool. Jenessa went across to him.

"There isn't anything going on between us," she said.

"What do you mean?"

"You know, Yvann. It's not sex, or anything."

He laughed, suddenly and shortly. "Why on earth do you bring that into it?"

"You're behaving as if I'm having an affair with him. It's just a job, just the work I've always done."

"I never said it wasn't."

"I know I've spent a lot of time with him and Luovi," Jenessa said. "I can't help it. It's, well . . ."

"The bloody Qataari. That's it, isn't it?"

"You know it is."

She took his arm then, and for several minutes they said nothing. Ordier was angry, and it always took some time for his moods to subside. It was irrational, of course, these things always were. Parren and his wife, since their arrival, had seemed set on changing the placid way of life he enjoyed, guilty conscience and all. The thought of Jenessa going over to them, collaborating with them, was just one more intrusion, and Ordier was incapable of dealing with it any other way than emotionally.

Later, when they had made some supper and were drinking wine together on the patio, enjoying the warm night, Jenessa said: "Jacj wants you to join his work too."

"Me?" Ordier had mellowed as the evening progressed, and his laugh this time was not sardonic. "There's not much I can do for him."

"He says there's a lot you can do. He wants to rent your folly."

"Whatever for?" Ordier said, taken by surprise.

"It overlooks the Qataari valley. Jacj wants to build an observation cell in the wall."

"Tell him it's not available," Ordier said abruptly. "It's structurally unsound."

Jenessa was regarding him with a thoughtful expression.

"It seemed safe enough to me," she said. "We climbed right up to the battlements today."

"I thought I told you—"

"What?"

"It doesn't matter," Ordier said, sensing another row. He raised the wine bottle to see how much was left. "Would you like another glass?"

Jenessa yawned, but she did it in an affected, exaggerated way, as if she too had seen the way the conversation was going, and welcomed the chance to let the subject die.

"I'm tired," she said. "Let's finish the bottle, and go to bed."

"You'll stay the night then?"

"If I'm invited."

"You're invited," Ordier said.

VIII

Four more days passed. Although Ordier stayed away from the cell in the folly wall, his curiosity about the

Qataari girl continued; at the same time he felt a growing sense of ambiguity, compounded by the unwelcome
presence of Parren and his wife.

The morning after these two had visited the house.
Ordier had been waiting for Jenessa to leave when a
distracting thought came to him. It was what Parren
had said to him on the ridge, about the unmarked, uni-
dentified scintillas. He had linked them to the Qataari,
and interpreted it to mean that someone else was observing them.

Ordier, listening to Jenessa in the shower cubicle,
suddenly saw the possibility of an altogether different
interpretation.

It was not that someone else was spying on the
Qataari . . . but that *the Qataari themselves were
watching*.

With their obsessive desire for privacy, it would
clearly be in their interests to be able to watch the
movement of the other people on the island. If they had
access to scintilla equipment—or had been able to manufacture it themselves somehow—then it would be a
logical way of defending themselves from the outside
world.

It was not impossible. The Qataari men and women
who had visited the northern nations had revealed a
brilliant inductive understanding of science and technology, and after only a few moments of hesitation had
been completely at home with such devices as elevators,
telephones, automobiles . . . even computers. Parren
had said that Qataari science was sophisticated, and if
that were so, they might have learned how to duplicate
the scintillas that had been poured so indiscriminately
over their homeland.

If the Qataari were watching the people of Tumo,
then they were certainly watching Ordier; he remembered the unmarked scintillas he was always finding in
his house.

Later that day, when Jenessa had left, Ordier took
his detector and scoured every room of the house. He
found another half-dozen of the unmarked scintillas,
and put them with the others in the quiet-case. But the

detector was fallible; he could never be entirely sure that every single scintilla had been found.

He spent most of this day in thought, realizing that this conjecture, if it was true, led to the conclusion that the Qataari knew he was spying on them from the folly.

If *this* was so, then it would account for something that he had always found naggingly strange: his unshakable conviction that the ritual was staged for his benefit.

He had always maintained the most scrupulous efforts at silence and secrecy, and in ordinary circumstances he had no reason to suppose that the Qataari knew he was there. But the girl had become a central figure in the ritual *after* he had noticed her in the plantation, and had watched her through his binoculars. The ritual itself invariably started *after* he went into the cell; he had never once found it in progress. And the ceremony, although staged in a circular arena, was always within his view, the girl was always *facing* him.

Until now Ordier had unconsciously attributed all this to simple good fortune, and had not sought a rational explanation. But if the Qataari were watching him, were waiting for him, were staging it for him. . . .

But all this speculation was denied by one fact: the famous dislike the Qataari had of being watched. They would not allow someone to watch them, far less encourage it by mounting an intriguing ritual for his benefit!

It was this new understanding, and its attendant enigmas, that kept Ordier away from the folly for four days. In the past he had fantasized that the girl was being prepared for him, that she was a sexual lure, but this had been the stuff of erotic imaginings. To have to confront this as a matter of actual fact was something he was not ready for.

To do so would be to accept something else that had once been an element in his fantasies: that the girl knew who he was, that the Qataari had *selected* him.

So the days passed. Jenessa was busy with Parren's preparations, and she seemed not to notice Ordier's abstracted state of mind. He prowled the house by day, sorting through his books and trying to concentrate on domestic matters. By night he slept with Jenessa, as usual, but during their lovemaking, especially in those moments just before reaching climax, Ordier's thoughts were of the Qataari girl. He imagined her sprawling across the bed of scarlet petals; her garment was torn away, her legs were spread, her mouth was reaching to meet his, her eyes stared submissively at him, her body was warm and soft to the touch.

She had been offered to him, and Ordier knew that she was his for the taking.

IX

On the morning of the fifth day Ordier awoke to a new realization: he had resolved the dilemma.

As he lay beside the sleeping Jenessa, he knew he accepted the fact that the Qataari had selected him, and he also knew why. He had met several Qataari in the north before he emigrated, and had made no secret to them of his work. They must have identified him here; he had been selected because of the scintillas.

But more than this: until this waking Ordier had feared the idea, for it implied that he was a prisoner of the Qataari will, but this new understanding actually freed him.

There was no further reason for his obsessive curiosity. He need never again agonize about missing the ritualized ceremony, because the ritual would not take place *until he was there to observe it*.

He need never again return to the claustrophobic cell in the wall, because the Qataari would wait.

They would wait for his arrival, as they would wait for others' departure.

Lying in his bed, staring up at the mirrored ceiling, Ordier realized that the Qataari had liberated him. The girl was being offered to him, and he could accept or refuse according to his whim.

Then Jenessa, waking beside him, turned over and said: "What's the time?"

Ordier looked at the clock, told her the time.

"I've got to hurry this morning."

"What's the rush?"

"Jacj's catching the ferry to Muriseay. The aircraft will be ready today."

"Aircraft?"

"To scintillate the Qataari," Jenessa said. "We're intending to spray them tonight or tomorrow night."

Ordier nodded. He watched Jenessa as she rolled sleepily from the bed, and walked naked to the shower cubicle. He followed her and waited outside, imagining her voluptuous body as he always did, but for once he was incapable of lustful thoughts. Afterwards he walked with her to the car, watched her drive away. He returned to the house.

Reminding himself of his new existential state he made some coffee, then took it out on to the patio. The weather was hot again, and the scraping of the cicadas seemed especially loud. A new crate of books had arrived the previous day, and the swimming pool looked clean and cold. He could make it a busy day.

He wondered if the Qataari were watching him now; if their scintillas lay between the paving stones, in the branches of the vines, in the soil of the overgrown flower beds.

"I'll never spy on the Qataari again," he said aloud, into the imagined aural pick-ups.

"I'll go to the folly today, and tomorrow, and every day," he said.

"I'll move from this house," he said. "I'll rent it to Parren, and I'll live with Jenessa in the town."

"I'll watch the Qataari," he said. "I'll watch them until I have seen everything, until I have taken everything."

He left his cushioned recliner and roamed around the patio, gesturing and waving, adopting elaborate postures of deep thought, of sudden decision, of abrupt changes of mind. He played to the invisible audience, remonstrating with himself for his indecision, declaiming his freedom to act at will, declaring with mimed tears his independence and responsibility.

It was an act, but not an act, for free will liberates the purposeful and restrains the irresolute.

"Am I interrupting anything?"

The voice, breaking into his ridiculous charade, startled Ordier, and he turned around in anger and embarrassment. It was Luovi Parren, standing by the door to the lounge. Her large leather bag was slung as usual across her shoulder.

"The door was open," she said. "I hope you don't mind."

"What do you want?" It was impossible for Ordier to keep the incivility out of his voice.

"Well, after my long walk I'd appreciate something to drink."

"Have a coffee. I'll get another cup."

Furiously, Ordier went into the kitchen and found a cup. He stood by the sink, resting both hands on the edge and staring into the bowl in mindless rage. He hated being caught off guard.

Luovi was sitting in the shade, on the steps that led down from the verandah.

"I thought you'd be with Jacj," Ordier said when he had poured her some coffee. He had recovered from the surprise of her unwelcome arrival sufficiently at least to make an effort toward politeness.

"I didn't want to see Muriseay again," Luovi said. "Is Jenessa here?"

"Isn't she with Jacj?" Ordier was distracted; he wanted his illusion of free will again.

"I haven't seen her. Jacj left two days ago."

Ordier frowned, trying to remember what Jenessa had said. She had left the house only half an hour ago, to see the ferry leave, she said; if Luovi had walked from the town they should have passed each other on the road. And didn't Jenessa say that Parren was catching the ferry this morning?

"Jacj has gone to charter an aircraft, I take it?"

"Of course not. The Qataari camp was scintillated three nights ago. Didn't you hear the engine?"

"No, I didn't! Did Jenessa know this?"

"I'm sure she must," Luovi said, and smiled the same sparse smile he had seen the day she came back from the folly.

"Then what's Jacj doing on Muriseay?"

"Collecting the monitoring equipment. Do you mean Jenessa didn't tell you any of this?"

"Jenessa told me—"

Ordier hesitated, regarding Luovi suspiciously. Her manner was as sweetly polite as that of a suburban gossip breaking news of adultery. She sipped her coffee, apparently waiting for his reply. Ordier turned away, took a breath. It was a time for instant decision: to believe this woman, or to believe the words and behavior of Jenessa, who in the last few days had done or said nothing that roused the least suspicion.

As he turned back to face her, Luovi said: "You see, I was hoping I would find Jenessa here, so we could talk things over."

Ordier said: "I think you should go, Luovi. I don't know what you want, or what you're trying to—"

"Then you do know more about the Qataari than you've said!"

"What's that got to do with it?"

"As far as I know, everything! Isn't that what the folly was built for in the first place?"

"The folly? What are you talking about?"

"Don't think we don't know, Ordier. It's time Jenessa was told."

Five days ago, Luovi's insinuations would have gone straight through Ordier's defenses to his guilty conscience; that was five days ago, though, and since then everything had become more complex.

"Look, get out of my house! You're not welcome here!"

"Very well." Luovi stood up, and put down her cup with a precise motion. "You'll take the consequences then?"

She turned and walked back into the house. Ordier followed, and saw her leave through the main door and walk down the broken terrain of the hillside toward the track. He was confused and angry, trying to put some logic into what had just happened.

Did Luovi know as much as she seemed to be implying? Had she really come to the house to see Jenessa, or was it just to make a scene? Why? What could her motives conceivably have been? Why should she imply that Jenessa had been lying to him?

The sun was high, and white light glared down across

the dusty countryside. In the distance, Tumo Town was shimmering in the haze.

Watching Luovi striding angrily away through the heat, her heavy bag banging against her side, Ordier felt a paradoxical sense of courtesy come over him, and he took pity on her. He saw that she had apparently lost her way and was not heading directly toward the track, but was moving across the hillside parallel to the ridge.

He ran after her.

"Luovi!" he called as he caught up with her. "You can't walk all the way back in this heat. Let me drive you."

She glanced at him angrily, and walked on. "I know *exactly* where I'm going, thank you."

She looked toward the ridge, and as Ordier fell back behind her he was aware of the deliberate ambiguity.

X

Ordier marched into his house and slammed the door behind him. He went out to the patio, and sat down on the cushions scattered across the sun-warmed paving stones. A bird fluttered away from where it had been perched on the grapevine, and Ordier glanced up. The verandah, the patio, the rooms of the house . . . they all had their undetected scintillas, making his home into a stage for an unseen audience. The uncertainties remained, and Luovi's brief, unwelcome visit had only added to them.

He was hot and breathless from running after the woman; so he stripped off his clothes and swam for a few minutes in the pool.

Afterwards, he paced to and fro on the patio, trying to marshal his thoughts and replace ambiguity with certainty. He was unsuccessful.

The unmarked scintillas: he had almost convinced himself that they were being planted by the Qataari, but the possibility remained that someone else was responsible.

Jenessa: according to Luovi she had deceived him, according to his instincts she had not. (Ordier still trusted her, but Luovi had succeeded in placing a doubt in his mind.)

The trip to Muriseay: Parren had gone to Muriseay (today? or two days ago?) to charter an aircraft, or to collect the monitoring equipment. But according to Luovi the aircraft had already done its work; would this have been carried out before Parren had his decoding equipment ready?

Luovi: where was she now? Was she returning to the town, or was she somewhere along the ridge?

Jenessa, again: where was she now? Had she gone to the ferry, was she at her office, or was she returning to his house?

The folly: how much did Luovi know about his visits to the hidden cell? And what did she mean about the folly being built for something "in the first place"? Did she know more about it and its past than he did? Why *was* there an observation cell in the wall, with its clear view across the valley?

All these were the new doubts, the additional ones for which he had Luovi to thank; the others, the major ones, remained.

The Qataari: did he watch them, or did they watch him?

The Qataari girl: was he a free observer of her, hidden and unsuspected, or was he a chosen participant playing a crucial role in the development of the ritual?

In his perplexity of free will and contradiction, Ordier knew that paradoxically it was the Qataari ritual and the girl that provided the only certainty.

He was convinced that if he went to the folly and placed his eyes to the crack in the wall, then for whatever reason or combination of reasons, the girl would be there waiting . . . and the ritual would recommence.

And he knew that the choice was his: he need never again climb up to the cell in the wall.

Without further thought, Ordier went into the house, found his binoculars, and started to climb up the slope of the ridge toward the folly.

He went a short distance, then turned back, pretending to himself that he was exercising his freedom of choice. In fact, he was collecting his scintilla detector, and as soon as he had the instrument under his arm he left the house again and climbed toward the courtyard gate.

He reached the bottom of the folly wall in a few minutes, then went quickly up the steps to his hidden cell. Before he went inside he put down the detector and used his binoculars to scan the countryside around his house. The track leading toward town was deserted, and there was not even any drifting dust to show that a car might have driven along it in the last few minutes. He searched along the parts of the ridge visible from here, looking for Luovi, but where he had last spoken to her was an area dotted with high, free-standing boulders, and he could see no sign of her.

In the distance, the town lay in the hot, pellucid air, seeming still and abandoned.

Ordier stepped back, squeezed between the two projecting slabs, and went through into the cell. At once he was assailed by the sickly pungent fragrance of Qataari roses; it was a smell he associated with the girl, the valley, the ritual, and it seemed subtly illicit, sexually provocative.

He put his binoculars on the shelf and opened the scintilla detector. He paused before switching it on, frightened of what he might find. If there were scintillas here, inside the cell, then he would know beyond any doubt that the Qataari had been observing him.

He pulled the antenna to its full height and threw the switch . . . and at once the loudspeaker gave out a deafening electronic howl that faded almost at once to silence. Ordier, whose hand had leaped back reflexively from the device, touched the directional antenna and shook the instrument, but no further sound came from it. He turned off the switch, wondering what was wrong.

He took the detector into the sunlight and turned on the switch again. In addition to the audible signal there were several calibrated dials on the side which registered the presence and distance of detected scintillas, but these all stayed at zero. The speaker remained silent. Ordier shook the instrument, but the circuits stayed dead. He let out a noisy breath in exasperation, knowing that the detector had worked the last time he used it.

When he checked the batteries, Ordier found that they were dead.

He cursed himself for forgetting, and put the detector on the steps. It was useless, and another uncertainty had appeared. Was his cell seeded with scintillas, or wasn't it? That sudden burst of electronic noise: was it the dying gasp of the batteries, or had the instrument actually been registering the presence of scintillas in the last microsecond of the batteries' power?

He returned to the claustrophobic cell, and picked up his binoculars. Qataari rose petals lay thickly on the slab where he normally stood, and as he stepped forward to the crack in the wall Ordier saw that more petals lay there, piled so thickly that the aperture was all but blocked. Not caring whether they fell back into his cell or out into the valley, Ordier brushed them away and shuffled his feet to kick them from the slab. The fragrance rose around him like pollen, and as he breathed it he felt a heady sensation: arousal, excitement, intoxication.

He tried to remember the first time he had found petals here in the cell. There had been a strong, gusting wind; they could have blown in through the slit by chance. But last night? Had there been a wind? He could not remember.

Ordier shook his head, trying to think clearly. There had been all the confusions of the morning, then Luovi. The dead batteries. The perfumed petals.

It seemed, in the suffocating darkness of the cell, that events were being contrived by greater powers to confuse and disorientate him.

If those powers existed, he knew whose they were.

As if it were a light seen wanly through a mist, Ordier focused on the knowledge and blundered mentally toward it.

The Qataari had been watching him all along. He had been selected, he had been placed in this cell, he had been meant to watch. Every movement in this cell, every indrawn breath and muttered word, every voyeuristic intent and response and thought . . . they had all been monitored by the Qataari. They were decoded and analyzed, and tested against their actions, and the Qataari behaved according to their interpretations.

He had become a scintilla to the Qataari.

Ordier gripped a piece of rock jutting out from the wall, and tried to steady himself. He could feel himself swaying, as if his thoughts were a palpable force that could dislodge him from the cell. It was madness.

That first day he had found the cell, the very beginning. He had been *concealed,* and the Qataari had been *unaware* of him. He had watched the Qataari, the realization of the nature of his stolen privilege growing in him slowly. He had watched the girl moving through the rosebushes, plucking the flowers and tossing them into the pannier on her back. She had been one among dozens of others. He had said nothing, except with his thoughts, and the Qataari had not noticed.

The rest was chance and coincidence . . . it had to be.

Reassured, Ordier leaned forward and pressed his forehead against the slab of rock above the slit. He looked downward, into the circular arena below.

XI

It was as if nothing had changed. The Qataari were waiting for him.

The girl lay back on the carpet of rose petals, the red toga loose and revealing across her body. There was the same crescent of pale aureole, the same few strands of pubic hair. The man who had kicked her was standing back, looking down at her with his shoulders hunched, and stroking himself at the top of his legs. The others stood around: the two women who had thrown the petals and bared their bodies, and the men who had been chanting.

The restoration of the scene was so perfect, as if the image of his memory had been photographed and reconstructed so no detail should be omitted, that Ordier felt a shadow of the guilt that had followed his spontaneous ejaculation.

He raised his binoculars and looked at the girl's face.

Her eyes, although half closed, were looking directly at him. Her expression too was identical: the abandonment of sexual anticipation, or satisfaction. It was as if he was seeing the next frame of a film being inched through a projector-gate. Fighting the feeling of associative guilt, Ordier stared down at the girl, meeting her gaze, marveling at her beauty and the sensuality in her face.

He felt a tightness in his crotch, a new tumescence.

The girl moved suddenly, shaking her head from side to side, and at once the ritual continued.

Four of the men stepped forward from the circle, picking up long ropes that had been coiled at the base of four of the statues. As they moved towards the girl, the men unraveled the ropes and Ordier saw that the other ends were tied around the bases of the statues. At the same time, the two women found their panniers of rose petals and came forward with them. The others began a chant.

In the rose plantation beyond, the Qataari were moving about their tasks, tending and plucking and watering. Ordier was suddenly aware of them, as if they too had been waiting, as if they too were a part of the ritual.

The girl was being tied by her wrists and ankles, the ropes knotted tightly and roughly around her limbs: her arms were stretched, her legs were forced wide open. She made no apparent struggle against this, but continued to writhe in the petals in the way she had done from the start, and as her arms and legs were tied, her movements changed to a circling of her pelvic girdle, a slow rotation of her head.

The garment was working loose from her body; for an instant Ordier saw a small breast revealed, the nipple as pink as the petals being thrown across her, but one of the men with the ropes moved across her, and when he stepped back, she was covered again.

Through all this—the tying of the ropes, the throwing of the petals—the solitary man stood before her, working his hand across his genitals, waiting and watching.

When the last rope was tied the men withdrew, and as they did so, the chanting came to a sudden end. All the men, except the one central to the ritual, walked away from the arena, toward the plantation, toward the distant Qataari camp.

The women showered petals, the man stood erect, the spread-eagled girl writhed helplessly in the hold of the ropes. The flowers were drifting down across her like snow, and soon only her face was uncovered. As the girl pulled against the ropes, Ordier could see the petals heaving with her struggles, could see the ropes flexing and jerking.

At last her struggles ceased, and she stared upward again. Looking at her through the binoculars, Ordier saw that in spite of her violent writhing, the girl's face was at ease and her eyes were wide open. Saliva brightened her cheeks and jaw, and her face had a healthy, ruddy flush to it, as if reflecting the color of the flowers. Beneath the petals, her chest was rising and falling quickly, as if she was breathless.

Once more she was seeming to look directly back at Ordier, her expression knowing and seductive.

The stilling of her body signaled the next development, as if the victim of the ritual was also its director, because no sooner was she staring lasciviously upward than the man who stood before her bent down. He reached into the heap of petals and took a hold on one of the red panels of the girl's toga. He tore it away, throwing into the air a cloud of swirling petals. Ordier, looking down, thought he saw a glimpse of the girl's body revealed beneath, but the petals drifted too densely above her, and the women were throwing more, covering the nakedness so briefly revealed. Another piece of the dress was torn away; more petals flew. Then another piece of fabric, and another. The last one came away with difficulty; this was the piece beneath the girl, and as the man snatched it away, the girl's body bucked against the constraint of the ropes, and bare knees and arms, a naked shoulder, heaved momentarily from the mound of petals.

Ordier watched as more and more of the petals were poured on top of her, completely covering her; the women no longer threw the petals with their hands, but up-ended their panniers, and let the scarlet flowers fall on her like liquid. As the petals fell, the man knelt beside the girl and shaped and smoothed them over with his hands. He patted them down over her body, heaped them over her arms and legs, pushed them into her mouth.

Soon it was finished. It seemed to Ordier, from his position above, that the girl lay beneath and at the center of a smooth lake of petals, laid so that no hint of the shape of her body was revealed. Only her eyes were uncovered.

The man and the two women stepped out of the arena and walked away, heading for the distant camp.

Ordier lowered his binoculars, and saw that throughout the plantation the work had stopped. The Qataari were leaving the valley, returning to their homes behind the dark canvas screens of the encampment, and leaving the girl alone in the arena.

Ordier looked down at her again, using the binoculars. She was staring back at him, and the invitation was explicit. All he could see of her were her eyes, placid and alert and yearning, watching him through the gap the man had left in the covering of roses.

There was a darkening around her eyes, like the shadows left by grief. As her steady gaze challenged and beckoned him, Ordier, partially drugged by the narcotic fragrance of the roses, saw a familiarity in the girl's eyes that froze all sense of mystery. That bruising of the skin, that confident stare. . . .

Ordier gazed back at her for several minutes, and the longer he looked, the more convinced he became that he was staring into the eyes of Jenessa.

XII

Intoxicated by the roses, sexually aroused by their fragrance, Ordier fell back from the slit in the wall and lurched outside. The brilliance of the sunlight, the heat of its rays, took him by surprise and he staggered on the narrow steps. He regained his balance by resting one hand against the main wall of the folly, then went past his discarded detector and began to walk down the steps toward the ground.

Halfway down was another narrow ledge, running across the wall as far as the end of the folly, and Ordier walked precariously along this, obsessed with the urgency of his needs. At the end of the ledge he was able to climb down to the top of the wall which surrounded the folly's courtyard, and once on top of this he could see the rocks and broken boulders of the ridge a short distance below.

He jumped, landing heavily across the face of a boulder. He grazed a hand and took a knock on one knee, but apart from being slightly winded, he was unhurt. He crouched for a few seconds, recovering.

A stiff breeze was blowing through the valley and along the ridge, and as Ordier's breathing steadied, he felt his head clearing. At the same time, with an indefinable sense of regret, he felt his arousal dying too.

A moment of the free will he had accorded himself that morning had returned. No longer driven by the enigmatic stimulations of the Qataari ritual, Ordier realized that it was now in his power to abandon the quest.

He could scramble somehow down the broken slabs of the ridge, and return to his house. He could see Jenessa, who might be there and wondering where he was. He could seek out Luovi, and apologize to her, and try to find an explanation for Jacj's apparent or actual movements. He could resume the life he had led until this summer, before the day he had found the cell. He could forget the Qataari girl, and all that she meant to him, and never return to the folly.

So he crouched on the boulder, trying to be clear in his mind.

But there was something he could not resolve by walking away. It was the certain knowledge that the *next time* he looked through the crack in the folly wall—whether it was tomorrow, or in a year's time, or in half a century's time—he would see a bed of Qataari rose petals, and staring back at him would be the bruised eyes of a lovely girl, waiting for him and reminding him of Jenessa.

XIII

Ordier climbed clumsily down the last overhanging boulder, fell to the scree beneath, and skidded down in a cloud of dust and grit to the sandy floor of the valley.

He stood up, and the gaunt height of the folly loomed beside and above him.

He knew there was no one about, because as he had been climbing down the rocks he had had a perfect view to all sides. There were no guards visible along the ridge, no other Qataari anywhere. The breeze blew through the deserted rose plantation, and far away, on the other side of the valley, the screens around the camp hung heavy and gray.

The encircling statues of the arena lay ahead of him, and Ordier walked slowly toward them, excited again and apprehensive. As he approached, he could see the mound of petals and could smell the heady perfume from them. Here in the shadow of the folly the breeze had little effect, and barely stirred the surface of the mound. Now he was at ground level he saw that the petals had not been smoothed to a flat surface above the girl, but that they lay irregularly and deeply.

Ordier hesitated when he came to the nearest of the statues. It was, by chance, one of those to which the ropes had been tied, and he saw the rough fibered rope stretching tautly across to the mound of petals, vanishing into it.

A reason for his hesitation was a sudden self-consciousness, a need for guidance. If he had interpreted the actions of the Qataari correctly, he had been tacitly invited to relinquish his hiding place, and to enter the ritual. But what was expected of him now?

Should he walk across to the girl in the petals and introduce himself? Should he stand before her as the man had done? Should he rape her? Should he untie her? He looked around again, helplessly, hoping for some clue as to what to do.

All these possibilities were open to him, and more, but he was aware again of the way his freedom was created by the actions of others. He was free to act as he wished, and yet whatever he did would have been preordained by the mysterious, omniscient power of the Qataari.

He was free to go, but if he did, it would have been determined that this would be his choice; he was free to throw aside the petals and ravish the girl, for that too had been predetermined.

So he stood uncertainly by the statue, breathing the dangerous sweetness of the roses, feeling again the rise of sexual desire. At last he stepped forward, but some residual trace of convention made him clear his throat nervously, signaling his presence. There was no reaction from the girl.

He followed the rope, and stood by the edge of the mound of petals where it became buried. He craned forward, trying to see the place where the gap for the girl's eyes had been left, but the mound was irregular and he could not make it out. The fragrance of the petals lay heavy; his presence stirred it up like flocculent sediment shaken from the bottom of a bottle of liquid. He breathed it deeply, embracing the dullness of thought it induced, welcoming further surrender to the mysteries of the Qataari. It relaxed him and aroused him, made him sensitive to the sounds of the breeze, to the dry heat of the sun.

His clothes were feeling stiff and unnatural on him, so he took them off. He saw the pile of scarlet material where the girl's torn toga had been tossed aside, and he threw his own clothes on top. When he turned back to the pile of petals, he crouched down and took hold of the rope; he pulled on it, feeling the tautness, knowing that as he moved it the girl would feel it and know he was there.

He stepped forward, and the petals stirred around his ankles; the scent thickened, like the vaginal musk of desire.

But then he hesitated again, suddenly aware of an intrusive sensation, so distinct, so intense, that it was almost like pressure on his skin.

Somewhere, somebody hidden was watching him.

XIV

The realization was so profound that it penetrated the pleasant delirium induced by the rose perfume, and Ordier stepped back again. He turned around, staring first at the wall of the folly behind him, then across at the plantation of roses.

It seemed to him that there was a movement some-where in the bushes, and, distracted from the girl, Or-dier walked slowly toward them. They seemed to be looming over him, so near were they. The bushes grew to an unnatural height; they were like small trees, and nearly all were taller than him. Convinced that someone was standing concealed behind the plants, Ordier ran toward where he thought he had seen the movement, and plunged into the nearest row of bushes. At once he was halted; the thorns of the branches snagged and tore at his skin, bringing spots and streaks of blood to his chest and arms.

Here, in the plantation itself, the thick smell of the roses was so concentrated that it felt as if the air itself had been replaced by the sweetness of scent. He could not think or focus his mind. Was there anyone beyond, hiding in the roses, or had he imagined it? Ordier peered forward and to each side, but was unable to see.

In the distance, just visible across the top of the plan-tation, were the screens around the Qataari camp.

Ordier turned away. He stumbled back through the prickly branches of the roses, and returned to the arena.

The statues faced inward, staring down at the girl buried beneath the petals.

A memory, surfacing sluggishly like waterlogged tim-ber through the muddy pool of his mind: the statues, the statues. Earlier in the ritual . . . why were they there? He remembered, dimly, the men gathered around the girl, the cleaning and polishing of the statues. And later . . . ?

As the girl walked into the center of the arena, some of the men . . . climbed into the hollow statues!

The ritual had not changed. When he returned to the hidden cell that morning, the Qataari had been posi-tioned exactly as he had last seen them. But he had for-gotten the men inside the statues! Were they still there?

Ordier stood before the one nearest to him, and stared up at it.

It depicted a man of great physical strength and beauty, holding in one hand a scroll, and in the other a long spear with a phallus for a head. Although the figure was nude from the waist up, its legs were invisible because of a voluminous, loose-fitting garment, shaped brilliantly out of the metal of the statue. The face looked downward, directly at him and beyond, to where the girl lay inside the petals.

The eyes . . .

There were no eyes. Just two holes, behind which it would be possible for human eyes to hide.

Ordier stared up, looking at the dark recesses behind the eye-holes, trying to see if anyone was there. The statue gazed back vacantly, implacably.

Ordier turned away toward the pile of rose petals, knowing the girl still lay there a few paces away from him. But beyond the petals were other statues, staring down with the same sinister emptiness. Ordier fancied he saw a movement: behind the eyes of one, a head ducking down.

He stumbled across the arena, tripping on one of the ropes (the petals of the mound rustled and shifted; had he tugged at the girl's arm?), and lurched up to the suspect statue. He felt his way around to the other side, groping for some kind of handle which would open the hinged back. His fingers closed on a knob shaped like a raised disc, and he pulled at it. The hinges squeaked, the back came open, and Ordier, who had fallen to his knees, looked inside.

The statue was empty.

He opened the others, all of them, all around the circle . . . but each one was empty. He kicked his naked foot against them, he hammered with his fists and slammed the metal doors, and all the statues rang with a hollow reverberation.

The girl was still there, bound and silent beneath the petals, listening to his noisy and increasingly desperate searches, and Ordier was growing steadily more aware of her mute, uncritical presence. She was waiting for him in the manner of her people, and she was prepared.

He returned to the mound in the center of the arena, satisfied, as far as it was possible to be satisfied in this state of narcosis, that he had done all he could. There was no one about, no one watching. He was alone with the girl. But as he stood before her, breathing the sickly fragrance of the roses, he could still feel the pressure of eyes as distinctly as if it were the touch of a hand on the back of his neck.

XV

A dim understanding was growing in him. He had always felt an unvoiced need to resist the fragrance of the flowers, dreading what it might do to him, but now Ordier saw that he had to succumb. He gulped in the air and the perfume it carried, holding it in his lungs and feeling his skin tingle, his senses dull. He was aware of the girl, of her presence and sexuality; the bruised eyes, the frail body, her innocence, his excitement. He kneeled down, reached forward with his hands, searched for her in the petals. The scent was suffocating.

He moved forward on his knees, wading through. The petals swirled about his sides and his elbows like a light, foamy liquid, scarlet-colored, desire-perfumed. He came to one of the ropes beneath the petals, and followed it with his hand toward the center. He was near the girl now, and he tugged on the rope repeatedly, feeling it yield, imagining it bringing a hand nearer to him, or spreading her legs marginally wider. He waded forward hurriedly, groping for her.

There was a deep indentation in the ground beneath him; Ordier, leaning forward to put his weight on one hand, fell instead, and pitched forward into the soft, warm depths of the mound. He shouted as he fell, and several of the petals entered his mouth. He reared up like a nonswimmer who falls in shallow water, showering flowers around him in a pink and scarlet spray, trying to spit the petals from his mouth.

He felt grit between his teeth, and he reached in with a finger and wiped it around. Several petals clung moistly to his hand. He raised it to look more closely at them, and Ordier saw a sudden glint of reflected light.

He sank down again on to his knees, and picked up one of the petals at random. He held it before his eyes, squinting at it. There was a tiny gleam of light here too: a glittering, shimmering fragment of metal and glass.

Ordier picked up a handful of the petals, felt and saw the same glistening presence on every one. He threw them up and let them fall, and as they flickered down, the sun reflected minutely from the scintillas embedded in the petals.

He closed his eyes. The scent of the petals was overpowering. He staggered forward on his knees, the petals rippling around his waist. Again he reached the depression in the ground beneath the petals, and he fell forward into the flowers, reaching out for the body of the girl. He was in an ecstasy of delirium and desire.

He floundered and beat his arms, threw up the petals, kicked and struggled against the suffocating weight of the flowers, seeking the girl.

But the four ropes met in the center of the arena, and where the girl had been bound there was now a large and tightly drawn knot.

Exhausted, Ordier fell on his back in the petals, and let the sun play down on him. He could feel the hard lump of the knotted ropes between his shoulder blades. The metal heads of the encircling statues loomed over him; the sky was brilliant and blue. He reached behind him to grasp the ropes above his head, and spread his legs along the others.

The wind was rising and petals were blowing, drifting across him, covering his limbs.

Behind the statues, dominating the arena, was the bulk of the folly. The sun's light played full upon it, and the granite slabs were white and smoothly faced. In only one place was the perfection of the wall broken: in the center and about halfway up was a narrow slit of darkness. Ordier stared up at it, seeing behind it two identical glimmers of reflected light. They were circular and cold, like the lenses of binoculars.

The petals blew across him, covering him, and soon only his eyes were still exposed.